BLOOD ON THE GROUND:

LIVING AND DYING IN NOD

A Novel

by

Merle Temple

Southern Literature Publishing
www.southernliteraturepublishing.com

Blood On The Ground: Living And Dying In Nod

Copyright ©2018 Southern Literature Publishing

ISBN: 978-0-692-19149-1

Printed in the United States of America

Unless otherwise noted, all scripture references are taken from the Holy Bible, New International Version. Copyright 1973, 1978, 1984 International Bible Society. Used by permission. All rights reserved.

Where noted, scripture references taken from the Holy Bible, King James Version, kingjamesbibleonline.org. Used by permission. All rights reserved.

Also where noted, scripture references taken from the Holy Bible, English Standard Version. Copyright 2001. All rights reserved.

Southern Literature Publishing
www.southernliteraturepublishing.com

www.merletemple.com

Book Reviews

"Bolt your doors. Don't make a sound. The monsters will follow you home and get inside your head."—Jim Clemente, *Criminal Minds*

"Every sentence, every word is steeped in real world experience. The feelings are fact. The thrills are fact…the book you've been waiting to take on the airplane and the commute. In real life it is a miracle that Merle Temple has survived and is thriving. His characters reveal the source of that spirit and determination. The book is terrifying and inspiring."—Walter Sterling, *Sterling on Sunday*, CBS Radio

"…a master weaver…amazing characters who lead you through their world. His ability to lace descriptive words and phrases through each page brings his book to life."—Susan Reichert, Editor-in-Chief, *Southern Writers Magazine*

"Takes the reader into each scene with him, with precise and riveting detail, forcing one to actually feel the danger…"—Jann Marthaler, Associate Editor, SouthernReader.com

"Inspiring people who'll become important people one day, a gift given the public on account of the gift given to him."—John B. Wells, *Caravan to Midnight*

"…a master storyteller, eloquently weaving actual events into fiction about the lives of a dedicated law enforcement officer and his associates as they fight crime in Mississippi in the 1970s. Great reading!"—Beth Kirkland, former Intelligence Analyst, Mississippi Bureau of Narcotics

"Enough stories for 100 books! The epitome of a true professional!" —Rick Ward, former MBN and NCIS agent

"A master at delivering spiritual messages within secular bindings." —K.B. Schaller, *Indian Life* newspaper

"To say Merle Temple's story is unique is an understatement. His books exemplify the statement: truth is stranger than fiction!" —Dana Todd-Banks, Mature Prenuers Talk-Australia

"In his latest book, *Blood On The Ground: Living And Dying In Nod*, Merle Temple takes the reader on a journey so realistic it frightens the soul while challenging the mind. The characters become real with the magic of Temple's ability to weave words into an understanding of depth, deception and determination. Another great book from a phenomenal writer."—Brenda Daher, *The Baldwyn News*

"Merle Temple has done it again with *Blood On The Ground*— penned a suspenseful and complex novel with characters who jump off the page. We are taken for a scary ride inside the seedy nightclubs and dark alleys—places we normally wouldn't venture, locales operated by drug dealers and the Dixie Mafia. It's a journey full of betrayal in a time when the line between criminals and law enforcement was blurred. It's a journey full of plot twists and landmarks most any Southerner will recognize. It's a journey I enjoyed from the first page to the last and you will too."—Jim Clark, *Lee County Courier*

"Merle Temple is spellbinding as he navigates his undercover encounters with characters one would never want to meet." —Wang-Ying Glasgow, Memphis Public Libraries

To Ken Fairly, a father figure when I needed one.

To Claude Stuckey, the truest friend I ever had.

To all the agents who thought it would never end.

To those who never let fear spoil the journey.

To wanderers longing for home.

—*Merle Temple*

PREFACE

The grizzled old crime reporter leaned back in his chair and turned the page on his notepad. Given to old habits, he wetted the graphite in his pencil with his tongue to get a darker line and make it flow like ink.

The springs in his chair creaked as he rocked back and forth and studied an old black-and-white photo of a young Michael Parker. He looked from the image to the old man sitting in front of him and then back again. James shook his head and thought about the high price time and trials exact.

"The first drug wars were a long time ago. Merle Temple has written all these books about your life. What do you think about them?" he asked, tugging at the chin whiskers of his gray beard.

Michael Parker laughed. "That guy is inside my head," he answered.

"What was it like when the Mississippi Bureau of Narcotics was brand new and still feeling those birthing pains? Y'all didn't really think you could win the war on drugs, did you?" the reporter asked as he handed the old photo to a silver-haired Parker.

Michael squinted as he tried to find himself in the image captured in the faded picture when youth was his armor and innocence his currency. Time was growing short, the clocks ticked loudly, and the hands spun faster and faster. Here he was when his life was little more than a minor footnote in history.

"I can't speak for the others, but I wanted to save the world, rescue damsels in distress, and slay dragons—errant knights, tilting at windmills, and all that. We were young, naïve, and thought we would outlive the stars. We didn't know we were drunk on our dreams until the world sobered us up. Maybe they'll wake us one day to say none of it was real, just a daydream or a nightmare. They say reality is overrated, but what do *they* know," Michael said with a sardonic smile.

"Some of your fellow agents died young, others ran afoul of the law, and some lost their families. Do you ever think of them?" the reporter asked.

"Their faces haunt my dreams. They gave all they had to give...so many temptations, living on the edge. We didn't think about consequences or the end of the road. Everyone wanted to go to heaven, but no one wanted to die. My professor gave me a note when I left Ole Miss. I didn't understand it, but I've kept it in my wallet all these years," he said as he read from a crumpled scrap of paper.

"I am sending you out like sheep among wolves...be as shrewd as snakes and as innocent as doves. Be on guard; you'll be handed over to the local councils and flogged...but when they arrest you, do not worry about what to say or how to say it. At that time you will be given what to say, for it will not be you speaking, but the Spirit of your Father speaking through you. Matthew 10:16."

"I can see how that must seem prophetic to you now," the reporter said. "But let's get back to the undercover days...when it was fresh and raw, and you were in the thick of the brambles and briars and unbowed. The war, the corruption, the temptations, the casualties...what did *A Ghostly Shade of Pale* leave out?"

Michael clutched the yellowed Scripture and closed his eyes. Emotions and images from a prodigal life came rushing to shore, messages in bottles set adrift by the castaways of yesterday. The past washed over the present, the barricades of time were breached, and a police radio crackled in the fog of yesteryear: "Come in, 822!" "Michael, are you there?" "He has a gun!" "Look out! Get down!"

He stumbled into the Last Chance Saloon, where a hollow-eyed bartender told him he'd already had his last chance, and there were no second acts. The undertaker leaned against the gates of hell and licked his chops while Delilah cut Michael's hair, but God came to where he was and fed him in the wilderness.

A man with a crown of thorns offered shelter from the storms as men cast lots for His garments. Weeds of sorrow were browned and frayed, flowers of youth wilted inside a ring of fire, and the lost begged for salvation and banged on the doors of heaven. Sparrows were falling, but God's eye was on them all. And Michael forgave it all, as he was forgiven.

Michael whispered, "Give us eyes to see Thee in our hour of need."

"Few of us ever live in the present. We are
forever anticipating what is to come or
remembering what has gone."
—*Louis L'Amour*

PROLOGUE

"America's public enemy number one in the United States is drug abuse. In order to fight and defeat this enemy, it is necessary to wage a new all-out offensive. I've asked the Congress to provide the legislative authority and the funds to fuel this kind of offensive."
—*President Richard M. Nixon, June 14, 1971*

"We rebelled in the late sixties. With us, it wasn't an apple, it was heroin, but it was the fall all over again. The serpent didn't tempt us, or at least we didn't see him, but we figured Adam and Eve were the first hippies, just looking to throw off their shackles like us. We rejected the God of the Garden, evicted Him. If He created Adam and Eve, He must have created the serpent...maybe the Vietnam War, social injustice, and the CIA, too. It didn't all work out as planned. Mistakes were made. Some, who we thought were friends, betrayed us with bad trips and dirty needles, that Cain and Abel thing, too. People overdosed and died. The blooms of flower power withered and wilted. People got sick, homeless and penniless, but we loved Communism. All that recoil, but we flocked like lemmings to the tree of knowledge and shook hands with the devil who was homeless like us. We wanted to be our own gods, knowing both good and evil. We smoked grass, and we wanted the green, green grass of a new Garden to cover the gravesite of America. We uncorked the jug and let the genie out of the bottle, and all the king's horses and all the king's men...you know. We sowed the seeds of destruction and the red, white, and blue was twisted by the whirlwind."
—*Milkwood Jones*

"They, looking back, all the eastern side beheld / Of Paradise, so late their happy seat…They, hand in hand, with wandering steps and slow, / Through Eden took their solitary way."—John Milton, Paradise Lost

"Fallen man is not simply an imperfect creature who needs improvement: he is a rebel who must lay down his arms."
—C.S. Lewis

CHAPTER ONE

"I stand amid the roar of a surf-tormented shore,
and I hold within my hand grains of the golden
sand—How few! Yet how they creep through my
fingers to the deep while I weep!"
—Edgar Allan Poe, "Dream Within a Dream"

"Forget the former things; do not dwell on
the past. See, I am doing a new thing! Now it
springs up; do you not perceive it? I am
making a way in the wilderness and streams
in the wasteland."—Isaiah 43:18-19

As the world turned in 1972, the cost of the average home in America was $27,550, the average annual salary $11,800, gasoline 55 cents per gallon, and a new Ford Pinto was $2,078.

Jesus Christ Superstar was playing in New York. The endless ground war in Vietnam appeared in living color on American TV sets every night, courtesy of NBC's peacock. Two-thirds of America's troops had returned home, but 20,000 North Vietnamese Army troops were massing near the DMZ to attack allied positions and force the South Vietnamese Army into retreat and chaos.

The New York Times had published the Pentagon Papers, a secret history of the Vietnam war leaked by Daniel Ellsberg. The White House "plumbers" unit burglarized a psychiatrist's office to find files on Ellsberg, and a group of shadowy figures plotted a break-in at the Watergate complex in Washington, DC.

But all that seemed foreign and far away to folks in the Deep South. In the land of cotton where old times were not forgotten, yesterday and today were almost indistinguishable until the body of some local boy came home in a coffin from Southeast Asia and neighbors needed comfort. Most Southerners just wanted to believe that the war, drugs, casual intimacy, and all the excesses of the counterculture movement had never happened. They saw a creeping infection that showed signs of metastasizing and seducing their young folks. They saw it as a breeding ground, a petri dish for evil, and they wanted it to go away.

But life chugged along at a lazy pace in Mississippi, where people were known to wear overalls to funerals and plan weddings around football schedules. Troubles could seem as big as a full moon. Chiggers, red wasps, boll weevils, and horsefly-sized mosquitoes were Southern crosses to bear, binding folks together in their common miseries. Neighbors celebrated the fragrant honeysuckle spring nights and stuck by their friends through the sweltering dog days of summer. Friends were friends through good times and bad…especially the bad times that seemed to come in clusters like sour grapes.

In Parker Grove, when her grandson, Michael, asked the time, Grandma Pearl Parker would smile and say it was half past a freckle, Southern elbow time. The forsythia bushes were showing the first blush of yellow bell color, and daffodils demanded that spring appear. Pearl opened her windows so "The Lord's wind can blow where He wills it to cleanse our homes and our hearts."

God's breezes were cooling a fresh-made egg custard pie on her window sill, and His channel catfish were frying on the stove. Alberta, the jolly woman with skin like premium milk chocolate, stayed with Pearl during the day and was tending to the kitchen. The smell of fresh hush puppies, the size of large dinner rolls but light as a feather, wafted through the old house high on the hill in the community where time stood still.

Alberta, who said she was going steady with Jesus, clapped her hands as she cooked on the ancient stove and sang *"Let the power of the Holy Ghost fall on me."* Michael listened to her, tapped his toes, and told her she could have been a great blues singer, but she vowed to sing nothing but the music of God. She hugged him and said, "Michael, the blues just leaves me blue, but gospel music leaves me as free and happy as a dog with two tails to wag."

While Alberta cooked and sang to the catfish, Michael's parents worked at the local Rockwell factory and the Citizens Bank to make ends meet. So former Lee County Deputy Sheriff Michael Parker held down the fort and played Pollyanna with Pearl—his buddy, confidante, and source of unconditional love.

Michael was a brand new graduate of Ole Miss and had survived a tumultuous stint with the local sheriff's department. Then Uncle Sam pointed at him right from the old iconic recruitment poster and said, "I want you for the new drug wars." Michael liked to tell his friends he'd been traded to the Mississippi Bureau of Narcotics by his sheriff for two first-round draft picks, but his cheerleader and once-upon-a-time first love, Dixie Lee Carter, had run off with the quarterback of an opposing team. Everyone who heard his sad story thought she should have been flagged for a personal foul; unnecessary roughness, perhaps.

Michael thought about drug wars and skirmishes of the heart as he watched Pearl counting the winning numbers needed on her next roll of the dice. Her face was weathered, and she had a bun full of gray hair. She didn't get around as easily as she once did. Pearl had struggled with a leg infection since she was a young woman, a case of dew poisoning in an open wound, she said. Horses came down with rashes they called dew poisoning, but when humans walked through heavy dew with broken skin, old-timers said the toxic action of the dew could lead to serious blood poisoning.

In the days when doctors still did house calls, Dr. Tannehill came regularly to treat her leg with salves and dressing, but even the beloved family doctor could not arrest it. It looked so grim at times that amputation was even discussed, but she never asked "Why me?" When Michael asked her why she didn't, she shrugged and asked, "Why *not* me?" She patted the Bible by her side and said, "Brother Spurgeon said within the Scripture there is a balm for every wound, a salve for every sore."

Pearl had lost her husband, Eula, in 1937. Times were hard, and her leg wound was what she called "God's thorn in her side," but she kept the farm going. She picked cotton, hoed her gardens, canned vegetables and fruit, and in the Great Depression, she still managed to feed the men she affectionately called "her hobos" who jumped the boxcars and walked the rails in the bottom land. She held her family together and sent most of her boys off to fight Hitler in World War 2.

Michael found the war diary that one of her boys had left with her. Uncle Ed was a bombardier and waist gunner on one of the old flying fortresses out of England, and his notes made history live and breathe, giving Michael a seat beside his uncle on the lumbering bomber. In a letter Ed sent to Pearl, he said, "Mama, when the flak was rocking our plane, fighters were strafing us, bombers were exploding in the sky around us, and men were screaming, I looked up and saw Jesus sitting beside me. He smiled at me, Mama, and I knew everything was going to be okay."

Michael was the apple of Pearl's eye in her old age. Her blue-gray eyes still sparkled when she talked about her father's exploits in the other war—the one she called the "War Between the States" or the "War of Northern Aggression."

Captain Wood Patterson was an officer in Moreland's Calvary in north Alabama, but as they played Pollyanna, her stories weren't about his daring missions or courage under fire. The stories were deeper and darker like her mood. She knew her grandson was soon to leave for the drug wars, and the air was scented with melancholy and goodbyes. Pearl's stories and the board game were interrupted when the old rotary phone sounded the jarring ring that could wake the dead.

"Get that, son, but don't tell anyone you were playing a dice game with your grandmother," she said with a chuckle as she leaned over the board to study her next play.

When Michael answered the phone, a familiar voice said, "Michael, this is Agent Clay Strickland, chief cook and bottle washer for Director John Edward Collins."

"Hey, Clay, how are you?" Michael said to the MBN's chief of intelligence.

"Good. Congratulations on passing the written exams and physical tests for the Bureau. Saw Sarge, your old partner in Lee County, and he asked about you. Did you know he's with the sheriff's office in Hattiesburg now? Hey, I know you're not due to report for another week, but I want to ask a favor," Clay said.

"Sure, Clay. Name it," Michael said.

"I want you to come down a week early and gather some intelligence for me. No enforcement activity, no drug buys or arrests...what some might call a little dumpster diving. I want you to go to two places for me, and tell me what you see, who you see, and what they say. Write your reports and I'll cover your expenses through my office. I dropped your fake driver's license and your car tag through the mail slot at the apartment you rented in Jackson. Both will be untraceable. You'll be Jim Patterson for this assignment. I thought you might like that last name," he said.

"Thanks, I do. Pearl will be thrilled," Michael answered.

"This is a secret venture between us and the director, Michael. No one else is to know. You'll be an intelligence agent for a day," he said.

"Whatever you say, Clay. They can drive bamboo splints under my fingernails and tie me to the gates of hell, but I won't give it up!" Michael said, laughing.

"Well, I don't know if it'll require all that, but I appreciate the spirit," he chuckled.

"Meet Rose Addington, one of our CI's, when you arrive in Jackson. If you don't know, a CI is what we call a confidential informant. Pick her up at her mother's house on 123 Blueberry Lane. She's been around the block a few times, but she has a good heart that's been broken too often. Rose will be expecting you.

"She'll take you to a big concert in a field near Brookhaven. They're calling it the next Woodstock, but I have my doubts. Just be observant, make notes of names, things that stand out, and any drug use you might see. You seem pretty observant and scored well on that portion of the old Secret Service exam you took at the Tupelo Post Office," he said.

Sensing Michael's surprise, he said, "Yeah, a friend over there pulled it for us. We don't miss much," he said.

"I guess not," Michael said.

"She'll also take you to the Leg Room at the Sun-n-Sand motel in Jackson," Clay said.

"The Leg Room?" Michael asked.

"Yeah, that's a moniker for a 'members only' type place. You'll understand when you get there. I don't want to tell you much more about it. I don't want to prejudice your report. They know Rose well there, but they will ask for the password, the secret sign. Rose will have it," he said.

"Should I know the code?" Michael asked.

"No, you can't show the password, only Rose. Again, you'll understand after you get there," he said.

"Send me the report by registered mail, return receipt requested. No editorializing, 'Just the facts, just the facts,' as Joe Friday always said on *Dragnet*. When you come to the Bureau to be sworn in, report to me. I'll have your gear, and I'll handle the voucher for your expenses. You got a piece to carry?" Clay said.

"Yeah, my personal, a .380 Beretta," Michael said.

"That'll do for now until we have our first training and you can qualify on MBN-issued firearms. One last thing: this is temporary, but stand at attention. Hold your breath, cross your eyes, and hold up your right hand. Do you solemnly swear to uphold the laws of the great state of Mississippi, so help you God?" Clay said with mock seriousness.

"I do," Michael said, trying not to laugh.

"You're good and official until I see you. Carry on and good luck!" Clay said.

When Clay hung up, a mockingbird outside Pearl's window began a cooing imitation of a mourning dove. Michael told Pearl he'd have to skip the catfish and leave for Jackson.

She looked out the window at Mississippi's state bird and said, "Captain Patterson had a way with birds, like you do. I think you inherited that from him. Before you run off, sit down for a minute, son. I don't know when I'll be able to talk with you again," she said, taking his hands in hers.

"You've seen a lot in your young life, some of it right here in this house. You had to be our little man when you were just a boy, and you had to grow up way too soon. That wasn't fair to a child, but you were our undercover agent to help us keep the peace in this home long before this bunch in Jackson hired you. I want you to keep on loving people, but keep your guard up, too. There's so much wickedness in the world," she said, the wrinkles around her nose and cheeks highlighting the sadness in her eyes.

"I know, Grandma. I'll be watchful," he said, nodding.

Pearl's attention drifted for a moment as her eyes searched for some faraway place and time. Michael knew that usually meant a story was coming.

"Did I ever tell you about our neighbors, the Pettigrew family, who lived down the road from us when I was a little girl? They were fine people. Mr. Pettigrew was a nice old man, but Papa told me he wasn't quite right in the head after Garrison's raiders came through here during the war. He told me that story and said the raiders were a vicious lot, a stain on the uniforms they wore.

"They first came through the Huntsville area when Papa was away in the war, and rode up to the farm where my mama, Rebecca, lived with her family. They started for the henhouse, but Mama stood in the doorway with her axe. She told them those pullets were all her little brothers and sisters had to eat, and they would have to kill her to get to her chickens. The captain waved his soldiers off. She was lucky. If he'd killed her, I wouldn't be here, and you wouldn't either, Michael. I miss Mama, just as you'll miss me one day. Maybe after hearing her story, you'll miss her, too, though you never knew her," she said.

Listening to Pearl, he realized he still thought he would live forever and was too young to have ever considered the vulnerability of life, the twists and turns that change timelines and eliminate lives that might have been.

"The raiders were still looking for food and for silver or gold to steal when they moved down from North Alabama to the Tupelo area. Mr. Pettigrew had buried his silverware and gold coins deep in the woods of Parker Grove. People were so afraid of the raiders they would turn in their neighbors to save their own hides. Some locals told them Mr. Pettigrew was the one with the silver.

"When the raiders came to his farm, Mr. Pettigrew denied he had any precious metals. He told them, 'I don't have any, but if I did, I wouldn't give them to you.' He had a big ole strapping boy named Peter, who was thirteen but looked older. The angry captain of the raiders eyed him and said, 'He's a Confederate!' Mr. Pettigrew said, 'No, he's only a child.' But just that quick, the Yankee captain drew his revolver and shot poor Peter right between the eyes, blowing his face off.

"His mama and sisters began to shriek, to wail and moan, and when Mr. Pettigrew rushed to his boy's side, that captain threw a noose around Mr. Pettigrew's neck and hoisted him up on a limb of the big oak tree in front of their house. Then the murderers rode off and left him hanging there. The family finally cut him down, but he had hung there too long, not enough air to his brain.

"I can still see Mr. Pettigrew shuffling around the yard of his house when I was just a girl of four or five. He was never quite right after those men strung him up. The sour smell of defeat and brokenness was on him. He would sit under that old tree almost every day and call to his dead son late into the night, just repeating over and over…'Peter, where are you?' At his funeral, the people who turned him in were the ones crying the loudest," she said.

Michael saw her weathered hands clenching and twisting her apron in what might have been anger or just too much sorrow revisited. He knew there was a purpose to this reliving and retelling of a painful past.

"Papa said when General Forrest learned what the raiders had done, he went after them. He chased them into Alabama and almost to Georgia, killing as many as he and his troops could catch. The general rode so long and hard that he fell out of his saddle more than once. He always had to be alert and careful, because the Union troops used attacks on civilians to lure him into traps to kill him.

"General Forrest was waiting for the Union Army at Brice's Crossroads. It was wet and muddy, and the Yankees were slogging through the mud and the humidity, and they were tired. It was pretty much a slaughter, but the supply wagons and the raiders who'd attacked the Pettigrew family took off for Memphis. They got bogged down in the mud, and our troops caught up with them near Ripley. With the memories of Mr. Pettigrew and people like him fresh on their hearts, so much anger and hate was boiling within them. They dismounted and clubbed those Yankees to death that day. It was a scene from a nightmare. Papa wasn't there, but some men who had fought with him in North Alabama were present, and he said they used to tell that story and weep. It haunted and tortured them until they died," she said.

She closed her eyes and shuddered at the thought of that day and the horrors of that time. The mockingbird landed on the window sill, looked at her, but ceased to sing.

"The Civil War wasn't civil at all, Michael, and this world isn't either," she said quietly.

"All those old stories of atrocities are why some folks have a hard time forgetting and forgiving. It drove some into the arms of the hooded haters, but they aren't the answer. That was the one word I never heard Captain Patterson use...hate. The only answer to that kind of pain, to all pain, is Jesus Christ. There's so much darkness in the world, son. I want you to be vigilant but to go on loving people like you do. Hate is a cancer that eats you up. It doesn't hurt your enemies, but it'll consume you and keep you separated from God," she said.

"The world will offer you thirty pieces of silver, tickle your ears, and whisper sweet nothings to you, Michael. They'll disguise lies as truth, but when the devil's lies are exposed, it'll always be an ugly and indecent exposure. Seek the good and the glorious, son, and cling to the old rugged cross. When the storms come, just listen for the whispers on the wind and the rhythm of raindrops slapping the earth around you. It might be Him, His feet on the same ground as yours. Put it to the test: 'If it doesn't glorify God, why am I doing it?' Promise me you'll keep your eyes wide open, and watch out for those people who want to steal your soul," she said, her voice pleading with him to hear her truth.

"I promise, Grandma," Michael answered.

"Once, when I was a young girl, I was fishing on the banks of Parker Pond. My cousin was fishing nearby. He was catching fish, one bream after another, but I noticed he was keeping the small ones and throwing the big ones back. I asked him why he was doing that, and he said, 'The big ones are too big for my frying pan,'" Pearl said.

"So many people live their lives like that. God is sending big blessings their way, but they think their pans are too small to handle anything but the small fry. Do you understand, Michael?" she said, her Southern turn of story and Gospel diction always edifying and precise.

"Yes, ma'am, I think so," he answered.

Michael packed his clothes in the little back room of the house he grew up in and tucked the Beretta under his belt. Alberta's goodbye hug dusted him with flour from head to toe. When he came back by Pearl's room with his suitcase, the wayward March winds were blowing the curtains on her open window, and he saw the sadness written across her face. She was wiping her leaking eyes and nose with the embroidered cotton handkerchief she always kept in her apron. It was her one "extravagance."

Pearl took his hand and held it in wrinkled palms that felt like velvet or soft, warm butter. She placed a package of King Leo peppermint sticks in his hand, her cure for all ills, and said, "In your life, the war won't be between states, Michael, it will be between your heart and your head. Take these in case your get up and go has got up and gone, and you need a little bit of zip-a-dee-doo-dah!"

When he packed his car to leave, he looked in the backseat, and there was a giant iron frying pan she had tucked away for him.

As he slowly coasted down the gravel drive, parting pinched his heart, and a blackbird sang its musical trill of "*pack up all your cares and woes.*" The day raced toward twilight, and the sun melted from its weariness. The old frame house was enveloped by the shadowy reflections of evening shade, the willows by the pond were weeping, and Michael thought about fish and blessings just jumping into his big skillet.

CHAPTER TWO

"I long to hear the story of your life which
must captivate the ear strangely."
—William Shakespeare, The Tempest

"There was a lot of things I probably
wouldn't do now, you know, if I had it
to do over again."—Tanya Tucker

When Michael pulled up to the modest ranch-style house on Blueberry Lane, the lawn was still wet from a midnight rain. A soggy *Clarion Ledger* newspaper was disintegrating in the middle of the drive, and he saw the front window curtains part ever so slightly. Someone was peeking out at him.

Before he could knock on the door, it flung open, and a young woman with long, dishwater blonde hair and lots of freckles gushed, "Hi, I'm Rambling Rose! You can call me Rose or Nosey Rosy, my other nickname!"

The sudden smell of spoiled food, bacon grease, and garbage overwhelmed Michael. The sink was piled high with dirty dishes and glasses, a dead fly garnished a platter of meat on the stove, and a carton of soured milk warmed in the heat of the house. Cigarette ashes dusted the couch, and a half bottle of Jack Daniel's sat on the kitchen counter.

The smiling Rose before him was a nubile nymph with a headband, a large peace symbol, enough beads for three rosaries, a miniskirt, and white go-go boots. Clay had warned him she had a penchant for falling in love with agents, one agent describing Rose as a tart with a heart. Rose and her friend Molly had become mainstays for agents looking to buy drugs from dealers in Jackson.

"I bet you must be Michael! You're just as handsome as Clay described you," she said.

"This is my best friend, Molly, and this is Carla, my mom," she said.

Molly, a redheaded woman in her early to middle twenties, had high prominent cheekbones, giving her face a hollow look. Her eyes were dark green and wide set, accentuated by her long Betty Boop eyelashes. Her strong presence had an air of petulance. She grabbed his hand in the new interlocking-thumb hippie handshake and said, "What's happening?" Her eyes were probing and appraising, sizing up the new agent.

Rose's mother, Carla, was thirtyish, a bleached blonde, barely five feet tall, and wore hip-hugging bell-bottom jeans, a ton of cheap jewelry, and a halter top—a look she just wasn't pulling off.

"Hello, Agent Michael," Carla purred as she batted her long, fake eyelashes.

She saw him looking at her outfit and said, "You know, I once bought high-waisted jeans as chastity belts and birth control for my daughter and her friends. It didn't work, so I gave up and joined them. How do you like my lowriders?"

Michael smiled and nodded as Carla rattled on.

"Get my baby home early, and we can party later when y'all get back," she cooed, jangling her junk jewelry.

"Yes, ma'am, I'll have her home early," Michael said.

"Ma'am?" she said indignantly, her hands on her hips. "I was only fourteen when I had Rose. Everyone says we look like sisters," Carla protested.

"Would you like something to eat before we go, Michael?" Rose asked, trying to change the subject.

Eyeing a potato that appeared ready for planting, a loaf of bread with fuzzy green spots, and a plate of hard black pebbles that once might have been beans, Michael tactfully replied, "No, thanks, I've already eaten, and we'll probably get some dogs at the concert later."

As Michael and Rose were leaving, Carla called out, "Hey, Michael, did we just click, or was that the sound of your handcuffs snapping around my heart, Mister Narcotics Agent Parker? Come back anytime if you need to frisk me. I might be concealing something intoxicating."

Michael flushed red, and she laughed uproariously.

Carla sucked in the tiny roll of fat above her low-cut jeans, and the girls shot looks at each other and rolled their eyes. As Michael walked out the door, he saw her hitching up her pants to cover lacy black undies peeking above the lowriders. The hip-huggers exposed not only her imperfections but a red rhinestone in her belly button and futile attempts to recapture a wasted youth.

As the door closed, Carla said, "What can I say? Vanity is my favorite sin."

****

After they left the house, Rose talked nonstop on the trip to the concert, her monologue interrupted only by an "and then" bridge between stories. She talked so much and so fast she was stumbling over and choking on her own words. Occasionally she would take a breath and ask, "Are you listening, Michael?"

They drove down I-55 to Brookhaven and took a county road to the middle of nowhere. As they traveled the narrow blacktop road, it seemed bluebirds and crows had cornered the market on fence posts. Perched atop each post, the black and blue surveyed their kingdom with regal dispassion while turtles lined the logs of every pond.

They passed an old cemetery where mourners in dark clothes hung their heads over freshly tilled dirt and supported loved ones when their knees buckled. Their pastor stood with an open Bible, mouthing the words, "Ashes to ashes, dust to Mississippi dirt."

When they rounded a curve in the road, they passed the mourners' small church. A sign out front read *Every home in our county has a Bible and a loaded gun.*

It was a rural area in transition. A muddy stream divided the county and once provided the mineral-rich water that made the local moonshine taste so sweet. The shine fueled the "brown bag" hymns of those who drank the brew concealed in brown paper bags while singing hymns of repentance. When a new generation arrived, they still sought the escape of altered states, but they snorted the white powder and smoked the homegrown while country parsons preached the brimstone.

Michael and Rose passed a roadside memorial with flowers and crosses to mark the spot where someone had died in an accident. Michael never quite understood why it was comforting to make a shrine of a place of death. But locals viewed these places as way-stations or exit doors from the here and now, temporary portals to the hereafter. The makeshift crosses were tributes by family, warnings by the grieving, and tardy, dead-on-arrival messages of "I love you" and "IOU."

One sparsely worded tribute had all that and roadside poetry, too—*Here exited Johnny Bell, who took a detour to hell. He shot that dope and lost all hope.*

It was late in the afternoon when Michael and Rose heard the music wafting across the fields bordering the road they were on. When they topped a green ridge brushing a sapphire sky, they could see the giant stage. Towering speakers framed the mosquito theater and boomed like thunder with each bass guitar lick.

When Michael paid their entry fee and inquired about the lineup of musicians, he learned a dozen acts had cancelled due to the promoter's failure to pay the entertainers. As they walked down the hillside toward the stage, vultures circled overhead in a lazy spiral, black brush strokes on a pale-blue palette. They seemed to be painting a ghastly mural, and Michael thought they were following him.

A small crowd of revelers was dancing in various stages of undress, and some openly used drugs. Several music fans walked past Michael, marijuana smoke literally seeping from their noses. A fog of vapor circled their heads like halos, and the scent of hemp clung to their clothes. Michael thought the long-haired young men looked like Tarzan but smelled like Cheetah.

Tanya Tucker was performing as they neared the stage. As Michael stood beneath her, someone hurled their underwear at Tanya and caught her full in the face as she belted out the high notes of "Delta Dawn."

She coughed, sputtered, and stammered.

Then the young blonde singer picked up the jockey shorts, looked at Michael, and said, "Are these yours, honey?"

"No, ma'am," Michael said.

She doubled over with laughter, resting her hands on her knees. "Ma'am! Did you call me ma'am? Well, aren't you a gentleman among thieves! You're just Southern fried precious," she said.

After making the rounds and mentally noting things for his report to Clay, he saw the concert was fizzling and told Rose it was time to go.

When Michael and Rose were leaving the concert area, he looked up to see the rootin'-tootin' sheriff of the county lumbering down the hillside toward them. He was overweight, balding, and a huge silver belt buckle accentuated the thickness around his middle. He had massive arms and shoulders. He wore arrogance like an overcoat and brooding anger like a badge of honor. The High Sheriff was looking for someone to harass.

Michael and Rose walked on, but the sheriff caught them from behind. He grabbed Michael roughly by the collar and spun him around.

"What're you hippies doing down here in my county?" he asked in a foghorn voice.

"Just listening to good music, Sheriff," Michael said with a winsome smile.

"Uh-huh. You sure you aren't here to smoke dope, get that sticky THC tar down in your lungs so you can cough like a coal miner and get high as a kite?" he demanded.

"No, sir," Michael answered, still smiling at the sheriff's mouthful of accusations.

"You laughing at me? You smile when things ain't funny," the sheriff said.

"No, sir, I just don't want to wind up like my cousin when he talked to the police. His mind took a vacation, and his mouth started working overtime," Michael said.

"Uh-huh, you're faster than Nabisco baking cookies, aren't you? You hippies are like bad weather these days. Y'all are blowing in and raining on decent folks' parades. Who's this cheap little harlot you got with you?" he asked, trying to provoke Michael.

"She's just a blind date, Sheriff. Never met her before today," Michael deadpanned.

"Uh-huh. She's probably a motherless orphan, and you're nothing more than a love child of your mama and some itinerant Romeo who jumped the line ahead of the daddy that raised you," he said.

"No, sir, I look too much like both of them," Michael said calmly.

"Want to know why I stopped you? My deputy ran a 28 on your tag, and the state shows that tag has never been issued. Can you explain that?" the sheriff asked.

"No, sir, I can't. Government efficiency, maybe," Michael said with a bewildered look.

"Let me see your driver's license," the sheriff said.

Michael handed him the one Clay had left in his mailbox.

He snatched it from Michael and looked it over.

"I'm going to check you out with a fine-tooth comb. You don't rile easy, do you, son?" he asked as he made notes before handing the license back to him.

"No, sir," Michael said.

"Uh-huh. Boy, have you thought about what you're going to ask Jesus when you meet Him?"

"No, sir, I'm more concerned about what He'll ask me," Michael said with his best boyish grin.

The sheriff looked at him for a long time without saying anything and then said, "You have this look, like you know something the rest of us don't. Maybe you do, and maybe you don't, but that can be pretty irritating. Go on, get out of here, but you remember this—don't deal your dope down here in my county, and don't look at our girls with lustful eyes. If you do, we'll dress you in stripes and put you in our jail for some rehabilitation that'll wipe that smile off your face," he said.

"I promise you'll never catch me selling dope or messing with your girls, Sheriff," Michael said.

Michael heard a dog howling in the distance, and the sheriff cocked his ear in that direction, forgetting himself for a moment.

"Well, I got to go now. That's my old dog, Blue. It gives me the chills when I hear her in pain. She done treed something or somebody. She's gotten old, and sometimes it's just in her head. Her belly and breasts are dragging the ground, but I can't bring myself to put her down. Dogs, deadbolts, and the divine are about all a man can depend on to keep safe in this world," the sheriff said.

He looked back at Michael as he turned to walk away and said, "You know something, Jim? If silence truly is golden, you may wind up a rich man!"

With that parting advice, he took off at a brisk pace as the howls of his dog became more plaintive. "Coming, Blue!" he shouted.

Rose was quiet as they walked along. She studied his face before speaking.

"Your voice was soft, and you smiled a lot, but you pushed that cracker pretty good. You're a gambler, a risk-taker, aren't you," she said.

"Sometimes, when it's warranted, Rose," he said.

"Do you roll the dice, you know, shoot craps on the dice tables, too?" she asked.

"No, I only roll dice in high-stakes games of Pollyanna," he said with a smile.

"What's Pollyanna, and who do you play it with?" she asked.

Michael thought of Pearl and said, "I can't say. I promised someone."

"You got so much warmth about you, Agent Parker, but underneath it all, I think you're freezing to death. I could thaw you out," she said.

Michael thought of Dixie Lee and a roaring fire and said, "Thanks, Rose, but I'll be fine."

Rose looked at him again as he opened the car door for her and said, "I know you're afraid I want you to say you love me, but I don't really. I just love you narc agents!"

Michael said, "We love you, too, Rose."

CHAPTER THREE

*"I don't think he enriched himself. But he did have
a lot of thieves around him. He spent himself.
He tore his passion to tatters, as Shakespeare
would put it."—Raymond Moley*

*"He was a crook...a corrupt politician...a
demagogue—but he kept his campaign
promises."—Drew Pearson*

The sky was bathed in shades of purple and peach when Michael and Rose arrived at the Sun-n-Sand motel. The first peek of distant stars in the heavens looked as if Tinkerbell had been to the dust mill to gather and sprinkle fairy dust across the twilight to light the way to the moon.

The motel was a place of secret deals, illicit rendezvous, legendary mixed drink concoctions, and Black Forest cake. The Sun-n-Sand was only a block from the Capitol building. State workers and pretty young women milled about outside, hoping to wrangle an invitation to the Leg Room.

A big man with a hard look, square jaw, and close-cropped salt-and-pepper hair was working security on the door of the Leg Room. He was wearing a tight suit that accentuated his barrel chest and thick neck. It was obvious he was a cop, perhaps one of the highway patrolmen who worked security at the Capitol. When he opened the door, he recognized Rose. He didn't ask for the sign, but she gave it anyway.

Her eyes never leaving his, Rose raised her skirt above her knee and said, "Slender legs." Michael understood then why Clay said he wouldn't be able to show the sign.

"Hello, Rose," the man said dryly.

"Hi, Bobby, how's your wife?" Rose asked with a sly smile.

There seemed to be some history between the two of them, and he quickly waved Rose and Michael through without further conversation.

The air in the suite was smoky and stale. A crowd was gathered in the rear of the suite around a redheaded man in a crisply pressed gray highway patrol uniform. His polished badge gleamed under the garish bar lights where the mixologist created storied concoctions he served with the hottest tamales in town for patrons with iron stomachs. As a Ways and Means Committee member once said, "There are many ways and many means over drinks and hot tamales across the street at the Sun-n-Sand motel where souls are sold and deals are struck."

Michael recognized the freckle-faced patrolman as Red Winter. Winter had been at Jackson Memorial Stadium when tests were held for applicants hoping to become MBN agents. The revelers in the suite were loud, raucous, and far removed from the fresh-faced youngsters at the stadium.

"Tell us about the stop you made the other night near Canton, Red," asked a man wearing a state representative name tag.

"Yeah, it was about midnight. I stopped this big ole black guy. He jumped out of the car, and Mary Jane smoke came boiling from the open door. He lumbered toward me, and I swung my heavy flashlight with all I had and hit him right upside of his head. It would've dropped an elephant to its knees," the animated storyteller said.

"Yeah, yeah, what happened then, Red?" one of the eager partygoers asked.

The officer grinned a boyish smile and said, "That big ole boy just blinked, shook his head, and said, 'Don't you do that again.'"

People laughed. They laughed too loudly. They were desperate to have a jolly good time, and all the noisy heehawing primed the pump of their storyteller.

"So I pulled my revolver and told him he could go peaceably, or I would just kill him right there, drag his body into the woods, and bury him where no one would ever find him. He assumed the position, and that was that," Red said.

Applause broke out, sodden toasts were made, and nervous young women watched their powerful escorts for cues and clues, so they would know when to laugh and clap.

"Tell 'em about you and the Natchez Trace park ranger, Red," another intoxicated politician called out.

"Yeah, I was called to work a wreck, and the shortest route was to jump up on the Trace to get there as quick as I could. I had my blue lights on and was whipping down the Trace when this ranger dropped in behind me with his blue lights on. I got off on the state highway and he followed me. I stopped to work the wreck. He pulled over behind me and just sat there.

"When I finished, and the tow trucks and ambulances were gone, that old boy walked toward me with his ticket book. I asked him what he was doing, and he said, 'Writing you a ticket for speeding on MY highway, a federal highway. I'll need your driver's license.'

"So I pulled my license out, and as he reached for it, I pulled it back and said, 'I'll need *your* license!'" Winter said.

Everyone laughed. Legislators slapped their knees, paid Winter over-the-top compliments, and their paramours giggled spontaneously this time.

"Yeah, it was funny," Red said, laughing and soaking up the adulation from the crowds.

"The ranger stuttered and asked, 'Wh-wh-what? Why do you need *my* license?' I said, 'Because you were speeding on MY highway, a state highway!'" Red said.

More guffaws.

"Yeah, he gave me his, and I gave him mine. He'd write a little in his ticket book, and I'd write a little in mine. He was fuming and about to explode. Then he said, 'You son of a...!' He jumped in his car and roared off toward his federal highway, fishtailing all over the road and slinging gravel," Red said.

Men were stomping their feet and slapping Red's back.

One of the silver-haired legislators said, "That carpetbagger federal scum. Yankees sent down here, I bet. Give us his name, and we'll get the local sheriff to roust him, and the tax assessor to revoke his homestead exemption. We'll fix him good."

Switching gears seamlessly, the legislator asked, "Say, Red, you got us some more of that smooth drinking whiskey tonight, the good stuff?"

"Yes, sir, I got a trunkload of the prime stuff. I stopped two trucks out of Kentucky and told 'em I might overlook their broken taillights—which I broke—if they'd give me two cases of good Kentucky bourbon," he bragged.

"Son, you're the best. What about some new girls for the Leg Room?" the man asked.

"Oh, yes, sir, they'll be up here later. I found some who're eager to work off their speeding tickets. These racehorses could run at Churchill Downs," he said.

Then Red looked up, saw Michael, and did a double-take. His face turned the near-orange color of his hair. Red looked away nervously and then quickly left the Leg Room, but Michael stayed to watch and mentally record events as Clay had asked.

Young women in tight skirts and low-cut blouses entered the suite, and some went into adjoining bedrooms with legislators in their sixties and seventies, men who had left their long-suffering wives back home in the districts they represented. Michael thought there were more double and triple chins in those bedrooms than a board meeting of the AARP.

Men were passed out on couches, and the room was filled with a pungent smoke that smelled like burning leaves or a skunk that had rolled in ragweed. Michael thought he would never be able to pass a dead skunk on the road again without thinking of that stench.

Sin, gin, and the tin men who were intent on staying near the troughs of the public till filled the Leg Room, and Michael's idealism was under full assault.

A tall, slender man with a melon-shaped head entered the room, and everyone deferred to him. Men rose to greet the man with Harry Truman spectacles, and the groupie girls appeared nervous, eager to be noticed and anxious to please. People were lighting cigarettes off the electricity in the air around the man. A bartender handed him a glass of whiskey and a fresh-rolled cigarette, one of those with the funny smell, and he glad-handed the crowd as he sipped whiskey and took long draws off the cigarette.

Michael heard someone call him Senator Ball just as he said, "Yes, this re-po-tah asked me if I was interested in foreign affairs. I said, 'No, not at all, son. I prefer American women myself.'"

Everyone laughed uproariously, and he basked in the adulation until he spied Rose and walked toward her with a grin on his face like a man with a sideways banana in his mouth.

"His name is Cornelius, but you can call him Corndog. Everybody does," Rose whispered to Michael.

"Well, Rosie, who's this you have with you today?" Senator Ball asked, his smile exposing large, crooked teeth that looked like a beaver after an all-you-can-eat buffet of hardwood trees.

"This is Jim from Tupelo, Corndog. He's an old family friend in town to visit," she said.

"Howdy, Jim, did you kids bring us any good reefer?" he asked, looking over his glasses at Michael with a warm smile that did nothing to change his cold eyes.

Michael looked at him and then at Rose.

"Don't mind Jim. He's kinda shy," Rose said with a wink.

"Oh, don't look so shocked, Jim. We got to have some fun here in the Leg Room. It ain't all about the girls. We got to get mellow, too. We have a stressful job, and we do our part," the senator said. He constantly cleared his smoke-filled throat before returning to a fixed smile that reminded Michael of the faked happiness of a Miss America contestant who'd just learned she was first runner-up.

"You'd better be careful, Corndog. You were the co-sponsor of the bill to create the Mississippi Bureau of Narcotics, weren't you?" Rose coyly asked.

"Why yes, honey, I did. The voters were demanding it. So we took the path of least resistance. But honey, that's just for the little people. Such restrictions don't apply to us. We're entitled, don't you know?" he said with a chuckle.

He took a drink of whiskey, swished it around in his mouth, gargled loudly before swallowing, and said, "Rose, darlin', you're right, though. You're always worried about your old Daddy Corndog, and that's why I love you. I do worry sometimes about creating ole Frankenstein. When he gets up off the table and starts lurching about, will he recognize his creator and obey his master?

"But I've known Director John Edwards Collins since he was an ATF agent, head of the LEAA, and a reporter for the *Clarion Ledger*. Democrats have done well by him, and Governor J.P. Coleman swore by him. Collins once liked the bottle more than he should have, but we stuck with him. He owes us, but he's also stubborn and independent. That team of college boys he's hired couldn't manage a flea circus, but it could be hard to put the genie back in the bottle once it's been uncorked.

"What irritates me is how we let him bamboozle us into setting such tough requirements to be an agent. Their resumes should only contain the important qualifications. Did you vote Democrat, who do you know, who you kin to, and what're you willing to do for us when asked. We have to replenish our voter base. Not everybody who votes Democrat has a home address in the graveyards, but the dead are among our most loyal voters.

"Our county sheriffs will still nab the boys with a couple of joints or maybe even a pound of weed and send 'em straight to Parchman. That won't interfere with the cooperative players who fly their planes to and from Belize from our crop-duster airfields in the Delta. The feds don't care too much as long as their gun-running mercenaries have the state's remote airfields to launch their flights. They can fly under radar all the way to Central America and back," he said.

He ignored Michael and touched Rose, brushing her hair lightly. Michael noticed every time she got near Corndog, he seemed compelled to touch her.

"Rose, you're a sweet little girl, but you think too much of these new kids on the block. If they get contrary and impudent and try to get off the leash, it may take us a while, but there're ways to hobble them when they do. That'll never interfere with our recreational activities here in the Leg Room and down at Moondog Square. We're like gods here in Jackson. Sure, we play poker with the devil. His deck is stacked, but he's always happy to accept our IOUs," Corndog said.

He took another long toke on the joint he carried, held it, and began to talk in a squeaky voice, like a constipated man who had snorted helium.

He smoked. He drank. He talked. He bragged...too much.

"You know, son, I grew up in the Delta, picking cotton in the hot sun, dragging that heavy sack, my hands bleeding from them sharp cotton burrs. My pants would be full of cockle burrs, and my back would hurt so bad from stooping over to pick that sometimes I had to crawl down the rows. I knew I had to find a way out, and I vowed to never crawl again for no man.

"It was hard because I was nobody...a poor student, a sickly child, but the local political boss told me I had a certain charm and a way with words. He said my future might be in the pulpit or...in politics.

"I just couldn't see myself as no polecat preacher. So I cleaned myself up and decided to go right to the top. I'd run for the state senate slot held by the Honorable Justin Johnson, the man who wore bow ties with seersucker suits and looked like he had sucked on a persimmon.

"He had a mistress in every county in the flatland of the Mississippi Delta. They'd put on their best cotton dresses and sit on the front porch of their little shanties and wait for him. They'd see a cloud of dust across the cotton fields and know he was coming. He'd give them some little token of his affection when he left and leave some poor man to raise the children he sired," he said.

The Delta politician gestured wildly, like a man swatting at flies. He weaved a bit, steadied himself, and then continued his recollections. Power and pot had seduced him into believing his self-manufactured legend, and every telling of his tall tales got better and better.

"Senator Johnson crushed me twice, and he mocked me one day in public…in front of my friends. That old boy laughed in my face and told me I'd better pick up my sack and get on back to the cotton fields. Right there and then, I swore I'd get him.

"I prayed and prayed for God to let me defeat him and be elected to the legislature, but it wasn't happening. One night I had this dream where I was in this big stew pot, and the cannibals were about to eat me. Then the head cannibal came up to the pot and sprinkled some dust in the stew, and he told me, 'It's all in the seasoning.'

"I finally realized that praying for the seat wasn't how God works. I figured God helps those who help themselves, and it was better to ask for forgiveness than permission. So I found out one of his girlfriends was mad at him. He'd done her wrong. I convinced her to season his stew with this animal tranquilizer I got from an old veterinarian. She did, sprinkled it in his bowl right there in a famous Greenville restaurant.

"Senator Bowtie got violently ill in public. It was on him like skunk spray, and he collapsed to the floor of the restaurant like a glass-jawed boxer who had just run into Marciano's right hook. It wasn't pretty, but I had hit the perfecta. All my nags had come in under the wire, and all his chickens had come home to roost. It ain't about breaking even, it's about *getting* even. That's what I told Johnny Vaught after Ole Miss lost a game. Coach, it's all about winning and scoring touchdowns. Don't you kids ever forget it!" he said.

Rose said, "We won't, Corndog." But Senator Ball was stoned in the end zone, his tongue thick but loose.

"God knows we're just souls in animal bodies, and right or wrong, the animal wants what it wants. So I asked God to forgive me for my methods, and here I am. I have men picking up satchels full of money for me in every county. I've been milking the cows better than Johnson ever did. I just give 'em what they want and tell 'em what they want to hear.

"While I've been oratatin' about the boogeymen taking their jobs and defiling and deflowering their women, the voters are still stuck on stupid. While they're reading romance novels and the tabloids and pretending their pathetic little lives matter, I've been deep drilling and it's thrilling," he said.

He let out a big whoosh of smoke, and his eyes rolled back up in his head for a moment.

"Twenty years later, and I'm still here. The story about what I did to Bowtie got around, and now no one will run against me. It's all about cannibals and the seasoning. That's my theology, son…that and the Leg Room here in Jackson. I'm still fishing, and my political worm ain't lost his wiggle. I'm making out like a peg-legged pirate on the deck of the Good Ship Lollipop.

"We're the heaven and hell party, Jim. Support us, and it will be heaven on earth. Go against us, and the fire can get pretty hot. I had to explain it to the pup from Arkansas who's running McGovern's presidential campaign. I told Bill there ain't no way a socialist is going to carry Mississippi or be President, and the national party had better recognize our regular slate of delegates to the convention, not this rabble of pretenders down here.

"He smiled a lot and had this catch in his voice, but the boy wasn't dumb. He was a Rhodes scholar, but I heard Oxford University 'rode' him right of England when he got rough with some girl. I can't fault him too much for liking the ladies, but I told him the forecast for McGovern's chances are about as good as the chances for a snow blizzard in hell," he said.

A man came up to Corndog to whisper in his ear, something about Bad Eye Tutor's wife dying and him being released early from Parchman Penitentiary.

"Don't worry me about cotton-picking, nitpicking nonsense. Just alert the sheriff and our local boys. They'll take care of it. I'm off the clock, on R and R time now…rest and recreation and rock n' roll," he said.

"Rose understands, don't you, darling? She's a veteran of the Leg Room," he said, patting her leg.

She smiled vacantly and mouthed the required words with mock sincerity. "Yes, sir, Senator. You're the best."

"Sure as a chicken's got feathers, that's right," he said as he slapped her backside.

"I was a lowly whitetail, but here in the garden of good and evil, I'm a god, the baddest buck in the forest. I'm as lost as Alice and as mad as the Hatter, but I'm a bad boy senator, and the bad girls like me and my foreign cars. All of us in this room know we've offended the gods and are cursed, so we're prepared to appease them, to throw some virgins into the volcano here in the Leg Room.

"But that means girls like you don't have to worry, Rose!" he said with the cackle of a lunatic who had sold his soul to the devil.

He wandered off but called out to Michael as they were leaving. "Just remember, kids, everyone talks about rooting for the underdog, but it's the top dogs they follow. You have to choose carefully which dogs you gonna bark with when you howl at the moon. They say you can have it all. That's a lie, but I do have everything that old Delta patrician once had, and winners get to write and rewrite history books and epitaphs. Remember, it's us versus them," he said.

"Who are them, Senator?" Michael asked.

"Anyone who ain't us, boy. Don't you be falling in the ditch with them," he said, giving Michael a hard look.

"There are ditches on both sides of the road, Senator," Michael said with a big smile.

"Well, son, I guess you'll have a shoulder to cry on either way, won't you?" Corndog said.

On the way to Rose's house, Michael didn't talk much.

Rose said, "Those old men got a bad case of the sweet tooth for booze, drugs, and girls, but it was good having you as my escort. It was our first date," she said with a big, sad smile.

When he didn't respond, she said, "You know they're really not such bad people, Michael. They just like to have a good time, and they've been kind to me. They don't hurt nobody unless they deserve it."

Michael looked at her and said, "Rose, I was born at night, but not last night. Those guys are as twisted as old phone cords. It's hard to believe the people of Mississippi cast their pearls before such swine. I'm not buying what they're selling, not even on double Green Stamp days, and you shouldn't either. They tell you a lot, too much, and one day they may start wondering how much they told you when they were high on drugs or their brains were numbed by lust. You need to be careful."

Rose smiled an innocent, childlike smile and almost swooned. "I knew you cared about me, Michael. I just knew it," she said.

He looked at his sweet and harmless CI and thought she struggled to stay in touch with reality, that this was all grand theater and the stuff of romance novels to her. She most likely suffered from a mild case of manic depression and appeared to be circling the drain of life. It broke his heart for her, and he wished the MBN didn't have to use girls like Rose.

"Crack the window, Rose. We both need to breathe some fresh air after tonight and clear our heads of Corndog's game of smoke and mirrors."

Michael thought about the Leg Room and politicians like Corndog. *Ticks are not the only bloodsucking creatures in Mississippi.*

CHAPTER FOUR

*"Funny, I don't remember no good dope days. I
remember walking for miles in a dope fiend
haze...shooting up in the bathroom and falling out
at the park...overdosing on my bedroom floor...my
dad having to break down the door...thinking today
was the day that his baby had died...feeling like I
lost all hope...giving up my body for the next bag of
dope...getting down on my knees and asking God to
save me cuz I don't want to do this no more!"*
—Delaney Farrell

*"He who is not sage and wise, humane and
just, cannot use secret agents. And he who
is not delicate and subtle cannot get the
truth out of them."*—Sun Tzu

After his visit to the Leg Room, Michael took a long, hot
shower and stayed up late to watch *In Harm's Way*, an old black-
and-white movie starring John Wayne. He drifted off to sleep in
the wee hours of the morning he was to officially report for duty at
the Mississippi Bureau of Narcotics.

He awoke from his dreams, snoring like a stalled chainsaw,
just as the ship he and the Duke were on was pitching to and fro on
stormy seas, and the officer on duty was sounding battle stations—
"All hands on deck! This is not a drill! Man your battle stations!"

The Duke's character, Captain Rockwell Torrey, snatched
the pillow from under Michael's head and said, "In case it slipped
your mind, gunnery stations at 0830, mister!"

When Michael arrived at the intersection of Lakeland and
Ridgewood, the last gasp of winter warred with the first hints of
spring. Tiny green buds adorned the branches of young trees
bordering the nondescript buildings. Beams of sunlight struggled

to break through the morning haze, and sudden gusts of wind formed dust devils. A lazy rooster crowed about the dawning of a new day and a new era in Mississippi. A silver morning mist enveloped the secret headquarters of the Mississippi Bureau of Narcotics. Michael thought it gave his new place of employment the look of a slumbering giant nestled in a cocoon of fog.

Down the street, young boys practiced on the diamonds of the Dizzy Dean baseball league, and a chain gang from the Hinds County Jail worked the highway to the east. Men in orange suits, many incarcerated for dope crimes, dragged their trash sacks behind them and sang the blues as they worked the swinging rhythm of sling blades to weed Lakeland Drive. The inmates and the baseball players were unaware that agents commissioned to "save" them from themselves were gathering around the corner at drug enforcement central.

The MBN was a hollow army with more troops on paper than trained agents in the field. The agency was struggling to get up to speed. Recruitment of fresh young faces straight out of college and veterans just back from the rice paddies of Vietnam was at full bore. The director appointed control agents to be temporary supervisors until a management assessment center could be developed.

While the MBN built the agency from the ground up, it had to depend on local police departments and federal agencies to develop informants to work with MBN field agents. Until the agency was operating at full speed, this was a risky but necessary startup proposition that attracted spies and prying eyes. Clay Strickland's new intelligence unit worked around the clock analyzing raw data to build a matrix of the state's drug business.

****

When Michael stepped out of his vehicle at headquarters, a group of scruffy young men milled about the parking lot. Some showed pistols under their arms or on their belts when they bent over the trunks of their cars to load forms, typewriters, weapons, and other tools of their trade. Like Michael, the agents appeared eager, anxious, and chomping at the bit…horses straining to break out of the starting gate.

Most, like Michael, had long hair and scraggly beards in the early stages of development. The motley crew clustered around the front of the main building were smoking, dipping, chewing, and jawboning. They were cool cats full of testosterone and false bravado, young men who thought they had nine lives and would always land on their feet.

They were a murder of cawing crows pretending to be a parliament of wise owls, modeling and imitating their heroes—high school football coaches, John Wayne, and Clint Eastwood. Michael thought they must have loved their mothers because they mentioned them often. Every day seemed to be Mother's Day to them.

They were probationary agents, survivors of rigorous trials the previous summer at Jackson Memorial Stadium. The agents had cleared a trying gauntlet of tests—weight and endurance exercises, hundred-yard dashes, IQ tests and psychological exams. Most applicants had failed either the physical and mental screenings or the exhaustive background investigations. The men in the parking lot were among the "lucky" ones, the chosen few.

The reasons they signed up for President Nixon's "War on Drugs" were as varied as the eclectic congregation of men gathered at MBN headquarters. Most were blue-collar gladiators running to or away from something. Some were empty vessels in need of filling up with a good cause or the faith of their parents many had abandoned. They were a diverse crew of warriors—college graduates, street cops, crusaders, and businessmen looking for adventure. Some were trying to leave the war behind, and a few husbands, who had married too young, were trying to leave their regrets behind when the seven-year itch arrived.

Life had rolled snake eyes for some gamblers who had come to Jackson to let it all ride. They opted to shoot the longshot boxcars, draw into an inside straight, or thumb a ride on the road to a new life. If that failed, the backup plan was to pursue a formula of GW+GE equaled salvation—good works and good enough to squeak into heaven before the angels sealed the gated community.

There were early signs of some simmering resentment and friction between those who went to war in Vietnam and students who had taken deferments to attend college and avoid Selective Service. Some agents were older and had tried other careers. This was their second lap around the track, and they were hoping for a sprint to the finish line. Others were just good ole boys who wanted to have power over someone because they'd grown up powerless and figured it finally must be their turn.

Most weren't prepared for what lay ahead of them, and many of the narco-pilgrims didn't know God, but they were seeking Him or something transcendent, some meaning they couldn't quite define. The MBN was their last chance to make it right, to do penance, and they'd come to Jackson like errant sinners to be washed of their sins…heroes-in-waiting looking for adventure.

They would soon mouth the mantras of the day: "Deny everything and demand proof. Parchman and graveyards are full of people who admitted to stuff." "Close only counts in horseshoes and hand grenades." And one more favorite: "Everyone you meet is guilty of something."

The requirement that agents have a degree or at least two years of college plus experience had been a magnet to attract recent graduates. It was a new paradigm for state law enforcement in Mississippi. It was no longer who you knew, who you were kin to, or what politician you were willing to do dirty deeds for that guaranteed employment for young cops. The mold was broken when John Edward Collins birthed the MBN, and "Mr. Merit" arrived in Mississippi.

As Michael walked up to the group, he heard a veteran cop talking to the rookies about the need to have a backup gun, a second untraceable and unauthorized gun to drop by a perpetrator in case things went sour in a shooting. Most of the new recruits were idealistic and rejected the idea. The officers pitching the second gun idea had seen too much. They had been used and abused by politicians. They were told to look the other way, instructed on who they could and could not arrest, and then abandoned to the high and dry hangman when things went awry.

One agent was holding court on the finer points of policing and requirements for search warrants. Agent Dave Best was a big-boned guy with a scraggly blonde beard and a hard face with darting eyes. He referred to his mama with almost every breath and danced around his audience in a snake-bit tango like a Mexican jumping bean in a hot skillet.

He must've loved Jesus, as well as his mother, because he used them both repeatedly as exclamations and expletives. A scantily clad young woman bounced out of the nearby convenience store and hopped into her convertible with two six-packs. Dave stopped his sermon on policing when he saw her and shouted, "Oh, Mama! Jesus!"

Michael thought...*No, not your mama and not Jesus, more like Jezebel.*

Dave resumed his lecture on policing and said, "When I see a redneck living in a trailer with a rebel flag, it's all the probable cause I need for a warrant. He's bound to be dirty!"

"Dave, he could be just an Ole Miss fan who's down on his luck," Michael joked as he walked up.

Dave stopped and sneered at Michael as he picked slabs of meat out of his teeth with a rusty nail.

"We were just talking about you, college boy. Where were you when I was in Nam fighting for freedom? You at Ole Miss? Dating them coeds, I bet. You're too pretty to be a cop anyway, just a kitten among big hungry dogs. These druggies will eat you alive," he barked.

Dave preened and strutted for the group and cut his eyes back at them with a sly, possum grin. "Hey, Michael, me and the boys here are getting up a shovel party. We gonna go out digging tonight, see if we can find where they buried your gonads," he said.

The agents all laughed and eagerly waited to see if Michael would pick up the gauntlet.

Michael laughed and said, "Sounds great, Dave! I'll go with you. I know exactly where they are. They buried them right next to your brains."

Dave flushed red and got real quiet. The other agents raised their eyebrows and looked at each other. Michael looked behind their eyes trying to see them, to see who they really were, to see if they were as uncertain as he was behind all the false bravado and male bonding rituals.

The group broke up and left Dave alone in the parking lot.

"Catch you guys later," Michael said as he turned to walk away.

When Michael entered the front door, there were no emblems, no flags, or anything in the sterile reception area to suggest this was the headquarters of the state's first agency with full state police power. Sheriffs and chiefs of police had lobbied against such authority since time began in Mississippi.

Just as he was about to speak to the lady at the front desk, two agents loaded with gear came bounding down the stairs from an adjacent townhouse. Carl Burns and Dean Smith, two agents sporting Beatles hair styles and the smiles of broke college students with their first paying jobs, called out to Michael. They were his classmates in the criminal justice program at Ole Miss, but they no longer looked like the clean-cut students he remembered.

"Hey, Michael! Hotty Toddy, we made it!" Carl shouted.

"Won't Dr. Tim Charles be proud to know so many of his boys are agents in the state's first drug enforcement bureau?" Dean asked, shaking Michael's hand from underneath the carrying case for his new Remington shotgun.

"Yeah, he'll be so proud and so surprised it's us!" Michael quipped.

Everyone laughed, and the new agents said in unison, "You got that right!" When the reunion ended, they took their gear to their cars. The blonde receptionist with a pixie haircut looked up at Michael from her desk in the foyer. She had small, dark eyes, reminiscent of the hint of bullets when you stare into the barrel of a gun. Her name tag said *DeeDee*. She showed a mild but muted judgment, revealing unspoken words...*Boys will be boys*.

Michael began to speak, but she raised a finger to shush him as she answered the phone. "Yes, Governor Waller, I'll put you right through to the director's secretary," she said with crisp efficiency, a voice like a rusty wheel in need of oil.

"Our new governor," she squeaked proudly.

At that moment, the door opened and out walked U.S. Senator "Big Jim" Eastland, smoking the longest and fattest Cuban cigar Michael had ever seen. The man, who some called the "Political Godfather of Mississippi," walked hunched over with an awkward, shuffling gait. He reminded Michael of Winston Churchill. He nodded to DeeDee and ignored Michael. His aide opened the front door, Eastland flipped the burning cigar on the sidewalk, the aide stepped on it to snuff out the fire, and then they were gone. Michael thought of news blurbs: *New Drug Agency HQ Goes Up in Flames: Senator's Cigar Suspected, Film at 6!*

DeeDee cradled her active phone, looked at Michael with no visible emotion, and asked, "Now, may I help you?"

"Agent Michael Parker here to see Agent Clay Strickland," he said.

"ID, please?" DeeDee asked with an extended hand.

Michael showed her his temporary credentials. She examined them carefully before pressing a button under her desk. The door behind her buzzed like a frustrated bumblebee and opened with a loud click.

"Yes, Agent Parker, go through the secretarial pool, up the stairs, turn right, past the director's office, past Chief Burnside's office, and down the hall until you reach the Bat Cave. When you finish, you can come back to this side of the building and go up to see Cliff in property to requisition your weapons, ammunition, and your car. You can stop by Legal, too, for your manual of dos and don'ts," she said with precise machine-gun diction.

She dismissed him then, but Michael thought she showed the faintest glimmer of a smile. He reconsidered and decided it could have just been indigestion.

He opened the door and stepped into the main floor, where a large secretarial pool was banging away on their Royal typewriters. In unison, the women looked up at him as he entered the room, then looked at each other and nodded. They adjusted the tiny earpieces around their heads, and the clicking and clacking of transcription began again.

The rhythm of the typewriters was hypnotic. The percussion backbeat burrowed into Michael's head like the songs playing constantly in the jukebox of his mind. The music in his head often framed and inflamed his mercurial moods with odes to yesterday, summertime, unchained melodies, and suspicious minds.

An open staircase with black wrought-iron railings to his left led to the second floor and the director's suite, what they called the Loft. On the wall behind the stairwell was a large sign—*Help is on the way.*

As he slowly ascended the stairs to the second floor landing, he saw a lady above him who wore a string of pearls like Beaver Cleaver's mother, and he heard her say, "Mr. Collins, the *Washington Post* is on line two."

People going up and coming down the stairs squeezed past him. Everyone was in a hurry. There were so many new agents to absorb—names, faces, and socials to change so no one would know how to find the men and women who were here today and gone tomorrow. The staff had to process operatives bound for the main streets of the counterculture, a netherworld of drug dens, nightclubs, and flophouses.

MBN headquarters had the air of Ellis Island of old. The punctilious staff worked like immigration officers. They were stern-faced and serious about their schedules, figures, and reports. Michael saw them as the shepherds of bureaucracy, herding refugees from normalcy into an unchartered new world, changing the identities of new agents until they became disappearing ink.

Today the MBN staff was the broom, and the new agents were the dusty sweepings of restless youth swept along on the ragged edge of a grand new adventure. It seemed overwhelming, but he took comfort in Tim Charles' parting advice for him when he left Ole Miss: "Just chew the meat and spit out the bones, Michael."

Good advice, but it was tricky. The whole MBN buffet had a new car smell.

CHAPTER FIVE

"...a cerebral, intelligence-based,
relationship-based service, i.e., all they
do is recruit people to get information
out of them."—Charles Cumming

"When we are tired, we are attacked by
ideas we conquered long ago."
—Friedrich Nietzsche

Outside of the Intelligence Unit, known as the Bat Cave to new agents, there was a sign with a large eye. Below it were the words...*The I of the MBN Is Upon U.*

Michael walked down the long hall toward the sign and prowled the nooks and crannies of this new world. People in tiny offices along the way looked up at him from their standard government metal desks. Some looked bewildered, others choked down greasy sausage biscuits for breakfast and chased their meal with double handfuls of Rolaids, and a few stared at mountains of paper in their inboxes and looked overwhelmed. A few waved, several scowled, and two belched like foghorns.

This is it. I'm really here, he thought as he walked into his new life. Stray thoughts ran wild through his mind like feral animals, barking and mewing at him, demanding his attention and his indulgence.

He entered the intelligence branch's fortress of solitude at the end of the hall, turning sideways to ease through the rows and rows of file cabinets and racks of ink stamps used to assign levels of secrecy to raw intelligence data. On the far walls of the command center were giant maps reminiscent of the war room on D-Day. Like ornithologists plotting bird migration routes, huge maps showed the flyways and smuggling routes used by cartels in

Mexico, Central America, and South America and the type of drugs by ports of entry. Laid over the routes were all the small airfields in the Magnolia State. By land, sea, and air, all the arrows on the maps converged on Mississippi.

He heard the grinding of an industrial-strength shredder and turned the corner to see an intelligence analyst feeding files stamped in red and marked top secret through the hungry, paper-munching machine. Above her on the wall was the motto of the unit's analysts: *Read between the lines. That's where they hide the truth.*

The analyst looked up from her task. She had an oval face, long, sandy-brown hair that glistened and flipped at the end, and a broad, genuine smile. She extended her hand and said, "Hi, I'm Pud Goody. You must be Michael Parker. The essay you wrote on protecting and serving made me cry when I typed it for submission to your permanent file. You sure have a way with words. Go on in, Clay's waiting for you."

Clay Strickland was sitting at his desk, reading a newspaper and eating a pepperoni pizza, when Michael knocked on his door. He had grown a beard since Michael met him in Tupelo, and when he turned a certain way, he had the visage of an Old Testament prophet or a young Abraham Lincoln.

"Come in, Michael. Eating on the run...in the crust we trust," he laughed and offered him a slice.

"I was reading this story about the Japanese soldier who just surrendered after twenty-eight years in the jungles of Guam. I wonder if he could even comprehend what's happened in all that time, or what he'd think of the images the Mariner spacecraft is sending back from Mars. Who knows? Maybe that'll be us one day. They'll have to come find us in these jungles they're sending us to. Shucks, by then they'll probably tell us the Martians landed in Jackson while we were away fighting crime and evil!" he said, laughing.

Michael smiled, made the Spock sign, and said, "Live long and prosper, Captain Kirk!"

"Well, you may ask Scotty to beam you up when you find out what you've signed up for!" he said, laughing again.

"Pull up a chair. Good job on your report. I know this was a wild ride just out of the chutes, a baptism by fire, but it's better to have your bubbles burst sooner rather than later. The director read your report, and we'll file it away as need-to-know only and shred the paper trail in case someone might be tempted to leak it to their political friends looking to blackmail their rivals.

"It's a thin line we dance along when we look at elected officials. The people must have the right to elect people of their choosing, even if they're scoundrels, but we can't translate that as carte blanche immunity for them to run criminal enterprises and harm the people we're sworn to protect. Lots of folks are wearing masks, and it's hard to tell who's who in this murky world, to distinguish friend from foe. Some of them would sell their own mamas down the river for a tart or a snort," he said.

"What about the cop I saw at the Leg Room?" Michael asked.

"We know Red's a player with powerful sponsors who want him over here to spy on us. He's already reached out to say he saw you, but promised to never tell his patrons who you are. We'll address it as it comes, but right now Chief Burnside wants me to run through this orientation with you. He thought it appropriate, since the director and I met you in Tupelo, and we invited you to apply to be one of the 'The Knights of the Dope Table,'" Clay said with a sideways grin.

Clay suddenly stood up and pulled out an old sword with a Vietnamese inscription along the blade. He drew it from its sheath and commanded, "Stand up, Michael."

Michael stood, and Clay touched the tops of his shoulders with the blade. "I hereby christen you, Sir Michael."

Michael said, "Whew! I'm glad that's over!"

"I knew the old sword from Nam would come in handy someday. The North Vietnamese colonel I borrowed it from in the Mekong Delta was long past caring if it was ever returned," he said.

The noise outside his office grew louder as people scurried by carrying files and equipment, talking to personnel in other parts of the complex through the hissing static of walkie-talkies.

Clay closed the door.

"Sorry, it's a little crazy here right now—chickens with our heads cut off, you know. The director has rounded up some good folks, and we're trying to prepare them for what lies ahead. The director doesn't want agents to wander onto the primrose path. Orientation is all about instruction, so there won't have to be correction later. Mr. Collins believes the only thing we ever want to be guilty of obstructing is the obstruction of injustice. He wants us to survive and live to be old men who are not consumed by our grievances, only our gratitude for serving. As my old commanding officer in Nam used to say, 'There can be no mist at the top, or there'll be fog in the ranks,'" Clay said.

He pulled a fat file from his desk drawer. Along the top was a label marked *Thrush*.

"This is your file, Michael. We now know more about you than anybody, except maybe your grandmother Pearl. Pretty impressive, huh?" he said.

"Yeah, it is. Why is it marked 'Thrush'?" Michael asked.

"That's your code name as long as you work undercover," Clay said.

Clay opened the file and scanned a condensed version labeled *Executive Summary*.

"Let's see. Where to start? A few highlights. You've been to Washington and met J. Edgar. You got stabbed protecting your former girlfriend, Dixie Lee Carter, and your friend Cheri on New Year's Eve, 1966, and your nose was broken defending your friend Harold Smith on the side of the road in Maryland. You also crawled out on a thin limb to protect people from the home siding scam by the mob when you were a deputy sheriff in Lee County working with your partner, Sarge," Clay said.

Michael raised his eyebrows.

"True?" Clay asked.

"All true. I plead guilty," Michael said.

"I'm just reviewing and regurgitating, standard orientation. There are lots of gravel road kids and blacktop boys coming into the MBN. When you live behind the picket fences of family and faith, it's easy to get lost when the barriers come down and the forbidden sin vendors come rushing at you. The dark side of the street will find the chinks in your armor and offer you their temptations on a silver platter—drugs, money, and easy women. That's their bounty for looking the other way—to not see some things or to un-see others. It'll sneak up on you before you know it, and the old line about the ends justifying the means will become the drug to numb aching consciences. We must prepare agents for what will come at them," he said.

He took a breath and laughed. "Sorry, I get distracted and begin to sound like a preacher at a tent revival meeting, don't I?" he said.

"Are you talking about me?" Michael asked.

"No, but I know the visit to the Leg Room was shocking to an idealist's view of the world. Politicians support us when it suits them and may point us to some cheap busts to make them look good. They'll give us a dime bag or an ounce of grass case, all while their buddies or bosses are driving trailer loads right past us and their planes are scraping the roofs of our houses as we sleep. They're also cons and shakedown artists who'll turn on us the minute they figure out we're not reliable agents of the status quo or their personal posse," he said.

"I kinda got that drift in the Leg Room. It was unsettling, for sure," Michael said, nodding in agreement.

"Speaking of which, I understand you had an interesting session with the Bureau psychologist—ink blots, sleepwalking, family issues, rescuing the broken, alcoholism, and things from your past like the incidents in Washington I mentioned," Clay said.

"Whew, yeah. It was more detailed than I might have imagined. I'm not sure I subscribe to all of it, but the background investigation and tests were exhaustive," Michael said.

Clay picked up the folder again and flipped through it for a moment.

"Don't take this personally, but you know the shrink recommended we not hire you?" Clay asked.

Michael was stunned. He said, "No, why?"

"The psychologist made the recommendation for your sake, not to protect the agency. He said you would be tireless and true, but it was not the life for you. Sorry, didn't mean to rhyme, just came out that way. He worried you couldn't sustain it, even though you passed the tests with flying colors," he said.

"But why, then?" Michael asked with question marks in his eyes.

"What did he ask you about your early home life?" Clay asked.

"He wanted to know about my family, about my father's drinking, how it all shaped my view of drug and alcohol use and abuse and my desire to be a police officer. I thought it was intrusive and irrelevant," he said, bristling a bit.

"Most of it was straight from your old FBI background check for your job in DC after high school. Other info came from our own investigation and stories from your relatives and neighbors. It may intrude on your privacy, but you're about to be given a gun and awesome powers that affect the lives of others," Clay said.

Michael nodded and said, "I understand. I don't mean to whine."

"The report said your job as a child was to find your father's stash of gin and water it down while your mother and grandmother distracted him. How old were you when that started?" Clay asked.

"Seven or eight, I guess. I would go to his favorite hiding places...the outside garage, the chicken house, the barn, or under the seat of the tractor," Michael said.

"Pretty scary stuff for a little boy and maybe confusing, betraying your father on some level. Lots to unpack there," Clay said.

"Yes, I loved him, but Pearl and Mama needed me to protect them, and that's what big men and little men do, isn't it...protect women?" Michael asked.

Michael paused and asked again, "Isn't it?"

"Did those responsibilities make you want to save the world, to right all wrongs, Michael? Is it all on your shoulders?" Clay asked as he leaned forward and rested his arms on his desk.

"Maybe. I hadn't thought about it that way, but like I said, Pearl and Mama needed me," Michael answered defensively.

Clay sighed and said, "I suspect your daddy and mama did the best they could. Pearl did, too. When you walked in your sleep as a child, you'd go to her room for comfort, wouldn't you? You love her, don't you?"

"Her room was my refuge, a place of peace. I used to wake up there, and yes, I love her very much," he said.

"The shrink saw a pattern, and I do, too. Your old boss, Bill Shrecker, at the Lyric Theater in Tupelo told us about the man who came in the theater while you were working your way through college as a doorman. That man abused you as a boy, didn't he?" Clay asked.

"Wow, this is a clearing of the decks, isn't it? Yes, I was at the old Tupelo Theater when I was about ten to watch a Walt Disney movie. Mama was working at Citizens Bank, and I walked down to the theater by myself. It was packed with kids my age. I was sitting there in the dark watching the movie when this big man plopped down beside me in the dark and suddenly grabbed me roughly by my privates," Michael said, squirming in his seat.

"You talk about it dispassionately," Clay said softly.

"Don't mean to. It was terrifying and still hard to recall without a feeling of violation and confusion. I tried to run, but he had an iron grip on me. He whispered to me to be still and he wouldn't hurt me. I relaxed to fool him, and he eased his grip.

Then I bolted out of my seat, broke past him, and ran out of the theater. I sprinted all the way to the bank," Michael said, fidgeting with the buttons on his shirt.

"You were a resourceful little boy. How did it affect you?" Clay asked, watching Michael intensely to see evidence of the kind of scars that don't show.

"Mama asked me why I was back so soon from the movie, but I couldn't tell her what happened. I just told her I didn't like it. I was so confused. She and Pearl had taught me to respect adults, and the assault was a betrayal of my upbringing, a shattering of trust," Michael said.

"What happened eight years later when he walked into the theater where you worked?" Clay asked.

"I was stunned. I knew immediately it was him, older but not as big as I perceived him to be when I was a child. He still had this look about him like an addict looking for a fix, a creep straight out of central casting. He didn't recognize me because I wasn't a kid anymore. He just walked right up to me. I wasn't who he was looking for. My heart was pounding. Anger flushed up into my heart and overflowed into my throat. After I took his ticket, I watched him from behind the curtains to the side of the theater area, and I could tell he was casing the place, surveying intended victims. It was a kids' movie, and parents had dropped their children off with us for safekeeping. We were a cheap babysitter," Michael said dryly.

Michael twisted around in his seat...crossing and uncrossing his legs as the memories came rushing to shore.

"I told Mr. Shrecker what was going on, that the monster was in our theater. I told him I didn't want to get him sued. I said I would watch the man until he made his move. Then I would mop up the floor with him, and the police could have what was left," he said as he saw Clay staring at his hands.

Michael realized then that his fists were clenched into tight red balls. His heart raced wildly like a runaway metronome—tick, tick, tick, thump, thump, thump. He dropped his hands to his sides and breathed deeply. The pounding of his heart subsided, and the pulsing roaring of blood in his ears changed from a raging wave to a gentle, lapping surf.

"I found a place in the shadows to watch and wait for him to make his move, but suddenly he froze like he had eyes in the back of his head. He whirled around and saw me before I could withdraw. He began to shake and looked as if he might explode. He acted like a trapped animal and suddenly bolted from the theater. I could smell his fear, the same odor of terror I felt the day he trapped me," Michael said, wiping the sweat from his upper lip.

"How'd you feel about your response?" Clay asked in a low, soft voice.

"Too responsible, too much the Goody Two-Shoes. Part of me thought I should've exacted vigilante justice, but I didn't want to get my boss in trouble. I worked there for over a year, and he never came back. Maybe some kids were spared what I experienced, but deep down, I wanted to hurt him," Michael said.

"Sometimes there's no perfect way to respond, but all our experiences will shape our responses to the things in the murky world before us. That's why we have to dig them up and take a long look at them. Once we finish the orientation, the past is gone. You've been born again in the cradle of the MBN, a new man with a blank slate. You can be anyone you need to be. You've agreed to a hundred-hours-a-week job, but it's not a job, it's a crusade. One day you may wake up and think you've come to the end of yourself. You might think all your dreams have changed, but it will be the dreamer who's changed, not the dreams. This talk is just a little preemptive splash of cold water in the face and purging of old ghosts, so they won't ambush you later," he said with a smile.

"I understand. What about you, Clay? What were your dreams?" Michael asked.

"After Nam, I thought maybe I might teach. I went to Southern, got my degree, and the only job I could find in Jackson was working for Orkin as an exterminator. Then I met my wife, Pat, on a blind date. She was the one who saw the ad for the MBN and told me this new drug agency was hiring. I wasn't sure about it, but she told me I had the background in military intelligence and should try it. So, here I am. I guess we're exterminators of a different kind, huh? Lots of termites are eating away at the foundations of the country," he said with a chuckle as he pantomimed the "whoosh, whoosh" of an imaginary bug sprayer.

Clay laughed so hard that he began to cough violently.

"Are you okay?" Michael asked.

"I've had this nagging cough for a while. It's probably my allergies. My sinuses have been messed up since the jungle and all those defoliants. Not to sound morbid, but I told Pat I'll die young. I feel it in my bones. If the war and the MBN don't kill me, traveling with the director might. We drove to Colorado for a meeting, and I now know the location of every Dairy Queen between Jackson and Denver. It was always, 'Stop here, boy. Sign says DQ's coming up, Clay.' He loves soft ice cream," he said.

Agent Dave Best knocked on Clay's door and peeked in. "Needed to see you, but I'll be back when you're done with the college boy," he said.

Clay watched Michael, who was stung by the unprovoked jab.

When Dave left, Clay said, "You know, people aren't always who they seem. Dave was abandoned at an orphanage when he was three, raped repeatedly as a child, finally adopted, and then abused until he was emancipated. He lived on the street and was homeless for two years. He's made a big comeback but covers his pain with false bravado. He may be looking for revenge, just as you could be, hoping to find your abuser in every dope dealer you meet, or in his case, in everyone he thinks had it easier than him. What I've told you is not privileged information. Dave is still angry, and he has shared his past with anyone who will listen. He wears his past and his anger as a sort of badge of honor. Because of that anger and a vulnerability to the drugs he'll be around, we'll have to watch him and see how he does, just as we'll watch you," Clay said.

"Why hire someone with that much baggage?" Michael asked.

"Why would we hire you?" Clay asked, wrinkling his brow.

"Touché. I see your point," Michael said.

"Walk lightly on his broken heart, Michael. He's just a mutt looking for a fire hydrant to pee on, and you're handy. His mitts are too big and bruised to pick the lock on the door of the prison where he's lived most of his life. Dave doesn't see that the door to his cell is open. He sits on his bunk saying, 'I'm fine.' When I was criticizing someone once, my mama told me, 'But for the grace of God, that could have been you,' and she was right. She also told me forgiveness is swallowing when you want to spit," Clay said.

Michael nodded and looked down the hall where a brooding Dave Best was sitting alone at a desk.

Clay said, "Here's a file on Moondog Square, your first enforcement case. It's a cesspool of drugs and depravity run by a guy called Milkwood Jones, but he goes by other names, too. He's a former glue sniffer who used to eat paint chips for snacks along with his special brownies...an opportunist and a manipulator. He brags about turning shame into kink. Jones wants to parade his darkness down Main Street and peddle his depravity to kids. He's been around a long time, so be careful around him. Captain Kangaroo was just a private when Jones began pushing dope and pimping good-time girls.

"The street talk says you can get anything you want at Moondog—anything—not just drugs but all the pleasures of the flesh if you know who to see, where to look, and what to ask for. They throw sharp elbows on their court, so be alert. I know you met Molly. She will be the CI to take you in to try a buy. She used to live there and is taking a big chance by agreeing to help us. She asked to work with you after she met you."

Michael looked surprised and said, "Really? I thought she didn't like me."

"She must have liked something about you. If Jones won't sell, just get some good intelligence. Pick up your buy money and weapons and read the file. Get with Harry Johnson, your control agent, so the surveillance team can mike you and be close by in case you need backup. When you finish with this assignment, Sarge has an informant lined up to work with you in Hattiesburg. So much to do, so little time," he said.

"Will do. Thanks for the talk, Clay. Lots to think about," Michael said.

"Because of your childhood, you're a fixer, out to right wrongs and save fair maidens, leap tall buildings in a single bound, and be the hero. The rascals you'll meet on this job aren't so fair, and their pet dragons are pretty nasty. Sheriff Gill Simpson in Tupelo said you lead with your heart. He said you fretted about the self-destructive tendencies of your former girlfriend, and you got too close to the abused girl, Magnolia. He's afraid your big heart will get you killed, or worse, you'll try to baptize every crook you meet!" Clay said through his infectious chuckle.

"The sheriff was almost as good at studying people as he was playing his fiddle," Michael said as the tension of the interview eased.

"He agreed with us about your strengths. You don't look like a narc, and you aren't threatening. That's not a weakness. It can be an asset. You'll buy drugs from dealers who wouldn't look twice at most of these other guys. Your soft heart doesn't have to be a liability. Just manage it and make sure you aren't dragging around some dull axe from the past you might be tempted to grind on the hearts of stone you'll encounter," he said.

"I think I'm beginning to see the point to this digging up of bones and rummaging around in my past," Michael said.

"It's all about old paradigms and the templates we lay over these drug wars. We'll have to adjust the lens through which we see the world as we learn what the rules are to the game, the stakes, and the quitting time. There'll always be boundaries and times when we have to decide if we're going to cross the line for a righteous cause or just be timid people who stare at the line the rest of our lives. We'll be tempted to believe tomorrow will never come, that the consequences of our actions have been pardoned, and the moment, the here and now, is all there is. There'll be days when it seems like the sun just won't shine, but we'll always regroup, the sun will rise, and then we'll try again," Clay said.

Clay closed the intelligence file and said, "I learned in Nam that there are three kinds of people—those who'll stick by you in hard times, those who'll leave you in hard times when the bullets are buzzing, and those who'll put you square in the middle of hard times and then blame it all on you."

He opened his desk drawer and handed Michael a note. "I got this message for you before you came up. A young lady, Jan Lea Carter, called looking for you. She said she's Dixie Lee's sister. It's up to you if you return her call. Be careful about telling anyone where you are. We didn't acknowledge your existence as an agent but took her message. She'll be at Shoney's around 3 p.m. She said she'd wait there for you to call. Go meet your friend. You'll be too busy soon. Give me a call later. Maybe we can catch the new movie, *The Godfather*," he said.

He stood and shook Michael's hand.

"Just think, Michael, because some peasants in the fields of Turkey are bleeding poppies for opium and other peasants in the mountains of Bolivia and Colombia are turning coca leaves into cocaine, we've been brought together to repel this invasion of America. It's a time to cast away stones, a time to gather stones together. It's time to grab our Davy Crockett muskets and our quick-draw holsters, and break some new ground at the O.K. Corral," he said.

"Small world after all, isn't it?" Michael said as he turned to leave.

"Yeah, boy, just remember you can't save it. It doesn't want to be saved. You aren't perfect, you don't have to be. One perfect Man came to save the world. His name wasn't Michael, and look what they did to Him," Clay said.

"Thanks, Clay. By the way, why was Thrush chosen to be my code name?" Michael asked.

"People told me you've always liked birds, and thrushes are loners like you. They're secretive and difficult to detect. I thought it fitting for a secret agent," he said.

Michael walked from Clay's office to where Dave was sitting and said, "Dave, I will be undercover on a tough case tomorrow night. I'm going to ask my control agent if you can accompany the surveillance team. I'd love to have you on the team," Michael said.

Dave looked like he'd been punched between the eyes, and then he recovered. "I'd like that, Michael. Thanks," he said.

Michael walked away, thinking about making peace with yesterday, a peace that cannot be owned...only rented, a rent that comes due every day.

CHAPTER SIX

*"You cannot go back and change the
beginning, but you can start where you are
and change the ending."—C.S. Lewis*

*"Those who dream by day are cognizant
of many things which escape those
who dream only by night."
—Edgar Allan Poe, "Eleonora"*

When Michael walked into Shoney's on I-55 North, the marquee said it was "Strawberry Pie Special Day." An army of eighteen-wheelers had pulled into the service station next door, and long-haul truckers with tattoos on their biceps were walking over for a much-needed treat and break from the grind of endless highways and maddening mile markers.

None of them got the reception Michael did when Dixie Lee's younger sister, Jan Lea, saw him.

The tall blonde with big pools of blue for eyes was the youngest of the Carter girls. He called her "Baby Sister," and she called him "Big Brother." Her face lit up in a warm, dazzling smile when she saw him. She rose to greet him with a rib-cracking hug that almost whooshed the air out of his lungs.

One of the truckers, who smelled like an old tobacco pipe, said to his waitress, "Does that come with the special today?"

Jan Lea giggled and said, "Michael, we've all missed you so much." She held his hands and drew back to look at him.

"Wow, you look so different with the long hair and the thing trying to grow on your face," she said as she looked him over.

"You know, I finally understand how those glasses Clark Kent wore totally fooled everyone who didn't know he was Superman!" she laughed.

"Yeah, I hardly recognize me in the mirror, and I've missed y'all, too, Baby Sister. Seems like it's been forever since I saw y'all," he said.

"Too long, Michael," she said, motioning him to sit with her.

"I never should've left in a huff the night Dixie Lee and I broke up. I remember waking you on the couch to say goodbye at midnight. I'm sorry for abusing your family's hospitality. They were always warm and welcoming. But at least you didn't have to give up your bedroom anymore when I didn't come back," he said.

"No, I understood. We all did. Everyone says hello... Marijon, Nancy, and...Dixie Lee, too, if I knew where she was," she said tentatively.

They sat and talked over Cokes and strawberry pie for a long time, a reverie to old times and lost love. The truckers had long since moved on while Michael and Jan Lea revisited the days of yesteryear and tortured what-ifs, what might have been.

"After you left, we all gave Dixie Lee what-for about it. Mama and Daddy weren't happy either. Dixie Lee got cold feet and broke it off with the man she was to marry. She tried to reach you," Jan Lea said.

"So I heard," Michael said.

"When the big wedding was cancelled, Daddy kicked her out of the house. He put up a huge banner made of butcher paper in front of our house on Avalon. It was fifty feet long and wrapped all around the intersection in big red letters," she said.

"Really? What did it say?" Michael asked.

"'Dixie Lee is not welcome here anymore,'" she said, lowering her eyes.

Avalon: the name evoked so many memories. Michael thought about trips there. It was once his place of healing, like the land of Avalon was for a wounded King Arthur.

"I'm sorry to hear that. He shouldn't have done that," Michael said, briefly closing his eyes.

"There was always this friction between her and Daddy. We've lost touch with her now. I'm not sure where she's living, but before she left, she cried a lot and told me she longs to stand on the corner of Avalon like she used to and wait for you to drive down the street in your red Mustang. I saw her out the window of my bedroom once, just sitting on the curb…waiting. I think time stood still for her when you left, and she still looks for you.

"When she packed to leave, those cards and flowers you gave her on your last visit had faded and curled, but she kept them in a box. We heard she took them to a fortune teller in Memphis, spread them out on a table, and asked for a reading. The gypsy told her you'd return one day, but it would be a long, long wait," she said.

"Don't you think you might come back and rescue her, Michael? You might be the answer to our prayers," she said.

"Someone called home once, before I left for Jackson, and I knew it was her. She didn't say anything, but I knew it was her. I could hear her crying on the phone, but I'd given all I had to give and couldn't give anymore. I can't save her, Baby Sister. I can barely save myself. I've been lectured on that saving thing a lot lately. The door has closed…if there ever was a door," he said.

"Well, I brought some pictures I found. I thought you might like to see them. Here's Dixie in Washington with J. Edgar Hoover and her boss, Richard Hunska. Hunska stood in as a double for Efrem Zimbalist, Jr. on the FBI TV series. See, she wrote it all on the back of the picture."

Jan Lea read the writing. "Hoover asked me, 'Don't you have a boyfriend in the Bureau?' I was surprised and said, 'Yes, sir, he works in the Identification Division.' He said he'd met Michael at the Methodist Church on East Capitol Street. I was surprised he knew so much about us."

The images of Dixie Lee cut him to his core, but he just said, "I remember."

"I can't let you have that one, but I have this one with her and her boyfriend. It's a good picture of her, and you could cut him out of the picture if you'd like," she said.

Michael looked away.

"Baby Sister, I'd rather chugalug weed killer and go blind than to see her with him again. Once was enough, but I appreciate the thought," he said.

"How did it ever come to this, Big Brother?" she asked with sad eyes.

"Who knows? Sometimes I really miss what we almost had. I left a lot behind when we parted. I'm still figuring out how to be whole again. When I do, maybe I'll come see y'all in another lifetime," he said, shrugging his shoulders.

They hugged before she left, and Michael saw the tears beginning to overflow the wells of her eyes.

"What's wrong, Baby Sister?" he asked.

"Aw, I've got something in my eye," she said

She turned one last time as she opened the door and said, "Watch out for kryptonite, my sweet Clark Kent."

Then she was gone, only the fragrance of her perfume remained, and he was left alone with his thoughts. He wondered if he would ever see any of them again.

Michael lingered and had one more slice of pie for the road. Things had gotten slow in the restaurant, and the waitress asked if she could sit with him for a while. She looked like she could use a friend. Her teeth needed dental work, and she kept rubbing her jaw from nagging pain. A chronic tiredness hung on her like a bad suit, and her feet were swollen. Her eyes looked as though she had just finished crying and was about to begin again.

As they sat and talked, all of it came pouring out—a story of loss, broken trust, and disbelief. Her husband had run off with her best friend and left her with the kids. She told Michael she'd overheard bits and pieces of his conversation with Jan Lea and thought he might understand. She kept repeating one phrase: "What do I do now?"

Michael had no answers, but he listened and tipped her all the cash he had with him. As he drove away from strawberry pie and yesterday, the sinking sun turned the white clouds to gold. They melted and seeped into a gilded sky. He thought about all the pain in the world—from Pearl's story about the Pettigrew family to Dixie Lee's trials to Agent Dave Best's tortured life, and now this waitress, ironically named, of all things, Hope.

He retired to his apartment on Ridgewood Road to read the file Clay had given him on Moondog Square. When he finished, he wanted to throw up, but he read the newspaper instead, a review of the new film Clay had mentioned, *The Godfather*.

Then he watched an old movie, *The Graduate*, on his little black-and-white television. He pretended he was Benjamin Bratton and Dixie Lee was Elaine, and he'd arrived at the church in the nick of time to rescue her from ruining their lives, but the nick of time only happens in Hollywood.

With the movie and all he had seen to fuel his mind, he fell asleep on his couch, and his dreams were high-octane theater. Embers of regret smoldered on a giant hearthstone that was his heart.

A man with three giant clocks labeled yesterday, today, and tomorrow called to him. "Stop chasing ghosts, Michael," he said. "Yesterday, today, and tomorrow are intersecting. You're confusing my clocks.

"You're still dating Dixie Lee in Washington, but the buses aren't running. Efrem Zimbalist, Jr. keeps telling you the FBI is a Quinn Martin production. Pearl's got on her apron, but she's got no peppermint. Your mama's setting the table with paper plates and plastic forks. Your daddy's got the brooding blues and is smoking Lucky Strikes on the front porch. He's been to his stash of cheap gin to paper over his pain, but he's already got three unlucky strikes against him.

"Deliverance is coming tomorrow, but tomorrow is a long time. It may not be what you pray for, and what appears to be love may just be a cheap imitation. You are a hitchhiker, thumbing a ride on the merry-go-round. You're on your way, and the horses go up and down on the carousel, but you can't run away from yourself. Your mind is replaying what it cannot erase—the faces best forgotten, the best friends nightmares can buy, and the casual castaways tossed to and fro on seas of self-indulgence trying to numb their pain, but who will numb yours?"

The man faded away, and Michael wandered in a dream world that was gray and ashen. The fog soup was thick, and the air was like charcoal. He wore gleaming golden armor from head to toe. The silk ribbons of the damsels he'd saved were tied to his lance, but the scabbard for his sword was rusted and empty. The roads were covered in soot, and a moat to his right surrounded a darkened castle. The path to the moat was filled with the stiffening bodies of dragons he'd slain, their rigid feet pointing toward the sky like road kill armadillos in Texas.

The Lady of the Lake rose up out of the water and offered him Excalibur if he would promise to rescue Dixie Lee. The draw-bridge was lowered. Dixie Lee's long, braided blonde hair hung from the tower window. It was an enticement for any passing knight sworn to the Code of Chivalry and great gallantry toward damsels in distress. He imagined her as Sleeping Beauty, breathing softly in her sleep, her golden hair spread over her pillow…her warm breath escaping through the curve of her parted, honey lips, and he heard her whisper his name.

He looked away from the trap and came to a fork in the path where he stared at a map posted on a giant billboard: "Take the left fork where nothing is right. Take the right fork where nothing is left. Your heart may say right, but it has no brain. Your brain may say left, but it has no heart, and either way, your broken heart is like crumpled paper. Pearl is ironing it, but the wrinkles can never be ironed away."

He heard Pearl say, "Always take the high road," and a third road rose up before him. He stepped onto it, and the scrapbook pages fanned faster and faster—good times, bad times, sad times, and the wailing echoes of generations asking…"Why?"

Michael passed a flashing neon sign that said *Pearly Gates just ahead*. He arrived at the pearled gates of heaven, but they were bolted, and he saw friends and faces from his past strolling on the streets of gold, holding the broken mirrors of yesteryear and wagging their fingers at him.

His second grade teacher, Mrs. Reifers, came to the gate and asked him, "Why did you step in to fight the two big boys who were beating the helpless runt? Who told you it was your fight... that you just had to?"

Michael's FBI roommate, Harold Smith, asked, "Why did you take the blows meant for me the night the gang jumped us in Washington? I didn't ask you to. Can you still not breathe out of your broken nose?"

Cheri ran up to the gates and said, "You saved me and Dixie Lee from the gang on New Year's Eve, and we never even said, 'Happy New Year, Hero!'"

Then St. Peter appeared, checked his roster, and asked him, "Did you think you were just going to stumble in here with the smell of soot on you and blow smoke in the face of God? Come back and we'll talk after you've been here ten thousand years. It's not your time."

Then Michael fell from the doorsteps of eternity. As he fell, he watched the taillights of the gospel train disappearing, and thunder muted his muttering of a line from the movie review about offers you can't refuse.

CHAPTER SEVEN

"Hell is empty and all the devils are here."
—William Shakespeare, "The Tempest"

"The stuff of nightmares is their plain
bread. They butter it with pain...They
whispered to Caesar that he was mortal,
then sold daggers at half-price in the
grand March sale."—Ray Bradbury,
Something Wicked This Way Comes

Michael was scheduled to meet Molly at the Paradise Club in downtown Jackson. She'd promised to take him to the "funky kingdom," a place where she once lived and almost died—Moondog Square. It was a place of interest to the MBN and the haunts of randy politicians like Senator Cornelius "Corndog" Ball.

As Michael walked through the crowd at the club, Jerry Clower, Mississippi's country comedian laureate, was just beginning his first set. Michael thought it was a strange venue for Clower. It wasn't his kind of crowd.

The revelers were loud, lewd, and crude. The pungent smell of marijuana filled the air, and childlike clubbers with white powder on and in their noses passed Michael. Stoned partygoers sat in corners hallucinating, finger-painting their faces, and giggling while they swallowed tiny white pills. Others wandered aimlessly in a drunken stupor through the mass of humanity to grope and be groped, collecting kisses and things doctors dispense penicillin to cure.

Clower, who couldn't hear himself above the din of noise, tugged at his red suspenders, paced the stage like a caged tiger, and became increasingly frustrated and exasperated. He made repeated pleas for some respect and civility, all to no avail. He finally retired from the stage. There would be no encore and no second set.

The club went black. The darkness yielded to flashing strobe lights that made everyone flicker and dance in spasms of jerky movements. Stoned party people swayed as music blared from the club's giant speakers. An appropriate metaphor for the death of yesterday began to play as Don McLean sang a farewell to American pie, Chevys, levees, and good ole boys.

A pimple-faced teenaged zombie with dilated pupils staggered up to Michael and shouted over the music, "Hey, man, like, who was the old redneck dude on the stage?"

"Someone you punks don't deserve," Michael deadpanned.

As the young man scurried away, Molly walked up behind Michael and tapped him on the shoulder.

"Hello, Michael," she said.

"Jim, please," he said as he turned to face her. He saw she looked different than the day he'd met her at Rose's house. Her red hair had been brushed, and she was dressed in a two-piece dress with a gold necklace and matching earrings, but there was still a certain essence about her—dime-store perfume, old smoke, cheap liquor, and a trace of the kind of perspiration that won't scrub off. She had the look of wounded prey that had been toyed with and released one time too often until cheap cosmetics just can't quite cover the scars.

"It's okay," she said, leaning close to his ear, her red hair brushing his face, her hip touching his. He felt the sharp edge of a knife tucked beneath her belt. "No one can hear us over the music. I heard your time with Rose was eye-opening."

"Yeah, I met Tanya Tucker, and we ran into a sheriff with a belt buckle bigger than the ones Elvis wears," he joked.

"You do know Rose is in love with you?" Molly said with a look that suggested she enjoyed gigging him.

"Rose falls in love with every agent she meets," Michael said, rolling his eyes.

"Well, her mama is in love with you, too," she said over the loud music.

"What? She's married," Michael said, frowning under knitted brows.

"That doesn't matter. She dumped her old man who worked in the factory. He expected her to cook and clean and be his slave. Haven't you heard? Man, those days are gone. It's a new day, the Age of Aquarius—free love, peace, brotherhood, and no possessions. She missed the movement and communion with the world. Carla wants to be free, to make up for lost time, and she chose you. She said you're the prettiest man she's ever seen, too pretty to be a narc," Molly said.

"So I've heard," Michael said with a grimace. He looked at her and felt square, archaic, and out of his element. She was defiant and insolent, but it was all a front, he thought, to cover her vulnerability.

"Molly, none of that's love, and it ain't free," he said a little too loudly.

She laughed at his discomfort and said, "Ready to go to see the witch doctor?"

"Only if he says 'Ooo eee, ooo ah ah, ting tang, walla walla, bing bang,'" Michael joked.

"What?" Molly asked with a squinty grin.

"Never mind. My jukebox never sleeps," Michael said.

****

The sun was setting over North State Street as Michael and Molly passed by Jackson Memorial Stadium. Shadows were falling across Jackson, hiding its scars.

A purple haze rimmed the horizon as they took a left on Riverside Drive. The light was fading fast as they drove down the winding road to a wooded area nestled behind Bellhaven College. The surveillance team was positioned in the MBN van on a nearby hill for better reception of his body transmitter. It was as close as they could get to the drug house without spooking the inhabitants. Agent Dave Best was in the van as Michael had requested.

"So you've paved the way for me tonight? You feel good about the approach we discussed?" he asked. Molly appeared to be growing restless and jittery as they neared their destination.

"Yes, I told Milkwood you were my boyfriend from Tupelo, looking to score big, and you were a dealer yourself... someone looking to become a subcontractor of sorts," she said.

"Tell me more about how you have access to Moondog and to Milkwood," Michael said.

"They troll the bus station for runaways. They found me there at the Greyhound station in Jackson and took me in. It's hard to get out, but I finally did, and even though he wasn't happy about me leaving, he lets me back in on temporary passes because I bring so much dope business his way. Most of my girlfriends stayed, and now they're too old, too fat, or too dead to leave. They just kept doing what he said. He told us it was going to take a lot of his medicine to help us pretend we were anything other than the nobodies we really were.

"Some are hanging on by a thread, and you know it ain't going to end well for them. They lost it. We all lost it—whatever it was. I look at them now and think it could've been me. He promised us all heaven, but we found out that meant living in his hell. He used to track down every girl who tried to leave, but now he mostly just disowns them and bars them from returning," she said.

Michael listened, but his mind wandered as he watched the afterglow of the sun warring with the moon for dominance. Thousands of blackbirds crossed the twilight sky, flying in unison toward wherever it is birds go at sunset. There was a sundog on the horizon. It was the first Michael had seen since he and Dixie Lee saw one in Washington as a rain squall swept down the Potomac and across the mall.

For a moment, he was lost in his thoughts. *If a sundown can be lonesome, this one is.*

He returned to the task at hand and asked, "You know if we're successful, he'll eventually know you were the one who set him up. Does that worry you, Molly?"

"No, this is personal, a long time coming. He took everything from me. I can't be free until I take everything from him. I hope we bring him down, and I want him to know I'm the one who did it," she said with some bite in her voice.

After driving round and round the hillside, the moon showed itself from behind some dark clouds. Michael asked, "Where is this place, Molly?"

"We're just a moonlight minute from there. Turn here," she said, pointing to the entrance of a darkened street that looked abandoned, a descending avenue of no return.

The narrow lane was more tunnel than street. Scrub trees and tangled undergrowth lined the drive, and at one point, the tentacles of the vines were raking the roof of the car like a witch's fingernails. They finally emerged from the twists and turns into a giant clearing, a square-shaped cul-de-sac with one way in and one way out—the funky kingdom Clay briefed Michael on, the Moondog Square frequented by the senator and his friends.

The air suddenly became thick, dark, and sooty. The clear ether sky that had been a showcase for the moon and stars became occluded by a gloomy and murky aura. Stars were barely perceptible, and the moon was crying behind a dark nimbus cloud, collecting tears for a sudden shower. It was a night harboring hidden secrets, mystical messages, and a whole menu of creepy ambient sounds.

A long, black limousine hearse sat to one side of the dead-end lot fronting Moondog Square, a tiered row of joined buildings, part castle and part nightmarish dollhouse. It was a no-man's-land with private balconies, French doors, windows with wide-bladed plantation shutters, and landings with wrought iron railings.

A hand-painted sign on the back of the hearse said *Funeral Management, Grateful Dead Now Departing. Short-Timers, Reserve Your Ride. Long Lines Special—Mourners for*

Hire. Theater-Trained Flatterers—Weepers and Wailers Optional.
You stab 'em, we slab 'em. Quiet Please. The Dead Are Sleeping.

A raucous wind howled like a banshee and blew dry, rustling leaves across their path like lemmings scurrying to the abyss. Thunder rumbled like Thor striking his hammer. The loud peals muted Molly's gasps, but she jumped halfway off her seat with each timpani roll. Sudden flashes of lightning from a passing storm revealed windows that looked like jack-o'-lantern eyes. A hundred Halloween eyes followed their every movement. Michael felt a smothering presence of evil.

Michael looked at the hearse, which sat window-deep in weeds with rat-gnawed seats, and then at Molly, who was as white as a sheet. Her voice was husky-hoarse, her nostrils were flaring as she sniffled. He had to strain to hear her. "No pun intended, Molly, but you're a dead giveaway we're up to something," he said as he switched on his body mike for the surveillance team.

"Sorry, I'll get a grip before we see him," she said, brushing her hair from her face and dabbing at her swollen eyes.

The gloaming of twilight and the stillness of dusk reminded Michael of nights in Parker Grove when he would hide beneath the covers as a child, hairs standing up on his arms after an episode of *The Twilight Zone.* He always waited for morning light to break and banish the monsters, but as he grew older, he learned the monsters were never gone, only hiding in the shadows.

Michael heard the soft tapping of drums and what sounded like a Gregorian chant coming from the compound. In the midst of the barren landscape, there was one tree outside the buildings.

"What kind of tree is that, Molly?" Michael asked.

"That's an apple tree. He planted it when he first came here. He says his apple didn't fall far from the tree of good and evil. Milkwood says this is his garden of serpents and angels," she said.

As they approached the buildings, the chanting and drumming stopped, and a mournful, disembodied voice from somewhere deep within the bowels of the compound began to sing a song from an

Italian opera, "O Mio Babbino Caro," but the words were in English rather than Italian. "I am pining and I am tormented, Oh God! I would want to die! Daddy, have mercy, have mercy! Daddy, have mercy, have mercy!"

Clay's warning about hard landings in alternate universes suddenly hit Michael right between the eyes.

An evening fog obscured the steps leading to the stairwell, and mud squished beneath his feet as they entered the breezeway connecting the buildings. The incessant chirping and barking of an army of tree frogs was almost maddening. Michael felt the weight of hidden watchers peering out at them from the darkness. On cue, a black Halloween cat with ragged ears crossed their path and hissed spittle at them from behind yellow eyes.

A sign at the interior gate suddenly loomed large out of the mist: *No Trespassing. Forgive us our trespasses as we trespass against you for trespassing against us.* A few steps further, a miniature teepee sat by the stairs with another sign that said *No fire sticks allowed.*

A rusty lantern hung on a nail by the withered gray stairwell, and it squeaked in the breeze as the wind rocked it back and forth in an eerie horror-flick rhythm. Michael realized he was sweating buckets. He rubbed his wet hands on his jeans and mopped his brow.

As he and Molly ascended the stairs, each step creaked and groaned its protest as if they were living entities pained by the weight. On the second floor they passed room after room, each sideshow with its own story. Some doors were barred and windows shuttered, others were ventilated for those mixing homemade drugs and cutting what appeared to be heroin in their sinks. Michael smelled arsenic, and there was so much marijuana smoke in the air, the night bugs were stoned and buzzing erratically.

The air was damp, musty, and lifeless and had the overpowering smell of human misery, the aftermath of intimacy, and excrement. People were sleeping in boxes for beds in this half-dream world of merciless visages. Rooms were filled with faces that looked as if they had entered the belly of the beast and never left. Some were bloated, while others looked like mummies straight from King Tut's tomb—distended bellies, patchy body hair on pasty pale ghouls, and sundry faces as thin as old garden rakes.

Some were playing dominoes on egg crates, one-eyed jacks were playing five-card stud, and amputees, stumps courtesy of the war in Southeast Asia, were playing checkers. They were all playing solitaire as they were digested by evil with barely a belch. When they died like beasts abandoned by kennel masters, there wouldn't even be a record they'd ever existed. A belly full of rats gnawed at Michael's innards. It wasn't hunger or fear, but the images of life reduced and degraded to this sin-soaked back alley.

One girl, who had skin like coffee with a little cream, was hunched over a rickety table, drinking soup with her fingers. The sole decoration in her room was a poster of a smiling Che Guevara that read *If Christ himself stood in my way, I would squish him like a bug.* She had the vacant look of the walking dead. She looked up at him with hollow, zombie eyes and made a suggestive obscene gesture, the eyes of an addict looking to finance her next fix.

The next room had three young women, all in various stages of undress. One girl rose from her bed naked. She was a small Asian girl, trim, almost emaciated. Her cheeks were scarred and pitted from acne, her nails were bitten down to the quick, and her pallor was close to the Madame Tussauds waxy look of someone who is not quite real. Miss "skin on bones" called out to Michael in an accent he thought was Vietnamese.

"Hi, cowboy, want to come in? I like girls," she cooed provocatively, motioning to the others.

"Really? Me, too," Michael deadpanned.

That jarred her out of her fog. "What? Aren't you looking for a good time?" she asked with a puzzled look.

"No, ma'am, I'm just passing through, but thanks for asking," Michael answered.

"Ma'am? Are you for real?" the girl asked.

Without a trace of irony, he said, "I'm just who I have to be tonight."

As they moved on, Michael heard the squawking of a parrot, and he stopped before an open doorway. He thought a young woman was smiling at him, but then he realized it was not a smile but the fixed stare of death. She was dead, the hose still around her arm, the needle still in the vein. It appeared she had also opened her veins and bled to death.

The floor was painted with her blood. People shuffled by, but no one seemed to notice or care. Michael picked up a blanket in her room and covered her with it. He knelt down to close her eyes and saw the note pinned to her threadbare blouse…*I just want someone to tell me they love me. Is that too much to ask? I don't want to do this no more. Free at last.*

Michael knelt by her and squeezed his eyes shut.

She had the chubby cheeks of someone's little girl. Is this why we're doing what we do? She would never smile again, never smell lavender in the spring, or cock her ear to the early morning tune of a mockingbird. Were her last thoughts of home and family? Was she afraid or relieved? Did she feel the parting, the separation as her soul left her body behind?

Molly called to him. "Come on Mic—Jim, let's go. You're scaring me. Her name was Carol Annie. We named her Little Orphan Annie. She heard the knocking and answered. She didn't know it was death knocking at her door. Annie let him in, and he took her. The Reaper is roaming and checking off his list, and he'll be back for us if we don't leave her room."

There was a loud knocking at the door, Molly gasped, and the parrot screeched loudly and said, "Annie's not here. Annie's not here."

Michael walked away from the girl's altar of death and gave Molly a hard look.

"You should be afraid," he said as they walked down the hall.

Michael heard a siren in the distance. Molly's breathing was labored, and he thought she was on the ragged edge. She suddenly seemed fragile and vulnerable as they moved through the shadows of what was offered to her as a refuge but became a wretched prison. She exhibited all the signs of an abused and confused woman.

"You don't understand. I was still here when that girl arrived. She got on this new drug the bikers push called methamphetamine, and her mind got messed up. She left her husband and children for her female drug dealer, who used her addiction to control her, lure her away from her family, and get her money. The dealer left Carol Annie for another sugar mommy when the money ran out. Then Milkwood found her and brought her to Moondog.

"He pulled her back from the brink, and she owed him. He named her his Gomer. She became a working girl for him, but she always dreamed of reuniting with her husband and three little girls. Milkwood got her out of the mental ward at Whitfield where he found her. She was in a straightjacket," she whispered to him.

"That makes me feel so much better," Michael said with dripping sarcasm.

As they walked down the corridor, a stammering man with a shrill Truman Capote voice called to Michael from behind the screen door to his room.

"W-w-welcome, stranger. If you're searching for the highest of h-h-highs to go along with your chemical nights, I have just the thing for you. It'll make you forget that ghastly thing you just saw, too," he said as he opened the creaking door.

A small blonde girl with a freckled nose peered around from behind him and clutched his trousers. She had deep-set, pale eyes. Her hair was stringy, and her skin had a yellow, jaundiced tint. No more than eleven or twelve, Michael guessed, but her eyes looked older. Her nails were discolored and cracked, and she was painfully thin.

The man dressed like someone playing at being a hippie. He had shrubs of hair in his ears, bushes in his nose, and masses of oily, black armpit hair visible from the edges of his tank top, but he couldn't grow hair on his head. His face was pimpled, and under long, pale lashes he had "Chihuahua eyes" partially hidden behind glasses with thick lenses. He was a short, sour little man who wore elevator shoes to compensate.

"Ar-ar-arnold's my name, Arnold Case. She's Ch-ch-charity. I-I-I call her my charity case, g-g-get it? My daughter likes men your age. I'm sure we could arrange something to our mutual s-sa-satisfaction," he said.

"Daddy, don't," the girl pleaded softly. She was standing on her tiptoes. Michael suspected she had probably walked that way all her young life.

Michael paused at the doorway. He looked at the little girl, who was gnawing on the back of her knuckles, and asked the man, "This is your daughter?"

"Yes, this is my b-b-baby. I have custody of her. I convinced the judge up in S-sen-Senatobia she'd be better off with me than her mother, who got religion and ran off to some Christian commune. She and my older daughter wouldn't mind me, and I had to discipline them. They learned that no chair under their doors could keep me out. So my older girl ran off with some boy in the middle of the night, and her mama decided she'd rather live with J-Jesus than with me. The judge was a man of science like me who didn't believe in all that mumbo-jumbo," the man said.

Once more the little girl tugged on his trousers and begged him, "Daddy, don't, please don't. I don't want to."

Arnold showed a flash of the brute he was and slung the girl to the floor in a rage. She coiled like a snake on the floor and held her belly as half-empty whiskey bottles rolled around her and water bugs ran across the butts of marijuana roaches littering the floor.

"N-now, you hush, ch-child, and do as Daddy says. Daddy's conducting business here," he said, trying to recover in front of his "customer."

"J-j-just like her ma-mama and her sister. They can't understand the urges of a man, the temptations. They make me do rough things. After all, I'm just a man, and I have needs," he said as he reached down and patted the girl on her head.

Michael seethed with an instant and burning anger. Different face, a different time, but he was the monster who had grabbed Michael in the darkened movie theater when he was a child. Michael's teeth were clenched, his fists were balled up into clubs, and the pistol under his jacket demanded attention.

He was washed overboard in his mind, drowning in the flood waters of anger. He screamed loudly on the inside, but it was a futile cry. Then he felt the tug of Molly on his arm as she tried to steer him away.

He looked at the man and the tortured little girl and said, "No, thanks, but maybe I'll see you later."

As they walked along, Molly whispered to him, "Let it go. We're not here to save the world."

Michael looked at her and asked, "Then what are we here for?"

CHAPTER EIGHT

"...a dog growls when it's angry, and wags
its tail when it's pleased. Now I growl when
I'm pleased, and wag my tail when I'm
angry. Therefore I'm mad."—Lewis
Carroll, Alice's Adventures in Wonderland

"Flirting with madness was one thing;
when madness started flirting back, it
was time to call the whole thing off."
—Rohinton Mistry, A Fine Balance

They stopped before a red door labeled *The Oven*. Molly knocked in a sequence to match the knocking of her knees and in a rhythm that suggested she still had the keys to the dark kingdom and maybe Captain Midnight's secret decoder ring, too.

A metallic male voice on a speaker next to the door said, "Enter, oh Sesame!"

They stepped into a dimly lit room, and after Michael's eyes adjusted to the darkness, he saw the man sitting in a lotus position on a beanbag in the center of the room. Next to him was a pile of hot stones and a mattress lined with nails. As they drew closer, Michael could see the pockmarks on his arms and the red marks from the stones.

The drug lord was quite the sight. He had long, black hair—so black it appeared to be blue under the single neon light in the room. Near the hairline, Michael thought he could see something moving, fleas maybe, running in and around the dyed roots of his hair.

His hair was slicked back with Dippity-do, so Michael thought maybe it was only Dippity-do bugs. The lord of the manor wore a short-sleeved mohair suit with a priestly collar; his eyes were deep caverns fogged by the cocktails of drugs he ingested, and he was sweating blood.

He was older than Michael would have thought, perhaps an old beatnik who became a guru for the hippies who followed his generation. Jones had obviously cut his teeth on crime long before his hippie adherents were out of the crib. A silver spoon hung around his neck, dried blood caked the edges of his nostrils, and his feet were soaking in a tub of hot water with steam rising around his ankles.

"Greetings and blessings to you. Enter! Do your feet need baptizing? Do you think I've held mine under water long enough? I don't wish to drown them, but I've eaten so many grasshoppers, like John the Baptist, I can't tell anymore when they're done and need to hop," he said as he examined his reddened feet and continued to ramble.

He dabbed at the beads of sweat on his upper lip with a white handkerchief stained with spots of reddish-brown.

"Pardon my bleeding, but I have hematidrosis. I sweat blood. When my junkies and ghouls here first saw it, they thought I was a god or a prophet, and they knelt before me and worshipped me. I became their graven image. Who was I to dissuade them? It worked for Manson, didn't it? Now they wait on me hand and foot, brush my teeth, and I never go to the throne alone. One day when I fall off my throne, bust my gasket, and they buy the casket, they're gonna carry me to my grave, and it's gonna be grand. People will talk about it for years while sharing a joint, and my ghost will show up and get a ghostly high.

"But I digress. I trust you like our little home here. I came here years ago. I was just an old mutt looking for a porch to sleep under, a place to scratch my fleas, and a warm place to sleep and die. The old woman who owned this place took me in. I made her happy in her last days by making her feel young again. So she left me this place, her old bed and breakfast, and I renamed it Moondog Square.

"I took others in, as she did me, and they made me feel young again and round and round it goes. Others just helped to pay the bills here at our flophouse, drug den, and bordello. You do know bordello is not an Italian dish, don't you, Jim? Isn't that what Molly calls you, Jim from Tupelo?" he asked before rattling on.

"Besides, my old lover knew she couldn't sell the place. There was a triple homicide here in the fifties. No one would buy it from her because of the bloodstains and the rumors it was haunted. Sometimes I think they're right. We hear funny noises and smell things, too. Pardon the smell. Stinky ghosts, people say. The ghosts must've ate tainted beans that killed them because the flatulence gets pretty bad at times," he said as he threw his head back and brayed like a donkey, "hee-haw, hee-haw."

"I'm sorry. The drugs make my mind wander and my tongue loose. My name is sometimes Milkwood, but you can call me Joiner. Pleased to meet you," he said.

"I'm Jim Patterson," Michael said, extending his hand, which Joiner refused.

"Sorry, germs, you know. What have you come here for, Jim, and who do you think you are—Super Fly, Don Corleone, or are you Dylan knocking on heaven's door? Dylan can speak it, can't he? Me? I ain't knocking or tapping or rapping, I'm banging on the gates. How about you, Brother Jim?" he asked.

"I'm just looking to get something to ease my pain. Joiner, you said?" Michael asked.

"Yes, the revolutionaries call me Milkwood Jones for the poison juice we made for their use from the Jamaican bush, but my real name is William Stone Joiner," he said, his eyes focusing in and out like the lens of a camera.

"My father was William Stone, Senior, and I'm William Stone, Joiner," he said.

Michael searched the eyes of the strange man before him for a clue to who he was or what game he was playing. *Was he mad, or was this a script?*

"Please excuse me. I'm high right now, but I ain't coming down from my treehouse for you or anyone. We live on our own planet, Jim, and just pull down the shades in the penny arcade to shut out the world. I see you searching my eyes. Many have gotten lost there, you know, and never found their way back. Once I lived in the salty waters near Biloxi with the rest of the rolling stones of the sea, where I trained the sharks to avenge the rape of mama earth by land people. Then I came here. You aren't one of the land people, are you?" he asked, leaning forward like a movie director, framing Michael's face with his hands.

"No, sir, I'm just a bird flinging myself out into the cold world on nothing but feathers and wings," Michael said to the man who was weird, wired, and in the midst of a drug-fueled sermon and confession.

"You called me sir. I like that. We haven't seen that kind of genteelness here in a long time. I return the favor. I hope you read our signs. You don't have any fire sticks on you, do you, Sir Jim?" he asked.

"I have some fireballs, you know, jawbreakers. Do they count?" Michael asked with a smile as he continued to make eye contact with him.

"Good one, Jim. Those aren't tears of misery you see in my eyes, Sir Jim. They're tears of joy for all my misfits, my girls and the high-heeled boys here, too. So many youngsters are giving away their charms these days. It has hampered our business, but we are creative, and thankfully, there's always the stoned, the sexual misfits, and the politicians. We make up deficits with an influx of cash when the legislature is in town or the Marcello Mafia boys breeze in from New Orleans. They all come—the bored and the mischievous all drop by to smoke dynamite, snort TNT, and take our magic carpet ride.

"Our motto is we feed the body but starve the soul. I leave the other to the preachers. We judge no one, not even the child traffickers. I watched your arrival here with my binoculars and my periscope from my submarine. Did I sense disapproval of Brother

Arnie? I hope not, for that would be so conventional. He was abused, and now he's the abuser. It's his turn. That's fair, isn't it? Was it Eve who picked the apple or Adam who ate it? Which came first, the chicken or the egg? The radicals and the killers stop by and stay here, too. Everyone cries for Abel, but Cain needs love, too, doesn't he? All are welcome in my tribe at Moondog Square, Sir Jim. I may have to put you on probation if I discover you're nothing more than a smallminded puritan.

"If we weren't loving and accepting of all, then Molly would have died. I remember little Molly there in the bus station, as sweet as sin, a little lost lamb in her make-believe world, making and sailing paper airplanes to a paper moon," he said.

He turned to her and said, "Look at you now, Molly. Here you are, darling, with your tall boyfriend, wearing your party dress and flying first class in your very own cardboard airliner. Is that a flicker of your flames I see? Maybe it's a softness to replace the coarseness of knowing too many men too intimately. You're a cute little porcupine with a 'pet me' sign now. Does it prick him when he pets you? When you left me, would just any man do? I bet not. I bet he's the pilot of your plane now," he said, madness oozing from him like sap from his Milkwood bush.

Molly didn't answer, but looked at the floor and scuffed her sandals like a kid with gum on her shoe.

"Aww, look at her hang her head, Jim. I still remember when I picked up the little runaway at Greyhound's house. She was a former Sweet Potato Bowl junior queen from Vardaman. She blossomed here, but one day she felt she had to go. I let her go, but she can't stay away. She loves me truly, but she fears me, and fear is really true love, isn't it?" He smiled through brown, rotten teeth.

The nerves in Molly's face began to spasm, and the color drained out of her.

"She's in the storm. Can't you hear her roar, Jim? Are you afraid of storms, pilgrim? You know I sit up here and watch everyone who approaches our little island here. I watched you as you moved through the shadows, Sir Jim. They don't engulf you.

You light them up. Are you reflecting the Light? I probably wouldn't sell to you if I wasn't so wasted and nodding, but I like you, and if little Molly vouches for you, you must be okay. Isn't that right, Polly Wolly Molly?" he asked.

He glared at her for a long time, saying nothing, as if he were reading her mind. "I can feel your brain ticking, Molly. She knows one hole, one leak, can sink a ship when you're dying to live and living to die. Did she tell you I had a hard time getting her to raise her skirts? But after a while, dancing the hootchy-kootchy just became like second nature, didn't it, country girl?" he said.

A tear trickled down Molly's face and wet her lips.

"Oh, isn't that precious, Jim? Did you think she was virginal? Yeah, she was breaking her teeth on the vodka bottles, so many of those hesitation marks on her wrists, and all the blood in the sink. Molly was shaking so bad I knew something inside her was broken, and I healed her, but then she told me she had to forsake me and graduate from Moondog University.

"She said she couldn't get over me if she was under me. She said outrageous and blasphemous things. Molly told me to stop pointing my gun at people, knowing full well I'm a pacifist, and she told me to claim all my babies my doctor friends had disposed of for me. I had a dream after that where the aborted babies were sitting on a table with their legs crossed, pointing at me and accusing me like Molly. So I let her go because I'm a sentimentalist, because she was disturbing our tranquility, and I wanted the dreams to stop," he said.

He took a long breath, reset, and started again.

"I have two jobs, Jim. I manage the broken ones here and the voices I hear in my head. One voice I hear is soft and full of light, but it asks too much. The other voice has grown louder and only tells me to live my carnal life and be happy. It's easy and asks nothing but to have a good time, that if it feels good, it must be right. What can I say? I'm weak and rotting within, but I own my weakness.

"Besides, happiness is just a sugar rush. It spikes you and drops you just when you think it's real, but holiness lasts forever. Are you a holy man, Jim?" he asked.

"Well, I got holes in my jeans," Michael said with a slight smile.

"Yeah, I hear you, got air-conditioned britches, too, but I ain't drinking from the gospel stream. I ain't looking for no pearly gates and streets of gold. Now, I ain't talking trash. I'm just a penthouse pimp counting my cash. If I'm wrong, I guess you'll be seeing the Son rise when I'm sitting down to breakfast in hell. No matter, I already fell into that pit. I already fell for a million years. It got hotter and hotter. The voices of the damned were raking my mind, and the executioner was waiting for me, but I put the needle in my arm, felt the rush, and forgot about it. I know my destination, and I'm going to live like hell until I get there. What other choice do I have? Do you think they serve heroin in hell, Jim?" he asked with a quizzical stare.

"I've never thought about it, Joiner," Michael said.

"Well, there're all kinds of habits and all kinds of prisons, aren't there? Who's your jailer, Jim? Are you in touch with the Commander-in-Chief? God tried to get in here once and came dressed up like this boy preacher, but we locked God in the attic. He bumped around up there, made some joyful noises, but he got quiet after a while, and began to smell. I smell so bad myself from my rot within, but I didn't know God could decompose, did you, Jim?" he asked, toying with Michael.

"No, I didn't, Joiner," he said to the madman, who stunk like a dead oyster at low tide.

"You know, I thought you were Jesus when you walked in with your long hair and your kind eyes, and the soft rhythm in your soul, but I know that can't be true because Molly don't know Jesus. Do you, honey?" he asked, looking at her.

Molly had regained a tenuous grip on her composure. She looked him in the eye and said, "No, never met Him."

"Hmm, look around you, children. These are the tombs and sepulchers of conventionality and the old way. We're the future, Jim…in schools, in the newspapers, even in pulpits, everywhere, man. Everybody else is trapped in their ghettos and don't know what they're missing. They only know people just like them in their echo chamber, the same old song. How holy they think they are. They'll never know the rush of heroin or the lusts of the flesh, but deep down they want to, Jim. They want to.

"There's no good and bad, no giant compass in the sky to guide our way, just the white-hot emotions of hate and lust and the seven deadly sins. We facilitate what the world calls sin and cover it with the blood of the poppy plant when the silver spikes pierce the veins, forgiving our excesses, seventy times seven injections.

"They've kept us in the shadows so they could play in the dark, but we're moving uptown and downtown. We're changing the world, not so much with bombs like our Weathermen brothers and sisters who crash here, but one day, we'll be the norm. Television anchors will speak our language, bands will play the messages to make the hearts and libidos of new generations throb, and our graduates will teach in schools and hypnotize children to make them children of the world, in it and of it. Our children will speak the words of wisdom—'To forbid is forbidden.' It's all so well-choreographed, and the curtain is rising on the final struts and bows of the old actors. Jim, who's biting the poison apple doesn't matter as much as who owns the orchard," he said.

Madness leaked from his heart and darkness seeped from the seams of his mind where reality was an infrequent visitor. Michael thought Joiner's cheese had slid off his cracker a long time ago. He also thought Joiner and his ideology were equally dangerous.

Joiner smiled, his head tottered, his eyes fluttered, and then he came back to the moment to stare at Michael.

"Are you scrubbing away the horizon, Jim? Who told you that you could? The night is closing in on us. The sun was no longer shining in the miserable lives we took in. We're just lighting a few lanterns for them. I was born into this life to help them, and if I am meant to drink or inject poison to fulfill my great commission, then I must. I don't suppose it really matters why Jesus died, does it, Jim?" he asked.

"Oh, I'm pretty sure it does, Joiner," Michael said.

The more the man talked, the more Michael could feel his skin crawl, and Molly seemed to be shrinking before his eyes.

His host leaned back and sighed.

"But I am remiss in my hospitality. Welcome, pilgrim. Here at Moondog, we don't care who's sleeping under what bridge or what some politician is doing. When I paddle around my pond, all I care about is, are the fish biting? My only ambition is to live until I die and then to just die in my sleep, and when you're dead, you're done, aren't you, Jim?" he asked.

"Could be the end, could be the beginning, I hear," Michael answered.

He looked at Michael and said, "You've got a quiet swagger, a hard face to read. I'm an old card shark, and you got one of the best poker faces I've ever seen, but you better be careful, Tarzan. The higher you swing, the more it hurts when someone cuts your vine and you fall. But you got a stiff neck, though. You sleep on a rock for a pillow? Are you thirsty for the well of living water? Are you dying for a breath of heaven's air? Will His blood wash out with soap and water? How do you know you won't burn in heaven, too, Sir Jim? Well, you hang around our barbershop long enough, you gonna get a haircut!" he shouted.

As fast as lightning, he whipped out an old .38 revolver and pointed it at Michael. "Would Jesus still love me if I killed you? Maybe I should put this pistol right in your face and blow your brains out!"

Michael saw his trigger finger tighten.

Molly shouted, "No! Don't!"

He smiled and said, "Tell Jesus I'll be needing air-conditioning and tell Lancelot that Guinevere has been unfaithful! Goodbye, Jim!"

There was a loud click. Molly screamed and clasped her hands over her ears, but nothing happened.

Then the drug lord doubled over laughing as Michael tried to calm his racing heart and show no emotion.

"Gets 'em every time! Don't worry, Jim, they weren't tombstone bullets. I don't think Jesus would let me kill you anyway, but I had to see if you were connected to the Commander-in-Chief. Is the Carpenter coming to rebuild your house? You might be an undercover agent for the cross. I think you must be, so it wouldn't be nice, would it, sending you to the potter's field, but I can't make a habit of doing kind things, else I might get used to it," he said.

He caressed his pistol and then carefully holstered it. "I shot a man dead once just to see how it felt to watch him die. You can learn a lot from the dying, Jim, that moment they cross over. I leaned over to him and asked, 'Whatcha seeing? Who's there?' But he didn't answer. One time I leaned in so close the door to the hereafter opened, and I thought I might get sucked in before I was ready. But that was another time, Jim, before the witches got new brooms to dust the wiccans, before the Satanists wore satin. I saw so much, too much, on the other side, and I don't want to see no more," he said in a scratchy voice.

He pulled out a bag of white powder, dangled it in front of Michael, and then tossed it to him.

"Here's what Molly said you wanted. Leave your donation in the offering plate and please be generous. No hand-to-hand transfers cause there's these new narc agents crawling around now, and that's their game. Besides, I never count my tithes until the saints come marching in. You come back often. Any friend of Molly's is a friend of ours. I love her, and she knows my rule… snitches get stitches. She can't betray me until the roosters have crowed three times," he said.

"I'm gonna have to go back here now and warm myself by the fire after our session. You can talk to Madam Rachel now, and she will assess our future prospects. She's not Jezebel, and she's not really a madam, but she *is* a mother to these young girls with broken wings. They just call her bad names behind her back. She's bitter, but she's not poison. She's aching to talk to you. I OD'd six times, and they brought me back. Rachel has only OD'd twice, but she's a late bloomer. I got a head start on her. She'll get there. I must go now. I promised the sweet young things, and they're summoning me," he said, cocking his ear to a lyrical chant that had begun somewhere outside the room.

"Come again, pilgrim. Come to visit or come to stay. We're all just trying to find a little peace of mind, aren't we? Remember, Jim, trust no one but me, and keep me on probation. Even your shadow will leave you just when things are darkest, and your teeth will bite your tongue when you're not looking. How do I know? I speak fluent shark!" he said.

Joiner stood and bowed at the waist. He parted swinging beads that served as the doorway to whatever lay beyond. He faded into the darkness behind the beads. A tall woman with long black hair emerged from a doorway to an adjoining room with a herd of black and white cats close behind. The cats were dressed in their piebald tuxedos and mewed in unison for Moondog's version of Eliot's Jellicle Ball.

CHAPTER NINE

"Nearly every day life leans over and says,
'Come on down!' "—Craig D. Lounsbrough

"The thrust is…to live on the far perimeter
of a world that might have been."
—Hunter S. Thompson

Rachel, the high priestess of the drug den, entered the room to sit cross-legged across from them, her sundress tucked under her legs. She could have been forty. She could have been eighteen. Rachael and her cats studied Michael with a gaze so intense that it made him squirm.

"He didn't tell you about my cats, did he? They represent my nine lives, and my true nickname around here is Miss Kitty Litter," she whispered, and then she seemed to change into a different person before Michael's eyes.

"What's your price, Jim?" she asked, her x-ray eyes boring into his heart and seeding nightmares in his head.

"I don't have a price," Michael said.

"Everything and everyone's for sale. There's a price tag hidden on all of us. Some just hide it better than others. Me, I'm marked down. I was suckled on sin and baptized in a tub of vinegar while I sucked on a sour pickle," she said, her eyes challenging him.

"We feed these junkies lies, convenient truths we call it, and they lap it up, like starving waifs trying to eat soup with forks," she said.

Michael looked at her and said, "Hiding the truth is like trying to hide the sun, isn't it? The truth eventually shines through clouds of lies."

"Truth?" she screamed.

"Don't speak to me about truth!" she snapped, her yellow cat eyes piercing him as she grabbed his wrists and dug her nails into his skin.

"They murdered truth on the Cross in our names. The wounds on our wrists never heal, and you're next in line to be crucified," she snapped.

She raised her dress along one leg, and there, tattooed on her thigh, was Revelation 17:5. "And on her forehead was a name written, Mystery, Babylon the Great, Mother of all harlots and abominations of the earth."

"Heroin is our god, and it is a jealous god," she said.

"Who're you trying to convince, me or you?" Michael asked.

She tilted her head, cocked her eyebrow, and said, "Something about you, you a preacher? Bet you were raised on cornbread, butter beans, and good morals."

Before he could answer, she said, "You don't belong here. Have you come to save us or to be saved, preacher? Maybe you come to raise me from the dead?"

"I can't save you, and I don't think you can save me. Maybe I've come for communion, or maybe I'm just a wayward undertaker," Michael said.

"Are you making fun of me?" she asked.

"No, ma'am, I don't think there is anything funny about you," he answered.

Without warning, she pitched forward on all fours, threw her head back, and hissed. Her cats hissed in unison with their mistress like wet air leaking from a room full of balloons. The evil in her eyes was paralyzing, the thing from the back of a cave measuring its prey. Then her eyes cleared, and she looked like a child for a moment.

"Are you heaven sent? Isn't this how I speak to your God, on my knees? Jackson's got so many churches. Why then does heaven seem so far away? I don't know, cause this is how I've been ticking along for so long on this rocky road. We're all just hitchhikers, thumbing a ride to heaven or to hell as the days thunder by us, trying to make it through this demolition derby. We're all on our way. Be it heaven or hell, we are on our way. Get out while you can, preacher, before they learn who you really are. This is not your altar, nor your pulpit," she pleaded.

"You can leave this place, too," Michael said. He noticed for the first time that her lips were cracked, her nails were dirty, and her breath was sour, like rancid meat, like rotten eggs.

"No, it's too late. I'm just an imposter, a worthless imitation of the baby my mama gave birth to. I was hungry, but the hunger ate me. I tried to buy love off the shelf, but you got to grow it from the seed. Molly knows. It don't matter what I do or where I go, I can't run away from me. I tried to touch the hem of His garment, but I got into a foot race with the devil, and he caught me. I'm nothing more than filthy rags, and unless you're packing industrial-strength holy bleach that can clean my innards, I must bid you goodnight," she answered as she slowly closed the door.

"Those who live on the fringe only need to touch the fringe of His garment as he passes by," Michael said.

She stopped for a moment as a giant cockroach crawled over her foot, and with one bloodshot eye peering at Michael through the door crack, she said, "I bet the girls chase after you, don't they? Just beg to sleep on your doorstep or eat the crumbs from your table? I can tell by the way you look at me I'll be living rent free in your mind for the rest of your life. If you ever need me, I'll be here with the rest of the cockroaches." With that, she squashed the roach with her boot, and the door creaked shut.

The last thing Michael saw were those eyes, eyes like old sandpaper, eyes that had watched as all the luster of life had been scrubbed out of her soul.

He looked at Molly and said, "The Summer of Love and the God is dead movement doesn't look so pretty at ground zero, does it?"

CHAPTER TEN

*"In keeping people straight, principle is
not as powerful as a policeman."*
—*Abel Hermant,* Le Bourgeois

*"Childhood should be carefree, playing
in the sun; not living a nightmare in
the darkness of the soul."*
—*Dave Pelzer,* A Child Called "It"

As they walked down the corridor with the dope Michael came to buy, the wind through the breezeway chilled him as it dried his sweat. He sensed Molly wanted to break out into a sprint to safety. Neither of them said anything, but when they reached the open door of the man peddling his daughter, Michael stopped.

"Don't look!" Molly whispered, but it was too late. Michael had already seen too much.

When he looked in the room as they passed by, he saw Arnold "shotgunning" his daughter. He was cupping his hands over her mouth and blowing concentrated Acapulco Gold marijuana smoke into her mouth and nostrils. A table beside the girl was covered in porn and how-to manuals.

"Daddy, don't!" the child begged, her voice muffled behind his big hands.

"This will help you to r-re-relax and be nice to our friends," Arnold said.

"What're you doing?" Michael called to the man in an angry voice he didn't recognize.

"I-I-I'm getting her ready for some clients, l-lo-loosening her up. She likes it. Hope you found what you were looking for. The clients are running w-w-way late. There's time for you if you've changed your mind. We're open for business every day and twice on Sunday. That's just to st-st-stick it to the Ch-chr-Christians who stole my wife. They're the real child abusers, planting all their nonsense about an imaginary God in the heads of children and telling them they're going to hell if they aren't good. We all know there's no hell," he said.

Michael said, "This is hell for her!" The image of a poster in the study of his childhood pastor flooded his mind. It was a picture of Jesus with His whip expelling those who defiled the temple. This little girl was made in His image, the temple of God.

"No, no, Charity's a happy girl," Arnold said.

A mountainous, pasty-white woman in her underwear appeared from out of the gloom of a back room. She had short curls dyed a putrid yellow-green. Her bitter bug eyes, set in a fixed stare, were so close together they threatened to cross. The woman looked like the Pillsbury Dough Boy's wicked stepsister and gave a whole new meaning to the term "put on your big girl panties."

She carried a syringe and a cloth reeking of ether.

"That's B-b-Bug-eyed Bertha Bates. She helps me. She's like a mother to the girl," he said.

He walked the girl over to Michael. Arnold had her pulled up tightly to his left leg. She looked beaten down, dazed.

Michael gritted his teeth. *The mission, the mission, they say.*

"She likes you, don't you, honey? She's a d-da-daddy's girl," he said.

Michael looked into her eyes floating on a sea of tears, and those eyes were pleading. He stepped into the room, and Molly reached for him. She grabbed his arm, but he pulled free because, like Jesus, he was in the midst of his own "temple tantrum."

He walked over to the depraved man. Arnold smiled and said, "Sp-sp-special rate for you, maybe fr-free the first time, just a taste."

He reached out in the common handshake to lock thumbs. Michael took his hand and pulled him close in a hug.

"I j-j-just knew you were a kiddy lover," the man said through the foulest breath Michael had ever smelled.

Michael held him tightly in a long embrace, until the man became uncomfortable and tried to pull away.

"W-wha-what're you doing, man? I don't swing that way," he said, his arm and back muscles tensing.

Michael pulled Arnold closer as he began to twist and squirm, pressed the nose of the .380 in his army jacket pocket against the man, and drove it up under his ribs.

"H-h-hey, what're you doing? W-w-hat's that?" he asked, trying to wrestle free of Michael's grip.

Michael slipped the gun under the man's belt and said, "These are mean streets, Arnold, and a man's not safe without his gun. You're going to send this child to her mother tonight. If I come back and she's still here, there's going to be an amputation by Dr. Beretta," Michael said.

"W-w-what? W-who do you think you are, the Great Sez Who? You can't do this to me. I'm p-p-protected. I'm somebody," he whined as he tried to kick at his captor's shins.

Michael snapped the safety off and said, "Look into my eyes. We can have a Fruit of the Loom adjustment right now."

Arnold turned white at the sound of the arming of the gun, and urine ran down his leg and puddled at his feet.

He began to cry and muttered, "Aw right, aw right! Oh God, help me!"

"I thought you didn't believe in Him, Arnold," Michael said.

The background music at Moondog Square droned on, the crowd too stoned to notice except for a man who wandered out holding an SDS newspaper and one pale man who sat back in the shadows, watching. Molly was shaking.

The little girl looked at Michael and ran to him, hugged him, and spoke to him for the first time.

"I want to go with you," she said, looking up at Michael with desperate eyes.

"No, honey, I can't take you, but this man is going to get you on the bus to your mama tonight. You do know where her mother is, don't you, Arnold?" Michael said.

He was outside, throwing up over the rail, but nodded and said, "Yes, f-f-first thing. I have the address. The girl was getting too old, anyway. They like 'em y-y-younger these days."

"I should put you out of your misery tonight, but remember, Arnold, you can't run far enough that I won't find you," Michael said.

"You made me s-s-soil myself and ruin my new pants. You took my little girl away, and you ruined my business. Satisfied, b-b-big man?" the pedophile asked.

Molly called out, "Jim, don't!"

Michael paused and turned to the man.

"No. Now that you mention it, I'm not!" he said.

He planted his feet, squatted a bit, and delivered a swift uppercut to Arnold that snapped his head back, broke his jaw, and landed him on the seat of his pants. Arnold wasn't moving, barely breathing, and a trickle of blood was running from the corner of his mouth and his nose. His eyes fluttered, and he began to moan.

"Now I'm satisfied," Michael said, rubbing his sore knuckles.

Bertha shuffled toward him, eyes bulging like one of the aliens from a fifties sci-fi movie. Michael turned toward her with his hand in his jacket, the nose of the revolver pushing against the cloth like the head of an angry serpent.

"You wanna dance, Bertha?" he asked.

She dropped the syringe, put her palms out, and then her hands over her head as she backed away, shaking her head left and right in a vigorous "No!"

Then Michael heard the applause. The Moondog community had awakened from their stupor, and they were standing in the breezeway and hanging out their doors and windows, applauding and cheering. Michael thought it was probably the first time they'd let themselves care about anything in a long time. *Even dope addicts and members of the oldest profession hate a child abuser. They once were children, and most were abused themselves.*

Michael bowed briefly before them, turned to Molly, and said, "Our work here is done, Tonto."

At the bottom of the stairs, they met the two men who were running late and on the way up to see Arnold. They had prominent mustaches accentuated by unfiltered cigarettes dangling from their mouths in plastic cigarette holders and brightly colored shirts. Michael blocked their way and said, "Arnold is closed for business. Vice and the FBI are up there and looking for you. Get out while you can and spread the word!"

The men looked at each other and ran away so fast they slipped and fell in the mud, ruining their new leisure suits, tangling the gold chains they wore around their necks, soiling their ostrich boots, and mussing their perfect gentleman's-club haircuts. Michael got their tag number for the vice cops as the perverts sped away from Moondog like the devil was hot on their tail.

As Michael and Molly walked to the car, a soundtrack of omens was playing. A lonesome train whistle sounded down the nearby rail line, and midnight bells tolled from one of the big churches downtown. March winds blew cold with a fine mist, chilling Michael to his bones.

The parade of horrors at Moondog Square seemed to have lasted forever. Michael felt like he was slogging through thick, putrid molasses. The madness of the night had left him nauseous, morose, and in need of a long, hot shower, but he thought Moondog's days were numbered. Child trafficking and dead girls melt political protection like butter in July heat. Milkwood had strayed from the original blueprint of hookers and drug addicts whom few in government care about.

He was questioning his choice of professions and thinking about his options. The night had scared Molly out of her wits. She shook violently and chain-smoked on the way to her home. She blew smoke rings out her window but said nary a word on the trip. Molly was crumbling. Her former tormentor still had a hold on her.

As he stopped to let her out at her apartment, she exhaled loudly with a nervous whoosh and relieved her smoke-filled lungs.

"What's wrong, Molly?" he asked.

She turned to him with wild, angry eyes and spat her words. "Agent Parker, I don't know what kind of perfect world you grew up in, but this is the neighborhood you signed up to take a stroll in.

"Am I scared? Yes. You were lucky tonight. He never would've sold to you if not for me and then only because he was stoned. You took too many chances tonight, and it could've gotten us both killed. I felt sorry for the little girl, but you can't save them all, Michael," she said.

"I might save one here and there, Molly, and who knows how many that one or two might save in their lifetimes," he said.

"You don't know. You just don't know. You think you know me, but you don't, and you don't know this world. Look at me!" she said, the rushing blood visible in the veins in her throat and on her temples.

Michael looked at her, and she pulled up her blouse to expose her breasts. He looked away quickly.

"No, look at me. That's what I mean. Your provincial values tell you to look away. Some women will take that opportunity to stab you or shoot you. Look at me, Michael," she asked with a softer voice.

He looked at her as she lifted her breasts to expose old needle tracks and the scarring beneath her breasts.

"This is where I shot up heroin when my other veins collapsed and to hide the marks when the health inspectors asked to see my arms. It's ugly, isn't it? Ugliness offends your romantic view of the weaker sex, doesn't it, purity and all that, huh? It worked well for me in the small veins in my breasts with my 31-gauge diabetic syringes. Then the veins began to blow. The abscesses came, and they got infected, but I didn't stop. I just moved on to my armpits and the tops of my feet. Besides that, I had to tend to the bleeding from the holes in my nose that the coke had eaten away when it was my drug of choice.

"Milkwood used to use the dorsal vein in his privates. Yeah, that's right. It shocks you and makes a man wince, huh? It repulses you, but this is what life, or its facsimile, looks like on this side of town, and this is what you chose, Michael. No one forced you to look at this godforsaken world or pretend you could walk a mile in the moccasins of our citizens," she said.

She lowered her blouse, sighed deeply several times, shook her head like a wet dog, and then her voice softened.

"I lied to you. I heard about you before you came to the MBN. Cal Mattox from Tupelo used Moondog as a flophouse when he was running moonshine, so did James Streeter when he was running to New Orleans to hide from the assassin stalking him. That ghostly pale freak Fredrick Hammel came through here hunting Streeter. He hurt the girls, cut some with a stiletto he carried trying to get information. He even scared Milkwood, who called the freak's handler, Ace Connelly in Memphis, to get him out of Moondog. He still stops by, I've heard.

"I wanted to work with you, but I'm not so sure anymore. I've seen them all, the cowboys and the badge-toting Don Juans, but you're different. You're on some kind of mission, marching to your own drummer. You cross the line and you care too much. I got hurt so much I stopped caring, but you make me want to care about life again, and that could get me killed. You got scars, the kind you can't see. There are shadows and memories following you, and they're warring for your soul," she said.

Michael smiled and said, "I guess we're all teetering on the wire and twisting on our hooks, but it'll all work out, Molly. Sleep on it. Besides, what would you do without the money the Bureau is paying you?" he asked.

She shrugged her shoulders and looked older than her years.

"Oh, I can always go back to the blood bank and sell more of my blood. I'm about dry, but I can always bleed a little more, I guess. Isn't that what the vampires of this world want…to bleed us dry?" she asked with a flash of sad resignation.

Distant lightning crackled across the night sky, and she watched the fingers of light run against the palette of black.

"What will you do, Michael? You seem to live in a world of black and white cats while everyone else sees a mixed-up and mottled calico world. The Bureau is not going to be happy with what you did tonight," she said.

"It'll be fine. They give rookies 'get out of trouble free' cards for the first year," he answered with a smile.

She squeezed his hand for a moment and said, "Bless your heart, Agent Parker. You still believe people like me might have a chance, that broken people can be recycled, too, just like cans, bottles, and old newspapers. I did, too, once, but all those high-minded Jesus dreams about redemption were like my mama's boyfriends—gone by the first light of morning.

"While I hid from Mama's monsters under my covers, I kept waiting for life's other shoe to drop. I tripped on those old soulless running shoes I wore out trying to flee from Jesus. So I left my dogs and cats behind and caught a Greyhound to the land of cotton, to Jackson and Moondog Square, where old times are forgotten or at least obscured by the haze of drugs. I thought I had hit rock bottom, but I kept on digging.

"For a long time I was waiting, but for who? Maybe it was someone like you, a prince. I was like you once. I thought all I had to do was believe, but my prince never came. The pushers came. The abusers came. Milkwood came. I kissed so many frogs, and none of them were princes. Sometimes I would pretend it was love, but then I'd wake up to find twenty dollars on the nightstand. I knew I was trapped in an earthly hell, sleeping on dirty sheets, just a leftover in a disposable world, knowing I had nothing left worth giving away.

"It's funny and bizarre, but you know when I knew I had to get out? Milkwood came to my room after he told one of those casual men that if he liked me, he would trade me to him for a Jimi Hendrix album. I remember staring at him, seeing him for the first time. Of all the things he did to me, that was the moment. He always told me that we're all living in hell, just riding the elevator to different floors. I knew then I was living on the basement floor next to the rest of the rejects, worth no more than a rock-and-roll album. I knew right then I didn't want to ride that elevator with him no more," she said, shuddering and hugging herself.

Michael felt compelled to offer an encouraging word, but he didn't want to interrupt the purging he was witnessing.

"My puppies and kitties are probably sitting around in heaven now, just waiting for me to die so we can play again like when I was a kid. I used to think about that when I put the needle in my body and felt the rush. I wondered if that might be the last wave to carry me home, but I wondered which home that would be. I dream sometimes that I'm standing in front of a door with my bags packed, and I can feel the heat coming from the other side," she said.

She paused, looked far away into yesterday, and said, "I feel like I'm standing at a crossroads, Michael. Don't know if I'm staying or leaving or coming in or going out, but my soul's tired of walking stooped and bent toward the grave."

Then she exited the car and leaned in the open passenger side window. "I lost myself trying to please everyone else. Now I'm losing everyone trying to find myself. I was one of those girls who honky-tonked on Saturday night and churched on Sunday. I wore a cross around my neck but had a cuss word hung in my throat I tried to wash down with hard liquor and harder living. I can't live that way no more. I can't do crazy no more. I long for the days when I was passing love notes in school instead of passing joints and needles and passing out," she said.

Molly looked a hundred years old. She struck a match and gazed at the flame. "You know, Michael, I've torched a lot of bridges just to watch them burn. My only regret is that my enemies were not on the bridges when they were burning, but you, 'Sir Jim,' bless your heart, you would run into the blaze to rescue your enemies, wouldn't you?" she asked, shaking her head and dabbing at the edges of her eyes where the dam threatened to burst.

She looked like a woman who wanted to cry, a seeker on the verge of some strange, inevitable revelation, a rightness she longed for. Molly was, once upon a time, a coarse and casual woman of incomplete pleasures, standing on the outside in the cold, looking in at some warm place. She was a ghost of a woman without truth who sensed it was near.

"I guess my arms are too short to box with God anymore," she said in a husky, scratchy voice that betrayed her weariness and resignation.

A long sheaf of red hair fell across her face, and she threw it back with a snap of her head and walked away, shoulders hunched, never looking back. He watched the little runaway walk toward the house under a lifeless evening sky, a night that seemed to be cloaked in mourning.

Michael thought about a kinder time before lost lambs like Molly and Carol Annie punched tickets of regret and shame to ride the Greyhound line and follow their dreams. Busloads of girls came to Jackson bound for Moondog Square, where kindness was killed and dreams dried and died. They were seduced by a would-be god who played at being immortal while he sheared the wool from his bleating flock of black sheep and auctioned their souls.

CHAPTER ELEVEN

*"As cops, our job is simple: do the right
thing, at the right time, for the right
reasons."—Gavin Reese, "Alex Landon"*

*"If you must leave a place that you have
lived in and loved and where all your
yesteryears are buried deep, leave
it any way except a slow way,
leave it the fastest way you can."*
—*Beryl Markham,* West with the Night

After he left Molly's house, he went to the rendezvous point to meet Harry Johnson, his control agent, but when he pulled up to the lone car sitting on the backside of the Ramada Inn, there was no control agent, only John Edward Collins, the director of the Mississippi Bureau of Narcotics.

Collins swung his 15 EE cowboy boots out of his car and leaned his massive frame against his gray Ford without saying a word. He took one last drag off an unfiltered cigarette, dropped it on the ground, and ground it into the pavement with one of the two steers that died to make his large footwear.

Michael swallowed hard. The man scared him more than the people at Moondog Square, because he respected him and wanted to make him proud.

"What was that about in there tonight, Agent Parker? I came by the surveillance post and listened to most of it. You could've blown your cover and put your informant in jeopardy," Collins said in his gravelly voice.

"I made the buy, a little girl may have been delivered from harm's way, and I think the surveillance team should have a mountain of intelligence on their recorders for Clay to decipher, sir," Michael answered.

"Agent Parker, Whitfield is full of people whose minds have been scrambled by drug use, and the mental health people are demanding we do something. There's a world of folks who don't mean us well, and they're looking for excuses to clip our wings before we get this agency off the ground. Some corrupt politicians want dirt on us to get us to back off, to control us, and we have to pretend we don't know what they're up to, because we need the appropriations, the purse strings legislators use to strangle us. I think you may have met some at the Sun-n-Sand. They want to use us to placate the public, but they really want us to be their goons and protectors of the status quo.

"There is an element at the Mississippi Highway Patrol who wants these jobs that you boys earned. They're used to getting ahead by who they know or who their kinfolks are, and their patrons call me every day asking me to lower the requirements, waive the background investigations, and take their boys over at MHP as agents. If they had their way, men like you wouldn't be here. Once they get their toes inside the door of the MBN, the hopes I had for an agency free of politics will be finished.

"The civil liberties groups are looking for an excuse to come after us. They think we're a cross between the KGB and the Gestapo, and in the midst of the agency launch and all these hurdles to clear, the new agent thinks he knows best tonight? You're new to the game, and you're going to tell me what to do?" he asked. It was a rhetorical question, and Michael remained quiet.

"To do all we have to do, we have to be like the man I met when I was an ATF agent. He was covered in tattoos, tattoos of eight different women. I asked him if he was really dating eight different women, and he said, 'Yes, I just thank God I'm man enough to handle them all.' That's us, Agent Parker. We have to manage it all—the enforcement part, the political part, and the public relations piece—if we are to survive," he growled.

Collins looked up at the clouds brushing the moon and crossed his arms as he leaned against his car.

"Tim Charles at Ole Miss speaks so highly of you and your integrity, but he said you're a man apart, not a pack animal. Boy, you need to get your legs under you and learn to walk before you run. We'll all get there together in the end. This ain't a foot race. Take the long view and don't get in such a hurry. You'll catch on fire and burn out too soon. I don't want you boys to always stay within the fine lines and be scared of your own shadow's temptations, but I do want agents who will stand in the gaps for what's right and for folks who can't count on anyone else to do that for them.

"Are we singing the same hymn, Agent Parker? Are we on the same page in the same hymnal? Are you even familiar with hymnals, Agent Parker?" he asked, finishing his long sermon on life in the Bureau.

"Yes, sir, we are on the same page, and yes, I am familiar with hymnals. That's what the mothers would hold up and shake at their daughters when I picked them up for dates," Michael said.

Collins narrowed his eyes and said, "Explain that one to me, Agent Parker."

"Their mamas told them there should always be a hymnal's width between our hips when we were alone," Michael said with a grin.

Collins couldn't help himself. A belly laugh snuck up on him and overwhelmed his serious face.

"So tell me, Agent Parker, would you have shot that child molester tonight?" he asked.

"No, sir, but it was only important that he believed I would," Michael said with a faint grin.

Collins laughed again.

"I think the dope dealer was right. I bet you are a good poker player. By the way, I've arranged for a health inspector to go by the place tomorrow to make sure the child is gone. A sheriff I trust will watch to see she arrives on the bus. The inspector will discover the dead girl on a routine inspection and get her out of there. He'll see if next of kin can be found. Jackson P.D. will look into the story of the missing pastor, too. Does that suit you, boy?" he asked.

"Yes, sir, it does. Thank you. One more thing, Mr. Collins," Michael said.

"What's that?" the director asked.

"When I looked into the abuser's eyes tonight, I didn't see a soul there," Michael said.

Collins nodded and lit another cigarette.

"You had better get on to your assignment in Hattiesburg. You're late, but try to get some rest along the way. You look like you've been rode hard and put up wet," he said.

He paused at his open car door and looked back at Michael.

"Agent Dave Best told me in the van tonight he was wrong about you, and your informant just called Clay. She told him she didn't want to work with any agent but you. Something about you lifting her up when life had let her down, something about you needing Tonto," he said.

He smiled and said, "Good job...Michael! Happy trails!"

Michael watched his red taillights disappear into the night. He was left to wonder if Collins had ever been there.

****

As he drove away, a radio evangelist on Michael's radio warned his listeners that man had evicted God from the public square, and He might soon hang out a No Trespassing sign in heaven and turn on the flashing No Vacancy neon. "It's time to put a dent in the devil's resume and fight him right where you are. Don't fuel his fire with sin; put out his fire with gospel gasoline," he said.

Michael turned off the radio sermon and stopped at a bridge over the Pearl River on his way out of town. He walked to the center of the expanse. It was partially illuminated by a dim streetlight casting a yellow glow across the bridge. As he looked up at the rotating heavens, a shooting star streaked across the strange night skies like a puff of fire from a roman candle.

Pigeons stirred from their roost beneath the bridge, and a breeze ruffled his long hair. He took a deep breath and wondered how the earth and all its troubles looked to God from up there, past the stars, beyond the Milky Way…high above it all.

The rush and gurgle of the water drew him back to the moment, and he stared at the waves and foam of the muddy river. He pulled out his wallet, took Dixie Lee's picture from the secret place he kept it, and fingered the frayed edges of the image. He also removed the lock of her golden hair he'd kept since Washington.

That romance and those dreams seemed light-years away from what he'd seen at Moondog Square and the Leg Room, but the two extremes provided perspective and focus. He had loved Dixie Lee, her flaws and perfect imperfections. All of her was mapped in his mind…how her lips would swell as they touched his, how his fingers smoothed her tangled blonde hair, and how she whispered his name. The memories suddenly seemed more like manufactured illusions, buoys dropped in the sea of time to mark a forgotten path he'd once traveled, stale breadcrumbs from yesteryear.

Michael startled. He almost thought he heard her call to him, but it was a homeless man who had been sleeping under the bridge.

"Hey, mister, can you spare some change?" the skinny man asked as he held his hat in his hands and smoothed the scattered wisps of gray hair on his head.

"Sure, buddy. Here's something for breakfast," Michael said, handing him a five.

"Wow, thanks, mister! I can eat all day on that! I won't spend it on booze, I promise. Everything has been backwards. My nose ran, my feet smelled, and I had to duck below my knees to pee and cough. Drunk me was always trying to starve sober me, but I'm sober me now and hungry," the man said, licking his cracked and bleeding lips.

He looked at the picture of Dixie Lee and said, "She's pretty." He gave Michael a big, toothless smile.

"Yes, but she's gone, and she won't be coming back," Michael said.

"You're hurting, aren't you, mister, wearing that ball and chain? You're all alone, too, aren't you?" the drifter asked with a Gabby Hayes lisp.

"Maybe I'm a voluntary prisoner," Michael said, looking at the churning water below.

"Anything I can do for you?" the man asked.

"Only if you're near Memphis and see her. You can tell her goodbye for me. We never had a proper goodbye. Tell her to leave the light on for me, just in case," Michael said, smiling, but the words tightened his throat and pricked his heart.

"I will, sir. You know, along my travels, I once saw real love," he said.

"What did it look like?" Michael asked him.

The drifter said, "It looked like everything I'd lost long ago, come back to me. I used to jitterbug when I had a handful of nickels, but I lost them and the jukebox went silent, and I couldn't dance no more. I laughed and then I cried, but someone gave me the Good Book in a homeless shelter. It said we're forgiven if we ask, and I wondered if that meant me, too," he said.

Listening to the tragic figure before him, Michael realized that every time he thought he'd hit the bottom of the well of separation, the bottom grew deeper. Maybe it was a survival instinct or part of him trying to find something normal and good to offset all he'd seen. Memories look better from a distance than up close.

He'd ceased to wonder about who was right and who was wrong, only what was left. He wondered if the day would come when the bad would be forgotten and only the good remembered, affections elevated by time to a pedestal where love stories become larger than life. It was the lofty perch of the Romeo and Juliet altar to which no flesh-and-blood human could hope to ascend.

Michael turned toward the river and began to rip the picture into small pieces.

"Wait! What're you doing, mister?" the drifter asked frantically.

"Saying goodbye," Michael said. "It's over."

The full moon came out from behind the clouds, and the light illuminated the shards of the photo as he released them. They fluttered down to the river like silver confetti, riding the wind like tiny dancing feathers in the night air.

He imagined for a moment he could see bits of her reflection in the water, a piece of a dazzling smile, a bit of a sparkling eye…all water under the bridge.

The man said, "I see you got hair, too. If it's hers, we could burn some cornbread on her. Burn her hair over a piece of cornbread and get the hex off you and put it back on her. She might have belonged to the devil, and he might want her for himself. I learned how to do that from a shaman when I was in Angola prison. Burn that bread with her hair, and you can cross her off your list if she's a double-crosser and a trampler of hearts. Do it unto others before they do it unto you. Isn't that in the Bible?"

At that moment, a sudden blast of wind blew Michael's jacket open, exposing his .380 under his belt and the gold shield he had just clipped there in case a local cop rousted him.

"You a cop! You a cop!" the man screamed as he ran off into the pitch black of night, flailing his arms above his head like the devil was dive-bombing him.

"Come back! I won't harm you," Michael shouted, but the man disappeared into the gloom, and Michael was alone again.

The sky was bleeding regrets, and goodbye was raining in his heart. The pieces of the picture had settled on the water and were swept away into the murky churn. Then he called a truce with goodbyes and their memories which begged and pleaded to stay, barricaded his mind against self-indulgences he could no longer afford, and touched her face with his mind.

I guess the warmest loves have the coldest endings, and Molly was right about life. It's no romance novel, but some stars seem to be etched into skies of stone. Just forget her name, forget her face, wait for feelings to fizzle, and go hide in this underworld to wrestle with the demons living here so I won't have to look at my own. I forgive it all and set it free. Goodbye, golden girl.

He released her hair into the wild winds. The yellow threads unraveled and swirled round and round in the churn like a mini-tornado. A sudden shudder swept over him and chilled him to his bones.

For a moment, he understood the cravings of the junkies. He thought, everyone is looking for their fix, a tender cure they can afford. He turned his collar up against the brisk wind and hopped in his car to head to Hattiesburg.

His car radio snapped and crackled, and the pastor said, "Well, it's time to sign off here on our little AM gospel radio station. We usually play a recording of the 'Star-Spangled Banner,' but tonight I want to play something I taped earlier: my six-year-old son, Billy Joe, reciting the pledge of allegiance. Let's see if we have it ready to roll. I think so. Take it away, BJ," he said.

The recording began with hisses, pops, and whispers of encouragement from a father to his son, and then, after clearing his throat and bumping the microphone a few times, the little boy began.

"I led the pigeons to the flag and to the Republic for the wishes it fans, under God, Who's invisible, with liver-tea and just ice four all. Amen."

The child's innocence countered all Michael had seen at Moondog Square. He laughed and laughed again as he felt the tension drain out from his body. Then he paused and said, "Invisible."

CHAPTER TWELVE

*"Sheila said she loved me, she said she'd
never leave me…"—Tommy Roe, "Shelia"*

*"I wanted to die in a ditch. I wanted to
disappear. I wanted a different history and
geography. In rhythm with the wheels
I said I want I want I want I want
I stayed on the train."*
—Lewis Nordan, Music of the Swamp

While Agent Parker was being baptized in the river of reality, the curtain was rising on another drama near Hattiesburg, where men were falling into an ancient bottomless pit. The fires got hotter and hotter, and they could not quench their thirst…

The midnight dew was heavy, and night creatures drank their fill from blades of grass and tiny flowers in a secret world born in darkness. Bugs, frogs, and nocturnal birds chirped and croaked in a symphony for no one.

A weighty stillness clung to the darkness. A cool spring breeze crawled down the bayou on the edge of the Leaf River. Silver light from an enormous full moon illuminated the bleached skeletons of splintered trees lining the slope leading to the rendezvous site.

A recent tornado had ravaged the landscape and ripped up huge trees, leaving moon-like craters, like something after an atomic war. It was duck and cover all over again when the F-3 twister roared through the countryside.

As Otis Wayne "Bad Eye" Tutor walked down the path in his straw hat and gray tweed coat, the kerosene lantern he carried bobbed and swayed with each step. At a distance only the lamp light was visible, as if it were borne by some disembodied spirit, perhaps the ghost conductor that locals had seen trying to flag down the trains on the tracks to warn of danger ahead.

Otis dressed in all black one night and waved the light at the train crew, just to keep the story alive. *For what is life*, he thought, *without ghost stories and tall tales?*

They called him Bad Eye because one of his eyes looked the wrong way after a bar fight. He always told folks, "You shoulda seen the other guy. He didn't have no eyes left!" They put a steel plate in Otis's head after the fight. After that, compasses began to spin round and round when he walked by.

A giant, emerald-green bug, winged and hard-shelled, splattered into the lantern Otis carried, leaving his lamp with a distinct green hue. Otis looked at it and thought he was now the "Green Lantern." He threw his head back and smiled, exposing the snuff stains on his decaying teeth and long hair growing from his nostrils, near combing length.

Lantern in one hand, his father's vintage World War 2 Browning Automatic Rifle (BAR) in the other, a .44 revolver under his belt, and a four-shot derringer in his boot, he moved toward an old outhouse the storm had left untouched, dragging a big iron sheet behind him for a shield. Otis came prepared because there were always leaks, and he had a price on his head.

The moon played hide-and-seek behind puffy white clouds. The moonlight slid down his craggy face, and shadows crept across the knoll like inky fingers. There were eroded mounds along the slope of the hill, and Otis could sense the restless spirits of Native Americans questioning his right to walk among their dead. He knew this ground's bloody history, and he'd put on his war paint to honor the blood of his ancient tribe.

He wasn't afraid of the night, but two white barn owls flushed from a nearby cottonwood tree startling him. They floated moth-like through the night, like ghosts or menacing specters of doom.

Otis was born under a bad sign, the night of a blood moon. He was afraid of the dark as a child until his mother told him the dark was afraid of him. But he knew shadows can blind you, and the things hiding in them can kill you.

His family gossiped and said his mother's cornbread wasn't done in the middle, but as Otis always told people, "Mama knew things!" He would point to his brain and say, "She's got kidneys, man, kidneys!" Otis also told his friends his mother was smart because she only drank milk from contented cows, just like Carnation Milk said in their ads.

He looked up at the moon as he lumbered down the incline and thought the face was mocking him. He had the urge to draw his pistol and fire a projectile at the big Swiss-cheese ball in the night sky. What if it reached there by some cosmic accident? Could he be charged with murdering the man in the moon? He kept his powder dry and laughed out loud at the vagabond moon, a homeless wanderer like him. His massive belly fat jiggled like a tub of Jell-O as he chuckled and bounced along.

The wooded and cambered knoll had been the home of a local gypsy fortune-teller known as Glosswitch. Bad Eye's wife, Sheler, once visited her for charms and poultices. There were always strange smells and smoke near the shack, and animals veered around her place. No one knew what happened to Glosswitch. Some said she'd been seen holding hands with the ghost conductor. Others said they'd received bills for card readings, and they were postmarked "Hell."

Her outhouse was all that was left after the storm. Otis thought a witch's outdoor toilet was an unlikely place to meet the narcotics agent, Michael Parker, but that was the beauty of it when Sarge picked it. No one would think to look there, and Parker was Sarge's partner as a deputy sheriff. Sarge said Parker was a young pup, but fearless and honest. Besides, he said Parker was qualified because he grew up using an outhouse in Parker Grove community south of Tupelo.

Narcs and outhouses; Otis's mind was bouncing like a BB in a barrel as he trudged along, and he thought of his favorite joke as a child. When asked by his teachers what books he'd read, he took great delight in startling the proper old ladies by answering, "Hundred Yards to the Outhouse, by Will E. Make It!"

A fine drizzle began to seep from the night sky. In what passed for deep spiritual introspection, Otis wondered if he had insulted God and the wells of heaven were overflowing with His tears. He wrote a letter to God once and mailed it to Washington, where they talk about Him a lot, but it came back marked "Addressee Unknown." Otis figured they must not have known God after all, or they were too busy impersonating Him.

He looked up as the mist sprinkled his face. *Maybe this is how they do it these days. No direct answers, no choruses of angels. Someone in heaven just punches D-6 on the big jukebox in the sky, "Play Misty for Me."*

There was a time when Bad Eye never gave a passing thought to God, but that was before the drug thugs moved in, paid off the local lickspittles, and robbed him of the political protection he'd always enjoyed for his bootlegging business.

It was before his time at the Delta farm, Parchman prison. It was before his brain got a little scrambled by the 100-proof shine special he called "Dixie Fried Hootch."

It was before...Sheler, before the Stone brothers, the drug lords, took her from him.

****

Sheler, who had eyes like cat's-eye marbles, eyes that shifted from green to indigo, was born near Chickenbone, Mississippi. Her mama, Melba Jane, meant to name her Sheila, but spelling wasn't her forte. She had a thick country accent and the tendency to add extra syllables to words. So Sheila morphed into "She-ler."

Sheler seemed cursed from the beginning. Hard times hadn't merely touched or brushed her, they had seized and assaulted her. She survived attempted rape at age eleven and once told Otis the stars had ceased to shine for her that awful day. She said light from the celestial flames in the night sky had burned out long ago, just like hers. Sheler said any semblance of a smile people saw on her face was only an echo of yesterday, dead starlight still traveling to their eyes.

"Mama Melba" still turned heads. She was a beautiful woman with sleek legs and hair like strands of gold spun from the sun, the kind of woman men dream of meeting when dusk stirs the longings and desire comes barreling down the tracks like a runaway train.

Melba fled Chickenbone and her husband's abuse when Sheler was ten. She took little Sheler with her to a shack outside Swiftown, Mississippi.

"Mama, I can see light between them boards," Sheler told Melba when she first saw her new home.

"Aw, honey, that's just air-conditioning for us in the hot Delta summers," Melba told her.

The precocious little girl studied her mama for a moment, put her hands on her hips, and said, "Mama, you aren't shoveling me cow chips again, are you?"

When winter came, they huddled before an open wood stove they cooked on and used for heat on December nights when the wind whipped across the Delta, making wooing and whistling sounds through the cracks in the shack. Sheler thought ghosts were trying to get in, but Melba held her close and told her daughter it was only the house breathing and hissing.

The first summer in Swiftown, they sat out on the back porch that backed up to the edge of a small pond they called the Raccoon Lagoon in honor of all the masked bandits of the night that visited regularly. Some nights they'd feed them scraps, watch the sunset burn a hole in the horizon, and sing along with a tiny transistor radio, especially when the Platters came on. They made sweet harmony, and the raccoons would applaud, the chickens would cluck in time, and stray dogs would howl along. "When the twilight is gone and no songbirds are singing, you come into my heart and here in my heart you will stay..."

Melba got a job waiting tables at a local restaurant, and there she caught the eye of a local politician. He started coming round to the house to see her. He eventually stayed the night and began to pay the rent on the shanty where Melba and Sheler lived.

Senator Justin Johnson came by regularly for the services he paid for, and it went on that way for some time, but Melba found out he had other women on the side, much younger women. He came around less frequently, and getting him to make a commitment to her and Sheler was like trying to nail Jell-O to the wall. Though Melba described her blood and her attitude as "Be Positive," the bloom was off the rose.

So it seemed providential when a man everyone called Corndog offered her some money and some revenge. All she had to do was doctor the senator's chili when they went to Doe's restaurant in Greenville. While Senator Johnson was in the men's room, Melba dusted his chili with what Corndog told her was PCP. She thought about the senator's other women, and she dusted it some more. Johnson threw up on the table, soiled his seersucker suit, and fell into the chili. His bowtie was submerged in the doctored bowl of capsicum, PCP, and woman scorned. Melba later called it "Swiftown Revenge," a dish best served cold.

The story of the senator's unfortunate public display spread far and wide across the Delta. Old ladies lit up telephone party lines with the gossip. Chuckling old men could barely concentrate on games of checkers at local country stores. The timing was exactly what Corndog hoped for. The telling and retelling of the story peaked just as the election rolled around. Corndog ran against the senator and ousted him by a surprising margin. No self-respecting Delta resident wanted a senator who puked in public, sullied a local dining establishment, and ruined a perfectly good bowtie.

Sometimes games continue with new faces. Corndog promised to take care of Melba Jane and Sheler, but he wanted the same fringe benefits Senator Johnson had been receiving. It seemed natural to Melba because men had always used her, and Corndog was kind to her and to Sheler. He bought pretty things for Sheler, the daughter he told Melba he wished he'd had. He bought

Sheler a used car when she hit her teenage years, about the time folks in the Delta noticed that Sheler had inherited her mother's good looks.

That's the way it remained, almost like a soap opera. It was like one of Melba's romance novels or one of those stories she read in the *National Enquirer* until Corndog took her with him to Jackson to meet his friends at the Leg Room. She thought he was taking her to the big city to propose, to give her a big diamond ring. All he gave her was a sack full of silver dollars to play the slot machines in the backrooms of a place called Moondog Square. She knew it was his way of telling her the money was payment in full for her part in poisoning Justin Johnson. Debt cancelled.

Sheler wasn't sure what went on in Jackson. Her mama wouldn't talk about it, but Melba was never the same. She began to talk a lot to Sheler at night, and one night when they were sitting on the back porch throwing marshmallows to the raccoons, Melba turned to Sheler, stroked the black hair Sheler had inherited from her father, and said, "You know I was young and pretty once, just like you, Sheler. I had dreams, but look at me now, a kept woman."

The night train from Greenville almost hit Melba Jane one night when she was walking down the railroad tracks in Greenwood in a flimsy nightie. It was one of those nights with a full moon so big and bright you could see the craters. That's why the engineer saw her and sat down on the horn. She fell from the tracks into the muddy waters of the Yazoo River and was fished out by a local emergency squad. The conductor told the sheriff Melba looked like a woman who had more grief than his freight train could haul.

Then one day, she disappeared. Melba was last seen far from Swiftown, along the banks of some slues south of Greenwood. Search teams scoured the area. Senator Corndog had them bring in the bloodhounds from Parchman to an area where a hitchhiker swore he saw her walking into the bayou under the pale moonlight. Men searched into the wee hours with lanterns, calling her name, but all they found were gators and snakes.

Then they found her slippers and a pile of silver dollars on the banks of one of the bottomless Delta bogs. They figured she had given up the ghost, so they gave up the search. Senator Corndog laid a wreath on the murky waters as her final resting place and a bowl of chili on the levee for her ghost as a gesture to old times.

Corndog was grieving and couldn't be found for a while. Rumors spread that a man named Milkwood Jones had given him a place to lay his head, and something and someone to make him sleep and forget his deadly sins, to ease the pain of Satan's pitchfork pricking Corndog's rear.

After Corndog disappeared, Sheler was left alone in the ramshackle tenant house to fend for herself as best she could. She drank water from an old artesian well in the field, stole food from nearby farms and barns, snatched eggs from beneath setting hens, and abducted plump chickens for her grander meals. She also stole a pistol, a Smith & Wesson .38 revolver, out of a farmer's pickup truck.

Her mama's sister, Doris, eventually came to take care of Sheler, but Sheler was wild by then. After Doris died in 1963, Sheler gave birth to a baby girl sired by her high school principal, who denied parentage. Then one day, her drunkard father showed up. Slick still had hair so black that Melba once said he'd been dipped in the devil's inkwell. He broke into the house where Sheler and her baby lived. He pointed to her daughter as proof she'd always been Lucifer's child, that she'd tempted him to do what he had done.

The Le Flore County deputy sheriff who answered the call found Slick lying belly up on the steps of the front porch, a big round hole in his chest and an even larger one in his back where the round exited the remains of the rapist. Sheler sat calmly in her rocking chair staring at the corpse, the smoking pistol by her side.

He asked her if she had killed him. Sheler didn't blink and she didn't stutter. "Yes, sir, and if he gets up and comes back to my house, I'll kill him again," she said.

The deputy called the sheriff, who called the county prosecutor, who called Senator Corndog. They decided justice had been delayed but finally realized. No charges were brought against her. All the highfalutin folks huddled together, agreed it was justifiable homicide, that it was clear poor Sheler was a half bubble off plumb when she shot him. The Le Flore County grand dames decreed that no more would be said about it without social consequences. After two women broke the pledge, they were disinvited from local book club meetings and barred from the annual cotton ball at one of the larger plantations. Justice was swift, and that was that. Deterrence was achieved.

After the whispers died down and the tongues stopped wagging, Sheler married a local boy just back from the war in Southeast Asia. They had a daughter of their own, but her husband, who was wound up high and tight like the military cut over his jarhead, was an alcoholic. He unplugged the jug when the hard times of Vietnam visited him in his sleep, and he became violent.

His nightmares and flashbacks got worse. One night she awoke to find him choking the life out of her, convinced she was Viet Cong. She only survived thanks to the ice pick she kept by the bed. He survived the shallow stabbing, which missed his arteries. There were no hard feelings, but pretty soon Sheler was on her own again.

She figured she couldn't outrun the scandals in her sandals, so she moved south to Moselle and enrolled at the University of Southern Mississippi. She studied to be a nurse and worked at a local garment factory in Hattiesburg to provide for her girls. Then one day, she walked into McDonald's and met Otis. Love at first sight mugged them, and they were married three weeks later.

Otis couldn't stop thinking about Sheler and her past as he stumbled down to the old two-seater outhouse. He talked to himself, trying to unpack it all, remembering the woman who told him she was born on Friday the Thirteenth, and that life had been paying her with bogus thirteen dollar bills ever since.

CHAPTER THIRTEEN

"The sound of a kiss is not so loud as that
of a cannon, but its echo lasts a great
deal longer."—Oliver Wendell Holmes

"If you wanna do good, you better stay off
old Parchman Farm."—Bukka White,
"Parchman Farm Blues"

It seems like only yesterday when I bought her a Big Mac and asked her out. Some said she wasn't a classic beauty, but when you got up close to her and looked again, you could see what a beauty pageant judge called her Apollonian symmetry. I wasn't sure what those words meant, but I liked it and knew they were right.

I rehabbed and sold houses and apartments on the side to supplement my bootlegging business. She went with me one day, and even though I was sweaty and dirty, she suddenly turned and kissed me hard when we were putting up wallpaper. She bruised my lips and stuck to me like the sticky paper stuck to the walls.

After we married, she won a beauty pageant in Hattiesburg—Mrs. Golden Eagle. Despite having two children, she still had an hourglass figure, long smooth legs, and a red-bronze tan. She was one of those women that when you see them, you immediately have this burning resentment for every man who has ever held them, a feeling of anger and envy for men you never knew, all at the same time.

She reminded me of the girl on the old Mickey Mouse Club. Sheler was beautiful, just like Mouseketeer Annette Funicello, who I had a big crush on. Them were good days. Sheler once put on some Mouseketeer ears and sang that old song for me. Sheler could make the sun shine at midnight.

She was like one of them plants that turns toward the sun. She always turned to the light of attention, to bask and brown in it. Just after sunrise and sunset each day, I would find her on our deck when the sun's light bathed everything in a soft orange glow. She was like that...harmony and light on the surface but turmoil beneath her eyelids, one cat's-eye blue and one green.

I didn't talk much, but she was a chinwagger, a jawboner, and a gossiper. That's dangerous in my line of work. It made me worry, and trust and worry can't live in the same house, but I loved her. Her daughters were like my own, and she was so pretty, a beautiful treasure to my hungry eyes. So I forgave her tongue-wagging, told her that her past didn't matter, and we were married right away.

Things were good at first, but she got twisted bad before she met me. She got into the Bible for a while, but pretty soon she had twisted it, too. I caught her practicing before a mirror. She would watch herself cry so she could imitate real emotions she'd lost along the way. She wanted to become someone else and leak fake tears on demand as weapons. I thought I could love all that out of her. They say love is blind but marrying her was an eye-opener. It gave me 20/20 vision for sure when we were united in what my friends called holy acrimony.

When I first courted her, the beauty with curved lips like Cupid's bow, she asked me to drink beer from her slipper. But after only a few short years of running with the Stone boys behind my back and snorting and shooting their chemicals, she was leaving her teeth in a glass of water, snoring like a freight train, and smelling like four dead skunks had died under the house—something dogs drug up and cats wouldn't have.

The Stone boys and their druggies fueled her madness on the wild side of town. They were using her all along, slipping her the drugs and luring her to their beds in exchange for the drugs that fed her habit. When she wasn't sleeping, she was always making naked chocolate chip cookies for them, cookies with no chocolate chips. She said the Stones liked their cookies naked like their women. Sheler used to wear white for purity, but over time her frocks became dirty and dingy, and she stole my key to her chastity belt.

She had a death wish, and I finally told her I couldn't sleep in that grave with her no more. I always thought it was about sprinkling a little love, planting some payback, but I was barking up the wrong tree. Then the cops on the take from the Stone brothers came after me to get me out of the way. There was nothing Sarge could do to save me.

Folks around Hattiesburg used to sleep with their doors unlocked, but that changed when the drug gangs came to town. When Sheler took up with them, they put little white pills in her drinks and paid local officials to send me to prison.

To survive prison, I had to cease babysitting the bitterness that had consumed me. I just put it over there somewhere, on a shelf where I could get to it one day if I ever needed it. There was so much blame to go around, I didn't know where to place it all— her father, mother, her mama's men friends, and her friends—but I'm pretty sure a big chunk of it could be laid at the feet of those Stone boys, who had smooth, velvet voices, like butter over grits.

Death may be waiting for me tonight. Maybe I'll recite my mother's ancient prayers as good practice for any sudden, unscheduled appointment before the Judgment Seat in heaven. They keep telling me it's later than I think. They might be right tonight. I hope I haven't led the narcotics agent into an ambush, but I got a bad feeling.

****

The moonlight bled through the cracks of the outhouse where "Bad Eye" sat in the deluxe four-seater, but then it was gone, hiding its face behind a bank of clouds as the night poised to expire.

When they framed me, and I had to go away to Parchman, I couldn't protect her anymore. I had crossed the wrong people. The politicians who took my bootlegging money were gone. The new big bosses who liked drug money wanted me to kiss their rings, but they didn't tell me they kept them in their back pockets.

Prison was hard. The jailers demanded conformity, worship of the world, and tribute to the political gods who gave them their jobs, but life with Sheler had been a prison for me, and my incarceration left her on her own and even more vulnerable to the drug boys.

While I was away, she got in deeper with the Stones. Just to torture me, one of the prison guards told me his friend with the highway patrol had stopped the Stones and she was in their car—stoned with the Stones. "Somebody's taking care of Mama while Daddy's away," he said, laughing at me, mocking me.

I told him she was still my wife, and if loving her was a crime, then I'd just have to do the time. I also told him I didn't want to kill him, but it was still on my list of possibilities. He left me alone after that.

I wrote Sheler often. Though I never understood those romance novels she read, I told her I still loved her, and the sun was still shining just for her, but she said, "I'm lost, don't find me. I am drowning, let me sink. It don't matter if you have the most marbles when you die or if you've lost your marbles, you're still dead! The big toilet in the sky will soon be flushed, and we'll all be gone. What does any of it matter?"

Otis figured there was a deep message in there somewhere, but it eluded him. All he knew was the fight, the brawl. The bell rings and you come out fighting.

His darling companion and beauty queen wrote him one last time.

Dear Otis,

What happened to us and to our town? I came here to Mayberry to escape, but now it's Peyton Place. I have lived in the darkness so long and can't find my way to the light. I sent my girls away to live with their cousins. The Stones were

after them, too. I took the gun I killed
Daddy with and threw it in the river. I
was afraid of what I might do when I was
alone, and Satan was whispering in my
ear. I been committing slow suicide
anyway with the Stone boys. I once told
you that you were driving me to the
grave, but it wasn't true. I was driving
that train bound for hell. I have much to
answer for. It won't be long now. I hear
the coachman calling...all aboard.

Sheler

****

Then the day came Otis had dreaded in prison. A somber-faced warden who looked like Henry Fonda and walked like a long-legged man stepping over cotton rows came to see him. The warden had the death row look, the face that says, "Time's up" or "I regret to inform you."

When the warden said there had been a high-speed chase and a bad wreck, Otis's fists clenched and unclenched, and a cold, oily sweat began to pour from his brow. "I'm sorry to tell you that your wife was thrown from the car and killed instantly," he said.

Otis never looked up but spoke from the back of his grief-clogged throat. "Who was she with?"

"She was in the car with Tim and Terry Stone," the warden answered, looking at the floor.

"Did they survive?" Otis asked dryly.

"Yes, they walked away, I'm told. They were released from the Forrest County Jail when they sobered up and bonded out," he said.

There was a long pause where neither man said anything. They just marinated in the stew of it all.

"We were going to release you, Otis, but we decided it would be best for the community if we delayed it until after your wife's funeral. She's in the ground now. Some people down there thought that would be advisable, given your volatile and violent nature, but I do have something for you," the warden said.

The warden handed Otis a picture from her funeral. He told him the mortician said no one attended the service, not even her daughters. The warden said they'd disappeared from the Clarksdale home of Sheler's cousin, and no one knew where they were. Some said a relative came for them. Others said some rich man had sent them away to a private school in Tennessee.

Otis looked at the picture for a long time. Sheler was in a casket for real this time, but it wasn't her. There was nothing any mortician could do after such trauma to make her pretty again. Sheler had nine lives, but the girl who had plowed such a rocky field in life had finally used them all up.

The warden said, "There's someone here to see you before you leave."

Senator Cornelius "Corndog" Ball walked in the room. The warden almost bowed before him and left Corndog alone with Otis.

Corndog had attended their wedding, and Sheler had told Otis the whole story about the senator and her mother. If the warden had the death row face, Corndog looked like a man delivering the news to a condemned man that "the pardon from the governor is in the mail…if you live long enough to get it."

"Otis, I wanted you to know you have my deepest sympathy for your loss," Corndog said, pursing his lips into the fake smile of a funeral home director who'd just gotten the call to come to a multi-car pileup with no survivors.

"Thank you, Senator," Otis replied.

"They're about to set you free, and I wanted to give you a little free advice. Anger and a thirst for revenge are poisonous to the soul. 'Vengeance is mine,' sayeth the Lord. You remember that, and if you ever have any thoughts about avenging Sheler's death, I want you to put it out of your mind," Corndog said in his best "Father Knows Best" imitation.

"Is that right?" Otis sneered.

"Yes, it is. I understand because she was like a daughter to me. I loved her and always tried to help her," Corndog said as he gave Otis a jolly-boy, Chamber-Rotary pat on the back.

Just as the camp loudspeaker announced chow time, Otis gave Corndog the stink-eye look with his bad eye.

"Let's see, you took Sheler's mama to Moondog Square and drove her to an early grave. Did that help Sheler? Just all in the seasoning, huh, Senator?" Otis asked in a pointed reference to the infamous story of Corndog's poisoning of his rival.

"Now, that right there is the kind of attitude I'm talking about. You don't know anything about the past. Her mama was complicated. There were generational curses at play in that line of folks. It was inevitable they all would die young…tragic, but inevitable," the senator snapped.

"Inevitable," Otis said, nodding and slowly rubbing his jawline.

"Yes, son, that's right, and you don't want to go messing around in things you know nothing about. There are people in the Delta cooperating with people in Hattiesburg and New Orleans right now, and many of them are rough people, Otis. You don't want to fool with them and upset any apple carts," Corndog said.

"Who are you, the Boogie Woogie Bugle Boy of Company B sent here to blow your horn for the syndicate?" Otis asked.

"I only want to assure my friends that you are a reasonable man. I want to help you like I helped Sheler win that beauty contest in Hattiesburg. We all knew she was out of her league, but a few calls here and there to the judges leveled the playing field," he said with a patronizing smirk.

Otis flushed red and jumped up from his chair. The shackles on his ankles almost tripped him, but he steadied himself and wagged his finger at Corndog.

"You didn't help her win! She won on her own, and I won't sit here and listen to you take that away from her. So you get on back to your Leg Room and to Milkwood Jones and his girls. I'll take care of my business, and if you *become* my business, I'll force-feed you your famous chili until your guts wear out," Otis said, his eyes boring into Corndog's head.

Corndog backed away from him like a zoo patron who realizes he has stepped too close to the lion cage.

Corndog said, "You're a beast, a simpleton. No wonder Parchman had to use 'Black Annie,' the old leather strap, on you for rules violations. That's why I sent Sheler's girls away to Memphis to one of the finest private schools, so they wouldn't be left at the mercy of Neanderthals like you."

Otis closed his eyes and thought of the girls who he considered to be his daughters, the girls who looked like little Shelers. At least he knew they were all right and that he could find them when the time was right.

"Killers and gofers are cheap, especially those just getting out of Parchman with no prospects. What they gonna do? What you gonna do except play ball and work for us? If you go against us, you're a fool," Corndog said.

As the senator walked toward the door, Otis said, "Yeah, and if a frog had wings, he wouldn't bump his behind when he hops, would he?"

At Corndog's request, the warden held Otis a few weeks for more "processing and paperwork." When the courts were about to object, Otis was quietly released on good behavior. Bad Eye was given a King James Bible with his name inscribed on the cover. The warden warned him again to "let bygones be bygones," to "let those sleeping dogs lie so their fleas don't start feeding on you."

Otis sat on his bunk the day he left, trying to bend over to put his shoes on. It had become an ordeal to tie his shoes because his stomach had become so swollen while in prison, the result of malnutrition, poor medical care, problems with digestion, and the hell that was Parchman Penitentiary. The prison had provided shoes with Velcro straps because he couldn't reach his shoes to tie them.

Inmates waved goodbye to Otis and wished him well when he prepared to leave. Some of them had worked outside too long when the crop-dusters were flying overhead, spraying the poison that made the sky bitter and sticky. Otis used to watch the lifers raring back and sniffing the air like glue-heads to get a cheap high or to commit slow suicide.

"What you gonna do when you get home, Bad Eye? Bet you going to eat good food like a hungry horse and sleep at least twenty hours a day on a real mattress, huh?" yelled one inmate whose brain had been fried over easy.

"I'm gonna eat a ton of good food and pick the meat off the T-bone, just for you boys, but I got lots to do to make up for lost time, plenty of time to sleep after I'm dead," Otis answered.

When the bus pulled up to the gates of Parchman, all the passengers gawked at Otis when he handed the driver money for his ticket home. It was a long ride, and Otis had plenty of time to think about bygones and sleeping dogs. He had his freedom, his health, and he had money hidden away. He had everything he wanted—everything but Sheler. She had a face that would've been beautiful until sixty or seventy had they not turned her into a different person, killed her, and ruined his life. When he napped on the trip, Otis woke up repeatedly thinking about what to do about those who had wronged him. He decided there were questions that had only one answer…murder. Cain figured it out, and so had Otis.

CHAPTER FOURTEEN

*"You don't hunt turkeys because you
want to; you hunt turkeys because
you have to."—Tom Kelly*

*"What sorrow awaits you teachers of
religious law and you Pharisees.
Hypocrites! For you cross land and sea to
make one convert, and then you turn that
person into twice the child of hell you
yourselves are!"—Matthew 23:15*

Otis had a layover in Jackson before arriving in Hattiesburg early the next day. He hailed a taxi and reported to his parole officer to assure him he wanted no trouble. The bored officer seemed relieved and wrote "harmless" across Bad Eye's file.

After a brief meeting with Sarge, Otis retrieved a dilapidated, fenderless car a friend had kept for him and went straight to his stash in the storm cellar behind an abandoned house he owned. He used to hide his stash of guns, ammo, and currency there in his heyday of bootlegging, along with his original 45 rpm recordings of Elvis from Sun Records in Memphis. All his treasures were there and perfectly preserved. He retrieved his weapons, so carefully wrapped in oilcloths, and reassembled and loaded them all. He also found and tested his turkey caller.

Otis gazed at his prized record collection and said, "Elvis, there will be some good rocking tonight. Feel like it's time to go hunting and thin the flocks. Too many turkeys ain't healthy for the species."

He cut through the dense woods to his stills, the ones the Stone boys had found through Sheler. Otis came up the wooded slope and could smell the smoke and exhaust from the stills. He crept close enough to see the Stones working the stills and packing drugs for their runners. They all looked alike, like Pete and Repeat—big and beefy with red hair and red necks. Otis took his turkey caller and simulated a "gobble-gobble."

The boys stopped, got real quiet, and he repeated the call again.

"Sounds like that turkey's close," Terry Stone said to Tim.

"Yeah, boy! I could use some turkey tonight. Get your gun, Terry," he said.

Otis gobbled again and then moved away from his position as the Stones honed in on the sound of the "turkey."

He flanked them and waited, hidden by the dense, green foliage.

"Where is that bird?" Tim asked Terry.

"Sounds like he was right here. Don't know where he could be," Terry answered.

Otis rose up behind them and said, "Right here, boys!"

A flicker of recognition and fear crossed their wide eyes as they turned, just before the 00 buckshot from Otis's shotgun opened them up and blew their bodies down the hillside. A giant oak stopped their slide, and Otis propped them up in a sitting position against the tree. They had the look of one of those old Western photos of outlaws in their caskets, pistols across their chests.

Otis wiped his mouth, looked down at the dope dealers, folded their hands over their bleeding hearts, and said, "Gobble, gobble. I guess you boys are the turkeys."

He chuckled and said, "I killed two Stones with one turkey call. The shepherd boy, David, ain't got nothing on me!"

He had business to tend to, so he decided to leave them where they fell. After all, he thought it only fair, because he loved animals, and *coyotes and buzzards get hungry for fresh steaks just like the rest of us.*

****

Otis drove down to Hattiesburg Heaven House, a local funeral home with lots of long black hearses. It was the mortuary that prepared Sheler's body and held the service for her. It was just about dusk when he eased through the back door to deal with the mortician, State Representative Arthur Percy. Percy was friends with Corndog and attended lavish parties thrown by the Stones.

The Stone family had asked Percy to keep it quiet and not advertise Sheler's funeral. Percy had crudely commented on Sheler's body parts while he embalmed her, according to Sarge's informants. Percy usually saved those comments for the young males he preferred.

Otis eased into the preparation room of Percy the Pervert, as people called him. The undertaker was preparing a boy of sixteen who had been killed in a car wreck. Otis listened from the shadows as Percy murmured to himself about the young boy's privates. Percy sighed deeply and shuddered as he touched the defenseless corpse.

A wave of righteous anger seized Otis. It was as if Percy was molesting Sheler.

"No, no, you don't," Otis said as he grabbed Percy from behind.

Otis knocked Percy to the floor and force-fed him a giant bottle of formaldehyde, glutaraldehyde, and methanol. Percy screamed about the terrible pain in his mouth and stomach. He went into violent convulsions, and then he went limp. The undertaker needed undertaking.

Before Otis locked up the mortuary, he wrote a letter to the family of the boy and left it on the front desk. He thought about Sheler lying in her coffin. He thought about Percy's death. Otis smiled as he walked away, and thought Corndog might be right about "Bad Eye the Beast."

Percy squirmed and struggled, but he won't be commenting on dead people no more. He's perfectly preserved now. Everyone will stand over him at the funeral and say, "He looks so natural."

****

Otis had one more visit to make, one more debt to collect… from the Right Reverend Peter Houston of the People's Temple in Hattiesburg. The pastor laundered drug money through the church for the Stones and their bosses in New Orleans and contributed to the campaigns of Arthur Percy and Arthur's political godfather in the state senate, Cornelius Ball.

Houston had counseled Sheler in her darkest hours and was just one more man who took advantage of her when Otis left for prison. She gave up on Jesus because she thought Houston spoke for Him.

When Otis slipped into the church late in the evening, no one but Pastor Peter was there. The preacher's silver hair was piled high and sprayed into place. Otis thought bullets would have bounced off the coiffed 'do.

Otis stepped into his office suddenly and said, "I need some counseling, Pastor."

"What? Oh, it's you! You scared me out of ten years of life. I didn't know you were out. They were supposed to let us know. What're you doing here? Have you come to repent, my son?" the pastor asked, flushing red.

"I have come for atonement, Peter, not mine but yours," Otis said.

"What do you mean, my atonement?" Houston asked.

"What I mean is…Tim, Terry, and Percy are all dead, and I've come to kill you, Peter," Otis said.

"What? Now, you wait just a minute!" Houston said as his hand moved toward the desk drawer where he kept his small pearl-handled pistol.

"No, no. If you open that drawer, I'll kill you where you sit," Otis said, aiming his shotgun at Houston's chest.

"You're drunk!" the pastor said. His eyes were wild, and his nostrils were flaring.

"No, I'm as sober as a judge, just drinking big gulps from an old bottle of revenge. It has fermented and tastes pretty good," Otis calmly replied.

"You know you'll go straight to hell, don't you? You're still following the devil," Houston pleaded.

"Peter, you should know, because you been two-timing Jesus and dating Lucifer for a long time. Your collar is empty. Just because you turn it around and pretend you're getting direct broadcasts from heaven doesn't make you a man of God. If I go to hell, I'll see you there, won't I...you two-bit hypocrite!" Otis said.

"Just be reasonable and tell me what you want, Otis. I'll do anything," Houston said. He ceased to demand and began to bargain, the last step before begging.

"I'll tell you what, Preacher Man. I don't cotton to killing no man who claims to serve the Lord. Maybe you did long ago before you got to wading in the shallows of sin, but that water was deep, wasn't it? You were drowning in your trespasses, the devil threw you a lifeline, and you sold your soul. So I won't kill you if you get up right now, get in the old church bus out back, and just disappear," he said.

"Disappear? Wait, what are you saying?" Houston demanded.

Otis suddenly raised his shotgun and aimed it at the signed picture of Houston and Lyndon Johnson on the wall behind the preacher's desk.

Boom! He blew it to smithereens! Glass shards and splinters filled the air and rained down on Houston, shiny glass fragments peppering his head and sticking to his heavily sprayed hair like glitter.

Houston jumped to his feet, hugged a lectern next to his desk, and covered his ears. A tiny trickle of blood oozed out of his right ear, and a small leak puddled on his designer shoes as his bladder surrendered to this unthinkable horror.

"No, no! Oh, Jesus!" he cried as violent tremors shook his body.

"You better cry out to Him. I bet it's been a long time since He heard from you, and He may not remember your name. It won't be in His book of life, will it?" Otis sneered.

"You're going to write a letter to Maude, the church secretary, that nice old lady who has no idea about your secret drug accounts, and you'll give her all the cash in the safe and a check for everything in the bank. Tell her it's for the church's mission work. Just say something came up. A new mission field called, or you had to go away for your health. That last part would be the truth," Otis said.

"But...but, Otis, how will I live?" he whined as he dabbed at the blood in his ear with his handkerchief.

"You'll live upright, above ground, breathing in and breathing out. That's how it's done. Better than the grave. You been playing at being the engineer, but you've been demoted to the caboose," Otis said.

Houston began to weep, and sobs racked his body.

"There, there, Houston. Dying, it's hard to imagine, isn't it...just not being anymore? It happens to everyone else, but deep down, you think maybe you're special, but you know you're not. So think about it. We've both done things we regret, but I'm trying to be kind now. You've got to be cruel sometimes to be kind. That's what the Hamlet guy said. It was one of the few things I remember from English class," Otis said.

"Now you get in the bus before my generosity runs out, and if you ever come back or I hear you're preaching your scam religion somewhere else, I'll track you down and arrange a face-to-face meeting for you with Jesus. You can't hide from Him, and you can't outrun me," Otis said.

Bad Eye rubbed his chin, scratched his head, and sighed deeply as he watched the cloud of black smoke from the oil-guzzling pickup truck disappear over the horizon.

Four down, more to go, Sheler. The dice were loaded, but now we're making field bets and rolling sevens and elevens. Now it's off to meet Agent Michael Parker in an old witch's outhouse.

CHAPTER FIFTEEN

"I would'st not harm thee, brother, but thou
standest where I am about to shoot."
—Unknown

"A man who desires revenge should
dig two graves."—Unknown

Otis settled in at the ancient wooden outhouse. He thought of the nights he and Sheler listened to the distant midnight train whistles in their love nest, her warmth cradled in his arms, two hearts pounding in unison to the rhythm and blues of life.

He crooned a song by the Mills Brothers. He sang it every night in his bunk in prison, just before he whispered, "Good night, Sheler."

"I'm gonna buy a paper doll that I can call my own, a doll that other fellows cannot steal. And then the flirty, flirty guys with their flirty, flirty eyes will have to flirt with dollies that are real. When I come home at night she will be waiting..."

The buzzing of red wasps on their nest in the dark of the outhouse and the thump-thump of the band's bass from the nightclub across the creek brought him back to the task at hand. There was a sign on the outhouse that asked whoever used the privy to dump the sacks of lime into the hole. The smell of lime was overpowering as he checked his weapons.

Memories, what good are they? They're as useless as a dull knife and an empty pistol, just deadwood. I got to finish this and stop dragging the junk in my trunk around with me. It's weighing on me, dragging me down, but soon all the anger will be satisfied, and I'll be free of my demons. You can't cry over spilt milk. Just take your rag, mop it up, and squeeze it out for the dogs to drink.

So here he was, waiting for Agent Michael Parker.

Sarge wanted me to meet the man he used to work with in Tupelo. He said Parker was a good partner, honest and trustworthy, and full of All-American enthusiasm. He said the boy could skate on cracking ice and never get wet. He said Parker could find himself way out there on some thin limbs, but he was one of the few who could crawl back. I promised Sarge I'd give the law a chance, but my blood lust won out today, and I had to answer the call of the beast in me.

Otis mashed a mosquito whining in his ear and fumbled with the dial on his transistor radio to find the St. Louis Cardinals. They were his favorite team. He never missed Stan the Man. He lost the static-filled station and turned to a rebroadcast of the old Orson Wells show "War of the Worlds."

He listened to the program that spooked the nation, and it unsettled him in the confines of his rendezvous house. "The Martians are coming, death rays, destruction, the end of the world..." Otis loved the old shows. He thought he was made for another time. His mama thought so, too.

Then he saw the advancing lights through the cracks in the boards. Lights moving down the slope—one, two, three or more, waving back and forth as men or Martians walked toward the outhouse.

Them Martians got dogs with them, too, he thought as he raised the heavy iron slab in front of him as a shield. The lights stopped and held steady for what seemed like forever. He could see the outlines of the men in the darkest corners of the shadows.

"That you in there on your throne, you old bootlegger?" a shrill voice shouted.

"Is that you out there, you piles of sticks and stones, or are you a bunch of Martians come to zap me?" Otis answered as he released the safety on the BAR.

"No, you old fool, it's Sammy and Marty Stone, come to set things right," Sammy Stone said.

"Well, David needed three smooth stones to slay Goliath. You are about two shy to slay me, aren't you? Those stones don't roll no more, do they?" Otis answered.

"You have to answer for our brothers Terry and Tim. We come to kill you, old man," Stone said.

"They had to atone for Sheler, and you can pay, too, if you've a mind to. Besides, they made the prettiest corpses you ever did see propped up against that tree! Who found them first, the hogs or the buzzards?" Otis said, taunting them.

"Your woman was a big ole piñata that begged to be beaten," Sammy Stone countered.

"Taunt me all you want, sonny boy. This is not my first rodeo. Is this really the hill you children want to die on, or you just come here with your heads full of mescaline to sniff round and hike your legs like the mongrels you are?" Otis shouted.

"You're the one who's gonna die tonight, old man," Stone said.

"Well, you gonna get on with it or just talk me to death?" Otis shot back.

"You go to hell, old man," Stone answered.

"Been there, boys. The devil sent me back. He couldn't handle me, and you and your army can't either," Otis said.

Bad Eye heard the cursing, the baying of the hounds, and he could sense their hesitation and fear. He peered through the cracks at the outlines of the men who had come to kill him. They'd sloshed through the swamp to the west of him and were wearing wading boots, hip-huggers that only left a little white v-outline up front.

Otis studied them for a moment as they hesitated and argued. He said, "You boys sure are pretty. You always wear diapers or just when you come after me?" he asked with a chuckle.

"Well, no matter. It's still an improvement over the sheets you wear when you're out burning crosses," he added.

A voice in the dark whined, "Sammy, you gonna let him talk to us that way?"

"Come and get it then, you little green men! Your brothers are waiting in hell for you!" Otis shouted to egg them on.

He began to sing Tommy Roe's song "Sweet little Sheler..."

He could hear the Stone boys and others running toward the outhouse as the first pink hues of morning showed. The *click-click, shick-shick* cocking and arming of their automatic weapons filled the night air, and their epithets punctuated the false bravado of men who had come to kill or be killed.

He raised the BAR, pulled it firmly against his shoulder, and clicked A for automatic, just as the whining bullets from the guns of the Stone brothers riddled the walls of the outhouse and pinged and plinked against his metal shield.

Splinters filled the air, and Otis brushed the residue from his eyes. He laughed out loud and thought his prison chaplain would be so happy to know he finally got the plank out of his eye.

That was larruping good. My tongue lashed my brain.

Then the night exploded in light and fire from the chug-chug-chug of his Browning. The rounds blew the door off its hinges. The recoil of the weapon kicked like a mule and increased with each round fired. He emptied one magazine, slapped in a new one, and started again.

Moans and screams filled the night air, dogs yelped, ejected shells bounced off the walls, and somewhere in the dark, someone was crying for their mama.

"I'm hit! Oh Mama, help me, Mama!" someone moaned.

The din of the battle was deafening, and the smell of gunpowder poisoned his senses. He became one with his weapon and thought the barrel of the gun was so hot it would melt down. Blood ran down his brow into his eyes, and there was a deep burning in his left side.

Am I hit?

He couldn't tell. He was running on anger and revenge. The smell of sulfur and charcoal filled the night air. An outline of a pentagram appeared on the blood-soaked hillside. The thief of the night, the roaring lion, was already sweeping the hillside in the tease of dayglow, collecting souls and announcing to Jesus, "None here for your heaven, only kindling for my fire."

This was a dead end on the road of broken dreams. In that moment of horror, everything slowed to a crawl. Misery was magnified, and each molecule of air floating by him was a grain of sand seeping from the hourglass of life.

He thought he caught a glimpse of Sheler, young, beautiful, and without stain. Amid the carnage, a bright light appeared, a tunnel opened, and a man emerged from the light with his arms outstretched.

Otis thought heaven must be a ghost town tonight, and then he thought of his Doberman named Jesus. Thieves who came to steal his homebrew and raid his stills used to hear his growl in the dark and run away crying, "Jesus is coming! Jesus is coming!"

He thought Michael Parker was missing a great party, and the last thing he remembered before he passed out was that smell again...formaldehyde.

CHAPTER SIXTEEN

*"Listen, you got any more of those
secret agent spy-scopes?...the secret
agent spy-scope, man. That pulls in
the moon, the sky and the planets...
and the satellites and the little bitty
space men?"—Wolfman Jack,*
American Graffiti *(the movie)*

*"No doubt every crime scene is a
disaster for someone, it's only a
question of scope."—John Houde,*
Crime Lab: A Guide for
Nonscientists

When a dirty, venal world seems to be closing in on you,
and you're a square peg trying to fit into a round hole, there's
something about long, solitary drives in the wee hours of the
morning that can clear the mind. The hypnotic flashing of broken
white lines, the hum of tires on the pavement, the smacking and
creaking of shocks was just what the doctor ordered for Michael.

He felt like he had eaten all the Cracker Jack but found no
prize. He wondered where the line was that Clay spoke of and how
he'd know if he crossed it. He lost himself in the night, and the
headlights became beacons to cut through the darkness to illuminate
approaching grace. The bump-de-bump rhythm of the road
provided a backbeat for a tangled tune of questions without
answers. The endless night was a churning black lake where a man
fishing for answers could cast his nets. It was a wishing well where
a forlorn driver, longing for yesterday, could toss coins in a
heavenly fountain.

Michael felt he was the fly that had escaped the sticky web
in the house that Milkwood and Rachel built. The late-night trip to

Hattiesburg provided solitude and time for Michael to digest and dissect all he'd seen at Moondog Square and the Leg Room. He bumped along Highway 49, singing a song about a long, lonely highway, a tune he played on the jukebox in the FBI Identification Division cafeteria in 1966 when he was a fingerprint tech.

He felt he was still on that long highway, trying to straddle two horses, to reconcile his life with the imitation of living he'd witnessed that bled regret and decay. It was a puzzle with missing pieces. Had all of life been just a preamble, preparation for Milkwood, Rachel, Corndog, and Molly? Like others before him, he asked time to slow down and wait for him to figure out this uncivil war Pearl spoke of, but time is always in a hurry and waits for no one.

As the mile markers zipped past him like tracer fire, he yearned for the simplicity of the black-and-white world he once lived in, when those "for sale" signs on politicians like Corndog weren't so obvious, before the "kick me" signs on the rumps of politicians were replaced by ones that read "bought and paid for."

****

Michael spun the dial on his AM radio to find clear-channel radio stations. The disc jockeys on the 50,000-watt stations provided soundtracks for nocturnal creatures like truckers, insomniacs, smugglers, and narcs. Late-night radio was alive with chatter covering North America and edging over the horizon on skip. From dusk till dawn, they were the best friends of night owls and lonely hearts.

A southbound freight train passed Michael, and the engineer sounded the blare of his horn just as the Grand Ole Opry crackled through the static on Nashville's WSM. A white cottontail bounded across the road when Art Roberts chimed in from WLS in Chicago, and even the night critters were afraid when Wolfman Jack howled on the mega-blaster station south of the border near Del Rio, Texas. Some said he'd left XERF for Tijuana, but no one knew for sure. That was part of his mystique.

The Wolfman dimmed lights for miles around the station when he keyed his mike to play underground music and sell coffins and baby chickens. He offered autographed pictures of Jesus and an absolutely free "How to Get to Heaven" packet for shipping and handling of $5.95. An advertiser promised to restore men's vitality with injections of goat testicles. As proof positive of the results, the good "doctor" asked listeners, "Who's ever seen an impotent billy goat?"

Michael rested the dial on the booming broadcast of WWL, transmitting from the south shore of Lake Pontchartrain. It had intrigued him since he first found it in 1960 when he was twelve. He was a fan of the TV show *Route 66*, and on one episode, Tod and Buz were listening to WWL as they crossed the bridge into New Orleans.

WWL's overnight country music program, "The Road Gang," was aimed at long-haul truckers and was in full swing when Michael found their broadcast. They offered companionship, weather, good humor, and weather reports for truckers along the main U.S. corridors and tonight for a narcotics agent on Highway 49.

The eighteen-wheeler vagabonds who listened to the station were a long way from home, trying to stay awake without gulping the "West Coast Turnarounds" dealers peddled to drivers at truck stops. If the long hauls and time away from home weren't bad enough, drivers were often threatened by businessmen who vowed to take their business elsewhere if drivers didn't pick up drugs for them. Drivers had families to support. Their livelihoods were jeopardized by men who sat on the front pews of churches, the loudest voices in the "Amen corner" when their pastors condemned drugs.

Drivers called in to WWL to request songs and to send messages to their families back home. The host, Charlie Douglas, also delivered messages to the drivers from loved ones and their trucking companies. Michael listened as Charlie read love letters from around the country. "Timmy says, 'Daddy, hurry home soon.

We miss you.' Mary said, 'Bobby, I'm sorry. I'll make it up to you when you get home.' Judy said, "Jerry, we all pray for you. Terry, Toby, Wayne, and I miss you, too.'"

Then, amid the messages, Michael almost ran off the narrow two-lane road when Charlie said, "This one's for a guy who's not a driver, but I hear he's a hoot owl out there somewhere who listens late at night. It's from a lady named Dixie Lee in West Memphis. She says, 'Michael, where are you?'"

Charlie said, "This is a new song from George Jones. I'll dedicate it to all you long-haul warriors who may have taken a wrong turn and gotten lost, and to Miss Dixie Lee and Michael. Let her know where you are, buddy."

Michael leaned over to turn up the volume, and the Possum began to wail. "Me and Jesus, we got our own things going. Me and Jesus, we got it all worked out...I know Jesus isn't gonna forsake me now."

After the song, Charlie leaned in close to the mike. His voice rode the hissing, shushing radio wave like a surfer on a rolling sea. "Sometimes treasure slips right through our fingers, and until we can see it at a distance, we don't know that it sparkled like diamonds and glittered like 24-karat magic. Friends, if this shoe fits, wear it, and buy an extra pair," he said. Then Charlie and his message of reconciliation washed out on the waves of the radio tide to the fathomless depths of the sea of forgetfulness.

****

Michael neared the meeting place on the backside of Hattiesburg. He passed a long strip of businesses that had fallen on hard times—a rundown motel, an old bowling alley, and a truck stop that had once thrived until truckers took the new routes the government built. A greasy spoon advertised homemade fried apple pies, beer, and live bait to go on its flashing neon sign that read—"Dixie Darlings: if we ain't got it, you don't need it."

When Michael arrived at the wooded area a mile past the strip, a citrine sun was rising, a pale moon was still lingering in the morning sky, and a lone star in the western blue refused to surrender to the light. The sun colored the morning with a yellowish hue, and a carpet of thick, wet grasses waved in the breeze along the ridge. Looking at the sun and the moon, Michael smiled when he remembered a story Pearl had told him about Mister Sun loving Miss Moon so much he died to let her shine every night.

With no sign of a car or the informant, Michael walked toward a gothic arch cut through the hedgerow that ringed the ridge. Before he entered the opening in the bushes, a cardinal whistled a spring mating call, and a potential mate answered from a distant tree, but when he stepped through to the other side, birds weren't singing, and there were no sounds or signs of any life.

A scattering of ragged trees along the slope of the hill appeared to be recovering from wind damage. Their splintered shadows caressed and shadowed the windswept upland, which looked as green as the felt of a pool table. The long fingers of the shadows cradled the descending grade in a tender embrace.

The grass was wet and squishy with morning dew, and he stepped carefully in the dim light. There was a strange smell riding the breeze; a wave of disturbance assaulted his senses and seeped into his lungs. He bent down to the turf and smelled gunpowder and the stink of violence and death on the hard-boiled ground.

There was blood on the weeds. When he looked closer, he saw small pieces of bloody body parts, a piece of an ear here and a fingernail there. In the distance, he saw the remains of the outhouse riddled with bullets. The curtain of light was rising, and the morning sun was revealing sins committed under the cover of darkness, acts demanding accountability and adjudication in a higher court.

He knew he was in the middle of a crime scene. It should have been cordoned off with yellow tape and crawling with cops wearing gloves and carrying evidence bags, but he just had to know more. Curiosity was an essential part of a cop's makeup as long as it didn't kill the cat or use up too many of his nine lives.

He walked gingerly across the field of death to recreate the scene in his mind. There were skid marks from people slipping and falling, depressions in the grass where at least one man had crawled a short way on his hands and knees, and outlines in the grass suggested someone had dragged another man by his heels.

He bent over and examined a bloody imprint of a large boot. There were two smaller shoe prints in a patch of mud across the way. The feet turned inward. Michael assumed the man was bowlegged. The distance between footprints suggested people may have been charging or running toward the outhouse. Upon closer inspection of the dense carpet of green, he found shells from a 12-gauge shotgun, a 9mm, and many spent .223 casings, likely from an AR-15.

Mixed in the residue was a patch of bloody blonde hair, and higher on the hill he found a tobacco juice stain, a Marlboro cigarette butt, and the stubs of cigarillos. Not far away he found an empty whiskey bottle with a large muddy thumbprint on one side and an index finger on the other. Nearby, he saw a piece of a plaid shirt, a baggie with white powder, and an apple with one large bite mark.

Michael ran all of it through his mind, turning it over and over as he mapped the scene. He could almost hear the curses, moans, and shrieks of those donning the death mask. He hypothesized that there were at least five men—smoking, drinking, and getting high at the top of the rise before charging the outhouse. Three had likely been wounded: one with blonde hair, one in a plaid shirt, and another who was pigeon-toed.

He walked down to the outhouse to pick through the ashes and splintered boards. He found a large number of .30 caliber casings and four empty box clips for a BAR. In the midst of the pile of debris and bullets, he also found one bloody shoe with Velcro straps. On one of the boards still standing, Michael found a carving of numbers...*101.*

It was part of the code word for Michael to use when meeting his informant...101 Damnations, a little humor on the part of Sarge and Clay and a takeoff on Clay's favorite Disney film, but there was nothing humorous about this plot of ground.

He squatted on his haunches and looked up and down the knoll. A loud hum or howl burrowed into his inner ear, an echo of something, a residual of temporal residue. A sudden disturbance benighted and overtook the hillside. A roaring, bursting rush of wind rustled and tumbled the brown leaves that had mulched the ground during the drabness of winter. Michael's long hair was whipped around his head. There seemed to be faces or dark shapes in the disturbance, souls sucked away by a force like a giant vacuum cleaner scrubbing the wounded ground.

Suddenly the zephyr died down and the howling ceased. It became eerily quiet, and Michael's watch showed he'd been there for nearly three hours. He decided it was time to scrape death off his shoe and call Sarge.

CHAPTER SEVENTEEN

"Oh, we have 12 vacancies. 12 cabins,
12 vacancies."—Psycho

"Until you guys can be trusted every time
and always, in all times and conditions, to
seek the truth out and find it and let the
chips fall where they may—until that time
comes, I have the right to listen to my
conscience…"—Raymond Chandler,
The High Window

Michael called Sarge but got no answer, and Clay was in a meeting. He left a cryptic message about the crime scene on Sarge's answering machine and told him he was en route to the meeting place. He made notes of what he'd seen before checking into a local roach motel where a reservation had been made—another joke by Clay and Sarge, all part of Michael's indoctrination and introduction to the dark end of life's street.

The motel advertised day rates, night rates, and thirty-minute specials. Each cheap and sour room had a Magic Fingers vibrating bed that shook the teeth out of users' heads while promising relief from the stresses of life or assistance with a low-rent rendezvous, all for a quarter.

The manager, a sallow man who looked undernourished, was washing his car when Michael arrived. It was more a caress than a wash of a car of his own creation, a 1967 Mustang painted black with a Batman emblem replacing the pony. Along the side was a giant yellow stripe that read "Batstang."

Hal, the manager, had a deep voice and spoke like a stretched audio tape constantly dragging, and he liked to use words like "far out" and "groovy." He said that Sarge told him to be expecting "Jim." He said he'd been saving his best room. His slurred speech and peculiar phrasing suggested Southern drawl on a slow, downer crawl, but he brought along fresh sheets as Michael demanded. Michael suspected the frayed, gray sheets might once have been white.

When Hal opened the door to unit 6, Michael saw a narrow bed for his clean sheets and a green army blanket with three holes in it. There was an upholstered chair in the room, worn around the edges with questionable stains on the arms. The chest of drawers was a thrift-store reject. The room had one narrow window with a view of swarms of green flies around a giant garbage bin that looked as though it was last emptied in World War 2.

There was a lamp on the table by the chair that had no shade, just a clear bulb with the flickering filaments exposed. He turned it off and on by pulling a long, rusty chain that wanted to stick each time. He tried the bed, which had a deep depression in the center of the thin, sagging mattress. It felt like it was filled with rocks or sacks of potatoes. In the corner of the room near the bathroom, he saw a used syringe.

Michael walked to the bathroom just as a tiny, gray mouse stuck his head out and wriggled his nose as if to ask, "Will you be bunking with me?" The walls were paper thin, and the rhythmic squeaking of bedsprings in the room next door increased as the wind whistled a mournful imitation of a Broadway tune through the cracks in the wall. To Michael it sounded like *The Man of La Mancha*, Don Quixote dreaming impossible dreams, fighting unbeatable foes.

There were bugs everywhere in the motel—the crawling kind, the flying kind, and the human kind. Michael doubled over and laughed out loud at the "glamorous" job his friends thought he had, the ones who imagined that he was playing baccarat in Monte Carlo casinos while fighting off some beautiful Russian spy. He didn't think Sean Connery ever had to stay in places like this.

Michael asked the manager, who looked more and more like a refugee from the movie *Easy Rider*, if he had ever made improvements to the rooms. Hal said, "There's no need for major surgery to correct a pimple or two, now, is there?"

Michael stared at him, and Hal asked, "Will you be staying with us for a while? We have two sheet schedules—optional and occasional."

"How long have you been in the motel business?" Michael asked.

"Three years," the manager said.

"What did you do before creating this lovely home away from home?" Michael asked.

"I was a traveling tent preacher, but I had to give up the Jesus juice. Yeah, I bet that surprises you, huh? I had to leave, man. It was like wrestling. What we did in the tents was phony. People sweating and swaying and falling out and then they bring out the shill and heal her. It wasn't organic, man, and it sure wasn't about Jesus. It was contrived and artificial, a scam. I fell in with the drug boys, but I knew before long that I had made a mistake. They mixed horse dung with their marijuana, gave it a fancy name, and charged more for it. If they had their way, there'd be vending machines with dope in every school. The daddy of a girl who used our dope was waiting for me on a delivery to her one day. He had a shotgun. He shot at me. I ran and never stopped until I saw this place that was dirt cheap. I fell in love with it, and I used the last of my savings from the old tent offerings, and here I am. There are nights I still sit around picking birdshot out of my behind. Let me know if you'd like our complimentary Pop Tart for breakfast," he said.

After the concierge from Hades left, Michael saw it was after 10 a.m. He'd had no sleep. Despite the accommodations, he fell fast asleep and dreamed about the time he searched for his great-grandfather's private cemetery in the woods near Shannon. In a place that time had forgotten, he had hoped to find evidence of the life and times of his great-grandparents and the burial ground of his great-grandfather's second wife, a Native American who had walked the Trail of Tears. Stories about her abounded in family lore, and she was always referred to as an "Indian Princess."

In his dreams, he walked through a dense forest to find the old graveyard at the back of a farm near Dotys Chapel. When he emerged from the woods, he saw the boneyard. The gravestones were tilted and worn in the untended cemetery. There was an old woman sitting on a hollow log amid the tombstones. He thought she looked like old sketches he'd seen of Pocahontas in history books.

She was reading a book with worn covers and yellowed pages. She looked up at him with expectant eyes when he approached her as if she knew him. He had the strange feeling she could hear him even when he didn't speak.

"Hello, I'm Michael Parker, and this was my ancestor's burial ground," he said.

She smiled, and when she spoke, Michael felt she was speaking to him in vowels while the rest of the world had only been uttering consonants—an open Bible vs. pulp fiction.

She looked through bottomless pools of brown that seemed ancient and said, "Yes, I've been waiting to talk with you."

"Oh, did the landowner tell you I'd be out here today?" he asked.

She didn't answer his question, but she closed her book and said, "You're searching, but you must be careful. What you're looking for may also be looking for you, and it may find you. Few of those you encounter will be who they seem to be. Sugar will look like the salt of the earth. Be humble. Remember always…God is great, but you're not. You can forgive people, and you can bleed for them. You can love them, too, but you can't save them. You are not Christ, but the Lamb knows your heart.

"Angels will sing loudest during your worst storms and trials. Listen for their harmony. From this day forward, you'll be surrounded by people, but you'll always be alone, even in crowds. Don't live in the tents of anyone's circus. The rent will be too high, and just like the tent next door, they all want your soul. The circus masters will have flowers at their carnivals, but they won't have a sweet fragrance. They don't want you to feel anything, not even the emotion of sorrow if it is not induced by the ringmasters. Their temptations will buzz around your head like evil avian spirits. In your darkest hours, these false prophets will leave you, and your shore will be deserted, but He'll still be with you. They'll try to bury you before they leave, but He is the true Planter, and you are His seed."

Just as he was about to ask her who she was, a loud knocking at his door woke Michael from the dreamscape. He stumbled to the door to find a smiling Sarge on the other side, one hand resting on the pistol on his right hip and the other taking a drag from his rancid cigar.

"Well, good morning, Sleeping Beauty. Sorry I'm so slow getting back to you, but I was baptizing prisoners in the jail and didn't get your message," Sarge said.

"Baptizing in jail?" Michael asked, rubbing the sleep from his eyes.

"Yep, got a big old wash pot and we dunk 'em right there. It's something to see, Michael," he said.

When Michael asked him if wanted to hear about what he saw, Sarge plopped down in the dilapidated chair and said, "Let 'er rip, tater chip."

Michael handed him his notes and told him about everything he'd seen and felt at the rendezvous site. Sarge listened intently while chewing on his cigar and then read the notes.

"Michael, there's been some strange activity around here, but no evidence linking Otis to any of it. He arrived from Parchman, checked in with probation as required, and went about his business. Two members of the Stone family have come up missing, but there's been no formal complaint filed. When I went by Mama Stone's house, she told me they'd all gone fishing on the river. A local pastor resigned and left his church, and his flock was quite upset until they discovered they have more money in the treasury than anyone could imagine. Lots of gossip, but these bouts of midlife crisis happen all the time, even to preachers.

"Oh, and a Hattiesburg undertaker seems to have committed suicide. Local police were tipped, and they found lockets of hair in a safe in his office, just as the anonymous caller said they would—snips of hair with pictures of the young men he'd prepared for burial. That prompted family members who'd used him for funerals to come forward to say he had made suggestive remarks about their sons and husbands as they lay in their caskets. None of this has been linked to Otis coming home. The rest is pure speculation and idle gossip," Sarge said with a wry smile.

"Hmm, I see," Michael said, nodding his head.

"What about the crime scene?" Michael asked.

"Investigators have been out there since you left me the message, but a hard rain fell before they arrived, and much of what you saw had been washed away. There were a few shells and such, and the outhouse was full of bullet holes, but it could be crazy kids out target shooting again. We have no bodies and no complaints… only yours," he said.

"I'm not complaining, just observing, Sarge. Where's Otis?" Michael asked.

"He was at his house when I went by there a while ago. He had a burn or scrape on his right temple, smelled of gunpowder, and he was exhausted, but otherwise, he looked okay. Given your message and all that's been happening, I asked him if I should read him his rights. He told me he had nothing to hide, that it wasn't his rights Miranda had protected, but the many wrongs done to Sheler and women like her," Sarge said.

There was a knock at the door, and Michael looked at Sarge.

"Perfect timing, that'll be him," Sarge said.

"Here?" Michael asked.

"Yeah, it's okay. Hal, the guy who runs this fine establishment, is one of my informants. He may not look like much, but I cut him some slack once when everyone wanted to hang him, and he owes me. I'm trying to wrestle him into my gospel wash pot. He's a work in progress," Sarge said, opening the door.

"Come on in, Otis," Sarge shouted.

Otis warily entered the room, looking left and right.

"Dang, Sarge, could you have found a worse dump for this important state agent to sleep in? I thought y'all was supposed to be friends," Otis asked.

"You must be Michael Parker," he said, extending his hand to Michael.

"Yes, nice to meet you. Sorry I was late to the party, I think," Michael said.

"Well, this whole talk is off the record. Sarge talked about Miranda so much this morning I got confused and thought you was Miranda, Michael Miranda," he said with a smile like a kid who'd just told a dirty joke.

They all laughed.

"So, everything we say here is just a story, a fairytale today. What's said here stays here. We'll save it for a rainy day, and since I was raised Baptist, once saved is always saved and exempt from prosecution," he said.

They all laughed again. Otis was on a roll.

"Yeah, we're off the record, just some good ole boys talking about Western movies, shoot-'em-ups and all. What movie did you see last night, Otis?" Sarge asked.

"Oh man, it was a good one, fellas. There was a movie about this guy who was done wrong. They messed with his woman. I never liked those revenge movies. They was always too predictable. You know in the end he's gonna hunt them down and kill them, and justice will be done, but I kinda liked this one. It was real. I could almost smell the gunpowder. The bad guys were straight-down-the-line evil, and the good guy tweren't so good, either, but I could identify with him.

"His blood was boiling with hate, and he lured them in. When you go fishing, you don't throw rocks and scare the fish away. He knew how to fish, all right, but he was scared, I could tell. He had a lump in his throat the size of the Yankee mini ball I once found at the Civil War site in Vicksburg.

"There was a big battle. He blacked out and came to amidst the wailing and screaming. It seemed like the earth was moaning, and ghosts were groaning. He heard the muffled drums and the thundering cannons shaking the ground. He saw the flashes of lightning and felt the blood running into his eyes. He thought he was dead at first. The battlefield was red with blood, and the wounded were crying for their mamas. Soldiers kept calling out, 'Medic! Over here, medic!' The hero was close to checking out of here and into the Motel Hereafter. Hopefully they'd give him a better room than Sarge gave you, Michael," Otis said with a flash of a weary smile. He was definitely on a roll now.

Then Otis got real quiet, and the false bravado faded. His hands trembled, and he rested his hands on his knees. His voice had taken on a crackly tone, like a hoarse itinerant preacher after a long tent revival meeting.

"Boys, the hero saw the gallows in the distance, and that big old scaffolding got his attention. They was all waiting in hell, those undertakers dressed in long black coats over fireproof robes. They told him they were driving the rope-a-dope hearse. But then over on the other side there was this white glow playing against a sea of snow, and in the brightness was God. He was shaking His head and wagging His finger at the hero in the movie. Then He said, in a booming voice like James Earl Jones, 'My Son died for you. Vengeance is Mine.'

"The hero told God he was just following the gospel of Jim Croce. You know, you don't tug on Superman's cape. You don't spit into the wind. You don't pull the mask off the old Lone Ranger, and you don't mess around with Otis, er, the hero I mean," Otis said, shrugging his shoulders and sighing several times in his movie narrative.

Otis sat there for a long while, saying nothing, and Michael and Sarge waited. Then Otis sighed again, long and hard, like all the air bleeding out of a dirigible.

"Boys, I've tasted the ice cream cone of life, and it has fallen on my tennies, but I checked myself and asked 'How are you, Bad Eye?' I answered myself and said, 'Above ground and vertical, ain't I?'" he said.

Sarge relit his cigar, puffed on it on a moment, and asked, "You know they'll be coming for you, don't you?"

"Yeah, Sarge, I know. They'll probably use their friends in probation to set me up for an ambush on the way to a meeting or find an excuse to put me back in Parchman, where there are plenty of folks dying for distractions. They'll kill a man just to pass the time. A life on the run with your hand on your gun ain't much of a life, but I wouldn't change a thing. I thought I saw her through the swirl of smoke this morning. She was in the clouds painting pictures, but she came out of the mist to hold me and dry my salty tears. I thought then and there that if I died, I would've already tasted a bit of heaven right there, dying in her soft loving arms," he said, resting his chin on his chest and stifling a sob.

Michael and Sarge looked at each other. They fought the tears that begged to come, and there was a long uncomfortable silence to honor a man who had lost everything. Michael walked over to the window to stare out at nothing in particular, just to give a man in mourning a moment to regain his composure.

Sarge finally broke the pall over the room. "I saw part two of that movie—addicts coming to emergency rooms in withdrawal because the Stones were nowhere to be found, drugs stopped flowing, and reported overdoses were way down. So I would say the hero saved lives, and he should think about that," Sarge said, squirming from an uncharacteristic display of emotion.

"Thanks, Sarge, but sin hardens a person, and sooner or later they begin to crack, to stumble and fall, and all the king's horses and all the king's men can't put Otis back together again. I guess that'll have to be ruled on at the great white throne of judgment," Otis said, blowing his nose on a yellowed handkerchief that must have come over on the *Mayflower*.

Otis stood and looked at them and said, "I think I'll go and rest some. My itching feet tell me it's time, if I'm free to leave, that is?"

"Sure, Otis, I'll check on you later," Sarge said, rising to pat him on the shoulder.

As Otis opened the door to leave, he turned to Michael and said, "Let me know when you're ready to make some buys from local dealers. We better do it pretty quick. Who knows what tomorrow brings? Oh, and make these cheapskates give you a better room. This is almost as bad as my bed at Parchman farm!"

When Otis had gone, Sarge hitched his chair closer to Michael and whispered secret things the thin walls could not betray.

"My informant in the Hattiesburg South Central Bell switching office was 'unofficially' checking for trouble on the phone lines and heard calls placed to an outfit I think you're familiar with: Moondog Square. I think whoever survived Otis's movie is holed up there. He said a man at Moondog told people here that he has doctors who treat trauma injuries. They don't ask questions and don't report such things to the authorities. My informant said they were promised the full buffet of treatments they provide, including voodoo dust from a witch named Rachel, and when they come out of Moondog, it'll be like it never happened. No warrants, no complaints, no bodies, no crime. It's like the movie Otis saw was never written."

"What now?" Michael asked, watching his pet mouse watching him.

"Meet Otis tomorrow, before this all gets a little too hot for him, and he'll introduce you to some local dealers who will try to step up and fill the void left by the Stones. It don't take long for the vultures to begin circling," Sarge said.

"What happens to people like Otis after we move on?" Michael asked.

Sarge stared at the floor and rolled the cigar round and round in his mouth and then launched into a bit of visionary eloquence Michael hadn't expected.

"I spect he'll drink just enough to numb his mind. He'll look over his shoulder and jump at the sudden slap of a screen door. He'll forget all her faults and the sorrow she caused him and elevate Sheler to the status of a saint. Each time he speaks of her, she'll grow more angelic. He'll remember her in them cotton dresses she used to wear, how she filled them out, how she couldn't get within five feet of him without a burning desire to touch her, and he'll cry where no one can see him.

"He'll let himself go, maybe get all grubby in his dress and hygiene, start living in his Chevy, and if his enemies don't get him, he may decide to take his Chevy to the levy, and nurse his pistol to check out of this life. Then they'll bury him along with his heartaches, and, like his movie, people will forget he ever existed," Sarge said.

It was a somber note to end on, devoid of hope, but then Sarge smiled from ear-to-ear and laughed until his belly shook.

"What a look on your face! You look like you just lost your best buddy, your girlfriend, and your backstage pass to Elvis concerts. Don't look so glum, son. He may survive and thrive like a duck in a pond of fresh water. I may dunk him in my big wash pot, give him something to live for, and he might become a great father to Sheler's daughters or the next great evangelist!" Sarge said.

"I like that ending much better, Sarge," Michael said, smiling.

"Yeah, me, too. Life can't break her heart anymore, but it's breaking his into tiny pieces," Sarge said, thumping his cigar butt at the tiny gray mouse that had edged up to his chair.

CHAPTER EIGHTEEN

"I know the law. The law doesn't know the streets"—Prince of the City *(the movie)*

"Although the world is full of suffering, it is also full of the overcoming of it."
—Helen Keller

After two weeks in the Hattiesburg area, Michael had bought drugs from six different dealers, mostly small-time pushers who had gotten their nerve up after news of the Stones' demise, and he had all the evidence his trunk could hold. It was time to turn it all in at the state crime lab and check in for orders from headquarters.

Otis had delivered, just as Sarge said he would. It was all business. He didn't say much to Michael except things like, "This guy deals cocaine. The guy over there likes LSD, and the pretty girl in the dorm sells to students at the University of Southern Mississippi." But the day Michael packed up to leave, Otis puffed his chest out, pumped Michael's hand vigorously, and said, "Our arrows will blot out the sun, and then we'll fight in the shade. Goliath is big, and we are small, but we got slings and smooth stones, and we won't give up until snowflakes fall in Mississippi in July. Ain't that right, Michael?"

Michael did his best John Wayne imitation and said, "Give up? That'll be the day!" He asked Otis to be patient, to give the law a chance…translation, no more of the Western movies on the hillside. He didn't think his plea penetrated the fog of obsession and revenge clouding Otis' heart.

****

Michael delivered the drugs to a harried state crime lab technician named Horace. Horace was near retirement and feeling overwhelmed. The bureaucrat thought his last few years as a state employee should be relaxed, a coasting time he'd earned. The creation of the MBN had destroyed his plans to kick back, drink coffee, peruse travel brochures, and work on his tan until he clocked out for the last time.

"You boys show up in Mississippi like a pack of wild dogs, barking and slobbering, running all over the countryside, buying dope and making criminal cases on people for things that weren't even illegal a few years ago. Then you show up here with all your dope, and you want it stored, and you want it tested. We don't even have the space to hold it all or the time to be running all over the state testifying when you arrest these drug merchants. You agents have this attitude. Yes, that's what it is, like what you're doing is more important than anything else. You march around waving the flag like Captain America. My cousin wanted to be one of you. He was politically connected, but he couldn't pass the tests. Your very existence offends the natural order of things in Mississippi, and then if all that's not bad enough, you have black agents and female agents showing up here, too. Unheard of! Things are going to hell, and don't get me started on those mini-skirts women wear," Horace ranted.

Michael let him wear himself out and then said, "They need to get y'all some help here in the state lab. I'll pass the word along to the higher-ups, and we'll try not to burden you more than we have to. We'd be nothing without you guys."

Horace sighed, lit a cigarette off the one hanging from his lips, and said, "Next thing you know, they'll have you boys arresting us for these cancer sticks. I know you guys give us job security, and yeah, a rising tide lifts all boats, but I want my boat to be treated like a yacht. I just want a little ring-kissing now and then. Is that so bad?"

On the drive to his apartment, Michael thought the man needed a tin of King Leo peppermint sticks. He thought he might bring him a can as a peace offering, no lab testing and no testimony required.

****

When Michael turned into the MBN parking lot, it had rained all night and was still pouring, the kind of downpour that conjures up images of arks and forty days and forty nights. The muddy water of the Pearl River was threatening to overflow its banks. He parked and ran for the door. Somewhere in the near pitch blackness of the angry sky, as he splashed through the pooling water, he heard the roar and whine of jet engines as an Eastern Airlines plane passed through the gloom on two wings and a prayer.

When he entered the building in his soggy shoes, he smelled hamburgers, french fries, and cigarettes. Ashtrays were full, and agents, milling around in the first floor secretarial area, looked like drowned rats, smelled like old dogs, and made o-ringed puffs of white smoke through pursed lips. They were throwing their voices and telling stories that deflected from their insecurities. Like big wet hounds shaking off soppy doubts or antsy travelers waiting on the rapture and pondering the scales of forgiveness and sin, they didn't look rested, just rusted from the rain.

Suddenly the director appeared at the top of the stairs and bellowed at the startled agents, "Gentleman, pardon me if I'm interrupting your social hour, but these ladies have work to do. If you boys don't have somewhere to go to buy dope from dealers poisoning our children, then get on up here and see me. I've got an opening for some deep undercover work at Parchman!"

The room cleared like a covey of quail dodging birdshot and lead poisoning on the opening day of bird season. Michael made a beeline to Clay's office.

Michael paused to knock on Clay's door and saw the intelligence chief at his desk playing with a strange device Michael had never seen. Clay had a death grip on it with both hands, twisting this way and that. He seemed mesmerized by the colorful, six-faced cube that was white, red, blue, orange, green, and yellow.

"Knock, knock," Michael said, rapping *Dragnet*'s "dum de dum dum" on the door.

"Come in, buddy," Clay said as he continued to work the device.

Clay sighed in frustration and said, "This thing is driving me crazy, but they tell me it's like weight-lifting for the mind. There is an internal pivot mechanism that allows each face to turn independently, mixing up the colors. It's a puzzle, and to solve it, each face must be rotated until the colors are uniform."

"What do they call it?" Michael asked.

"They call it a Rubik's Cube. This is an early prototype a friend at Foggy Bottom got for me," he said.

"Foggy Bottom?" Michael asked.

"CIA. He said it'll be big one day," Clay said as he tossed the device to Michael.

As Michael experimented with Clay's new toy, Clay asked him if he was familiar with purple martins.

"A little...they eat mosquitoes, I think," Michael said.

"Yes, we have gourds up for them to nest in at our house in the country. The original inhabitants of North America used to put them up. Those birds have a long relationship with humans, and they migrate here each year from South America. We see them here in the spring if they survive the winter in Argentina. Besides the hardships of migration, some people try to kill them for food down there. It's hard to understand why, because there's not much meat on those scrawny little birds. I guess if you're hungry enough, you'll eat anything. There's always somebody who wants to pluck your feathers and fry you in this world. That goes for birds and people," he said.

"I guess so. I knew folks who lived near Belmont who used to eat dirt because they were so hungry," Michael said, still wrestling with the cube.

"What's your favorite place to migrate to, Michael?" Clay asked, rubbing his sore fingers from his hour-long bout with the Rubik's Cube.

"Okaloosa Island at Ft. Walton Beach in Florida is my sanctuary," Michael said, wondering where the conversation was headed.

"Yeah, it's nice there. You know, birds and agents aren't the only migrant hearts, Michael. Broken hearts are continually searching, migrating here and there to find their place in this old world. Molly has a migrant heart, and I want you to be careful with her. She's begun to believe in life again, and I think she's looking for a place to nest," Clay said.

Michael stopped twisting the cube and looked at Clay. "Something I need to know?" he asked.

"Rose called me," Clay said, frowning.

"And?" Michael asked.

"You know how she is, insecure, a child in so many ways, and into all this boy-girl drama. If she didn't know so many dealers and have access to these crooked pols and all, I wouldn't use her. All the girly jealousy wears me out. I thought I'd seen the last of that in junior high, but we do what we must and take our information where we can get it," he said, reaching into his desk for a cassette recorder.

"She told me Molly's changed. Here's a little bit of the call I taped," Clay said.

The spindles of the cassette turned, there was a hiss of tape, and then Michael heard Rose. "It's bad enough my mama wants Michael to be her big dog now that Daddy's gone, but now Molly thinks Michael's her personal agent, but I saw him first, Mr. Clay. Now she's been to the beauty shop, bought new clothes, and is working on a big drug deal just to get to work with him again. It ain't fair, Mr. Clay. I was the one that brought her to your party. I think you should...what's it called? Excommunicate her or something."

Clay sighed, rubbed his aching ears, and said, "Now, here's Molly, who called later."

Michael heard popping, rattling, and static, and then Molly's voice. "Sorry about the noise, Agent Strickland, but I had to lock myself in my room. I'm having problems with Rose right now. She's stalking me. I'm working on a deal I think Agent Parker will like if he's available, and we can go back to Moondog soon, too, I think. I know y'all like to have at least two buys from each dealer to help your case in court. There's something going on over there, and I'll call back later to tell you all about it. I think I can get Michael in front of a big, female dealer, and I know she'll sell to him because women like him. You know, Agent Strickland, it's not fair that y'all use a guy like Michael undercover, because a girl would do anything for a man like him."

"Oh, boy," Michael said, shaking his head.

"Yep, the word has gotten around, too. Rose and Molly won't work with any other MBN agent. The Jackson P.D. officers say they've cut them off, too, and told the P.D. they're too busy with Agent Parker. The MBN agents who'd worked with them before you arrived have gotten a dose, too, and the agents are joking again about how you're just too pretty to be an agent. So expect some ribbing," Clay said.

"Oh, man. I don't have time for this," Michael said.

"Sorry to be the stinkbug at the party, buddy, but you needed to know," Clay said.

"I know," Michael said.

Clay picked up his folder stamped Moondog and said, "Molly called back and told me a lot about what happened at Milkwood's place. Combined with what the Jackson P.D. and the health inspector's office told us, we have a good picture of what's unfolding there since your buy from Milkwood and the events in Hattiesburg.

"In the last week or so, there's been chaos at Moondog Square. After your visit and the information you gathered, the health inspector showed up on a 'routine' inspection of the facilities. He found the dead girl, and we hear it was quite a scene. Jones expressed shock, and then he fainted for good measure and bad theater. The inspector called in the homicide unit of the Jackson P.D.

"They interviewed the residents about the girl and where her dope came from, but nobody knew anything. When they were knocking on one door, they saw blood and entered the room and discovered another body...the father you smacked," Clay said.

"Arnold is dead?" Michael asked.

"Yes, but you have an ironclad alibi. You're covered, even though it's no secret you two weren't exactly soulmates. Detectives found a bloody knife with what turned out to be a match for Bertha's big paw prints they had on file from a previous arrest. When the prints matched, they came back to arrest her. She took a swing at them, bolted toward the stairs, and fell over the railing. She's in St. Dominic's Hospital with a broken back. Bertha's confessed to the crime and told them he blamed her for not helping him when he was attacked. She told them a druggie staying at Moondog didn't like the setup with Arnold's little girl. She told the detectives she wanted to come to Arnold's rescue when the guy was slapping Arnold around, but the man had the wrath of God in his eyes," he said with a wry smile.

"Live by the sword, die by the sword. Hard to feel bad about Arnold," Michael said.

"Yeah, but that's not the whole story. The cops aren't buying her confession. They say she's scared out of her wits and would rather go to prison than to rat out the real killer. She told a jailhouse snitch it was Johnny 'Split Nose' Gagliano, one of the made men out of the Marcello Mafia family in New Orleans, who did it. He was staying there for some R and R and got wind of what Arnold was doing. Turns out the Mafioso had a daughter who was abused, and he almost beat a pedophile to death during a stretch he did in a federal prison in 1968. The guy lived but wouldn't press charges. Bertha said Johnny took Arnold's business personal, like someone had personally peed in his cereal. Jackson P.D. put a wire on their jailhouse snitch, and here's the recording of Bertha," he said.

As the recording began, Michael put down the Rubik's Cube and thought this must be the day for secret recordings.

"This is Lt. Robert Tullos with the Jackson Police Department. This is a recording made in the Hinds County Jail by confidential informant 6932 working for the city on the murder of Arnold Case."

Hisses, clanking, wailing, jail sounds.

The thin, squeaky voice of a female inmate said, "Bertha, who was this guy?"

A voice Michael recognized as Bertha Bates answered, "Split Nose is big and mean, skin so dark brown like somebody stained him with wild berry juice. He's got massive arms like one of them pro wrestlers on TV and a strange mark, like the mark of Cain, down the side of his neck. He has no soul behind his eyes, just emptiness above a crushed nose and broken cheekbones. His eyes look dead, and the scars all over his face make him look like he dry-shaves with barbwire. He's like those dime novel images of a cold, brutal killer, you know, over-the-top mean and scary. Arnold once took me to an illegal dog fight near Guntown. One of the snarling dogs lunged at me and almost broke free from its chain. That dog had the same look in its eyes as Split Nose, except his anger was mixed with the blankness of a shark, the kind of look that says, 'I'll rip your throat out just because I can.' After he killed Arnold, Split Nose looked at me with that gummy sneer and said, 'He was a bug tired of being a bug, and I was his windshield. Let's just call it bugacide.'"

Clay stopped the recording when the conversation veered into an X-rated monologue.

"Gagliano left for the Big Easy that night. New Orleans intelligence units tell us he delivers money to Meyer Lansky for the mob and bodies to the gators in the swamps for Carlos Marcello. Gagliano once greeted a rival boss from Chicago who came to New Orleans to make demands. He disarmed his bodyguards and broke their fingers. What cinched it between him and Marcello was the time the mob learned Gagliano's brother was a snitch for the FBI. Split Nose killed his own brother without hesitation and dropped him down a sinkhole in a remote field outside New Orleans. Maybe Bertha is right about that mark of Cain thing. She'll probably plead to manslaughter and serve a few years, figuring that beats the death sentence she'd get for fingering Split Nose. That leaves Milkwood to work things out with the Marcello family," Clay said, picking up a report from the Tunica County sheriff.

"The little girl took the last bus to freedom and is with her mother now somewhere near Tunica. The sheriff, who picked her up at the bus terminal at the request of the director, said the mother wept when she saw her daughter. She thought she'd never see her again. She said Charity told her about a man who tried to help her. The mother asked the sheriff to tell the man God will bless him for what he did and she'll pray for him every day of her life," Clay said.

Michael cleared his throat, gnawed on his lower lip, and stared at the window behind Clay.

"The inspector found a Bible in the attic belonging to the missing pastor but no sign of a body or of any real evidence of a murder. Milkwood told the police he had no idea perverts were living at his bed-and-breakfast, and he pledged to find out who would have done such a thing to Arnold, who he thought was a fine man who struggled with his demons.

"Behind the scenes, Jones is on a rampage and blaming all the wrong people. He was so stoned he barely remembers you being there and doesn't seem to connect you with any of it. This Rachel, who seems to be the witchy woman, apparently has shared none of her doubts about you with him, so we don't know what kind of game she's playing or if she's just hedging her bets.

"Then amid the mayhem, the wounded from the battle in Hattiesburg arrived at Moondog Square. There are at least two men in the anteroom above the second floor. Milkwood told the police there were cancer patients staying with him for holistic therapy, and they would be there until they went into remission. Molly said the men arrived with two body bags, and Milkwood disposed of them for the Stones," Clay said.

"Good grief! Is that all?" Michael asked.

"No, the city politicians, who have covered for him, are getting antsy about the place, too much activity and too many folks dying. Prostitutes and drugs are one thing, but their exposure has risen since you went tiptoeing through their tulips. Worse for their bottom line, the place is so hot now that we hear legislators are afraid to show their faces there.

"Your visit to Moondog was not a big event in the grand scheme of things, but it set in motion a lot of dominos that began to fall. All the little matters make the big things…big things. In any event, the director is torn between firing you, having you committed to the state hospital, or giving you a medal," Clay said with a chuckle.

"Undercover in Whitfield, I can see it now," Michael said.

"Well, at least it wouldn't be Parchman!" Clay said.

"Things are getting a little out of hand. We don't want to make any arrests at Moondog too soon and blow your cover around Jackson. Molly has other deals in the making and wants to take you back for a second buy when the waters calm. She'll tell you all about it. Speaking of water, the rain is supposed to stop later today, and a meeting is set for 5 p.m. She'll meet you in the end zone at Memorial Stadium. The gate on the south side will be open," he said.

As Michael rose to leave, Clay added, "She's a good source, but she's fragile. So no unnecessary roughness in the end zone, but don't allow her to clip the quarterback below the belt, either."

CHAPTER NINETEEN

"Amazing grace! How sweet the sound…
I once was lost, but now am found;
Was blind, but now I see."
—John Newton, "Amazing Grace"

"I think it is safe to say that while the South
is hardly Christ-centered, it is most certainly
Christ-haunted."—Flannery O'Connor

The rain stopped just before Michael saw Molly approaching. She looked scrubbed, polished, and pristine. Her hair had been cut, and her outfit was not counterculture casual but knockoff sorority girl. The wilted look of fear and fatigue and the hollowness he had seen during their ordeal at Moondog was gone. As she strode toward him, it was like viewing an image that had been double or triple exposed on film.

He saw the young girl with all her life before her, when all things were possible, and all the pages of the book of life were yet to be written. He also saw the jaded Molly he'd met at Rose's house and the confident, bespectacled young woman she appeared to be tonight.

"Well, good golly, Miss Molly, look at you," Michael said.

"You like?" she asked as she turned around, twirling and smiling like a *Vogue* model.

"I didn't know you wore glasses," Michael said.

"Yeah, I'm as blind as a bat, but no more vanity for me. I used my blindness to protect myself, to look away from the ugliness of my sins. I also wore my glasses tonight because they make me look like someone else. I don't want to be the old me anymore," she said, briefly looking at the ground.

"Well, they look great! What's changed? You were thinking about giving up the Mata Hari life, and you weren't sure you wanted to work with me anymore, either," Michael said.

She reached into her giant purse and pulled out a Bible.

"I found this old Bible Mama gave me long ago. I never used it. It was in the old suitcase I had when I arrived at the bus terminal, all dusty on the outside but pristine on the inside. When I found it, it had changed or maybe I had changed. It was almost like the book was speaking to me. I used to think it was lifeless, but I guess it was me who was lifeless. I was so empty the wind just whistled through where my heart used to be. I began to read the book, and I read it all day and into the night. Somewhere in there, in those words printed in red, I realized He wasn't calling me by my shame but by my name. It was a love letter written to me. My record player had been stuck on the B side of life, but I'm ready for the A side, the sunny side," Molly said in a long rushing, stumbling, gasping of emotionally packed words.

"That's great, Molly!" Michael said.

"Michael, did you ever love someone?" Molly asked.

"Yes, I thought I did, but right and wrong got tangled in her hair and lost in her eyes," Michael said quietly.

"Is she gone?" she asked.

"Yes, afraid so," he said.

"What happened? I think you're still carrying a torch for her. You have that look. Women can tell," she said.

"As the song says, love is a many-splendored thing, and it can get complicated. You ask too many questions," he answered with a smile.

She stared off into space, her arms folded, and then she cocked her head to study him from behind the tortoise-shell glasses that magnified her eyes. She teased him with an appraising or approving look, and he had the sudden urge to check his zipper to see if he'd left the barn door open.

"Michael, I've told you a lot and showed you too much, but I'm not that person anymore. I am the original Miss Judged. I ran out of gas on the road less traveled while I was eating devil's food cake for every meal, trying to slap the vinegar out of myself before somebody else did it for me. Oh, I'm speaking in riddles and sounding like Milkwood now. It's not coming out right. You make me stammer and tongue-tied," she said as her voice became low and raspy, tinged with the twang of the Vardaman Sweet Potato Queen she once was.

"You're doing fine, Molly," he said softly.

"Life's been dealing to me off the bottom of the deck. I was born right smack in the middle of Mama's mess, and my wires got crossed. I tried to play her tune, but it was a sour note, and every use of me by the abusers seemed like love because I was so starved for affection. I know you think I'm damaged goods," Molly said, looking at him with resignation in her eyes and voice.

"No, I don't," he answered.

"Yes, you do and you should. In the old days, I was a grifter, my language would've made a sailor blush, and I knew every filthy trick from rolling drunks to stealing from an old lady who had befriended me, but you're just tripping on the shadows of my past, the scars and the imperfections. He had scars, too, awful but beautiful scars. The more I listened to you the other night and the more I read, it was like seeing a movie in color after watching black and white all my life. I know it sounds crazy, but I've been thinking about cotton fields and cotton candy, magnolias and weeping willows, and a life where the living is easy. I felt drunk, but I was stone cold sober," she said.

He watched her as she talked...the muscles in her neck, the nerve twitching in her right eye, her shaking shoulders tapering down to a slim waist and the sudden flaring curve of her hips. A gust of wind whipped through the stadium, and a sheaf of red hair blew across her face. Tossing it back with a flip of her head, she gnawed on her bruised lower lip, reddened from an elusive echo of tenderness.

"I figure survival lies in just sealing off a part of your heart that the world can never touch. I did, and saved it for someone like you. That part of me has never been touched. I was going nowhere, but I could go somewhere, anywhere with you. I'm dreaming good dreams, sweet dreams, and we could dream them together, Michael," she said.

"Molly, I—" he began.

"No, hear me out, and then we'll be back to good old MBN business. I want to climb your mountains and swim in your seas, Michael. I know I sound like a corny, starry-eyed schoolgirl. I know it's forbidden, and I don't expect an answer tonight, but if you ever want to talk, just come and sit with me and let me tell you about my dreams and the empty nights I've spent watching my life crawl by," she said, stifling a sob.

"If that doesn't impress you, I want to tell you I know you're the kind of man who'd leave the toilet seat down for a woman, but I'm the kind of girl who'd leave it up for you. How many women would do that?" she asked with a shy smile.

"Not many, Molly," he said, returning the smile.

She sighed deeply and pressed the Bible against her cheek.

"Whew, I feel like a foolish schoolgirl, but I'm glad I got that off my chest. Oh, but you've already seen my chest, haven't you? Okay, enough of that mushy stuff. Back to business," she said.

She switched hats in midsentence and became his CI again. It was a seamless transition and a perfect example of compartmentalizing.

"I went by Moondog Square. Milkwood was always crazy, but he's off the chain now, Michael, no connection to reality. He was walking around the compound with a hatchet, handing out underwear and shoes to the working girls and the addicts. A man complained about his shoes being too small for his feet, and just that quick, Milkwood raised his hatchet, chopped off the guy's toes, and said, 'Fits now, doesn't it? Would you like to complain about your jockey shorts?' People are terrified of him now. The worship has turned to fear and hate.

"Milkwood saw me watching him and said, 'I'm glad you came home, prodigal girl. We're the lost tribe of Israel, and we must get on the ark and get home before dark, before the levee breaks. Adam has lost his apple, and I killed my brother. The snake bit my ankle, and I am Cain's twin, doomed to wander the barren land. Violence has risen up into a rod of wickedness, and I have killed myself. There are graves here they'll never find.'

"I asked him how he knew all these things, and he said, 'How do I know? A bird came down to prophesy to me, but I killed it, and then I saw the future in its entrails.'

"I knew again he's a monster, but that doesn't mean I have to be a monster, too, does it?" she asked.

He saw her trembling lips, the uncertainty in her fluttering eyes, and he said, "No, you don't, Molly."

"Milkwood's truly over the edge now, but I can take you back to see him if you want to get the second buy you guys like to have. I don't think he even remembers you, but if he does, he hasn't connected you to any of what's going on now. If we go in again, who knows what trouble you'll stir up this time," she said with a big smile and a quick squeeze of his hand.

She withdrew her hand quickly and opened her Bible. Michael saw the pages she'd turned down and the verses she'd underlined.

"I pray for you, Michael, and include the words I read in my Bible. 'There shall no evil befall thee, neither shall any plague come nigh thy dwelling. For he shall give his angels charge over thee, to keep thee in all thy ways.' That's one I like for you from Psalm 91.

"Another one is, 'Thou shalt be far from oppression; for thou shalt not fear: and from terror; for it shall not come near thee.' That's from Isaiah 54:14. I like Psalm 91:3, too, 'Surely he shall deliver thee from the snare of the fowler, and from the noisome pestilence,'" she said.

She talked and talked and the purple dusk gave way to a pitch-black night that suddenly crashed to earth and enveloped the football field in an inky darkness. Then someone turned on the stadium lights with a loud clack-chack, and a voice on the PA startled them.

"Take your time. Clay's paying the bills," the disembodied voice said.

"Gosh, I feel like we're having a Bible study. It feels strange but natural and good, too. Call me when you're ready to take another shot at the house of darkness or when you want to talk about dreams. I was used and abused, and taught to use and abuse others, to pass on my misery. I'm ready for some innocence, Michael, to eat cherry snow cones on hot August days and to twist again like we did last summer. I was always left-handed, but now I'm right-minded. I'd like to learn how to play second fiddle to others, and I'd like to say those three words people whisper in the night, words that make the world go round. I'd like to say them for free and mean them, Michael. I don't want Moondog Square to be my tomb, buried in the graveyard of the lost. I don't want evil to win," she said.

It began to drizzle as they were parting, and she thrust a piece of paper into his hand just as the stadium lights went out. Then a cold, hard rain fell as Michael scurried to his car. For some reason, he stopped sprinting and splashing through the puddling water and looked back. Molly was still in the end zone, standing in the monsoon. She was framed in each flash of lightning, the firmament's flickering strobe lights, and a frame-by-frame slide-show from heaven.

Michael watched her in the pouring rain. Her eyes were closed, and her hands were outstretched, reaching, and then straining toward heaven. The water was spattering around her and pooling in her hands, and her hair was plastered to her head. There was a look of serenity on her face as if God were cleansing her… the Custodian of the universe wringing all the dirty water out of a mop, making it as good as new, as white as snow. The stadium was a giant baptismal, and she seemed to hear a melody in the tempest meant only for her. While most would be frightened by the thunderstorm or the soaking from the deluge, she was feeling the caress of God in the torrent.

A squall blew through the stadium and drove Michael against the wall by the end zone seats. The goal posts rocked back and forth. They almost bent forward to the ground as if in a deep bow before the advance of God. Then a crack of light appeared in the storm, but it wasn't lightning, and it wasn't the stadium lights.

Michael had never seen anything like it. His mind was racing and his heart was pounding.

Look up, a better world may be drawing near.

The cold rain chilled him. He was shivering from the soaking and from what he had witnessed. In his car, he dried himself off with a towel he'd bought when the Hattiesburg motel towels didn't meet his standards. He fluffed his wet hair and opened the note Molly had given him.

It was Scripture, Hosea 1:2, and he read it out loud. *"When the LORD first spoke through Hosea, the LORD said to Hosea, 'Go, take to yourself a wife of harlotry and have children of harlotry; for the land commits flagrant harlotry, forsaking the LORD.'"*

CHAPTER TWENTY

*"There was a really big screen...sit inside
or outside the car. We had arrived at the
local drive-in."—Adine Cathey*

*"Once to every man...comes the moment
to decide, In the strife of Truth with
Falsehood, for the good or evil side. Truth
forever on the scaffold, Wrong forever on
the throne—Yet that scaffold sways
the future, and, behind the dim unknown,
Standeth God within the shadow,
keeping watch above his own."*
—James Russell Lowell, This Present Crisis

Michael was overwhelmed as he drove away from Molly. He wanted to believe in miracles, that what he'd seen was real, her transformation sustainable after such a hard life. But that was his heart speaking, the one that brought home stray kittens as a child and defended runts against schoolyard bullies...the one who believed in redemption. It was the soft part of Michael, the one Clay and Molly herself had cautioned him about.

He could already feel the subtle changes in himself after all the things he'd seen since he held his nose and jumped in this toxic pond. It felt like his DNA was being altered, and he wondered if he could ever be the person he used to be. He knew it would get harder and harder to retreat to the world he grew up in during the '50s and '60s, until one day he might lose sight of that foundation altogether and subscribe to the adage "When in Rome, do as Romans do."

In any event, he had a problem to deal with. How would he maintain contact with Molly on his assignments knowing how she felt about him? They hadn't covered that in his classes at Ole Miss.

He drove around for hours and parked for a while at the rest area on the Natchez Trace overlooking the Ross Barnett Reservoir, just to think and watch the remnants of the storm move across the water. While Michael watched the lightning dance on the water, he again sought the company of old friends on his radio.

The big border-blaster station south of Del Rio was lighting up his radio dial and rattling his car's cheap speaker. It wasn't the station it was during his youth, but it still owned the airways at night, booming through Canada, over the Pole, and into Russia, where the KGB used the dialogue, sermons, and ads to train their spies to speak English.

Through a maxed-out modulator, a snake-oil salesman sounded like he was spitting into the mike. He told listeners he felt their pain and could cure what ailed them and numb their aching hearts. He swore he could put hair on men's chests and heads and make aching prostates go to sleep. Quickie divorces were quick and cheap, and friendly banks sheltered hidden assets and asked no questions.

A radio preacher asked widows to send him their life savings because he was locked in hand-to-hand combat with Satan and needed an army of tithers to sustain his struggle. He preached the gospel of "a dollar before you holler" and "pay before you pray." The radio actors offered false hope and medical quackery for broken people, a metaphor for Moondog Square's dingy orphanage for the rejected and vulnerable.

Moondog Square's Dr. Feel-Good and the Del Rio radio doctors peddled the same fool's gold and preached similar counterfeit sermons. There was nothing transcendent on the radio, no woman at the well telling others about what she'd heard and Who she had seen.

Michael heard Pearl's admonition: "Lord, help us over the shining fence."

He drove to a phone booth to call Clay, who seemed to never sleep. Clay agreed to meet him at the Showdown Drive-in Theater on Highway 80 in Jackson.

****

When Michael arrived at the drive-in, the marquee advertised an all-night Elvis marathon. The man in the ticket booth handed him a Mason jar, like the ones Pearl used for canning. "Got a special tonight—free lightning bugs. If the movies don't move you, you can catch as many as you want to light up this here jar," he said.

The third feature, *Kid Galahad*, was just finishing when Michael pulled up next to a choice car speaker in the seventh row, center screen. Elvis was throwing punches, singing songs, and wooing pretty girls.

Off to Michael's right, no occupants were visible, but the car was rocking suspiciously. To his left, a couple sat transfixed by the music. He could see them sitting so close together the girl appeared to be in the boy's lap. The flickering lights from the big screen captured them in a Norman Rockwell moment—forever young and eating from the same popcorn box, their fingers brushing as they fished for popcorn. Just behind, he could see a car in his rearview mirror. The man was slouching in his slumber, his head out the driver's window, and he was snoring like a chain saw. Whining mosquitoes were on the hunt, and a stray dog was looking for scraps, sniffing the bags litterbugs had tossed from their cars.

The fourth movie of the night, *Jailhouse Rock*, was underway when Clay arrived. Elvis had just kissed the girl and told her, "That ain't tactics, honey. It's just the beast in me."

"Hey, Clay, sorry to get you out so late," Michael said.

"No problem. How are you?" Clay asked.

"You caught me hitting the hard stuff, Coke with peanuts and a Moon Pie, my comfort food," Michael said, holding up his "drugs" of choice.

"Well, glad you called. I was up writing a long, detailed intelligence report, piecing together the information in files from several agents. Plus, I was still fading heat after a trip to McComb with Chief Burnside today," Clay said.

"What kind of heat?" Michael asked.

"Oh, we were riding down the interstate giving the politicos at the MHP what-for, talking about all they're trying to do, and lo-and-behold, we discovered Larry's mike was keyed. It was all going out on an open mike on a channel the MHP monitors. It ruffled a few feathers, but it will pass. The truth hurts. And then we had to fire an agent for improper relations with his CI," Clay said with a sideways grin and an eye roll directed at Michael.

"Not me, buddy," Michael said.

"I know, but it can get out of hand, and it did for that agent, a good man. But I digress. How did it go tonight?" Clay asked.

Michael told him the story in great detail, and the back-and-forth lasted for a long while, long enough for another Elvis movie to begin.

"A girl who's shown everything to everyone is showing you a little ankle like Claudette Colbert in that movie…her heart really. She's lived in the bleak and now she wants the beauty. I don't know, Michael, but after all she's been through, I don't know if you can lose the hardness or unsee all the things you've seen and done. Survival is a part of our DNA, and it clouds your view of the world. She knows all the tricks and scams. Only you were there, only you can decide if her conversion is real. I suspect she believes it's real, and she believes in you. Maybe that's enough," Clay said.

Clay scratched his chin for a moment and then said, "She has a lot of connections. We need to get back in there and close the case on Moondog Square after a second buy from Milkwood. Sarge called to say Bad Eye has come up missing. That worries him and me, given his history. He's a wild card. Molly told me she has another deal in the making, one on some suppliers out of New Orleans. So I don't know what you do right now, except manage it and protect yourself. I've documented that you've notified us of the status, so you're covered.

"This thing with Molly reminded me I didn't tell you everything the MBN shrink said about you," Clay added.

"But you're going to now," Michael said.

"Yes, as food for thought. He liked you, but he said you have just enough gentleness for the women you encounter and just enough maleness or toughness, whatever that means, to be accepted by your male counterparts at the MBN. He wasn't so sure how that will work out, but he thinks women will love you and that may cause you problems. The good doctor thinks you awaken the mother instinct in them, too. They see you and want to cook for you, sew buttons on your shirts, and darn your socks. Men may be suspicious of you, suspect you might be a purist who'll tell on them, or they may feel you think you're better than they are, but you'll overcome the misgivings of agents over time. It's the vulnerability to women in this brave new counterculture that concerned the shrink," Clay said.

"They pay him for these insights?" Michael asked with a chuckle.

"Yeah, good work if you can get it," Clay said.

"Speaking of his observations, you can be persuasive with women. You like women and they like you. How do you know so much about women? I struggle. Is it lots and lots of practice and first-hand experience?" Clay asked.

"No, I just listen to my adventuresome friends and take notes," Michael answered with a grin, and his tongue planted firmly in his cheek.

They both laughed and then sat in silence for a moment.

"If I know anything about women, I suppose it's from watching Pearl and Mama, and maybe Dixie Lee. That may be too small a sample for this work," Michael said.

They stared at the final scenes from the last movie. It was the closing moments of *Blue Hawaii*, the wedding scene. Elvis and his bride-to-be were resplendent in their leis aboard the double-hulled canoe taking them down the lagoon to the wedding chapel. Elvis sang the "Hawaiian Wedding Song" and got the girl.

"You know, when Elvis filmed this movie, girls were still throwing their undies at him on stage. Some still do, but their drawers look more like parachutes now," Clay chuckled.

They both laughed, and then Clay got serious again.

"The director thinks you need to take a short break, a little breather to let things cool off. Los Angeles Detective Harry Falkner, who worked the Charles Manson case, is hosting a homicide seminar on the coast, and the director thinks you might enjoy the training and the salty air. It's only two days. Meet people, walk on the beach, and learn about murders and crime scenes, since you seem to wander into them so often. Here are the details. They're expecting you," he said, handing him his reservation.

"Thanks, sounds good. Lately I feel like I've been walking on a high wire with my eyes closed," Michael said.

"Yeah, I wish life was like these movies, but in the real world, happy endings can be hard to come by. Some folks are like contestants on *Let's Make a Deal*, always picking the wrong doors. Girls like Molly have walked under a hundred ladders, broke a thousand mirrors, and an army of black cats has crisscrossed the paths of their lives. They can't catch a break. They're tormented like Charlie Brown. People like Lucy in the comic strip want to see them fail or make them dependent. They keep snatching the football away before they can give it a good kick and then charge them a nickel for psychiatric advice or ten bucks for a dime bag of false hope called heroin," Clay said.

As the end credits ran for the movie, Clay said, "It never seemed so complicated in his movies, did it? Just follow that dream and live a little, love a little. Now there are people who'll steal your soul and then pretend to help you look for it."

A rooster crowed in the distance as stragglers hung car speakers on the posts. Clay watched them for a moment and asked, "What do you think, Michael? Are we here to win or just to beg for terms, to negotiate surrender?"

"Winning sounds preferable to me, Clay. There's a connection to alcoholism and winning y'all missed in my background investigation. My grandfather on my mother's side was an alcoholic, too," Michael said.

"Tell me about it," Clay said.

"Don't remember much. He died when I was very young, but I remember he made good fresh-squeezed lemonade in the summertime. I learned something else about surviving from a story that his wife, Big Mama, told me," Michael said.

"What's that?" Clay asked.

"During the Great Depression, my grandfather would go to Tupelo to collect the commodities they lived on...buckets of lard, blocks of cheese, and such. On one of those treks, he didn't show up for the longest time and drug in late that night. He was drunk as a skunk and had no commodities. Big Mama found out he had stopped at a house belonging to two sisters of ill repute. She tucked her revolver under her shawl and drove to their house.

"She knocked on the door, and when they saw her, they asked, 'Evie! What're you doing at our house this time of night?'

"Big Mama said, 'I've come for my commodities.'

"One of the sisters, who Big Mama said bought rouge by the barrel, mocked her and said, 'We don't know what you're talking about.'

"Then Big Mama whipped out her pistol, cocked it, and said, 'I *said*...I've come for my commodities.'

"The ladies squealed, 'They're right here under the bed, Evie. Let us get them for you,'" Michael said with a smile.

Clay said, "That's funny. Now that's what I call winning!"

Michael laughed, and Clay did, too.

"Man, we could've used her in the MBN!" Clay said.

He looked at Michael and said, "Pearl on one side, Big Mama on the other. No wonder you know so much about women!"

"There's another memory crowding my mind tonight," Michael said.

"What?" Clay asked.

"I remember Mama saving up her pennies and nickels, and I'd watch her drop them in a mason fruit jar with a slot cut in the top. She was hoping to take me to see Elvis at the fair," Michael said.

"You're going to be all right," Clay said as he shook Michael's hand and exited the car.

Michael watched his red taillights until they disappeared, and he thought one day the world seemed hot, and the next day it was cold. The meal was burned, or it was raw. If there was a rhythm, he was struggling to find it in this wilderness. He needed a field guide to this world like the ones bird lovers carry around. If you're ever lost or in doubt about who's who, just whip out your guide. There's a red-crested nit over there, and that's a blue-tailed flit brushing the clouds up yonder. If there's an answer high above the storm and all the lightning and thunder, he thought he sure could use it right then.

As he pulled out of the drive-in, he saw a turtle in the path of his car. The turtle looked at him and then pulled his head into his shell.

Maybe that's it, Michael thought. *Is that the answer, make like a turtle? Just pull our heads into our shells. Only come out when it's all over to ask, "Who won?"*

CHAPTER TWENTY-ONE

"On the streets...there are things you
learn that no book can teach you."
—Ramon Rodriquez, The New York Times

"...already whirling into the plunge of its
precipice...the first seconds of fall always
seem like soar."—William Faulkner,
Requiem for a Nun

On the way to his apartment, Michael drove through downtown Jackson. He saw the lighted Governor's Mansion in the distance and the abandoned King Edward Hotel. Locals swore it was haunted and ghosts shared the rooms with vagrants and junkies.

He turned on Amite Street that ran behind the King Edward and up to the Sun-n-Sand on Lamar. The Amite Street area had fallen on hard times, and there were still pools of blood in the gutters fronting a local nightclub.

Addicts were shooting up smack in the alleyways, and prostitutes were still out working the street corners in the wee hours. The bookmobile didn't make stops in this neighborhood. Enforcers of Jackson's Blue Laws wouldn't survive attempts to write citations in the part of town where sin merchants dozed but never closed, seven days a week.

On a street corner partially illuminated by a bar's flickering neon sign, two women were rolling a man in an expensive suit. Just as Michael passed them, one of the women flipped the intoxicated man onto his belly. She produced a knife and sliced open the back pocket of his pants to slip his billfold.

Michael stopped and approached the women and the man lying next to an empty bottle of booze.

"Evening. I think y'all should leave this drunk alone, and you'd better give him back his money, too," Michael said to the women.

They looked at him as if Scotty had beamed him down from the Starship Enterprise. "And who you think you be, hippie boy?" one woman asked.

"I'm a long tall Texan enforcing justice and the law," Michael said with a winsome smile.

The other woman worked her way around and behind Michael to flank him. Just as she pulled out a straight razor to slash him, Michael spun around and hit her full in the face. Down she went and her cheap wig came off, exposing her close-cropped, graying black hair. She sprang up and ran away, holding her mouth and screaming, "My face, my face! Pimp Daddy gonna be mad!"

Her emaciated partner in crime brandished her own blade and hissed at Michael, "I'm gonna cut you up good for hurting my sister."

She was skin and bones. Her eyes were wide and empty, an IQ likely in the sixties. The tracks on her arms, her puffy face, and runny nose were the telltale signs of an addict barely hanging on, doping herself into a stupor after every night on the dead-end streets of the asphalt jungle, awakening with no memories and no regrets.

The streetlamp above her flickered like a strobe light, buzzing and popping like a hundred bugs hitting an electric fence. She advanced toward Michael, teetering atop her high-heel shoes, swinging her knife left and right, and slurring her profanities and threats. "Who you think you be? You think you can come down here and mess with our biz-ness?" she challenged.

Michael pulled his pistol and said, "You think you can still work with a big hole in your chest? They're already warming up the meat wagon and digging the pauper's grave."

She dropped the knife, shrieked, and ran after her sister and the needle to make it all go away. She would find her kit, put the fire to her spoon, and feel the prick and the familiar warm rush.

When she woke up on the dirty floor of the rat-infested hovel she rented from her slum lord, it would all be like a bad dream, except for the bruising around her eyes from her pimp for coming home empty-handed.

Their intended victim, who reeked of alcohol, was higher and tighter than a newly set perm. He struggled to his feet, and his tongue tripped over his words as he tried to speak. He was hanging on by a spaghetti noodle and rolled his wild, bloodshot fish eyes at Michael.

"I dun know who, who you are, but you saved my bacon, brudah. Muh name's Hal, Hal Davidson. Who're you, some kinda avenging angel? Where did you come from?" the man said.

"The thermostat is set on boiling down here, mister. If you're going to stroll through hell, you'd better buy yourself a fireproof jacket, else the street creatures will be fighting over your charred corpse," Michael said.

As Michael turned to walk to his car, the man called out, "Well, God bless you, anyway, whoever you are. I'm gonna run fast and far from here."

Michael looked back at him and said, "Run faster. The race has already started, and Death is a lap ahead of you."

Then Michael heard a primal scream from somewhere deep in the inky blackness of the night, something ancient and evil, and shivers of vulnerability and mortality crawled up his spine.

He drove up the street toward Lamar. A breeze was blowing old newspaper sheets down the lane, and dust devils were forming in the alleyways, whipping grit and grime in a noxious swirl.

An old man with weathered skin the color of cinnamon sat on the pavement in front of the Faith is the Victory Tabernacle Mission. He sat cross-legged, cradling an ancient guitar in his lap. Empty wine bottles, nudged by the wind, rolled around him on the pavement with a rhythm matching the music he sang and the guitar he thumped.

Michael stopped his car in the middle of the street and rolled his window down to listen as the old man sang a song by

Blind Willie McTell about final goodbyes, women who grieve, and a last request to lay some flowers on his grave.

It was heartfelt and haunting, and as Michael drove away, the blues singer was still wailing and banging on his guitar, and it seemed a perfect soundtrack for the night. He never saw Michael, but Michael wasn't the intended audience. The man was singing to himself and to ghosts only he could see, maybe some from the King Edward Hotel. He was preaching his own funeral.

****

When Michael passed the Sun-n-Sand motel, he thought of poor Rose, the Leg Room, Red Winter, Molly, and powerbrokers who cooked all the books except the Good Book.

As he headed for his apartment, first light was breaking, and he thought about the theater of the macabre, a parallel world born at night with dreadful actors and deadly rules. Animals, the eight-legged and two-legged kinds, spun their webs of entanglement and scurried about in the darkness of a tragic sideshow, retreating to their dens like vampires avoiding the first blush of morning.

He drove along the streets of Jackson, and the neighborhoods changed. He saw a kid on a bicycle flinging papers toward the drives of darkened homes and a milkman placing glass bottles in doorways. When he passed St. Dominic's Hospital, a nurse was scurrying out of the emergency room to greet an ambulance with its lights flashing and its siren screaming…a nocturnal tale of different worlds just a few miles apart.

Looking at the hospital, Michael thought sick people in hospitals know they're sick, but the dead men walking, the sick people he'd met in life, just deny their illnesses. They miss the ambulances while waiting to catch hearses at the end of roads that run out much sooner than expected. They mark time and dread finality, unsure of what to do about it and where things went wrong. He thought of his father, and a salty tear surprised him, squeezed out of his eye, and trickled down his cheek. He figured that ever since the rebellion in the Garden, the whole earth had been one giant triage, and *we are all patients or attendants, sometimes both. Then one day we surrender our dog tags for toe tags, and we're pushing up daisies.*

There was a haze of smog across the rising daystar, and the clouds appeared to be pasted onto an opaque sky. There was a pulsing roar in his ears. His throat was parched and so tight it demanded a hard swallow that wouldn't come.

His arms were leaden, and his head ached right between his eyes. The man in the old Anacin commercials was inside his head with a sledgehammer pounding his anvil, and something was chiseling away his former self.

The whispers of the wind whistled and buzzed round the windows of his bureau car like angry hornets, and melancholy clung to him like flypaper. There was a nagging, nauseous feeling in the back of his mind that he'd left something undone…words unsaid, opportunities wasted, or doors unbolted.

Clay was right. Michael needed a break.

CHAPTER TWENTY-TWO

"In every outthrust headland, in every
curving beach, in every grain of sand there
is the story of the earth."—Rachel Carson

"Ladies and gentlemen of the jury, Sharon
Tate…Jay Sebring…Voytek Frykowski…
Abigail Folger…Steven Parent…Leno
LaBianca…and Rosemary LaBianca are not
here with us right now in this courtroom.
But from their graves, they cry out
for justice."—Vincent Bugliosi

Michael stood at the picture window of the Broadwater Hotel's third floor conference room looking out at the Southern Riviera. Two kids were sitting on a pier, their legs dangling over sparkling sun diamonds that danced on the blue-green waters of the Gulf.

It wouldn't be long before the summer steam pot arrived, and farmers who furnished eggs to local restaurants would give their hot chickens ice water so they wouldn't lay hard-boiled eggs. The restaurants would fry their oysters and green tomatoes on the sidewalk, and the sun would bake the sin right out of their sinfully delicious dishes. The tourists' sunglasses would fog up when they walked outside, and ladies would complain when their makeup melted and ran down their faces as they read their horoscopes on the beach.

Charter boats lined the seaside marinas and bobbed on waves lapping at their hulls. A pod of hungry bottlenose dolphins chased a school of silvery fish near the shore. Michael could almost feel the gentle caress of the sun and the distinctive smell of the Gulf—salt, surf, sweat, and a hint of dead fish—a blend whipped, churned, and mixed by the nautical winds sailors lived for.

Ponytails bobbed on the beach, and pimply-faced young boys followed the giggling boarding-school girls with dogged determination, hope that sprang eternal…the mystery of love and innocence. Seagulls drifted over the blue water. Children and the aptly named laughing gulls laughed, and in the distance the white sails of a boat rose and dropped on the choppy water.

The once pristine strip of land between Gulfport and Biloxi was still recovering from Hurricane Camille, which had devastated the Mississippi Gulf Coast in 1969. Debris and empty beer cans still littered parts of the beach and spoiled Biloxi's imitation of Florida. Thirsty, hungry dogs were panting in the heat, pink tongues lolling. They licked at cans and empty burger wrappers and chased sand crabs.

Tourism and organized crime were the two mainstays of the local economy. Tourism had suffered in the wake of the storm, but gangsters were selling sin day and night. Illegal gambling, sports betting, and prostitution were all out in the open. Local patricians hid in their antebellum homes and turned blind eyes to the menu of crimes on the coast, spicy and indigestible dishes sure to bring heartburn and heartache to paradise.

The surge of the water from Camille soaked the playground of northern snowbirds and gangsters. At high tide during the hurricane, expensive furniture floated out of the lobbies of the hotels. Bales of marijuana, illegal gambling tables, and dead hookers washed up on the beaches. It was not the image the Chamber of Commerce hoped for.

Michael read Clay's intelligence file entitled "Camille and Crooks." The coast was not the magical place Michael remembered from childhood vacations. The bayous, bays, and swamps belonged to the bootleggers, bank robbers, pimps, drug dealers, and smugglers. The enriched mobsters and politicians ruled a kingdom built on sand, sex, and sin.

Seeking the R and R the director recommended, Michael brought along an old pair of binoculars to look at coastal birds and dolphins. Through the field glasses, he also got a close look at nightclubs and strip joints with names like Horseshoe Lounge, Gringo's Lounge, Dream Room, Gay Paree, the Chandelier Club, and All Girls Revue.

The red, blue, and green neon flickered like flames against the roofs of the clubs at night. The bumping bass of the jukeboxes, the cackling laughter of the working girls, and the barking of the street pimps were unchanging—"Girls, nice girls. You like to meet some nice girls?"

Tourists came to eat at places like White Pillars and Mary Mahoney's, but others came to take a walk on the wild side of Biloxi. Locals wished everyone could've seen Biloxi before, meaning "before the hurricane." When the MBN said before, they meant "before organized crime."

In the midst of the crowded neon decadence of twenty-five strip clubs and tall billboards advertising girls and good times, Michael saw a small, lonely sign for Trinity Baptist Church with an arrow pointing inland. *Only one block away*, the sign read. The church promised relief from all that the strip offered, the things the pastor preached against every Sunday.

Michael looked away from the folly of man and searched out the colonies of the little birds called least terns. He watched them float, hover, and dive into the waters of the Gulf. They nested on the beach in a protected area. Through the long lens of the glasses, he could see signs that read *Nest in Peace* and *Please Tern Around*, signs that could have been warnings for the puritans and Boy Scouts who came to the coast.

A sudden disturbance caught his attention, and he saw a juiced-up guy running naked through the tern nesting area, scattering the birds. The young man glistened in the sun, still carrying a giant bottle of vegetable oil. Shocked women gasped and averted their eyes, and fishermen pelted the interloper with bait fish as he ran by.

Two police officers chased the oily streaker in a proverbial "greased pig contest," but each time they grabbed him, he slipped away. His name was probably Bubba. When the story of the "Butt Naked Bubba" hit the papers, mothers across Mississippi would hold their breath in a state full of boys called Bubba.

While he was watching terns, police, and greasy pigs, he also saw a familiar face. Senator Corndog was walking on the beach with two men who looked to be from the city down the road, New Orleans. From their dress and look, Michael thought they might be what Clay called "Marshmallow Men," slang for "Marcello Men."

One of the men was thin as a rake, badly sunburned, and looked like a lobster fresh out of the broiler. The other had a barrel chest, no neck, and thick arms too short for his body. His nose looked flattened and disfigured when he turned toward Michael's view. There was something familiar about him, the way he looked, but Michael couldn't pull it up. On a beach full of people in sandals, the Marshmallow Men looked like they might specialize in fitting people with concrete shoes. Corndog was smiling at them like a proud man with a new pair of dentures. The animated politician gestured wildly, painting pictures on the cool breezes that salted their faces and blew their hair.

There were lots of earnest looks, smiles, and handshakes. The body language often accompanying the sealing of deals and pledging of fortunes was written all over the three men. Michael wondered why they would be meeting on a public beach, but there were no bugs on the beach except for the sand fleas and the biting flies, and the conversation was out of the range of eavesdropping government shotgun mikes. Corndog was selling his corn out in the open, hiding in plain sight, and making a statement of power to the gangsters.

Michael suddenly felt he was not alone. He was jolted from his surveillance and musings when someone behind him said, "Pretty day, huh?"

****

Michael turned to see none other than Mississippi Highway Patrolman Red Winter standing behind him with a lopsided grin on his face.

"Yeah, I could get used to this," Michael said.

"You here with him?" Michael asked, pointing to Corndog.

He passed the field glasses to Red.

Red took the glasses and eyed the area where Corndog walked and watched the scene without comment.

"Who are those guys? They don't appear to be local Chamber of Commerce boys or emissaries from the local Welcome Wagon," Michael said.

"Don't know. He knew I was coming to the homicide training and asked if he could ride with me to Gulfport. Then he dismissed me. Said he'd find his way back to Jackson," Red said, handing the glasses to Michael.

"Do that often? Transport senators?" Michael asked.

"Now and then, I do. The lieutenant governor asks for party favors sometimes, too. Just some booze and booty for visiting businessmen and other entrepreneurs from New Orleans," Red said.

"Do you ever ask?" Michael asked.

"No, they don't tell, and I don't see. When I'm taking care of them, I'm struck deaf, dumb, and blind. I don't even see them anymore. They're the invisible men to me. You might not understand because you're a rookie, but here's the way I see it. I write speeding tickets to make a little revenue for the state to pay your salary and mine. I also police the little people in my universe—the drunks, dopers, derelicts, and hookers—and I'm good at it. These politicians live in a different world, and they take care of its inhabitants. It's not my concern," Red said with an air of cold disdain and feigned superiority.

"So you don't hunt the big game, and because you're good at shooting ducks in a barrel, I should give you a pass?" Michael asked.

Red bristled for a moment. Michael smiled and studied him, happy he was talking. Then Red's face softened and Michael felt a joke or tall tale was coming to lighten the moment.

"I'll tell you this. Corndog's obsessed with living forever and preserving his virility. He adds Miracle Grow to his bath water. He's convinced it's an aphrodisiac and a fountain of youth," Red said with a grin that scrunched up the freckles on his face and made him look like he had the pox.

Michael thought it was probably not the first time he'd told that joke, but they both laughed until their sides and their smiles hurt.

"I've watched Corndog a long time, ever since he ambushed the incumbent before him. I'll tell you, Michael, when he made his speeches at country churches, the womenfolk would get the vapors, and their hearts would throb right out of their blouses. They'd have to pull out their little compacts and walk behind the church to fix their tear-streaked faces, and the men were sure he was talking just to them in some kind of secret, special language.

"He'd attack his enemies, make his enemies their enemies, and convince them their enemies were his enemies. He'd get all worked up and rail against egg-sucking carpetbaggers and dirty communists who hated Jesus, and when that didn't work, he'd tell the poor white folks his opponents would give their jobs to black folks. Then he'd ask his audiences if they were going to let them get away with it, and they'd all shake their heads 'No' and say, 'We're with you, Corndog,' and then they would ask him to kiss their babies," Red said.

Michael listened to this poor man's history with fascination.

"He traveled all the rutted back roads and got to know every pothole in the dirt trails and every empty heart along the roadside and how to ease into and out of them all, how to play 'em till they ain't empty no more. And all them rusted-out old cars on blocks in front of every shack? Give him a little time, and he'd have them running and purring just like those little feline girls who flocked around him. He keeps his promises and lives up to his threats. People respect that and overlook his failings. He's like them. He once was them, without a pot to pee in," Red said with obvious admiration.

"Heck, he's got fan clubs in the Delta. One of 'em that don't care for revenuers has a saying—*Corndog on his stick wraps pigs in their blankets*," Red said.

Michael nodded and resumed watching Corndog with the binoculars.

"I saw Rose, the girl you were with at the Leg Room. She's mad at her friend Molly and let it slip that you've been inside Moondog Square and might know about Melba and her daughter Sheler. When Melba died, it changed the senator. Some might not have thought so, and maybe it wasn't true at first, but he was joined to her at the heart, not the hips like his other women. He found in her something his money and power couldn't buy. I'm not even sure the distance of death's separation can sever that kind of connection. I don't know what happened, but he told me he never should have taken her to Moondog Square.

"You know, when she came up missing, I was on one of the search parties. When I used to drop him off at his plantation, he had this big old pack of blue tick hounds, and when they saw him coming, they'd come running, tails wagging, grinning and slobbering at the same time, as only a hound can. Early that morning when he lost Melba, I took him home. Those hounds saw him, but they weren't wagging their tails. Their heads were bowed down to the ground. They knew.

"When Melba died, he began to change, but when Sheler died like she did, he went a little crazy; guilt maybe. Who knows? He began to believe his own press and got reckless, flaunting it all a little too much. He started smoking dope and had a big ole chip on his shoulder that made him lean to one side. He started daring folks to knock it off," Red said.

"I walked into the Capitol supply room one day, and there was Corndog wearing bib overalls and a straw hat, working a giant piece of licorice around the corner of his mouth, and running off copies of porn pictures on the mimeograph machine. He acted like it was the most natural thing in the world, no matter that all the secretaries were glaring at him and a couple of reporters, too. But those 'journalists' are too deep into the party favors to ever call out someone like him.

"He looked at me with dilated pupils and a big grin and said, 'The boys at the Leg Room have got to see this. It would make Huck Finn blush.' It used to be all in fun with him, but now his old dull knife of humor is bent and has a sharp edge to it," Red said.

"Where does that leave us, Red?" Michael asked.

They stood there for a long, uncomfortable moment, and then Red said, "Man, I want you to know I'd never rat you out to those guys."

"I appreciate that, Red," Michael said.

"I'm just doing what I have to do to survive in the system. A man's gotta do what he's gotta do to get a piece of the action. I'm not their hatchet man or black bag boy. They're all drunk on booze and girls, and I'm just a poor bartender, gopher, and pimp. I hope you understand. I try to be as hard to hate as I can. I'll try extra hard to never put you in harm's way or wiretap you, even if they ask," Red said.

"Thanks, but that's slicing the baloney pretty thin, isn't it, Red? Sometimes when you've swum with the sharks for a long time, you don't even realize you're wet anymore, until one day you're lunch. Being in 'a little bit' with people like Corndog is like being a little bit pregnant," Michael said.

"Naw, man, I'm managing it. I know where the line is, and I never cross it," Red said unconvincingly.

Michael paused and said, "If I agreed with you, we'd both be wrong, but as one of Corndog's favorite politicians from Massachusetts once said, 'We'll drive off that bridge when we come to it.'"

Red laughed and said, "Ha, ha. That's a good one."

Michael raised his binoculars again and focused a tight view of Corndog.

"Did you know I can read lips some?" Michael asked.

"No! What? Can you really?" Red asked. His eyes were wide, and he looked concerned.

"Yep, he's talking to the Mafia boys now," Michael said.

"What's he saying?" Red asked as he swallowed hard.

"He's saying…'I'm going to make you an offer you can't refuse,'" Michael said, quoting *The Godfather.*

They both laughed, and then Red grew somber.

"Man, I suddenly feel like H-E double toothpick, too pooped to pop. This philosophizing is taxing to the mind," Red said.

He looked out at the beach for a long time to plan his thoughts before speaking again.

"You know, I think you judge me. To you, it's all cut and dried, black and white, no gray in the world. You think people are right or they're wrong, a good guy or a bad guy, and if you're ever a bad guy, you're always a bad guy," Red said.

"No, I believe in redemption, Red, but the final act will soon be upon us. This isn't a dress rehearsal, you know?" Michael said.

"Well, they say the lust for power is the last temptation. I hope so because I am so tired of being tempted. We only live once, and man, that's more than enough for me. If we ever get crossways, Michael, and you're the one to come for me, I'll put up a good fight and won't make it look too easy. We've got to entertain the crowd and put on a good show for the readers of the *Clarion Ledger*, don't we?" he said with a catch in his voice.

If it was a joke, it fell flat, and Michael watched him as he wandered off to find his seat in the seminar.

The beach had emptied. Corndog and the gangsters had disappeared, along with the police and their one-man nudist colony. All that remained was the endless sea, the millions of grains of sand on the beach, and the least terns, the least among us.

While Michael watched the beach, a man who had cop written all over him pulled up to the front of the hotel's huge canopy in a beat-up Ford. He unloaded a box full of files, a carousel projector, several trays of slides, and two boxes of Krispy Kreme doughnuts from the store down the road.

The armpits of his shirt were stained with sweat, and he wore a loud tie that was too long and sloppily tied in a large double knot. When attendants came out to help him, he tried to look pleasant, but it was more grimace than smile. The elegant hotel, whose marina had just been graced by Paul Newman and Joanne Woodward, epitomized luxury and swank, but the man's appearance screamed *cop*. Michael figured this must be their speaker, Detective Lieutenant Harry Falkner.

As Michael entered the conference room, hotel staff were pulling up the screen for the slides and passing out pads, pencils, and cold Cokes. The speaker called the crowd to order and warned anyone with a squeamish stomach to look away from the crime scene photos.

Lieutenant Falkner was a small, stocky man with a round head. He had removed his tie. White neck and chest hair showed around his open collar, patches of curls so long they could've been braided. There was a roll of jowl under his chin that jiggled like Jell-O when he talked. He had tried to disguise a receding hairline with an artful comb-over of cotton-like wisps of fine hair.

The nicotine-stained mouth precariously balancing a bouncing cigarette under his nose was big enough for two faces and two cigarettes. He was a chain smoker, constantly lighting one cigarette while he still smoked another. Michael thought he had the look of someone who had seen too much and drank too often to forget a life that had worn him down. He wondered if he had abandoned the loftier idealism of youth and surrendered to the commas and conjunctions that interrupted his dreams. He wondered if he was a man waiting for full stop, the big period of death.

Falkner was a better speaker than Michael might have imagined. The detective introduced himself as a former fullback at a small high school in New Mexico. He left for the big city to play at USC, but a knee injury ended his football career. He said he left the gridiron for a bigger game where he was the one who threw the flags for personal fouls and unnecessary roughness.

The old detective was thorough and meticulous in his re-creation of the crime scene and the events leading up to the murders ordered by Charles Manson. The crime scene photos were horrific, a gallery of gore, sadism, and unchained madness. The slides were ghoulish images from a nightmare, fuel for Michael, who often dreamed in Technicolor and excruciating detail. His narrative, accompanied by the visuals, disturbed Michael, who wanted to save damsels in distress, like the once beautiful Sharon Tate hanging from the ceiling, neck broken and blood seeping from a hundred stab wounds.

It only got worse on the second day of the training. As bad as the pictures of the Tate murder scene were, the thing that finished any thoughts Michael might have had about working homicide was the audio tape of Susan Atkins talking about killing Sharon Tate.

I was holding her arms behind her and she's looking at me…begging an-and crying: "Please don't kill me. Please don't kill me. I don't wanna die. I wanna live. I wanna have my baby. I wanna have my baby." And I looked her straight in the eye and I said, "Look, I don't care about you. I don't care about your baby. You better be ready. You're gonna die and I don't feel a thing about it."

And then I proceeded to stab her, okay? And you know what? I just kept stabbing her and stabbing her 'til she stopped screaming. No, I thought you understood. I LOVED her and in order for me to kill her I was killing part of myself when I killed her. In fact, Charlie gave us instructions to mutilate them. We were gonna cut out the baby if we had time. And there's more. Before, one guy we cut his head off and uh, three more out in the desert...and more besides. At least eleven. Eleven they'll never solve. And there's gonna be plenty more to come. We're gonna pick out the biggest pigs and execute them and release them from this Earth. You have to have a real love in your heart for people to do this for them, you know?

"And that, gentlemen, was the face of evil," Harry said.

"They used Tate's blood to write *Pig* on the front door, and the next day they killed Leno Labianca and his wife, Rosemary, in their home, stabbing them repeatedly. They also stabbed him with a fork and left it sticking out of his belly, a fork they used to carve the word 'War' on his stomach. This savagery shocked all Americans, all except for the Weathermen. We hear they adopted the sign of the fork as their power symbol and had Sharon Tate's picture hanging in the hall at their 1969 War Council meeting in Flint, Michigan. It was there one of the Weather Underground leaders said, 'Dig it! First they killed those pigs and then they put a fork in the pig's belly. Wild! Offing those rich pigs with their own forks and knives, and then eating a meal in the same room, far out! The Weathermen dig Charles Manson!'

"Manson and his crowd are in prison, but these terrorists are still hiding somewhere in America. They could be in your state. Those of you who are working undercover and going in and out of these flophouses and drug dens, please be the watchmen on the wall and watch for these criminals," he said.

On the last day of the training, Michael held up his hand and gestured toward the images displayed in a summary of the training. "How do you work cases like this without it changing you? How do you unsee all you've seen and erase it from your mind?" he asked.

Harry said, "That's a good question, Agent Parker, but I'm not sure I have the time or the smarts to make sense of it for you or me, but I try to remember I'm not the first guy investigating a murder. Cain, the first murderer, killed his brother Abel, and he tried to cover it up, to hide it from God. So here we are living east of Eden, and blood is still on the ground. Not much has changed, except they don't use stones much anymore to kill."

CHAPTER TWENTY-THREE

*"Then the LORD said to Cain, 'Where is
your brother Abel?' 'I don't know,' he
replied. 'Am I my brother's keeper?'"*
—*Genesis 4:9*

*"The voice of your brother's blood cries out
to Me from the ground."*—*Genesis 4:10*

The long day of brutal images finally ended just as a mulberry sun lingered on the horizon and burned a hole in the Gulf, transforming puffy white clouds into air castles of pink, peach, and mango.

Even hardened homicide investigators left the room without the usual banter and false bravado officers use to survive the hard profession they'd chosen. Some went to the bar, a few called their wives, and others went to church. A few men wandered down to the beach, sat by the edge of the water, and melted into the orange haze that had glazed the Gulf.

Michael stopped to browse the offerings of the upscale boutique in the hotel and to look at the restaurant's tables of polished silverware, elegant china, and crisp linen. He watched the elegant waiters and waitresses in the starched white jackets they wore like dress military uniforms. Then he retreated to his room to unwind and stare at snowy images on the old black-and-white TV in his room, but the distractions weren't working. Even as the half-light of dusk faded to black outside his window, the vivid pictures from the seminar stuck to his mind like weevils on cotton bolls.

The walls were closing in on him. He could see Sharon Tate hanging from the ceiling of his room and hear the babblings of her executioner. He walked to the elevators. Fresh air off the

Gulf sounded good. Maybe he'd run into other cops who were restless, too.

He punched the elevator button and tapped his toes to the loud beeping as the elevator passed each floor. When the silver doors opened, there stood none other than Senator Cornelius "Corndog" Ball. Two comely young women dressed to the nines, one white and one black, were attached to him, a call girl under each arm. He smoked a cigar almost as big as Senator "Big Jim" Eastland's Cuban Partagas. Ball wore a "cat that ate the canary" grin, pointy-toed Western boots, and a ten-gallon cowboy hat.

Michael hesitated. Corndog weaved to and fro like the leaning tower of the Delta and said, "Whatcha looking at, boy? Don't you know there's lots of flavors of ice cream in every scoop? These girls are gonna show me how to make a banana split. Aren't you, ladies?" he said. The girls were holding him up and grinning like two possums that had happened upon a dead cow carcass.

Michael hesitated. The senator was stoned, but if he recognized him through the fog, Michael's cover would be blown at the Leg Room.

"Well, poop or get off the pot, son. As sure as I'm the Supreme Honky Cracker of the Exalted Order of Redneck Peckerwoods, me and my girls got places to go!" he said.

The girls giggled and jiggled under their tight jeans and low-cut blouses. Michael stepped on the elevator, turned his back to the trio, and hit L for lobby. He could feel the hard stare from behind him, and the smell of alcohol and the pungent odor of marijuana smoke was overpowering in the small and poorly ventilated elevator. Breathing in the elevator was like licking an ashtray.

"Say, son, don't I know you?" the intoxicated senator asked.

"Don't think so. Just passing through," Michael said.

"I never forget a face, even when I'm plastered. Of cush… ah, a curse of being a politician. I meet so many little annoying drum-beaters while I'm conducting my orchestra," Corndog said, slurring his words.

"But I am skunked tonight. If I died in the arms of these lovely ladies, and they cremated me tonight, I'd probably burn for a week," he said.

The girls laughed and cooed, "Oh, Corndog, you're so cute."

"Course, they might just drain me and use me for their own personal still," he said. More uproarious cackling ensued.

The silence in the slow elevator was deafening as each floor passed like thick molasses poured from a narrow-mouthed jug.

"You a cop?" the senator blurted out.

"I'm a tourist passing through town, a would-be beach bum. Do I look like a cop?" Michael asked.

"The whole hotel is crawling with cops, some kinda training, I hear," Corndog said.

The elevator doors opened, and Michael stepped into the lobby and said, "Y'all have a nice night."

As they brushed by him, the red-headed escort brushed up against Michael and pinched his buttocks hard. Corndog said, "You, too...Jim. Son, if you can't hang with the big dogs, you better stay on the porch. Tell our Rambling Rose hello."

Michael watched him walk away with the girls, and he wondered if the drunken politician was just guessing or if he'd been burned. As they walked away, all three of his elevator companions sang an off-key version of "It's Crying Time Again" and swayed in unison, hips bumping hips, moving like the plastic hula dancers on car dashboards, left then right, right then left. Hands were in places where hands shouldn't be.

Michael walked by a loud room where an Elvis impersonator in a white jumpsuit was singing to a table of older women whose flowers of youth had wilted. The ladies wore t-shirts that read "Bug-eyed Ohio Buckeyes."

"Elvis" dropped to one knee in front of the ladies to tell them he was all shook up, just as Michael spotted the piano bar ahead. The crooning of the impersonator faded away, and soft jazz music soothed the solitary figures in the Trophy Lounge, where the owner's horse trophies lined the walls. There was something for everyone at the grand hotel.

Michael saw Harry the detective sitting alone at a corner table. He was nursing a straight-up glass of the daily double in the hotel's signature red glasses. The famous double had shaved ice, lime juice, Cointreau, rock and rye, and 151-proof rum, and the top was sprayed with a dash of brandy. If you survived the drink, you got to keep the red glass as a souvenir. The ashtray by Harry's drink was full of butts, two still smoking so much the detective and the table were engulfed by a haze of blue-gray smoke.

"Hey, Harry, mind if I join you?" Michael asked as he walked up to him.

"Pull up a chair, young mister narc agent, and I'll tell you some tales and try to answer the question you asked in class. Offer you a strong tonic?" Harry asked.

"No, thanks, I'll have the house wine," Michael said, signaling to the waitress, who could go skiing barefooted. God had given her a firm foundation for a job that required her to be on her feet.

She sized him up right away and said, "Let me guess. Iced tea?" she asked.

"What else?" Michael answered.

"You Southerners speak your own language down here, don't you? Well, suit yourself," Harry said, motioning to the waitress for another drink.

The more he drank, the more he talked and the more war stories he told. But they weren't the routine war stories told by cops to numb their pain or to overcompensate for the normal lives they'd sacrificed for the job. The dialogue was more a warning to a young officer or a confessional meeting with a priest to say, "Forgive me, Father, for I have sinned."

Harry's breathing was slow and labored, and his voice was raspy from too many cigarettes. His speech was a bit slurred, but he was not drunk.

"I don't know, Agent Parker. You're just starting your career, and this may seem over the top to you or just plain nuts, but in all my years in homicide, I've seen human beings at their worst, and it's easy to get a little numbed by it all. You experience what you think must be evil, but then after a while you sense there's more to the equation, an unknown dimension, and you're not so sure anymore. You begin to question the randomness of it all, and see the missing piece as some black thing let loose in the world to exploit the frailty and weaknesses of humanity," he said.

Michael nodded and listened intently. Harry was the teacher, and Michael was the student. Class was in session.

"It starts off small, like when you're with guys you work with. Everything's good. You're having a great time, a lot of laughs, and then somebody, an outsider, joins the group and everything changes. Everybody is still laughing, but you notice it isn't the same kind of laugh. It's forced and uneasy, and then you're all at each other's throats. Then you see the newcomer is watching and feeding off the discord. You want to think he's just another garden-variety manipulator, but you sense everything's changed, even the weather. The quietness is deafening, and the birds have stopped singing. A haze or fog settles over your world, and it begins to follow you everywhere. It's hard to put your finger on it, to figure it out, but after a long while of working murder cases, you encounter that spirit or entity again and again until you come to recognize its spoor," he said, taking another gulp of his drink.

"The murder cases might be completely different but yet they're similar, too similar, and you know you've seen it before. Sure there are different faces, stories, and motives, but that presence or stink is the common thread. You start to think you're only spinning your wheels, and you're nothing more than a housekeeper who keeps cleaning up after it, almost an accessory after the fact. You wonder if you're not an enabler, that if you didn't show up to investigate, it might not kill at all," he said as he called to the waitress for another round.

Michael was riveted by the detective's candid testimony. It somehow resonated with Michael, his past, and his time as a deputy sheriff. It made him think of Streeter, "The Pusher," his untimely end and his purported conversion in New Orleans.

"You know, Michael, I noticed some murderers were genuinely bewildered at their actions. Not the usual denials and professions of innocence, but the times when you see their eyes change right in the middle of an interrogation. It's like something leaves them, an entity that jumps in and out of bodies like those old alien movies. It's not male or female but a dark, dark thing… ancient and terrifying.

"Who knows? Maybe it came on some UFO like those B movies when I was a kid, maybe out of the desert at Roswell. Maybe it's always been here since it slithered up to Eve in the Garden and destroyed the world with an apple. After a while, you think you've lost it, and you become detached to survive. You suspect everyone and trust no one because the one you trust might be the dark thing itself all dressed up to sneak up on you," Harry said as he held the cold drink to his fevered forehead and sighed.

While Harry talked to him, Michael noticed Harry seemed to be looking beyond him, maybe for the thing he was obsessed with.

"There was this one case I assisted on because I used to attend parties with the people involved. They were decent, sociable people, and I couldn't believe it. It was not murder but attempted murder twice. A man's wife tried to poison him. I interviewed him after they pulled him back from taking his last breath. He lay in his bed writhing in pain, alone and losing his bowels in the night, but after the hospital saved his life, he wouldn't believe his sweet wife could ever harm him. He thought it had to be a big mistake, and he brushed it off. Then she hired a hit man to kill him, but we were watching her.

"You wonder how that could happen. She was a successful Realtor, but one day she showed a house to a man, just a Realtor alone with her client. She fell in love or lust that day with a man she later described to us as the 'spawn of the devil.' Once upon a time, I wouldn't have believed her, but after all I've seen, I believed every word she said. Her husband did, too. She went to prison, and he waited on her all those years. He took her back and they're now living happily ever after. She told me one night that something dark had invaded her soul when she met that man. She said it wasn't love, and it wasn't just lust. It was the beast who told her the price of being with him was killing her husband. No one knows where that man or thing is now," Harry said, taking a long drag off his Marlboro.

"Whew, you've seen some stuff, Harry," Michael said.

"I'm just a sour old bloodhound that caught the scent. I don't know why I did and others didn't, but I get suspicious when cases seem too easy, too pat, and I feel like someone has handed me a gold-plated sledgehammer to kill a fly that isn't even buzzing anymore. After a while, I became a man obsessed and spent my spare time tracking this thing and cross-referencing cases, dates, places, and similarities.

"Once I bugged the house of a politician, someone I suspected of being the thing itself. While I was listening, he found the bug. I don't know how he knew, but he knew. He just knew. I don't know how. I could hear him breathing, his hot breath on the mike, and then, while I watched the house with my binoculars, he opened the window, sneered, and beckoned me to come in. Not much scares me, but I ran and never looked back. It's something outside the law of this world, savagery without a conscience. It broke me, Michael, but nobody cared or believed. Just clear cases, they said. Guilty or not, find someone to offer up as a sacrifice to satiate the public bloodlust," Harry said.

Michael's throat was parched, and his hand trembled a bit when he picked up his glass. He realized the waitress was suddenly giving their table a wide berth. He also noticed two men who had quietly entered the bar and were sitting at a nearby table. It was the two men he'd seen with Corndog on the beach.

"Clay Strickland, our Chief of Intelligence, told me he felt it when he was an officer in Vietnam. He said you could just smell it. Like you said, it might be a man who could subtly change every conversation, turn men against each other, and make them see each other differently. He said he could pit brother against a brother, or 'he' could be a woman who used men and played to their weaknesses until her darkness overwhelmed their light. It was all the same somehow. He said he and the other officers talked about such things one night when they bivouacked during an intelligence mission along the Ho Chi Minh trail.

"They captured a Viet Cong soldier who was babbling incoherently about meeting a thing in the jungle, something like the devil or what he called his number six Via. The translation of his language was hard, but it was related to fallen angels who had developed feelings of rebellion in heaven and were kicked out to roam the earth. He said the man was literally scared out of his skin and believed his three souls and seven spirits had left his body when he met Satan in the jungle. He kept hollering for those wandering, lost souls and spirits to come back. 'Please come back to my body now!' he cried over and over.

"Clay said it was some kind of strange mix of Christianity and Buddhism, but they found a pocket-sized Bible in his backpack with Revelation 12:9 underlined: 'And the great dragon was thrown down, the serpent of old who is called the devil and Satan, who deceives the whole world; he was thrown down to the earth, and his angels were thrown down with him.' When the man saw the soldiers reading the verse, he told them it was once accepted truth long before the great deception when Buddhism was introduced to them two thousand years ago.

"After the soldiers heard and saw all that, Clay said they peered into the night and checked their weapons. The jungle seemed to close in on them, but it wasn't the Communists they feared," Michael said.

"Yeah, that's some strong stuff...gives me chill bumps. It was like what I felt on the Manson case. You got the gun, the badge, and all the power, but you could sense it laughing at you, toying with you. You look into the pit, the black hole of this existence, and something there is staring back at you. You can smell it, taste it, and hear it like a humming, a shrill sound that won't stop when you cover your ears. That's when you suddenly realize how puny we are, how insignificant. We're just dumb prey, a herd of wildebeests on the Serengeti, and the beast is stalking, waiting to bludgeon us and drag us back to hell's kitchen to fry our souls," he said as he took another long drink and snuffed another smoldering cigarette into his overflowing ashtray.

"Harry, you're scaring me, or maybe I'm scaring me," Michael said, managing a weak laugh.

"I know. I scare me sometimes. By the way, who're those guys over there who seem to be watching us? They look at us like we're the slowest, weakest wildebeests in the herd, and they're Neanderthals fresh out of the caves with the biggest clubs," Harry said, instinctively patting the pistol on his hip.

"I see them. Not sure what the game is," Michael said.

"They're not here for me, Michael. It's you they're after," Harry said.

"I know, but let's get back to your tales of the supernatural," Michael said.

"Yeah, as I said, there were times I scared myself. I even suspected I might be him…it. I questioned the face in the mirror each day to see if it was still me or only an imposter or if it ever *was* me. You know the monster wasn't under the bed but in my head. I found myself home alone after my divorce, afraid the darkness would find me, and I got to thinking about nursing my gun barrel and checking out.

"I began to drink heavily and almost killed my liver, until I slowed my booze intake down to the pace of a sailor on shore leave. I kept asking the big casino Dealer to reshuffle the deck and deal again, hoping for a better hand that never came. Yeah, I had nothing left to believe in, so I decided to believe in Him. Sometimes I wish He would come back and cast all the demons into the swine and let them drown in the sea," Harry said, pointing upward.

Then he smiled at Michael and said, "Of course, if the demons left the dead pigs, they'd probably all come back as politicians in Washington!"

They both laughed loudly and broke the tension. Harry stood and weaved a bit before shaking Michael's hand, pumping it like the ancient handle on the artesian well in Parker Grove. Michael thought his arms even squeaked like the old rusty pump handle.

"Ever meet anyone like the evil I describe, Agent Parker?" he asked.

"Yeah, I think so, but they styled their hair to hide their horns and others wore a halo to hide the venom of a serpent. In a movie theater long ago, I met a man who didn't hide it. He had snake eyes, and when he looked at me, it was like watching a serpent uncoil," Michael said.

CHAPTER TWENTY-FOUR

"...and over it there goes forever—black-pinioned winging its solitary and hopeless flight, the raven of his anxious thoughts, and finds no place to rest, and comes back again to the desolate ark with its foreboding croak of evil in the present and evil in the future."—Alexander MacLaren

"Homo homini lupus est...Man is a wolf to his fellow man."—ancient Roman saying

Time had flown by listening to the L.A. detective. Michael bid Harry farewell and thanked him for the tutorial. Just before he walked away, the old detective motioned toward the men still watching them and said, "The big one with the scarred face looks like he's been coughed up from the bowels of hell. He could be the one. He could be it. Be careful, Michael. The viper hates you."

The crowd in the lounge had thinned. Fresh-faced airmen from Pensacola in their starched uniforms and military buzz cuts were filing out after dancing proper dances in the ballroom with their proper dates. If they hurried, they could catch a few winks before early reveille.

Leon Kelner, who had come to Biloxi from the Roosevelt Room in New Orleans, moved from the cadet ball to the piano in the lounge. He began to tickle the ivory keys in a haunting rendition of the theme from *The Godfather*, a tune dominating the airwaves on FM radio. He had a kind face that looked as though he had smiled through too much adversity. Music was his ticket to a kinder world, Michael suspected. A lighted rack of bottles of amber liquid shadowed his face as he looked up at Michael and smiled.

"This gangster melody is for you and for the gentlemen waiting for you. Walk softly and hurry along," he said.

The two goons watched as Michael and Harry parted. As Michael passed near their table on the way out, Michael glanced at them and thought the guy with the scarred face and heavy brows could have been a movie villain right out of central casting.

The man glared at him with empty eyes and said, "Evening, Officer." He wore a grayish t-shirt under his jacket bearing the word Mosca's, a famous mob restaurant in Louisiana.

"Excuse me, are you talking to me?" Michael asked.

"Yeah, Jim, I am, or is that even your real name? You're the one sitting with the famous L.A. detective, aren't you? Who was the old man telling you all his war stories, your brother of the badge or your daddy? Be careful you don't let those stories go to your head. You might get dandruff in Biloxi and your daddy may find you and your 'Head and Shoulders' in the local landfill," the man said, smirking, challenging.

Michael should have ignored him, and he knew it. *You don't bark back at every mutt that barks at you, but sometimes you just surrender to the urge to push back when you're pushed.*

Michael smiled back at him and said, "They might find the cradle your daddy rocked you in there, too. You know, the one with his initials carved on the side…666."

The man with the tracked face and strange mark on his neck stopped smiling. His eyes narrowed, blood-swollen veins protruded from his forehead, and he squeezed the glass he was holding so hard the glass cracked.

Then he threw his head back in a throaty braying, like a mule drunk on corn mash. "Death can't be prettified, pretty boy, and it must be respected. You're the reason we have pencils with big erasers and sharp shovels to bury the remains we've erased," he spat through clenched brown teeth. Little flecks of spittle rode his words like errant missiles and clung to his teeth and the corners of his mouth.

The darkness around the man was suffocating. Michael could barely breathe. *Move on*, he heard a voice inside him say.

"The holes they'll dig for us will all be the same size, but they'll probably bury you a little deeper to make sure you don't rise again," Michael answered.

The man didn't seem to blink as often as most people, but when he did, his eyelids moved in slow motion. The opacity of his eyes suggested that any small thing could trigger a hidden rage simmering at the back of those caverns. It was the type of face that gave society an excuse to cage other humans, the same feral look Michael once saw in a chained three-legged dog that had chewed off its leg to escape its tether.

The thin, sunburned man next to scarface scooted his chair back, reached for something under the table, and began to rise as Michael's hand moved toward the sidearm under his jacket. Scarface growled at his companion, "Not here, Jake the Rake."

As Michael turned to walk away, lobsterman said, "Okay, Split Nose."

The name stopped Michael in his tracks: Johnny "Split Nose" Gagliano. He knew he looked familiar when he saw him on the beach. Gagliano was the man who had murdered Arnold the pedophile. He didn't know whether to arrest him or give him a medal, but Michael felt vulnerable.

From what he'd read in the file, Split Nose had done the mob's dirty deeds since he was a kid working horse races, dope, slots, houses of ill repute, labor unions, and delivering kickbacks to cops and firemen before graduating to become Marcello's enforcer. He and his goons still controlled the wards in New Orleans and swung the balance of power to their political allies in local and state races. Everyone in his neighborhoods knew they needed to request help to vote, even if they weren't illiterate. Those who didn't play along wound up in the hospital or the morgue. He was a one-man crime wave.

"I bet they keep starry-eyed pups like you around for good public relations and trot you out with your earnest Boy Scout face to impress the gray-hairs in churches and civic clubs. You're a proper officer of the law, and you don't soil your hands with dirty deeds, do you? You want to arrest me, maybe gun me down like a dog in the street with no warning, but your sticky code of honor won't allow you to dispense private justice, will it?" Split Nose said, taunting Michael.

Jake the Rake bared his teeth and emitted a high-pitched heh-heh-heh hyena laugh.

"Maybe, maybe not, but sometimes enemies can be friends, or at least call a truce for a moment so they can stop men who harm little girls," Michael answered.

It might have been a sucker punch and the dumbest thing Michael had done recently, but for a brief moment, he saw that Split Nose was surprised, and his eyes softened. He spoke with more eloquence than Michael might have imagined.

"I heard there was a man who took up for the girl named Charity. Did the news of Arnold's death give you a secret, guilty pleasure, Mr. Policeman? Never mind. I don't care about the pushers and pimps there. The senator thinks he knows you from somewhere. If you mean him harm, that conflicts with our business plans, and we can't have that. Unless you want to dissuade me of my concerns, or if you're not prepared to be reasonable and go along and get along in the parade, then we're at an impasse, and what could be a victory parade will be your death march to the county morgue," he said.

"I've always been leery of parades and crowds. When you blindly follow the masses, the *m* is often silent," Michael said.

"All right then. As a courtesy, I'll give you a head start, friend. I'll also give you this pearl as a token of timeouts. They opened an oyster here today and gave this to me," he said as he held up the pristine white jewel.

"Thanks, but no thanks. I already have a Pearl in my life," Michael said.

"Then the clock starts now. This place and this hotel are on the Sin Strip. You had better depart the Broadwater, part the Red Sea, and run for the Bible Belt, else you might wind up like Judas for betraying us. This could be your Akeldama. Did they tell you I killed my own brother for crossing my boss? Why would I hesitate to kill you?" he said.

The piano music was no longer playing. The lounge had emptied, and no one was in sight. The staff had scattered. Michael could have called local cops to roust the men or tried to arrest the men himself, but he didn't feel that would go well, and wasn't sure what the charge would be. There was no warrant out for Split Nose that he knew of, and too big a fuss would destroy his value as an undercover agent far beyond his current cases. It looked as though his cover was already blown, but the damage could be contained. Corndog might have sicced his mad dogs on him just to see what they could pry loose. Split Nose could be faking and making idle threats, but when it came to violence, Michael didn't think he had to fake something so ingrained. It was easy to see him as the baby who reached up to strangle his mother's obstetrician during childbirth. He was born mean.

Michael nodded and walked briskly toward the elevator. Life was now measured in minutes, maybe seconds. The doors opened quickly. As he entered, he could see the men rising from their table. Michael got off on his floor but obeyed the sudden urge to abandon his overnight bag and get out of Dodge. It wasn't pretty or graceful, but he sprinted directly to the stairwell door and hurried down four flights of stairs that led to the exit door near the rear parking area.

Michael cracked open the exit door to the back lot and let his eyes adjust to the dim glow of two pole lights high above the cars in the lot. It was warm, too warm, and a foul smell was in the air. One light was buzzing and flickering on and off, a Morse code warning of impending disaster—three dots, three dashes, and three dots.

His eyes finally adjusted, and he waited and watched for a long time. Then he heard a noise in the stairwell above him, someone coming down the stairs fast. No, it was more than one and they were stumble-running. One shouted, "Slow down!" The other man cursed. There was a loud metal clanging, and the third floor fire extinguisher came bouncing down the stairs.

Michael pushed out of the door and ran for his car. He was out of breath when he dove into his state vehicle. The Ford cranked just as the two men burst out of the stairwell. He gave thanks for good batteries, slammed the gear shift to drive, and gunned the car right at them. They jumped out of his way, and the air turned blue from their curses as he roared past them.

Michael heard a loud pop, the report of a pistol, and the whining treble of a ricochet off his back window. He instinctively ducked his head as he shot down the drive, dodging a service van and barely missing a shapeless woman and a toothless man exiting the side door of the hotel. He ran through two shrubs, fishtailed left and right, and then bumped onto Highway 90, the main drive along the beach.

Improvising on the fly, his plan was to outrun them and lose them in the countryside. He would take Highway 90 to Highway 49 and head north toward Hattiesburg and Jackson. It was after midnight and traffic was light. As Michael sped down the highway, he could see lights of crabbers and fishermen moving down the beach, and beyond them the outline of a tugboat pushing a lighted barge.

Adrenalin and his pounding heart magnified all the night sounds. He could hear the humming and whining of his tires on the pavement until he ran through a fresh patch of asphalt laid that day by state road crews. Then his tires made sticky, squishing sounds, and he could hear the asphalt peppering the rear fenders of his car.

A giant white egret loomed up in front of his windshield, spooked from roosting by nocturnal beachcombers. He swerved to dodge the ghost-like bird and roared on toward Gulfport, passing the turn to the Ship Island ferry somewhere in the dark to his left. Campers had accidently burned down the island's old wooden lighthouse, but Michael had been playing with his own fire tonight and wasn't looking for flames at sea. His eyes were glued to his rearview mirror, searching for the lights of pursuers behind him.

He saw no one following him and breathed a premature sigh of relief. One moment they weren't there, and then they were. Bouncing headlights appeared and looked to be closing on him like a rocket. With his window down, he could hear the whine of the car's engine in the distance and the sudden interruption of sound when they shifted gears.

Michael thought of his drag races when he was a teenager, and he floored the bureau car, dodging construction barrels and hugging the tight curves on the coastal highway. Just before Long Beach, he roared into Gulfport and took a hard right onto Highway 49.

He fishtailed and skidded onto the sidewalk, narrowly missing two staggering drunk sailors and their dates leaving the Babylon Bar, a seedy club specializing in greasy burgers on cracked plates, hard liquor in dirty glasses, and local bands that worked cheap. A short thumping blare of "I'm a road runner, baby" came before the door closed behind the double daters with a "Beep-Beep, Schrooooam!"

The sailors were attached shoulder and hip to painted, halter-topped women who took a percentage of the drinks sailors and marines bought for girls in local joints. If need be, they weren't above rolling the sailors when they passed out after drunken intimacy. Shaded pink by the blinking neon lights that bathed the two couples with promises of heaven on earth, the women with red smears for mouths looked too old, too bitter, and too hard for the skinny young servicemen. In the harsh light of morning, the sailors might find their cheap musky perfume hard to wash out of their uniforms and nostrils.

Michael saw the streaking reflections of his car in the windows of storefronts as he sped through the mostly abandoned streets of old Gulfport. Michael thought the images looked like the Starship Enterprise when Captain Kirk engaged warp drive to bend space and propel his ship faster than the speed of light.

The headlights had turned with him, scattering the foursome at the club, and were gaining on him again. A homeless man with a bottle of wine was passed out near an inner city mission building whose flashing sign said *Jesus Saves*. Michael roared by him and the mission and through the crossing just as he saw the street sign that said *Dip*.

His tires left the pavement, and the car became airborne momentarily. When his tires hit the pavement, the shocks groaned and creaked, and he heard a metallic sound. Sparks flew from the rear of his car, lighting the dark night like sparklers and Roman candles at old family Christmas rituals in Parker Grove.

Michael didn't care if local police stopped him now; he was looking for late-night cruisers. He would welcome any relief, and the people in the car behind him weren't shy about flaunting traffic laws, either. They ran the light, and their car looked like Evel Knievel jumping a line of buses when they shot out of the dip. The car soared, bounced, and nosedived into the pavement, and showered a stray dog with sparks when it reconnected with the asphalt.

When Michael looked away from the scene in his rearview mirror, he saw a black cat with yellow eyes crossing the road in front of him. The big Halloween kitty had the "cat in the headlights" look and froze in the middle of the road. Michael swerved to miss it, and his left tires took a deep trench left open by a utility crew. Grit, grime, and sludge splattered his car and spun out from under the wheel wells, smearing the left side of his car and the side windows with mud and sludge. His tires spun and whined for traction, but he wrestled his car from the trench and corrected his path just as his pursuers hit the poor cat with their Mercedes and flipped it up and onto their windshield.

Michael was still thinking about how much bad luck that dead cat had to be when a young man in knee pads jumped the curb of the sidewalk to roller skate across the street in front of Michael. His eyes went wide and wild when he saw Michael's car. Michael wrenched the steering wheel hard to the right to avoid the skater and flattened a parking meter and plowed through two garbage cans. Garbage and other debris settled around the skater like rain, and the empty cans bounced into the path of his pursuers.

Michael righted his chariot, demanded all the state car had to give, and left skaters, cats, and drunks behind when he exited the city limits of Gulfport and hit the open highway. Exhaustion tugged at him, and his arms ached. He felt the need to prop his heavy eyes open with toothpicks.

He remembered a late-night speed trap Clay had told him about. The Mississippi Highway Patrol often ran radar just north of Gulfport to catch impatient Yankee tourists on their long trip south to the beach.

He sped through Landon, Nugent, and Lyman toward Saucier, but still no sign of a local cop or an MHP unit. Where's a cop when you need one? He was in open country on 49 under a canopy of stars. The starlight was his umbrella and compass in a high-speed race from death, light that had begun its journey to earth from frozen space around the time of the founding of America.

Houses, tin sheds, pecan groves, and scrub pines were blurs outside his window, and small American flags attached to mailboxes flapped in the whoosh of the draft made by his car. Telephone poles became a picket fence, lines on the road looked like dots before him, and the fender of his car scraped the guard rails on the small bridges he crossed.

His speedometer showed he was doing 86 miles per hour on a narrow two-lane road, but the Mercedes was hanging with him. It was so close he could hear the barking of their tires when they shifted gears and smell the diesel and the hot, burning rubber when they skidded around the curves behind him.

Then he saw a giant sign...*The Heart of Dixie*. Sticking out from behind the billboard was the front end of a gray MHP cruiser. He floored it again and zipped by a startled patrolman drinking coffee and eating doughnuts. Just as the fumbling patrolman dropped his sugar snacks and hit the blue lights, the gangsters whizzed by him, and the patrol car fell in behind them.

Michael cut on his hidden police scanner and heard the officer radio for backup. "This is unit 22. I'm in pursuit of two cars traveling north at a high rate of speed on Highway 49 south of Saucier. Request intercept from unit 24 and roadblocks by any available cars."

Every time the officer transmitted, Michael could hear the wail of his siren through the scanner. The trooper had the presence of mind to get Michael's tag number and he radioed it in with the tag number of the gangster car. Then the patrolman radioed that Michael's pursuers were pulling over. He said he needed backup and someone to head off the lead car.

"On my way south, ten minutes from you," another unit answered.

Michael knew it wouldn't be long until he met the southbound patrol unit. He saw one of the many makeshift fresh fruit and vegetable stands Mississippi farmers had erected along Highway 49 to lure hungry tourists. He whipped in behind the stand, cut his lights off, and played dead. *Run Silent, Run Deep* was one of his favorite war movies.

Two minutes later, he heard the approaching siren of the southbound MHP patrolman. He passed Michael's hidden position like a streak of piercing blue flame in the night. Michael jumped out of his car with his screwdriver and quickly replaced his untraceable tag with another spare tag Clay had given him.

He proceeded north on back roads, weaving his way toward Jackson. He only saw one MHP unit hidden in the shadows of an old barn. Oddly enough, the trooper only bumped his blue lights and didn't give chase as Michael passed him. Michael breathed a sigh of relief. All the action appeared to be south of him now. He listened to chatter on the scanner, and from what he could tell, his pursuers had been cuffed and were being transported to the local county jail for speeding, reckless driving, failing to yield to an officer, and possession of firearms.

As he entered the city limits of Jackson, the deep-purple shadows began to bleed a drizzling rain. The headlights of oncoming cars sparkled like diamonds, and he squinted against the glare. He felt dirty, empty, and damp from sweat and fear.

He heard the dispatcher for the Highway Patrol radio the first officer: "Unit 22, the tag you sent on the other car didn't come back. You must have copied it wrong. That tag has never been issued." Like the sheriff Michael and Rose had encountered, that impossibility had yet to register with other agencies as an MBN anomaly. It was a new wrinkle with no irons in sight.

He switched off his scanner and cut on his AM radio. He spun his dial to a station playing a tribute to Mahalia Jackson, who had just passed away. Her rich, powerful voice began to sing. "Didn't it rain, children? It rained forty days and forty nights. 'Brother Noah, can't you take on more?' Noah cried, 'No, you're full of sin. God got the key and you can't get in.'"

The adrenalin of the night had worn thin, and Michael was exhausted when he pulled into the parking lot and stumbled into his apartment. He tried his control agent but got no answer. He rang Clay, who did answer, and in a rushing, gushing pouring out of the events of the night, Michael recommended a return to Moondog Square before chatter from the coast found its way to Jackson.

As fatigue and stress slurred his words, he told Clay they needed to warn Molly and find out how much damage Rose had done. Clay startled him awake twice on the phone and advised him to get a good night's sleep and report to headquarters the next day.

Just as Michael hung up, the drizzle turned into a downpour. He had always liked the sounds of raindrops and thunder at night. It was a curtain to pull, a place to hide in the thick gray clouds of thunderstorms surrounded by the humid smell of earth and water. The driving rain was whipping the trees, cleansing the streets, and tapping a rhythmic lullaby on his roof to soothe an exhausted traveler. The water was pooling on the sills and lisping against the window panes of his apartment, saying *phat* when it meant *splat*.

With the rhythm of the rain, the peals of thunder, and the flashes of lightning, Michael ran out of juice and collapsed on his couch. He had literally dodged a bullet and survived a wild ride through the countryside.

Michael felt lucky. He felt blessed. He felt alive. He felt like a man who had found a pile of pennies, pennies from heaven. He fell asleep thinking of a murdered woman and her unborn child, a man called Split Nose who carried .45-caliber erasers, and the obsessions of old homicide cops haunted by their nightmares.

He dreamt of a broken girl named Molly, Sharon Tate, and a dogged L.A. detective. They were all pitching pennies into puddles of rain.

"Didn't it rain, children?"

CHAPTER TWENTY-FIVE

"…these vignettes I sketch for you—what
are they? Watercolors…yes and
dreams blurred with tears…"
—John Geddes, "A Familiar Rain"

"People who cannot receive a blessing
from God, will demand it of men."
—Rosaria Butterfield

While Michael was running for his life, MHP Officer Red Winter was pulling a shift for another patrolman near Hattiesburg when he heard all the radio chatter near Saucier. He had left the homicide seminar early after receiving word from Corndog that he wouldn't need his services. Red had seen the two women in the lobby of the Broadwater, favorites of the senator, and he knew it meant Corndog would likely stay overnight at a friend's condo in Long Beach.

Red was running radar south of Hattiesburg when he heard the description of cars MHP troopers were chasing and knew immediately who was involved. He often disappeared when he had covert or extralegal jobs to perform for his patrons. This time Red decided to make it official. He radioed headquarters to tell them he was en route to Saucier to assist fellow officers.

The radio chatter increased as he drove south. He heard Unit 22 radio he was pulling over a Mercedes with two occupants, and he needed backup. Red knew the officer would need plenty of backup if he was right about the men in that car. He heard the officer's request for someone to intercept the lead car still headed north on 49 at a high rate of speed. Red knew it had to be Michael and that he probably had a scanner to monitor the radio traffic, too. He tried to guess at what Michael would do.

Red figured Michael would lie low somewhere to avoid the southbound patrol unit, put on another unregistered tag, and then take back roads toward Jackson. He knew the perfect place to intercept the stuffy MBN agent.

Red remembered when he was first assigned as an unofficial aide to politicians in Jackson. Corndog was a new senator then, and he watched as the elder statesman of the Leg Room schooled Red on the finer points of living and dying in what they called…"Nod."

"We offer a specialized menu to the chosen few who opt to serve our needs, Mr. Winter. If you tell us you don't want to dine with us and eat from our menu of money, that's as bad as telling the chefs their menu is unfair to cannibals. We can remedy that, son. We can add you to the menu, and the political machine will eat you alive, and your career and life will be over…if you get my drift," the man said.

Red knew getting into bed with these people was like playing chess with pigeons. No matter how good you are, the pigeons will eventually knock over your kings and knights, poop all over the board, and then strut back and forth like they beat you at the rigged game they invented. But he figured he didn't have much choice. If you are offered associate membership and refuse, you are no longer neutral.

A life of "Yes, sir, Boss" began, and Red adopted his live and let live, go along and get along philosophy of hear no evil, see no evil, and speak no evil when his political masters were involved, but on a night when a fellow cop was running for his life, MHP Officer Winter chose to be a law enforcement officer again. Red had a feeling Parker was the fly in the champagne he'd been drinking, but he decided all that he saw, heard about, or things done or said by Agent Michael Parker were now buried in the same convenient case of memory loss once reserved for people like Corndog.

After Michael zipped past his hideout, Red decided not to chase after him. He bumped his blue lights once as a salute to a man all alone, running as hard as he could for the finish line, a man he begrudgingly admired. He radioed the "all clear" to other units looking for him. Red said, "No sign of him up this way. I think we've lost him, boys."

Then Red had a funny thought. *If I stopped chasing the wrong things, maybe the right things would have a chance to catch me.*

****

"What's that annoying sound?" Tupelo lawyer Reggie Morris wondered. His phone had been ringing for five minutes, but Reggie was in the grips of late-night toddies and his usual p.m. sedatives, and he slept through the noise until it finally burrowed into his pickled brain.

"Hello," he mumbled, as he rattled the receiver around on its cradle. "This had better be important," he spat.

"Reggie, this is Arturo Marcello. I've been trying to reach you for Don Carlos," the voice said.

Reggie sat straight up in bed, instantly sober and wide-eyed, when he heard the voice of the consigliere for the Marcello family.

"Yes, yes, Arturo, my friend. What can I do for you?" Reggie asked.

"We have a situation in this backwater town, Saucier, Mississippi. Johnny Gagliano and his associate, Jake Poretto, have been arrested, and the Don wants you to go there right now to bail them out and take care of this before it gets out of hand. The locals are playing hardball, and business will suffer as long as Johnny is in jail," the Mafia counsel said.

"Saucier is a long way from Tupelo. Don't you have anyone closer?" Reggie whined.

Silence…long…cold…silence.

"But of course I'll go. I'll get dressed and drive there immediately," Reggie said.

"A plane out of Memphis will land in Tupelo in thirty minutes to pick you up," Marcello said.

"So soon?" Reggie said.

"Cani abbaia e voi pasci. Cu' vigghia, la pigghia," Marcello said in Sicilian.

"I'm sorry, Arturo. I don't understand Sicilian," Reggie said.

"Dogs bark and oxen graze. The early bird catches the worm," Marcello replied.

"Yes, you're right. I'll be at the airport shortly," Reggie said.

Reggie jumped out of bed, mumbling curses and heart racing. His little white dog cowered in the corner as Reggie vented to his precious Peaches, who always listened intently. "Flying to south Mississippi in the middle of the night in this rain is crazy, Peaches! But the money's good, and I'm in, and you can't say no when you're in. There's only one way out after you're in. Same with the Klan when I went to Fayette to defend Tupelo's Grand Dragon when he went down there to kill Charles Evers. These guys don't play. I met Johnny, the guy they call Split Nose, at the Don's party at Mosco's. Only one man ever scared me more…Fredrick Hamel."

Peaches whined and hid under the bed at the mention of the name.

****

Corndog was snoring like a broken buzz saw when he startled out of a drug- and alcohol-induced sleep in a Long Beach condo owned by the Marcello family. He was screaming and calling Melba's name, then Sheler's.

"Melba! Melba! Where are you? Are you in the bayou? Little Sheler, where are you, child? Vultures are pecking your eyes out, and the gators are snapping at your toes!" Corndog cried, his eyes wild with terror and bleeding guilt.

The two girls sharing his bed were paid to keep him happy, and they were afraid. The one with hair like ripe red tomatoes protested in a voice that sounded like a broken flute, "Who, Senator? No one is here but us. Don't we make you happy, baby?"

They'd seen him in a bad way before, but never like this. One began to stroke his hair while the other whispered sweet nothings to him.

"Get your cold fingers of death off me, you gold-diggers! Get out! Get out now!" Corndog screamed.

"Okay, baby, but what did we do? We promised Johnny we'd be good to you. Don't tell him you're unhappy, or he'll hurt us," the girls pleaded.

"It's okay, just leave. Here's some money," Corndog said, grabbing a wad of bills from the nightstand and tossing the greenbacks at them.

The clueless girls gathered their things in a hurry and left the condo. Corndog sat on the side of his bed wondering how he got here, how he had become who he was. He had gotten word the DEA had intercepted his patron's cotton bales near New Orleans and Charleston. The bales were stuffed with white heroin, and the Feds were asking questions about his gin in Greenville. *Then this guy at the Broadwater tonight who had been in the Leg Room with Rose, and these mobsters always demanding more and more legislation, more parties, and more accommodations from business friends and supporters.* He put his hands over his ears to stop the voices shouting at him.

"It's a house of cards, and I'm holding only deuces and treys. I got the free stuff, but it had strings, and now the strings are choking me, the interest is compounding, and I'm paying and paying and paying," he moaned, holding his head in his hands.

He jumped up, threw back the curtains, and stumbled out the glass doors onto the lanai. His heart was pounding, his knees were knocking, and his hands trembled as he reached for the rail to steady himself. There was rough stubble of beard on his face, and his hair was cobweb wispy. His eyes were sunken, his posture stooped, and he suddenly felt frail and vulnerable.

The moon lingered over the Gulf, and the wind blowing through the lanai carried the pungent odor of decay and rot. If he wasn't killed or sent to prison, he suddenly saw what his future held. He and his fellow politicians would hang on until the sappy lines no longer worked, the young girls would no longer come around, and the phone calls would cease from party bigwigs and the movers and shakers in Washington.

Corndog and his contemporaries would juggle the balls until they began to squabble like children. They would no longer cut deals on major legislation but on who got the last jelly doughnut on the dessert tray at the Sun-n-Sand. They'd keep at it in the Leg Room until their parts wore out, until even their imaginative perversions wouldn't be enough to sustain their illusion of power.

Then they'd play bocce ball until their knees wore out or sit hunched over faded checker boards, pretending and remembering, waiting for the Debt Collector. As the end of the road and judgment drew near, they'd drink themselves into oblivion, and their doctors would point to images of their vascular system and make comments about clogged drains. Then finality would arrive, the day when no one crawled, bowed, and begged before them anymore. It would be over and a fate worse than death realized…irrelevance.

Corndog sighed, gagged, and then threw up over the rail, again and again. People on the lanai below him shouted at him, and he returned their obscenities. He wiped his mouth with the back of his hand and said, "It's all been one long, hellish hiccup. One day you're the big rooster, the cock of the walk, and the next day you're just a plucked feather duster."

****

"We gotta pull over, Johnny. Adam-12 is on us like fleas on a dog!" Jake the Rake shouted at Split Nose over the wail of the MHP siren. Skinny Jake was always the only one who could reason with the volatile Big Johnny. They were tight, Jake so skinny and Johnny so burly that Marcello called them "Mr. Thick and Mr. Thin."

"Tonight ends with this? We're roadkill for some hick highway cop?" Split Nose complained through gritted teeth.

When Split Nose and Jake the Rake yielded to the MHP cruiser bumping their taillights, Split Nose was furious that Michael had escaped. He knew this mistake would be hard to explain to his Godfather. After they pulled over, Split Nose was still pounding the dash of the car in a blind rage when the bullhorn from behind ordered him and his partner to exit the car with their hands up.

Other law enforcement units converged on the scene, and when the boys from New Orleans exited their car, a sea of blue lights surrounded them. Silhouetted against the flashing lights were men with sidearms and shotguns drawn and aimed at Michael's pursuers.

Spread-eagled on the car trunk, Split Nose protested as he was cuffed. "Where's the guy in the other car? You didn't get him, but you protect your own, don't you?" he spat.

The MHP officer said, "Our own? What does that mean?"

"Forget it. I want my lawyer," a sullen Split Nose said.

When they arrived at the jail, everyone came to see them. This was not just another routine night for the Harrison County Jail. Trustees had already alerted inmates some hard cases were coming in. The jail was full to the brim and overflowing with petty thieves, dopers, sex perverts, drunks, men arrested on old traffic and child support warrants, and inmates awaiting transport to Parchman.

After they were fingerprinted, Johnny was given his one call to his lawyer, Arturo, consigliere for the family in New Orleans, but Arturo told him friends of the Don had already called them, and Reggie was on his way.

"When you are released, come straight here. Carlos wants to see you," the consigliere said.

When the Marshmallow men entered the central lockup, the poor ventilation and pungent air were overwhelming. The whole place smelled dank and moldy. Split Nose thought it stunk like a tavern full of alcoholics had consumed a truckload of stale beer, used the lockup as a urinal, and died there.

A big inmate with a shaved head, beefy arms like tree trunks, and a mountainous belly with layers and layers of fat approached Split Nose. He was wearing a bright-orange jumpsuit, carrying a bottle of vodka peeping out of a brown bag, and walking with a swagger like he was the big dog of the jail.

"Well, what have we here? We heard some real-life gangsters would be staying in our hotel. I've never seen any real-life Mafioso. Y'all got any of those good New Orleans cigarettes with you?" the man asked. His dirty fingernails were yellowed from a fungal infection, and a truckload of grime was ground into the creases of his knuckles.

Split Nose and Jake the Rake stared at the man and said nothing.

"You Big Easy boys need to know the rules around here. I'm Booger Bob, the boss hog of this lockup, and there ain't nothing going to be easy about your stay here," Bob said, flexing the muscles under his meaty shoulders and tightening his muscles from jowls to buttocks in a display designed to intimidate new arrivals. It had worked so many times before.

"Excuse me, Bob, but Johnny's had a rough night. I don't think you want to mess with him tonight," Jake pleaded.

"Well, I'll be, boys. I believe this big guy is a ventriloquist and this little fella is his dummy. Mister, I couldn't even see your lips move when your dumb dummy was talking," Bob said to Johnny.

The inmates all laughed at Bob's jokes, even though they'd heard them all before.

"People who stick their hand in the fire get burned," Johnny said quietly to Bob.

"Did you hear that, boys? He threatened me. Are we going to have to do this the hard way, Johnny, or are you gonna be a good boy and kiss my big old caboose? Maybe you'd rather I come by later tonight and crack your skull in your sleep? You know, we heard those rumors about your boss killing Jack Kennedy. A lot of us here liked Kennedy, and I ain't a sitting duck for long-distance killers like you and your kind. You have to look me right in the eye when you come for me, Guido!" Bob said.

"Oh, geez," Jake said as he watched the darkness cross Johnny's hard-boiled eyes.

Bob turned sideways, grinned at the other inmates, and patted his posterior to taunt Split Nose. Too late it occurred to Bob that Johnny had the same feral look as the assassin on the cover of a worn pulp fiction novel circulating among the inmates in the jail.

In that moment of distraction and preening, Split Nose stepped forward as quick as greased lightning, hooked his right foot behind Bob's left ankle, and jerked it out from under him. Down the big man went like a beached whale with Johnny right on top of him—Captain Ahab on Moby Dick—hammering his nose and eyes like a man beating big slabs of meat in old slaughterhouses.

Splat, splat, the sickening thuds on flesh echoed down the halls of the lockup. Bob's arms flopped and jerked with each blow, and his face was a bloody pulp. Split Nose banged away with short machinelike blows. His head was lowered, shoulders rolling like pistons in an engine as he hammered sickening, murderous blows into Bob's face and chest. With each grunt of angry effort, Split Nose had not enjoyed anything as much since the night he killed Arnold.

Split Nose was the tenderizer tonight, a machine of rage as chunks of flesh were gouged out of Bob's face and teeth rattled around on the floor of the cell. The patterns of blood spatters on the floor from split lips and busted eyes were the work of an abstract painter capturing images to induce terror and revulsion.

Finally, breathing heavily, the rage of Split Nose was satiated in one last shuddering, climactic release, and he yielded to Jake's pleas for him to stop. He rose from Bob's body and stared menacingly at the inmates of the Harrison County Jail. His face was covered in blood, and spit foamed and dripped from the corners of his mouth like a rabid dog. Split Nose picked up Bob's bottle of vodka and did the bottoms up until the bottle was empty.

The inmates were plastered against the walls, cowering in fear, and some were throwing up and crying. They had never witnessed such savagery.

Johnny smashed the bottle on the floor, prized open Bob's battered and bruised eyes, and said, "He'll live—hospital, not the morgue. Anyone else got anything they think I should kiss?"

CHAPTER TWENTY-SIX

"Death is as near to the young as to the old;
here is all the difference: death stands
behind the young man's back, before the
old man's face."—Thomas Adams

"You may break, you may shatter the vase,
if you will, but the scent of the rose will
hang round it still."—Thomas Moore

It was raining in Jackson when the word came that Molly's mother had died a violent death in a flophouse in Memphis. It didn't matter that they hadn't spoken in years. She was still Mama, flaws and all. Her mother's death churned up all the regrets, the anger and guilt, and the "what-ifs." She was reliving it all, thinking about her past mistakes. The smell of beer from a six-pack already scented her apartment, and each time she looked in the mirror, her face was all scrunched up like a clenched fist.

Anger and grief were wrestling and warring for dominance. One moment she remembered the lullabies her mother sang to her when Molly was a little girl, and then she remembered the beatings and the mental abuse.

Molly called the request line of her favorite radio station in Jackson over and over after learning that her mother had died. Each time she asked them to play "Born to Lose." She danced as she sang along with the tune, her heels drumming the floor and keeping time: "Born to lose, I've lived my life in vain. All my dreams have only brought me pain." She called and called them until they finally busied out the request line.

She'd been dreaming about Michael when the news arrived about her mother, and it was confirmation to her that darkness and death were in the air. Such news always came in clusters, like plane crashes and UFO sightings. When the knock on her door brought the bad news, she had been dreaming Michael was in great danger. She also had a strong feeling of foreboding and absence for more than one life lost, but it wasn't Michael she feared to be dead. It was her mother, and "Good Golly Miss Molly" sensed Rambling Rose was gone away, too.

Oh, Rose, is your flower no longer blooming? Oh, Mama, you've been a ghost for so long, and now you are for real. There's a monster buried back there with you. I can't be that monster anymore, and I can't let Michael see her...ever. I don't want to be the girl in your twisted fairytale who helped a bullfrog to safety and kissed it, but the kiss didn't work. The bullfrog told the girl he was to have been her Prince Charming but changed his mind when he saw she wasn't pure of heart. I'll try to resurrect the little girl and let the monster rest with your ghost.

Molly lay on her bed and stared at the ceiling. Pain was her familiar pillow. The beer didn't mute the pain, the radio station wouldn't take her calls, and her Prince Charming was nowhere to be found. So she talked to her new friend, Jesus. His line was never busy.

****

Rose had been on the run since her jealous jabbering at the Leg Room had gotten out of hand. She stayed in the shadows because she was warned by a friend that she had talked too much and she was in danger. Then she was turned away by the big security guy at the Leg Room. She showed him the sign and a little more leg than the sign required, but he slammed the door in her face.

She was once a clean hippie, but she was living out of her car, and her palms and underarms were sweaty, her legs unshaven, and her cutoffs and halter top dirty. Her junk food diet had given her the green apple two-step, and her clothes were soiled. She desperately wanted a shower and fresh clothes, but she was afraid to go by her mother's house until it all blew over and everyone kissed and made up and agreed what an unfortunate and comical mistake it all had been.

She stopped to gather her thoughts at the rest area overlooking the Ross Barnett Reservoir and to find some clarity and a way out of the box canyon of her dilemma. Her last thoughts were of the Leg Room where she was in with the in-crowd and how she'd messed things up with the MBN and Michael. She thought about how the green-eyed monster can eat you alive.

Rose was drinking an RC Cola and eating a Moon Pie, Southern delicacies her daddy bought her when she was a little girl. She listened to a wren sing his song of faith from the upper terraces of a tall pine tree and thought of church socials, front porch stories her daddy told her as the sun was setting, and times when she was a kid and could still dream a kid's dreams. She missed her father and thought this storm would surely pass, and she could find him and tell him how much those cold drinks and Moon Pies meant to her.

The skinny little pothead never heard the man with the soft shoes when he walked up to her passenger window and shot her twice in her right temple with a .22-caliber pistol, the sound muted to a "thup, thup" by a homemade silencer.

All her emotional conflicts ended, she collapsed against the steering wheel. The tiny wren quit singing when her car horn blared the last sad refrains of a hippie girl's brittle flower power, answering the question, "Where have all the flowers gone? Girls have picked them every one. When will they ever learn?"

The man pulled her off the horn and looked all around to see if anyone had heard. He pulled out a switchblade and cut out her tongue, proof to his employers in New Orleans that "the snitch won't snitch anymore."

The killer placed her bloody tongue in a plastic bag and put his hand over his heart. Rose was slumped in her seat behind the wheel when he put the car in neutral and pushed it down the hill. He crossed himself and watched her old jalopy sink into the murky depths, her pool of sleep where the silent coffin would one day be the perfect bed for breeding fish. The site of her death would become a favorite fishing hole for anglers who would travel from places far and wide to compete in the fishing rodeos at the reservoir every year, and the gentry at the Leg Room would toast the commoner's memory and swear she was like a daughter to them.

As the car sunk to its watery grave, the water was a swirl of jasper and sapphire, and Rambling Rose with the corn-tassel hair was blonde and dead.

****

Otis was walking along the shoreline of the Ross Barnett Reservoir, thinking about his life. He had tried to forget Sheler and the men who had done her wrong and drove her into an early grave, but he couldn't. Revenge gnawed at his innards like a pack of hungry rats.

He stopped and picked up a mussel shell mired in the mud and rocks. He wistfully put it to his ear, hoping for the sound of surf rushing to the shore, but it was not a seashell like the one he found for Sheler when he took her to Okaloosa Island in Florida.

Otis had surprised her over dinner at Harbor Lights Restaurant in Ft. Walton Beach with a pretty shell he'd found when he was crabbing. She put it up to her ear and oohed and ahhed like a little girl, as if Otis had given her something that all the money in the world could not buy. She told him later the roaring of the ocean in her ears stuck there forever, just like every word of love he had whispered to her on those long sunset strolls along the beach.

He remembered how the orange glow of the setting sun was cast across the sea, highlighting the golden burnish of her hair and the soft sheen of her face. He could still see her smile, how her lips were wide and warm when she recalled those times. Her eyes sparkled again, and her face was lifted to the sky with a fleeting pang of the wonderment and innocence of the child who had been robbed of the happy endings she longed for.

Otis reckoned some dishes on life's buffet gave her cases of soul poisoning that never healed. It was her mental wiring the Stone brothers had poisoned a little bit at a time. An old vet once told Otis when you're giving a dog a pill, you disguise it in a piece of hamburger, and the dog won't even know it's eating medicine. That's the way it was with poor Sheler. One day she was fine. The next day she was addicted to their burgers.

Then the full presence of her visited him, and he remembered the day Sheler looked at him with sobs choking her throat and said, "You know I may have been born in a dumpster, but I'm not trash."

So he had come to Jackson to settle old scores, to cancel all debts, to seek the only justice he knew of this side of heaven. Revenge may have been a bitter stew, but it was the poison he craved night and day. He would go to Moondog Square for Sammy and Marty Stone, and he would go to the Leg Room for Corndog and his friends, and he would kill them all and anyone else who got in his way.

Otis was startled out of his obsessions by the blare of a car horn. He reached for his pistol and then eased up through the trees. He saw a man pull a young, blonde girl off the beeping horn. There was a blood spatter on her blouse and in her hair, and she appeared to be dead. He'd seen too many dead people, and she had the look of a soul that had lost its body.

As the man bent over the girl with a knife, Otis could see a holstered pistol and a badge clipped to his belt. The killer put something in a bag, and Otis watched as he bumped the car into neutral and pushed it down the hill. The man stepped back when the car picked up momentum and watched it careen down the hill and crash into the water with a huge splash and wake.

The car floated for a moment and then sank beneath the water. The man stood there with his hand over his heart as the air trapped in the car began to escape, sending bubbles to the surface. It began to sprinkle rain as the hit man policed the area for shell casings and any other items that might suggest an act of homicide had been committed on the lonely overlook of the big lake. He bent down to wipe the bloody blade of his knife on the grass and then walked away as if nothing had happened.

Otis didn't know the girl, but he had thought about killing the man then and there. Too many girls had died, and this was not an official act by an officer but the distinct look of a hit, a cold-blooded murder. Otis decided not to kill him because it would have interfered with his mission to settle his own scores, but he got his tag number, and he would never forget his face, the face of a killer.

After the man left, Otis stood there looking at the girl's watery grave. He knew nothing about her, but her death seemed to magnify his own loss. The look she had on her face haunted him, like a girl trying to figure out a puzzle. He walked down to the water's edge and threw a handful of wildflowers on the last place he saw her.

He wondered if she liked seashells and if someone had ever given her one. There was something about seashells. He wished he had one now. Maybe he could not only hear the tide rush in, but maybe he could hear Sheler's voice one more time.

As Otis drove away, he hoped he didn't get pulled over for CWD…crying while driving.

CHAPTER TWENTY-SEVEN

"When I waked, I cried to dream again."
—William Shakespeare, The Tempest

*"There are things we know we know. We
also know there are known unknowns; that
is to say, we know there are some things we
do not know. But there are also unknown
unknowns—the ones we don't know we don't
know…it is the latter category that tend to
be the difficult ones."—Donald Rumsfeld*

Michael was sleepwalking, like he did when he was a child. He stumbled blindly in the pitch black of night. He couldn't see who he was tracking, but his bare feet could feel the footprints he followed. He listened for his father's voice, but it was not his earthly father but God Himself. Then the footsteps ended, and all the yearning and searching ended. A light illuminated scarred feet standing before him…the feet of Jesus.

As he drew closer, he could hear Pearl's voice calling to him like she did at the Easter egg hunts in Parker Grove. "He's introducing Himself, Michael. Warmer, warmer, you're almost there. You're getting warmer, son. You're burning up. You're as hot as a firecracker! Nothing is by chance or coincidence. All of it is His masterpiece."

Then he felt something just outside the here and now, so close he could almost touch it. Brushing against him, a tap on the shoulder, a whispering or murmuring, it was a song on the wind he hummed unknowingly, a melody in his heart, a caress. Ordinary things became signs and wonders and a happy anxiousness, an urgency to tell someone and to laugh or cry. It was a light in the darkness, the missing piece, and a map or compass for the sojourner, an awakening from a long sleep. A vibrancy of colors, sights, and sounds replaced the darkness of the dream walk. It was a heavenly apothecary offering a balm of purpose for the aching loneliness and answers, the answer to all his questions. The light was transforming, altering, an invitation marked Father, home, love, and peace.

He thought God looked like Vince Lombardi, but he wasn't giving his famous back-to-fundamentals sports speech, "This is a football." His hands were outstretched toward Michael who felt a soft caress of his heart when God said, "This is a Bible."

When Michael woke suddenly, he was standing in front of his TV, and the old test-pattern image of the Indian chief in full headdress was staring at him from the studios of WLBT-TV. The ear-splitting sine wave tone had stabbed his ears and startled him from his strolling stupor at 4 a.m. The National Anthem at sign-off had not awakened him, but the shrill tone had done the trick.

He thought maybe it was a sign to let him know that when all of television land was sleeping, you should be, too. The image used by engineers to adjust picture quality was rolling and rolling, and Michael stooped to stop it with the horizontal button.

He looked out his window. A pale moon and a dusting of tiny silver-white stars had emerged after the storm and lingered over his apartment, and he thought the TV test pattern might be a wonderful idea for life. Just check your pattern each day, try to sharpen your image and bring the world into focus, maybe read a Good Book Someone gave you in a dream.

****

The golden pallor of dawn framed the horizon, and the dew was still on the grass when the summons came from headquarters. The steam was still rising from the thermos cup of hot chocolate Michael sipped as he drove down Ridgewood Road, and a gentle breeze moved tree branches in a lazy motion like the wave of a tired beauty queen in a parade. Yards full of buttercups perfumed the morning and lined the road along the way. Pearl always told him that God deposits His sunshine and dew to make butter for the birds and bees.

The flowers were in front of old home places razed to make way for new construction, and the yellow blooms had outlived the gardeners who had planted them. The green thumbs, along with their hopes, dreams, and aspirations, were long gone. Everything that had once seemed so urgent and vital was buried with them, but the prophets had written in their gardens with daffodils and forget-me-nots, a plea from yesteryear… "Don't forget me. My life mattered."

He was still blowing on his hot drink, trying to cool it, when he arrived at the MBN. From the cars he saw in the parking lot, he figured he must be the only undercover agent there at such an early hour. The other agents were probably sleeping in cheap motels in the remote corners of the state after long nights in the bars, clubs, and way stations of the lower places. He was glad to have made it home to his apartment, but he was still weary and could've slept until the second coming.

A scraggy dog with exposed ribs was watering a young tree near the entrance, and house sparrows nesting under the eaves over the front door were chirping a happy, good-morning tune when he entered the building. DeeDee, the receptionist, told him a big meeting of the brass was in progress, and she was told to ask him to wait until they called him. So Michael sat under the indoor shade of a giant ficus tree in the waiting room and finished the last of his hot chocolate.

Michael noticed DeeDee was sporting new layers of makeup that must have taken a long time to apply. He thought it made her eyes larger and somehow familiar. He smiled and decided he would secretly dub her "raccoon eyes."

"What's so funny, Agent Parker?" she asked, furrowing her brow.

"Nothing, just thought of a private joke," he said.

"Are you going to be trouble?" DeeDee asked.

"No, ma'am. I don't bite. I don't even bark," he said.

Her intercom hissed like a cat with a furball in its throat, and a tinny voice in the sea of static said, "Send Agent Parker up to the director's second floor conference room."

She buzzed the door open and said, "Sounds like everyone is waiting on you. I suspect you've been up to something. You must've been very good or very bad last night."

"You have no idea," Michael said.

****

When Michael ascended the stairs, the door to the director's conference room was open. Chief Larry Burnside, Control Agent Harry Johnson, Clay, and the director were seated around a long table. Mounds of paper and charts were stacked on the table, and diagrams of timelines were pinned to the wall. Pud Goody was seated in the corner with her notepad and pencil, and she looked like a mourner at a funeral.

"Come in, Michael. Have a seat…lots to talk about," the director said.

Just then Sarge rounded the corner with a fresh cup of coffee. Smoke was curling up from his ever-present cigar.

"Hey, Sarge, looks like everyone is here," Michael said.

"Yeah, the MBN always calls in the big guns when they're in trouble," he joked, but Michael noticed his eyes weren't smiling.

"Michael, I informed Clay that Otis has been missing since y'all made those buys in Hattiesburg, but out of the blue, he called me yesterday and said he was working on some big deals for you. He had tag numbers he needed names for. So I ran the tags and gave him the information. One came back to a Rose Addington on Bluebird Lane in Jackson," Sarge said.

Michael looked at him and then at Clay. Clay nodded and looked away.

"Thank God she's alive. Where is she?" Michael asked.

Sarge looked at Clay and then at his notes.

"The second tag was a Louisiana plate that had never been issued, but the numbers were consistent with those assigned to the New Orleans area," Sarge said.

The men in the room looked restless and uncomfortable. Pud Goody dabbed at her eyes with a tissue. Larry Burnside absently stirred the coffee in his cup, and the repetitive *tink-tink* of his spoon against the ceramic sounded a cadence of defeat.

"I asked Sarge to come over today to bring you up to date on all that has happened. It has been an eventful forty-eight hours," Clay said.

"Michael, Otis told me he saw a blonde girl in the car. She looked like a hippie, and she was hollow-cheeked, like she hadn't eaten well. He said the girl had a dried rose clipped to her rearview mirror. Otis wouldn't tell me where it happened...just that he saw a man kill her and dispose of her body. I'm sorry," Sarge said somberly.

Everything got quiet in the room. The ticking of the wall clock was deafening. Michael thought of what Rose had asked him the last time he saw her: "You went to college, Agent Parker. How many angels do you think can dance on the head of a pin?"

Michael dropped his head, rested his elbows on his knees, and whispered, "Oh, no. Please, no."

"Otis said if he got sucked into an investigation of her death, it might compromise his plans. He said he couldn't have that, but he said he would never forget her face or the cold mug of her assassin. Otis said the man was medium height, close-cropped gray hair, and had wide shoulders that looked too big for his body. He looked like an exercise freak with pale eyebrows against a deep tan. When the man turned toward him, Otis said he had a pinched, bitter mouth, just like a girl killer," Sarge said.

"He said the man had a large gold shield clipped to his belt and a pistol with a silencer he used to kill her. Otis kept telling me not to worry. He said he would fix everything. Otis said men have to answer for dead girls. He said he was sorry for lying to me about the drug deals, but he had to know who the dead girl and her murderer were. Otis said if we didn't get to him before he does, he would have to take care of this killer, too. He kept telling me too many girls had died, and someone must pay.

"I asked him how he could find the man since the tag didn't come back, and he said, 'You don't think I tell you everything, do you, Sarge?'

"I asked him to come in so we could talk it over, but he said, 'Life ain't all it's cracked up to be, Sarge. Don't worry about me.'

"I told him not to do anything rash, that the people he was messing with are dangerous and have connections in high places, and I told him the devil was tempting him, baiting him with a lust for revenge. But he seemed calm and at peace.

"He said, 'That's all right. The devil always squeals when you pull his tail. Besides, he may not be tempting me, I may be tempting him, Sarge. Have you ever thought of that?'

"I told him tempting the devil was a sin, too, but he was long gone, and I doubt I'll ever hear from him again. I think he's on a suicide mission," Sarge said.

Michael was shaking his head and drumming his fingers on the conference table. He muttered, "Evil walks the planet."

"What's that?" Chief Burnside asked.

"Just something an old detective from L.A. told me," Michael said under his breath.

"Sorry to spring it on you all at once in this meeting, but time is of the essence now," Clay said.

"Let me bring you up to date. Take a look at these charts of the sequence of events and what we know about the connections that tie it all together," Clay said as he rose and took a pointer to use on the charts.

"Reggie Morris from Tupelo, the same guy who showed up in Fayette to defend the KKK Grand Dragon when you were a Lee County deputy, also turned up in Harrison County early this morning. He came to bail out the mob guys who were chasing you, but the bail is pretty hefty. He has filed motions to reduce the bail, and that may buy us a little time.

"As we discussed before, the guy you had the run-in with in Biloxi is now a prime suspect in the murder of Arnold the child abuser at Moondog. Bertha has agreed to cooperate if the government will put her in witness protection. You know from the file I gave you that Johnny is prominent in the Marcello operation.

"Late yesterday, the DEA seized bales of Delta cotton at the ports of New Orleans and Charleston. There were hundreds of bags of pure heroin wedged into the bales. They were to be shipped overseas or diverted to inland routes through Louisiana or up the eastern seaboard. The cotton was ginned in Greenville, and the company that owns the gin is a shell company controlled by Senator Cornelius Ball. The DEA is interviewing and arresting people in New Orleans, Charleston, and the Delta as we speak. They haven't said how they got wind of the cotton-heroin connection, but things seem to be moving at a fast clip," Clay said.

"Gives a whole new meaning to wishing you were in the land of cotton, huh?" Michael said.

"Yeah, it does. Red Winter called me last night. He wanted to be in the clear, so we interviewed him in the wee hours this morning. Red said he doesn't know much, but he figured it must have been you they were chasing last night, and he waited on the route he thought you'd take. He not only didn't stop you, but he told other units he had that road covered so they would look elsewhere. He watched you drive by in the night and let you pass," Clay said.

"Good for Red. I needed a friend last night, but I didn't think it would be him," Michael said.

Chief Burnside leaned across the table and handed Michael a file.

"We can't be sure Otis is telling us the truth, but we can't find Rose anywhere. We looked at her known haunts, and agents went by her house. Her mother said she hadn't been home in two days and hadn't called. They believe her. She looked worried sick about her daughter. Also, in the midst of all this, Molly's mother died. She's topsy-turvy, but she was just in Moondog Square and doesn't think any of it has reached there. She said she thinks she can get you back in for another buy because they're cash poor right now and a little crazy. Are you up for it?" he asked.

"Let's set it up then. I'm ready," Michael said.

"She's waiting for you to call her. Remember what we talked about at the drive-in. She's more vulnerable than ever, so be careful," Clay said.

As everyone filed out, the director asked him to hang back.

"Michael, close the door and have a seat," he said.

"Good job last night, but be careful with this informant. You can't right all wrongs by bleeding all over your Ole Miss diploma, thinking you must fix everything and save everyone. Some things are exempt from earthly justice. There is a maze of mirrors in the world, lies and half-truths muddying our vision, and sometimes when we knock, the doors won't open. We wake up one day and realize we've just been peeking through the keyholes. The doorkeepers mean us harm and use the law when it suits them. It's easy for an idealist to get disillusioned and turn to bare legs in the sack for comfort," he said.

"No, sir, that won't happen," Michael said, wondering if the director had faced similar challenges when he was a young cop.

"It's not personal, just a word of wisdom from an old man who's seen it all. Good guys fall into traps all the time. We're surrounded by people who're so crooked they have to screw their socks on every morning before they put on their shoes," he said with a chuckle.

"Surrounded and outnumbered—I guess we got 'em right where we want 'em. They'll all surrender soon," Michael said with a weak smile.

"Uh-huh, as soon as they start construction on ice castles in hell," he said.

The director picked up a pen and pad and drew a line. On one side of the line, he wrote *wolves*. On the other side of the line, he wrote *sheep*. Then he drew an arrow pointing to the line and wrote *We are here*.

"That's what it all boils down to, Michael…sheep and wolves, money and murder. You want to look for the good in people, to trust and believe. One day, if you run into these people you want to save and they're on fire in the street, you won't grab your water hose. You may be tempted to grab the gas can. Keep your guard up. Remember what I told you: don't burn brightly and burn out, fight the long fight," Collins said.

"Yes, sir," Michael said.

The director stood and offered his big paw of a hand.

"One more tip: when the devil's team is running plays against you, don't take your eyes off the water boys. The ones who carry water for the other side may be wearing our jerseys. We have skunks on our team, too," he said.

CHAPTER TWENTY-EIGHT

"Forever does not make loss forgettable,
only bearable."—Cassandra Clare,
City of Heavenly Fire

"Some flowers must be broken or bruised
before they emit any fragrance."
—Robert Murray M'Cheyne

Thick gray clouds drifted low over the city streets near the park where Molly waited. Two men with hollow gray faces on a street corner were trying to light a cigarette, but their hands were shaking so badly the matches kept sputtering out. The men, like the neighborhood, were on the skids. Gray clouds and gray faces, no more fire, only smoke…

Michael tuned his radio to the same low-power AM gospel station he'd listened to the night he met the homeless man by the bridge, the first time he worked with a broken girl named Molly. A soft-spoken preacher named David Daniel James was discussing Genesis.

"My beloved brothers and sisters, we are all living east of Eden and have been since God served His eviction notice to the residents of the Garden. It's been a dog-eat-dog, brother-against-brother world since the serpent tempted Eve and then Cain, the first man born and the first murderer who killed Abel out of jealousy. The earth drank the blood he spilled, and all Cain could do was compound the sin crouched at his door by lying to God and asking, 'Am I my brother's keeper?'

"Can you imagine what it was like when Adam and Eve heard about the murder of Abel? They wanted to be like God and know everything, but they didn't even know what murder was and probably weren't sure why they had to move on down to the east side. Eve ate the apple and brought death into the world. Yes, she gave Adam the apple, but he ate it. They had over nine hundred years to think about it all, nine hundred years of pillow talk and finger-wagging, I imagine," the pastor said with a chuckle.

Michael laughed at the pastor's joke. He reached to turn the dial on the radio, but the speaker had hooked him.

"We've got to know where we came from if we have any hope of knowing where we're going. Our first parents' sins dog this fallen world, blood is demanded for blood, and on it goes. How long does the Divine curse go on? How deep does it pierce us through the ages?

"If you're struggling today, trying to make sense of the world and reconcile it with your faith, remember we inherited this fallen world, and we have now entered another chapter of a story as old as humankind. Just look around us. Free Will is not the title of some novel. Children are shooting dope and nodding in Nod. If there's malice in our hearts, there's no room for love, only the sin that led to blood on Cain's hands. Abel is still speaking to us about depravity, murder, and a world without his offspring. Blood is on the ground once more in a nation where men try to evict God from their little garden spot.

"We are all fugitives and wanderers, and in this world of groaning and trembling, the only thing that can protect you against what runs in your blood is the Blood that stained the Cross. The flashing sword still blocks the way to the tree of knowledge, but we have been rerouted to another tree where Christ died for us. Fix your compass on the eternal. This is not your home, and you can't save this wicked world. If you try, it'll gobble you up and spit you out, but you can be in it, not of it, and here's where it gets tricky. You can be for it by signing up as a soldier in the army of the Lord. He who is not with Him is against Him.

"We should remember that in the beginning Adam and Eve were both called Adam, but after the fall, he gave her the name of Eve or mother of all life. He could have called her death, but he didn't. She bore Seth, 'set in place of,' and named him in an expression of faith in a merciful God. Eve's prophetic life was fulfilled when her Seed came to swallow up death in victory. She was the first to hear the prophecy of the Cross when she confessed her sin and heard God say to Satan, 'I will put enmity between thee and the woman and between thy seed and her seed; it shall bruise thy head, and thou shalt bruise his heel.'

"She was the first woman, first wife, first sinner, and first mourner. Apples are still offered, and the battle with Satan continues for those who desire to bear God's image on earth, but we have a Redeemer," the pastor said.

He paused for what seemed a long stretch of dead air, and Michael fidgeted in his seat and adjusted his radio dial.

"There's someone listening to me right now on his car radio, someone lost in the fog of life and in the midst of a great struggle, a lionhearted pilgrim who needs the Carpenter to remove the splinters from his paws," the pastor said.

He paused again for a long, pregnant moment, and Michael squirmed.

"This is enemy territory, and he will oppose you, tempt you, and whisper in your ear his lie that he's innocent and Adam was but a myth. But remember this: if the first Adam was a myth, so was the second Adam, your Redeemer. Until next time, my dearly beloved," Pastor James said.

Michael's hand shook when he turned off his radio. He didn't know enough to be sure about the preacher's theology, but it echoed what he and the detective had talked about. As he approached the meeting place, he thought it all made his head and heart hurt, but it stirred his soul.

****

As he walked across the park, a gentle rain had begun to fall. Michael smelled the damp earth and the odor of Kentucky Fried in the garbage can. In the distance beyond the wooded hills, he heard the whining hum of the big diesel rigs on Interstate 55.

He saw Molly sitting in a Buddha pose on one of the covered benches. He first thought she was meditating. As he drew closer, he saw she was reading the Bible and dipping a child's bubble pipe in a bowl of soapy water. She was blowing bubbles! That single act softened the contours of the woman, and all he could see was the child she once was.

The soothing pitter-patter of rain played percussion on the tin roof above her bench. The sound of the raindrops on the rooftop reminded him of the Folger's commercial where the percolating coffee pot played a catchy plop-plop rhythm. But other than the soft singing of the rain, the solemn day was windless and seemed to be clothed in a shroud of silent mourning for a girl named Rose. Everything was eerily quiet, like the Head Librarian had shushed the day.

Molly heard him coming and looked up from her reading. He saw she was reading in Genesis. She looked worn around the edges, like her Bible. Her eyes were tired, but her smile was quick when she saw him. The light he'd seen in her on the football field had dimmed, but it was still there.

"Hey, Molly," Michael said with a quick smile.

He saw her face brighten. She rose and began to reach out to him. He could tell she wanted to hug him, but she caught herself and shook his hand instead. Her hands were cold and limp.

"Hello, Michael, long time no see. That's how it feels anyhow. I've been struggling since I last saw you," she said as she shoved her hands in her pockets and returned to her seat.

He sat on the bench beside her, and the rain got harder. A mist sprayed them when a sudden storm breeze appeared, and water puddled around the edges of their shelter. They retreated to the back side of the bench, and she shook herself like a wet dog.

"I'm sorry about your mother and about Rose," he said as she wiped strands of wet hair from her brow. He thought she looked childlike and innocent, and once again, he caught a glimpse of her as she once was before the world steamrolled her.

"Thanks. I mourned for Mama, but then I got to thinking about things that happened. When I was a little girl and started to show some cleavage, she made me bind my breasts and cut my hair short because she thought her boyfriends were looking at me 'funny.' She was jealous of her own daughter. She used to beat me, too, with a belt and sometimes the buckle end, but I took the belt away from her when I turned twelve and told her that would never happen again.

"I wanted to hurt her back, but I remember what her pastor told me. He said, 'Molly, you got to love your mama because she's too hard to like.' He'd known her forever, and I asked him how long she'd been that way. He said, 'Since she came out of the womb.' Isn't that sad?

"She pretended to be so holy, and all the while she was living like hell and clubbing me with Scripture. One day I got sick of her hypocrisy and said, 'You know the Catholics have got it all wrong about the Pope being God's emissary on earth because clearly you think *you're* His emissary,'" she said.

She laughed and Michael did, too. He thought Molly had been orphaned for a long time.

"Poor Rose may have messed it up for our work, and she sure messed it up for herself. All of it hurt and frustrated me, and I got a little angry at God and at you, too," she said with a shy, guilty smile.

"What happened to the happy girl on the football field?" he asked.

"One step forward and two back, sometimes. It wasn't just losing Mama and Rose. When things went south at Moondog, many of the girls returned to their old homes to start over. They saw what you did with the little girl, and when Milkwood no longer felt like a god to them, they left for the last places they had called home. You know, the wood-frame houses with white picket fences and victory gardens in tiny towns or country farms—but their parents didn't recognize them. The girls didn't look the same anymore, and their families looked at them like they were imposters who had abducted their long-lost daughters.

"The little girls who the parents grieved for were long gone. Oh, they all tried and pretended. Everyone cried, lied, and promised to be better, but the promises were all broken, and one morning the old folks woke up to find their babies gone again, gone for good this time. The girls gave up fighting their demons and came crawling back to him. They couldn't defeat the voices in their heads because they'd played with their imaginary friends too long. These motherless children were once too vital to be forgotten, but they made deals with the devil to peddle themselves and sing their bitter songs about empty hearts and veins full of heroin. They returned to Moondog to sing their false god's tune again," she said.

"I'm sorry," Michael said.

"Yeah, I am, too. One girl set her baby on fire when she and a new pimp were cooking dope. The little boy's in the burn unit now, and the state's looking for someone to foster him. Another girl left to be a pole dancer, but she'd just given birth. She couldn't care for herself, much less a baby. Before she came back to Moondog, she gave up her baby for adoption. When they asked who the father was, she gave the state a list of twenty-six names to test. The baby is now a ward of the state, but he'll have a better chance of surviving life now than he would have inside the walls at Moondog.

"Several girls told me their return was only temporary, living one day at a time while they waited for you, or someone like you, to come and rescue them. It was their fantasy and mine, too, I guess," she said.

She blew her nose on her handkerchief and started again.

"I was out driving last night and crossed the yellow line. A cop I know stopped me and asked me if I was drunk. He's got lots of hands like an octopus. We call him Mr. Stop and Frisky. I had one drink, but it tasted like turpentine, and it didn't stop the pain. I told the cop I couldn't lie. I was driving under the influence of love," she said with a grin and a wink.

"Molly, I learned the hard way that life is too short to leave the key to your happiness in someone else's pocket," Michael said.

"Gee, it was a joke, Michael! But yeah, all of it and then the news of Mama's death and poor Rose. It set me back, but I'm okay and ready to do business again if Rose didn't ruin it all with her stories about you and me," she said.

"She's really dead, isn't she?" she asked.

"I think so, Molly," he said.

"I've been studying Genesis today. Did you know Eve was misunderstood?" she asked eagerly.

"Yeah, I just heard someone talk about that," he said.

"Maybe that's my problem, too. I'm misunderstood and stained, too. I just needed a stain remover," she said.

"There's lots of craziness right in the world; out with the old, in with the new. Throw out the baby with the bathwater and burn it all down. I think we are losing our innocence, death by a thousand nicks. We're in the slow bleed, hip-deep in muddy water, and the flood waters are rising. I don't see it ending well," he said.

She nodded, and they sat quietly for a while thinking about it all.

"There's a big anti-war rally planned for Jackson by the SDS, and it's the only thing I've seen that excites Milkwood lately. He thinks it's the culmination of his life's work, his genius finally realized, and Moondog's business will be good again when the armies of the revolution march into Jackson.

"He fancies himself as the godfather of these radicals. Milkwood thinks the Weathermen will want to sit at his feet and listen to his wisdom. He says he knew which way the winds of revolution were blowing long before these weather forecasters. When they first came to Jackson to plan for this march, they stayed at Moondog. I heard them talking about establishing reeducation camps in the Southwest when they take over, brainwashing people who won't go along with communism. One of them said there were too many Bibles and too many crosses in Mississippi.

"They sat in circles smoking dope, talking about bombing buildings, killing police, and longing for the revolution and the day the Russian, Chinese, and Cuban Communists move in to occupy America. Milkwood asked them what they would do with those who won't accept the new way without God and Capitalism. They told him they would eliminate them. When Milkwood asked them what eliminate meant, they said resisters, as many as twenty-five million people, would have to be killed.

"These were smart people with graduate degrees from Harvard, Yale, and Berkeley, but this Communist communion scared me, Michael. This can't be of God. They all got stoned out of their gourds and got up and did this strange dance, twisting like serpents. Milkwood got up and danced with them and made hissing sounds," she said.

"Snakes writhe alike," Michael said.

"Rumor is they'll send us to infiltrate the crowd and gather intelligence about the drug dealers and SDS radicals. Any info you pick up on who's coming to dinner in Jackson would be helpful," he said.

"What will you do after we're done at Moondog?" she asked.

"They may send me down to a snoozer assignment in Tylertown. What could possibly happen there?" he wondered aloud, forgetting Clay's warning about loose lips sinking ships.

"The director is talking about putting resident agents or topside investigators in the field. Maybe I'll be assigned to one of those posts someday. Who knows?" he said.

"If you get one of those jobs, maybe I could be your CI there. I think professional CI might be my calling," she said.

Then she looked at Michael, rolled her eyes, and said, "Oh, don't look so pained. It was just a thought."

They both laughed an uncomfortable laugh.

"Well, wherever they send you, be careful. People's blinker lights are out of God's juice, and they'll turn on you without warning, and I ain't talking about cars. You speak truth and that makes enemies of people living lives of lies. Your truth may've been meant for my head, but it went straight to my heart, right past this weight of what-ifs smothering my lungs.

"So I think about all of it and try to see the big picture. I move the pieces around in my head like a jigsaw puzzle, but one piece or clue, the key slice of face and scene, is always missing.

It's a longing for the ordinariness of an ordinary life I've never known and can't fake. So I obsess about Mama and the abuse, but then I make myself stop. If the worst should befall me, just remember, it will be a relief. I'm claustrophobic, so don't let them bury me, Michael. Just have me cremated and put me on your mantle, because I would have done anything to be near you and still would," she said as her voice cracked and vulnerability spilled out of her heart.

Michael looked at the ground and scuffed his shoes like he always did as a kid when he was uncomfortable.

"I'll pick you up at eight tomorrow night. Once more into the breach, Agent Molly, dress accordingly," Michael said, patting the Bible she held in her lap with a "there, there" rhythm.

"Okay, sounds good. I'll wear my prom dress," Molly joked.

As he walked away, she began to blow bubbles again. A gusty wind remained after the rainstorm and blew paper wrappers across the park. A pale-orange sun, a force of nature like Molly, peeked out of the clouds to subdue the approaching dusk and paint the world in amber hues, and the wet asphalt shined like new money.

Michael thought about the daily acrobatic feat it must take for girls like Molly to leap over yesterday and live for today. He was left with the feeling he and his wounded CI had hugged, though they never touched.

CHAPTER TWENTY-NINE

"…our souls may be consumed by
shadows, but that doesn't mean we have
to behave as monsters."—Emm Cole,
The Short Life of Sparrows

"I'm not sure what they mean by 'revenge is
a dish best served cold.' But I do know
this—nobody's ever satisfied with a single
helping."—Clay G. Small, Heels Over Head

Split Nose sat in his jail cell, cracking his scarred knuckles and swatting flies. He'd been swatting flies of one kind or another all his life. Except for one ill-advised peace overture from a group of inmates who claimed they'd never liked Bob anyway, the braying donkeys Johnny shared his cell with had been silent since he dispatched Booger Bob.

The jailers found Bob unconscious and bleeding in the common area and asked the inmates what happened, but no one knew a thing. They transported Bob to the local emergency room, and the latest reports showed he'd been moved to intensive care. A jail matron told a trustee Bob's larynx had been crushed, and he might never speak again above a squeaky, raspy whisper.

Johnny and Jake waited. Jake read a dog-eared copy of a pulp fiction novel circulating among the inmates in the jail. The title of the book was *Mob Boss*.

"Hey, Johnny, you got to read this. It's so hokey," he said.

Johnny was fuming and would have none of it. They had served breakfast with warm, clabbered milk. The bacon was buried in a pound of grease, and the eggs were garnished with long dark hairs, courtesy of the kitchen trustees.

Their Jim Dandy to the rescue, Reggie Morris, arrived in Harrison County as the sun was rising. He set about filing motions and rounding up the large cash bond he knew the judge would require for such notable out-of-state gangsters. Once Reggie had the order from the judge and the bail was set, two somber men driving a black sedan with Louisiana plates met the mob's errand boy outside the bail bondsman's shop, the one with the flashing sign that read *Free at Last*.

Morning shadows were still cast along the street, and the men with cash in bags marked *Little Sicily Olive Oil Company* said little to Reggie beyond grunts and nods. It was business as usual for the men from the Crescent City, and Reggie could tell they'd probably done this many times before. The men with undertaker faces handed Reggie the bags and said, "Here's Johnny's get-out-of-jail-free card." Reggie laughed at what he thought was a quip, but they didn't.

Reggie phoned the consigliere who had told him to spring Johnny and Jake. The mob counselor told Reggie to make sure the boys knew the Don wanted to see them as soon as they got back to New Orleans.

"You tell him business is suffering and to leave this distraction alone. It's bad for business," Arturo said.

When the jailer came to inform Johnny and Jake their lawyer had arranged their release and they were free to go, Split Nose turned to the gawking inmates as he walked out of the cell and said, "If any of you street punks packing heat ever get into a fight, find a real man and give him your ammo cause you ain't gonna make it in this world."

Reggie met them in the waiting room and walked them outside. When he passed along the message from Arturo, Johnny stepped close to him. A tornadic wrath had consumed Johnny, and he constantly rubbed the mark on his neck that appeared after he killed his brother. It burned brighter and brighter and itched from the blood lust that had infected Johnny.

"You don't tell me what to do, you prissy little lawyer boy," Johnny said.

Reggie's tie was suddenly too tight. It choked him as his heart raced and sweat broke out on his forehead.

"I'm just the hired hand. Don't shoot the messenger, Johnny," Reggie said.

Johnny and Jake left Reggie standing in front of the jail mopping his brow with his handkerchief. Jake never questioned Johnny when he told him to drive to a local gun dealer who supplied the needs of men who hunted men. They pulled around back, and after a while, Johnny came out with a small arsenal of weapons and ammunition.

"Where we going, Johnny?" Jake asked.

"You know where we're going, Jake the Rake," Johnny answered.

So instead of heading to Louisiana, they turned north on Highway 49 for Jackson. Every tooth-jarring smack of springs and shocks in fresh potholes from the night's hard rain only aggravated Johnny's foul mood.

Johnny was a troubled child, and he fought hard against what Sister Margaret had tried to beat into him at the school for wayward youths. He came to envision good and evil as those moments of temptation when the two figures appeared over each shoulder. The one with the halo said, "Now, now. You know Sister Margaret wouldn't want you to do such things," and the one with the horns and red suit said, "Go for it."

Split Nose always chose the one with the pointy tail and pitchfork.

Why did I ever lay up at the hippie's piggy palace in Jackson? Whose idea was it to get involved with a senator who smokes dope and can't keep his pants on? The things we have to do, the people we have to associate with for the sake of the business. They aren't family. Cut them out, cut them up...these fat, greedy politicians. Now these punk Communists are hanging around and snot-nosed kids are rioting and flying Viet Cong flags. Kill them all, the senators and the crybabies, like we did Kennedy. Else nothing changes, the politicians still smile, chumps pay their taxes, and no one gets fat except the Rockefeller types who look down on us. This is the death of America, the little land where the politicians are selling us out to the highest bidders, and no one cares.

They passed a meat-packing plant in one of the small towns, and the stench of meat and blood wafted over the highway.

"Where are we headed, Johnny?" Jake asked again.

"We're going to the slaughterhouse," Johnny said.

****

The phone in the Long Beach condo rang loudly before the sun showed itself across the Gulf. Corndog grabbed it on the first ring. He nodded a lot, said, "I see" and "I understand" and "Yes, sir, I'll take care of it" in a one-sided conversation with someone at the Little Sicily Olive Oil Company in New Orleans.

Then a second call came from authorities at the port of New Orleans about the contaminated cotton from Corndog's Delta gin. Then a third call came from buyers at the Cotton Exchange in Memphis. A fourth call came from someone in the Leg Room in Jackson.

Corndog said, "I'll handle the Memphis *Commercial Appeal* and the Jackson *Clarion Ledger*. Yes, I heard both papers had stories about 'White Heroin in White Cotton.'" Then Corndog listened for a while, and tears seeped out of his eyes when he said, "Rose was just another girl at the Leg Room. I barely knew her and knew nothing about her work for the Bureau of Narcotics."

As he sat on the side of his bed, he began to sob, his shoulders hunched against the coldness of aloneness and the inevitable arrival of the Grim Reaper. A fifth call came in; it was Red Winter.

"Senator, are you all right? I know there's some trouble. Do you need a ride back to Jackson?" Red asked.

"No, Red. I have a rental car, and I need to take care of some things, to see people and make amends, but I thank you. You may be the only friend I have left right now. You are my friend, aren't you, son?" Corndog asked with an air of desperation, something Red had never heard in the voice of the Delta senator.

After a long pause on the line, Red said, "Give me a call if you need a ride, Senator."

When the connection clicked off, Corndog said to an empty line, "How quickly the worm turns."

Corndog forced himself to get up and shower, to put on a veneer of the old cockiness. The board of directors was meeting at the Leg Room, and he thought he could still make it if he hurried. Perhaps he could still calm the waters with a few stories and some IOUs. He was in such a hurry to leave, he left behind his Rotary pin and his favorite six-iron.

Corndog arrived at the Sun-n-Sand in the afternoon. He walked to the Leg Room and inserted his key, but it wouldn't work.

He knocked and knocked again.

The door opened, and there stood one of the burly security guys Corndog had hired.

"Well, Bart, good to see you," Corndog said as he tried to step inside.

Bart raised his hand and said, "I'm sorry, Senator, but you aren't welcome here anymore."

"Oh, come on now, Bart. Am I going to have to show you some leg to get in? Is this some kind of joke? If so, it ain't funny," he laughed nervously.

Corndog became frantic and suddenly lowered his shoulders like a lineman under Friday night lights and tried to bust through the door, but the guard put his foot and shoulder against it and refused to budge. The big man began to push Corndog back into the hallway.

Corndog could see the other members of the Leg Room inside, and he screamed at them, "You're all Dr. Frankenstein and I'm your monster. You've disowned your creation, and the mob is coming for me with their pitchforks and torches!"

Bart shut the door with a *whumpf.*

Corndog stood there for a long time, his nose an inch from the closed door. He finally put his hands on the door and then his face. He pounded on the door weakly and begged, "Let me in. I can fix it. I can fix it."

He straightened himself and wiped his nose on the sleeve of his custom-tailored suit. As he turned to leave, he saw two new girls approaching the Leg Room. Tall and pretty, they came swinging toward him with the confidence of youth. Both had a wilderness of long, teased blonde hair and perfect tans. They exuded a predatory vibrancy, and with their high heels, they stood eye-to-eye with him. They were just the kind of girls Corndog once could have charmed, but they had seen him turned away at the door of the Leg Room.

Corndog's boom of authority was once as loud as a cannon. Overnight, it had become nothing more than a creaky chime and the stinky snap of a cap pistol. Just as he mounted a feeble attempt at his old lines, one girl noticed his color was not good and he was sweating profusely.

"Are you all right, mister? Should we call someone to help you to your car?" she asked.

The other asked, "Do you need a doctor?"

He said, "No, no, I'm fine. It's just so hot in here. I was about to invite you ladies to dinner."

"We're busy right now. We have an appointment at the Leg Room. Have you ever heard of it?" one girl asked.

"Yes, I've heard of it," Corndog said flatly.

As they brushed by him, one said to the other, "Who was that poor old man?"

"I don't know. Maybe he used to be somebody. My grandfather looked like that just before he died," the other one replied with a shrug of her shoulders.

It was like a spear through his heart. At that moment, he saw the end and his short path to the finish line. He heard the sweeping sounds of the custodian of forever dusting away his footprints as if he'd never existed. He realized then how he had betrayed himself, and he heard a voice saying, "Nothing and no one is forever."

As he stumbled down the hall, he began to think of "life insurance policies"—notes and tapes he had secreted away, things that might give him leverage, bargaining chips to keep him alive and out of prison.

That's the ticket. I can make deals. I always knew how to cut a good deal. People owe me. I can do what I have to do, keep the Don out of it all, and avoid Johnny. Then I can go into a rest home for a while, kick this dope habit, and then go back to the Delta and retire...sit out on my veranda and think of Melba and Sheler and the good times. Reporters will come by to ask me to relive my defeat of Senator Bowtie and my rise to power. I might have a garden or raise a little cotton for one of those big corporate cotton companies. Those carpetbaggers and scalawags don't even live in the Delta anymore. I don't like 'em, but I might be an entertainment director or public relations man for them, maybe take buyers to hear BB make the blues guitar sing, or dine on the roof of the Peabody in Memphis. That wouldn't be a bad life, but I can't go back to poverty, to the rickets and nothing to eat, patches on my overalls and cardboard in my shoes. But then one day, no one will come by except the funeral home director and his boys in their shiny, long black limousine. Just got to have a plantation house, nothing fancy, just a clear view and clean sight for miles and miles of flat and treeless Delta where I can see if Melba's ghost leaves the bayou to sneak up on me...to haunt me. Who knows, I might even book passage by train or riverboat and follow my cotton to one of the ports and catch a ship to some exotic place where everyone wears fine cotton clothing. Wouldn't that be something? Cotton will always be king, and Corndog will always be the Delta's senator emeritus.

Corndog was sleepwalking through his misery, so lost in what-ifs he never saw the man watching him as he climbed into his car. The man pulled out behind Corndog to follow him as the sun set.

As he followed Corndog, the man fitted a homemade silencer onto a .22-caliber pistol.

****

The man watching Corndog was so intent on the job at hand he never saw the man watching him.

Otis staked out the Leg Room to find Corndog. Otis knew he had taken Melba there, and something bad had happened at the Sun-n-Sand and at Moondog Square. Whatever happened, it ended her life and put Sheler at risk for the rest of her life. Otis had come to settle all debts.

Otis was waiting across the street from the motel when he saw Corndog arrive. He thought he looked harried and disheveled as he shuffled into the motel. He wasn't the cocky man who had visited Otis in prison.

Corndog wasn't gone long. He looked as if his visit had not gone well. He walked to his car and sat there with his head on his steering wheel for a full five minutes. Then Corndog cranked his car and slammed his dashboard in anger over and over. He rolled down his window as he pulled out and rested his elbow on the driver side window frame. His air-conditioner was not working.

Otis was about to pull out when he saw a car following the senator. Corndog drove right past Otis's position and then the car tailing him did, too. Otis got a good look at the driver, and he recognized him. It was the man who had killed the girl at the reservoir. It didn't surprise Otis. Little surprised him anymore, and he just took life as it came. He only wondered who he was, why he was following Corndog, and how this might affect the plans Otis had for Corndog. Then he had the image of a man, two birds, and one stone.

A lazy sun began to settle over the apricot skyline, and chimney swifts appeared in the evening sky as Corndog and his convoy of surveillance drove north from Jackson on Highway 49 toward Yazoo City and Greenwood. Otis wondered what the game was with the guy ahead of him. If he was hostile toward Corndog, where would he make his play? Otis was sure of one thing:

Corndog was his to dispatch from this world, and no one would interfere with his plan.

North of Yazoo City, the sky grew darker and became a blue-black night with flecks of gold and purple on the horizon. The headlights of Otis's car played over the clusters of palmetto palms that grew wild and lined the highway.

Otis hung back. Any time the man he was following looked in his rearview mirror, he would see a different view of the headlights behind him. When they were working in Hattiesburg, Michael showed Otis the toggle switch that allowed bureau cars to change lights to look like a different car on long stretches of highway in a flatland like the Delta. Otis copied the MBN design and wired his car to switch from a set of headlights to one light on either side.

North of Tchula on a deserted stretch of highway, Otis had toggled to one light and then to no lights as he split the highway down the middle and focused on the taillights in front of him as his guide.

Suddenly the man following Corndog sped up and whipped into the left lane. Otis thought he would force Corndog off the road or pull up beside him and shoot him with the little pistol he used on the hippie girl.

Otis cut on his lights and sped up to catch up with the two cars now traveling side by side. Otis angled toward the gunman's left taillight and clipped the car with his front bumper. He learned the technique when he worked in stock car racing. He perfected it by watching police practice the maneuver at Parchman.

Because cars are front-heavy, the bump sent the car into a wild spin, rotating around the engine. Otis slammed on his brakes to avoid the car, and Corndog's car proceeded north on 49 like nothing had happened. The spin caused the man's engine to stall, and it bumped off the road into a drainage ditch, bounced, and rolled over once.

Otis stopped to watch and wait, his headlights resting on the disabled vehicle. Steam was rising from the man's car, and the wheels were mired in mud on the edge of a slough. Frogs silenced by the noise of the wreck began to croak again. After about three minutes, the driver's side door creaked open. The mud caught it, but the driver's hand appeared and then the rest of him as he squeezed his battered body out of the car.

There was blood on his forehead, and a rivulet of red trickled down his face, into his eyes, and around his nose. He looked dazed. Otis exited his car and walked toward the man. He didn't see the weapon the man had used on the girl, but the man had a badge clipped to his belt and a holster that held a snub-nose .38-caliber police special.

The man stopped when he saw Otis and weaved to and fro.

"I'm a police officer, and I'm hurt. Could you get an ambulance?" the man asked.

Otis did not reply, and the man could only see his silhouette in the headlights.

"Who are you? Did you see what happened? Did you get any tag numbers?" the man asked.

Otis said nothing. The man was trying to wipe the blood from his eyes as he sank into the muddy bog.

"I was passing another car. Did you…did you hit my car? Was that you? Someone hit me, but I don't know why," he said.

"I, ah…I'm going to need to see your license and insurance. Can you get me to the LeFlore County Hospital? I think I'm hurt real bad," the man said, clutching his ribs.

"Here's my insurance card," Otis said as he stepped closer to the man and raised his 12-gauge shotgun. "It's my license, too, my license to kill rabid dogs running up and down this highway."

"What? No…no, wait! I don't know what you're talking about. I'm an officer of the law, and the people I work for will reward you," the man protested.

"You're gonna drop names now? Don't make promises you can't keep. You're talking like you was big money, but you ain't even pocket change to me. What law allowed you to kill that poor girl at the reservoir and bury her in her car?" Otis asked.

The man weaved again and fell to his knees. His breathing was labored, and he was wheezing. *Punctured lung*, Otis thought.

"You were there? Where were you?" he asked.

"Watching, always watching what men like you do to innocent girls when you think nobody's looking. You killed that girl, and you have to answer for your crime. The jury just voted, and the judge has sentenced you to die tonight before you have a chance to kill the senator, because killing him is my pleasure and mine alone," Otis said.

"What? No, no! Wait a minute! Wait just a minute! We can make a deal. If you want to kill him, go ahead. People I work for want him dead, too. He's a liability now. The girl, that girl, I felt bad about it, but she talked too much. It wasn't personal, just a job. She endangered important people, people that matter, and she was a nobody," he said as he coughed up blood. Death was tickling his throat.

"Kinda like my Sheler was a nobody. That's what they said about her and her mama...nobodies. The ghosts of the dead and the grave are calling you to an unmarked grave for assassins that only grows weeds, not mourners," Otis said.

"You'll burn with me," the man said, bloody foam showing at the corners of his mouth.

"Maybe, but I've still got time to repent and make it right, but they're already stoking the fires of the inferno for your arrival," Otis said.

The man reached for the gun on his belt, but the explosion from Otis's shotgun lit up the night and the buckshot decapitated the killer of harmless and helpless girls.

Otis stood there a moment under the starry sky and looked up at the vastness of a universe that can numb a heart and make one death seem a smaller thing than a conscience says it is. He returned to his car to catch up with Corndog. He raced up the highway toward Greenwood, but when he saw the city limits sign, he knew he'd lost his opportunity.

Otis turned back toward the scene of the execution. He had to tend to the body, and he wanted to see what agency he worked for.

There was no traffic on the highway at that hour. When he arrived at the scene, he exited his car with his flashlight, but there was no body in sight. Though he knew the man was dead, he instinctively raised his weapon and sighted along the beam of the light.

Then he saw the drag marks. Something, some Delta denizen, had claimed the body. Killer was on the menu tonight, and the gators and giant turtles of the slough were having a feast. Pass the trigger fingers, please.

Otis looked through the car for papers or identification, but the car was clean except for the .22-caliber pistol with the silencer. The serial numbers had been filed off, and the whole weapon appeared to have been cobbled together in a gunsmith's shop. He took it because he thought he might need it for the Stone boys and Corndog, or maybe Michael might want it for forensics.

When Otis turned to walk back to his car, he saw Sheler's ghost standing by the roadside as if this field of death was her shrine. She extended her hand to him, beckoning him to go with her.

"I'm sorry, honey, but there are still miles to go before I rest and things that must be done before I melt my guns into plowshares," he said.

Her ghost waved a sad goodbye and faded away, and somewhere in the night, a gator belched.

CHAPTER THIRTY

*"Lest we forget at least an over-the-
shoulder acknowledgment to the very first
radical: from all our legends, mythology,
and history (and who is to know where
mythology leaves off and history begins—or
which is which), the first radical known to
man who rebelled against the establishment
and did it so effectively that he at least
won his own kingdom—Lucifer."*
—*Saul Alinsky,* Rules for Radicals

*"Killing a cop just because he's a cop,
that'll happen. And that should happen.
And there's nothing inhuman about it at all.
It's survival. It's the most human thing
in the world."—Bernardine Dohrn,
Weather Underground*

As Michael and Molly descended into the valley of
Milkwood, he looked up at the sky. A dirty, yellowish arc had
settled over Moondog Square like a giant circus tent Michael had
seen as a child in Tupelo.

Molly, who was visibly nervous, told Michael she'd
been reading Psalm 23, and it reminded her of a story Jesus told
about a man waylaid by thieves on the ancient road from Jerusalem
to Jericho.

"It was a trail winding through a dark and treacherous
valley, the Valley of the Shadow, a twisting, dangerous path of
thieves and murderers. I think sometimes Moondog Square is that
place, but we shall fear no evil, Michael, shall we?" she asked.

"Nah, it'll be a piece of cake," Michael said, but he
instinctively reached down to pat his gun that wasn't there.

"This may be our last assignment, Michael. Do you know my nickname for us?" she asked coyly.

"No, but I'll bite. What's our nickname?" Michael said.

"M&M. Her kiss melts on his mouth, not in his hands, but you may never know for sure," she teased, her eyes dancing.

"Pretty bad," Michael said. Then they both laughed to break the tension.

Molly had told him things had changed. Milkwood was paranoid, and his people would probably pat Michael down for weapons, so Michael hid his gun in the car before they arrived. He was wearing the discreet wire Clay insisted on. The surveillance team in the van up on the hillside was all ears.

The whole compound area had deteriorated since Michael's last visit, and the atmosphere around the dead-end street seemed heated and stagnant. Smells he'd noticed before had ripened and intensified. The odor of death, something like rotting corpses or carcasses, was in the air, and the whole area seemed to be marinating in a toxic stew. He could only imagine how it would be when the full brunt of July heat set in and the magnolias were melting. Molly said people downwind of the Square had started putting peppermint oil under their noses and no longer sat out on their verandas. The green flies were swarming down in the valley. The stench of decomposition had drawn them and the giant rats scurrying around the compound.

As they walked toward the front entrance, they had a sense of foreboding. The events of Michael's short tenure at the MBN and the return to Moondog had increased his feeling that there was a big bull's-eye on his back and that something or someone had him in the crosshairs.

He no longer felt the presence of life behind the walls of the buildings. The teepee was tilted, and the *No fire sticks allowed* sign was on the ground atop a pile of trash. A new sign had been nailed to the wall of the first floor: *East of Eden, Nod City Limits. You're no longer just trespassing. You're now a target.*

The stairs they climbed were green with mold and mildew, and many steps were cracked or broken in two. Michael's gait was awkward, his shoes sounded wooden, and somewhere within the complex, a blues harmonica was playing "House of the Rising Sun."

When they stepped onto the second floor, Michael could see that many of the rooms were empty. Cobwebs were in every corner, and dusty sheets covered cheap furniture. The rooms that weren't vacant were populated by pasty-pale people bearing the abrasions of loneliness, defeat, and the tracks of too many needles and tattoos of the occult and all things taboo. Their hygiene was gone, and they lived in filth and feces. Some choked on their own vomit. Their private parts were exposed, and they made half-hearted suggestive gestures that were not sensual, only grotesque.

Michael felt sorry for them, but there was danger, callousness, and feral desperation behind these objects of pity. He wanted to help them, but the cop in him knew some inhabitants of Milkwood's paradise would cheerfully bash his head in, stab him, or strike him below the belt and leave him incapable of fathering children. Moondog's zombies appeared to be in a collective stupor, as if they were waiting on something or someone they knew would never come. The snap, crackle, and pop had gone out of Moondog Square.

As Michael and Molly walked down the dreary hall of pain, an armed guard in military fatigues approached them, a man whose skin was so dark it was difficult to make out facial features in the dim light. His voice and demeanor suggested he was no one to mess with.

"State your business," the man growled. He had the look of a former Parris Island drill instructor.

"We're here to see Milkwood," Molly said.

"I know you, Molly, but I don't know this man," he said, fingering the 9mm on his hip with one hand and caressing a giant bowie knife tucked under his belt with the other.

He walked up to Michael, nose to nose, and stared at him to intimidate him as he patted his waist, legs, boots, underarms, and the small of his back for weapons. He was after guns and missed the small body transmitter taped inside Michael's underwear with the thin wire running up to his bellybutton.

"I'm Sergeant Bodacious. Do you see me or do you only see my color?" asked the man with breath like roadkill on hot July asphalt.

"No, I'd rather skip right past that tenth of a millimeter of your epidermis to get a long look at your heart, if you don't mind," Michael said without hesitation.

The man began to smile and then he laughed like a sailor who just got shore leave.

"You're a strange cuckoo bird, but maybe someone to share a shaky tree branch with when the storm comes," he said.

"You may pass this sentry. Second door on the right. Good luck," he said.

He spoke into a small walkie-talkie and said, "Two visitors coming in, sir. They're clean."

When they entered Milkwood's room, he was sitting on the floor picking raisins off an ancient fruitcake. The cake looked like the unwanted Christmas gift that keeps on giving. His skin was a shade lighter than Mountain Dew, and three of his ragamuffin followers were with him. The girls were wearing dirty, threadbare pullover gowns, and they were so thin their legs and arms looked like matchsticks.

They sat in a circle with their skeletal leader around an ancient Ouija board. The crumbs of what looked like psychedelic mushrooms littered the floor. The planchette was moving around the board for the girls as Milkwood watched. When Michael and Molly walked closer, it stopped moving, and the participants looked up at their visitors.

"Well, look what the Hounds of the Baskervilles drug up," Milkwood said, slurring his words.

"I remember you, Brother Jim, and still hanging on to pretty Molly, I see. Are you two still an item? I need money, and I was thinking of suing you for alienation of Molly's affection, but you can't demand what you can't win, can you?" he asked.

"We're very happy," Michael said, reaching to take Molly's hand.

"That's enchanting. Have y'all returned looking for a good time, a magic carpet ride? If so, I'm afraid you've come to the wrong place. Rachel has left me, and the child you were so fond of has flown the coop. Someone helped her father get his wings, too, but I doubt he's floating on a cloud singing 'I'll Fly Away.' Maybe he busted the gates of the inferno wide open, but I suspect that would please you, wouldn't it, Jim?" he said.

Milkwood wasn't pausing for responses. He was off on another one of his insanity-fueled monologues. Sweat poured from his body, and his drenched clothes stuck to him like a second skin, a thin man on a thin string barely keeping it between the ditches.

"No, you won't find any of them or the good times here anymore. My last two brain cells have been arguing with each other all day about how it all went wrong. The 'Man' with all his badges and all his agencies has insisted we walk his line and not step on the cracks. They say the Devil lives here, but what a tomfool idea. Everybody knows he's always hiding in the details. He's not even registered to vote, but he does attend church in disguise," Milkwood said as he looked down at his board and scratched his head with bony fingers.

"Sorry to hear it, but they say what doesn't kill us makes us stronger. Thanks for seeing us," Michael said.

"Why wouldn't I see you, Jim? Even Christ was willing to meet with the most prolific murderer of His people in the first century. Isn't that true? And no one here would ever cry 'Crucify Milkwood,' would they, Molly?" he asked.

"No, I'm sure they wouldn't," Molly said.

"Ah, little Molly, I was broken by your betrayals. I hope you won't betray Jim. I once thought of cutting her throat, Jim, but her tongue became so sharp I knew she'd do it herself one day," he said.

He stared at Jim for a full minute without saying anything.

"But I'm curious about something, Jim. We were just practicing a little witchcraft with our magic board and trying to get the spirits to show us the way. The last time we saw you, some said the board wouldn't work then either, and it stopped just now when you walked in. That's most unusual. Ouija was alive and buzzing and telling us all sorts of things, but as soon as you appeared, it stopped. The spirits don't like you, it seems. It may be your Via are too strong, as my girlfriend from Vietnam knows," he said, pointing to a girl in the circle.

"I don't understand because there should be plenty of spirits here in this private cemetery to overcome anyone with heavy Via. After you left the last time, the Ouija board came alive, and we could talk to many wandering spirits. What do you make of that, Jim?" he asked.

"Beats me, Joiner. I should get along with them. I'm a wanderer myself," Michael said.

"Oh, you remembered my other name. I'm not him anymore, but at least I know you were paying attention. You might not be the problem after all. We just watched Nixon on TV. He's enough to make any spirit ill, and then there's this guy who's been stalking our place. I've seen him lurking out there. Got him on tape one day, and when I showed it to the boarders from Hattiesburg today, they freaked out and started packing. I call them the Rolling Stones, and they can't seem to get no satisfaction here since I shared the tape with them. More lost revenue we need so bad. Look at the monitor, Jim. What do you think? Is the lurker an evil spirit or the devil in disguise again?" Milkwood asked, making horns on his head with his fingers.

Michael looked at the monitor when Milkwood punched play, and there the man was. Michael looked and looked again at the grainy images. It was Otis.

"What do you think, Jim? Ever seen him before?" Milkwood asked, studying his face.

"No, but he doesn't look like a spirit or much of a threat. Maybe he's a jilted lover or an undercover agent for the Better Business Bureau," Michael said.

"Hmm, you might be right. It's so confusing these days. If I had a dollar for every tear I've cried over it all, I'd be a millionaire. I feel like Paul after he was knocked from his horse. Who are you today, Jim, Saul or Paul? Which do you aspire to be? Do you want to destroy me, Saul, or do you wish to save me, Paul? We have to keep the old place humming because when the world feels cold, we all need someplace to go, don't we? I've cut down on costs and gone hungry for the budget. I've been trying to lose calories of the soul, Sir Jim. So I've been on a new 'No Jesus' diet. Nothing but the blood seems nothing but tap water to me. I've seen the light, though, and it blinded me," he said.

Michael thought he hadn't changed unless he was crazier than the last time he saw him.

"You know what I say about it all? Jiminy Cricket, that's what! Oh, excuse me, but Grandma always told me to say that when I was about to use the other JC's name in vain, same initials, you know? But Jiminy was Pinocchio's conscience, wasn't he? I lost my conscience somewhere along the way with my virginity and left them both with my heart in San Francisco. I knew way back then I didn't want to milk no more cows or slop no more pigs. So I ran away to my playground, but Woodstock's gone, John, Bobby, and Martin, too. It ain't no kind of life now, just struggle and strife, and I'm getting tired. There's got to be something better, huh? What's the answer? Do you know, Jim?" he asked, his eyes questioning, almost begging.

"No, I'm afraid such things are above my paygrade," Michael answered.

"I hear you, brother...me, too. I'm just a pharmacist or undertaker or matchmaker or hit man, whatever life demands of me at the moment. I'm looking for some glue to hold it all together. He who joins halves is glue. Are you the glue we've been missing here at Moondog, Jim? Maybe you should 'stick around.' Get it? Stick around?

"I worry for you, Sir Jim. Is your life thematically sterile? Have you come to Moondog Square to experience the shady side of the street, to look for sauces to spice up your life, or are you here as Elmer Gantry? Are you a migrant swallow here to fatten up or will you only spring and summer with us and then abandon Capistrano in our cold winters when we need the fire of your wisdom? Are you cracking your whip to save us from ourselves, or are you just walking through our minefield in your snowshoes? Surely you're not going to tell me crime doesn't pay? So what? I know that already. I hope you're not just another dull, dim-witted rent-a-cop in sheep's clothing sent to write me a ticket for violating the Ten Commandments," he said.

Milkwood drifted then, and an uneasy silence filled the room. A girl in the circle began to brush her hair, and it fell out in clumps from a body starving for food and sanity.

"Molly and I have come for more of the happy powder, if you have some. We want to have a party to announce our engagement," Michael said, squeezing Molly's hand.

Milkwood ignored him and cued up part two of his sermon of the damned.

"Brother Jim, the only hope I have is brought by the men and women who visited us here, the visionaries who brought their clairvoyance to our valley. They've broken bread with us and will come again for the big march in Jackson to change the world, burn the Bibles, and pull down the crosses. These agents of rebellion could be my sons and daughters. They may not carry the lineage of Cain, but they harbor his spirt. My work will go on through them. We'll be baptizing the great unwashed masses in the gospel of the world, and they'll be waterlogged and going under for the third time before they can whisper John the Baptist. Peace on earth, good will to the rebellious," Milkwood said.

"Are these the same folks who just bombed the Capitol? The ones who blew themselves up when a nail bomb they were making to kill innocent people exploded? Doesn't sound like a peaceful group," Michael said.

"You know a lot about the brothers, Jim. You sound like a government agent, just when I had hope for you," Milkwood said.

"No, I'm just a guy who thinks it's wrong to kill innocent people," Michael said.

"I dig it, Jim, but none of us are innocent, are we? Some always have to die for there to be peace and progress. The struggle has been going on for a long time. It's the Weathermen now, but after World War 1 and 2, they called themselves the Antifa. One day the Weathermen may fade, and the movement may reclaim the name of Antifa. We are all anti-fascists, and one day truth will only be what we say it is. This is the new Bethlehem, and they're our heavenly hosts coming down to us. Jim, I'm a minor prophet, and this is my bible," he said, holding up his copy of *Rules for Radicals*.

"The young are hungry for meaning and purpose, a revolution of the soul, and we must give it to them. Our major prophet, Saul Alinsky, says we are the religion for the have-nots, and we will organize them in hell, if there is a hell," he said.

"I'm not a theologian, but wasn't Jesus the real radical who defeated Satan?" Michael asked.

Milkwood covered his ears, and a tiny trickle of blood showed at the corners of his nostrils.

"Jim, you make my head hurt. No, don't you see? The great universities will abandon their Christian foundation, throw off the shackles of divine design, and offer classes in Milkwood 101 and graduate studies in what man now calls depravity. Che, Mao, Fidel, and Gus Hall will be celebrated. The last priest will be strangled with the guts of the last preacher. Cloistered Christians will mature, lay down their crosses, and step into the world. The captives will be set free from the old-time religion to worship at our altar. Children infected with love of country and an imaginary

God will be cured. We won't be preaching Mark to this sin-soaked world but his twin kept locked away in the attic, the black sheep of the family...Marx," he said, pausing to catch a wheezing gasp of air.

"What if these captives don't want to be set free?" Michael asked.

"The Weatherman reeducation camps will handle those straggling hard cases. If brain cleansing fails, the executioner will come to scrub the fruited plains clean of their infestation. For the institutions we loathe to bleed, people must bleed first. Who knows, I may get the franchise for the camps. But c'mon, Jim, it's in our DNA. We all want to pick up that stone. Everybody's a little evil, but you must be over fifty percent to play on our team. The head Weatherman says I'm a perfect 66.6 percent bad. Get it, Jim...666! The Weatherman's got a way with words. He must be the communications director for the devil," Milkwood said with a chuckle.

Milkwood began to cough violently. He covered his mouth with a soiled handkerchief, and Michael saw the fresh bloodstains on it. Milkwood wiped his lips with the filthy rag, blew his nose, and began again.

"The Weathermen told me the serpent must shed its skin to be petted by the world. Then they said in forty years we'll be in the White House and confusion will rule. Everything will be questioned. Division will reign, neighbor versus neighbor and brother against brother, Cain and Abel all over again with every tribe wandering in Nod. Adam and Eve will move back to the Garden where they were unfairly evicted by their Landlord, and they will plant a whole orchard of trees of knowledge, transform the world, and we will be our own gods. You can't unroll a little of the carpet without the whole rug wanting to unroll. The old Eden was a bore anyway, and people with their Christ are the real danger. Soon America will be red, white, and blue and gone," he said.

Milkwood sighed and shrugged his frail shoulders.

"But until the Promised Land arrives, we got to worry about paying the bills right now and beating back the wolves at our doors. Doom is beating its bass drum. The Italians and politicians have left us. The wounded Stones will soon leave, too. Is your God punishing me, preacher? Nothing to do but put out the vacancy sign, offer free goodies for weary travelers, and hope for the best, I guess.

"So I'm having a markdown sale, Jim. I'll sell you all you need. I'll give you the last of it on hand for the right price," he said.

Milkwood motioned to a girl, who brought out a large bag of white powder. It looked to be a half pound of heroin, purity likely weak as Milkwood had cut the mix again and again, stretching his resources to survive his drought of misfortunes.

"How much you got on you, Jim?" he asked.

"I have two thousand dollars for me and Molly, not nearly enough for what you have there," he said.

"I tell you what. You can have it all for free if Molly agrees to come home to us," Milkwood said with an evil grin.

Molly looked terrified and glanced at Michael with fearful eyes.

"That's not going to happen," Michael said, rising to leave.

"No, no. Don't get on your high horse, Matt Dillon. You can keep Miss Kitty and have the smack for your cash, too. It's a cleansing, and I like you, Sir Jim. Go get wired with friendly friends, celebrate your wedding and matrimonial bliss, and prepare for the revolution. I will put in a good word for you with these guys who can shoot flies off the barn at fifty yards. I'll make sure they don't kill you if you and the other sheep will just chew your cuds quietly. What about it, Slim Jim?" Milkwood asked.

Michael handed him the money, and Milkwood handed him the bag of dope, hand-to-hand just like prosecutors preferred and all on audio tape in the surveillance van if Clay's technology was working.

Milkwood weaved back and forth as if he was about to pass out. Then his eyes focused, and he looked at Molly and said the magic words. "Miss Molly, when I first met you, heard you speak, and then heard you singing in your room here one day, I thought you sounded like what good bourbon tastes like," he said, pausing.

"Rain makes flowers bloom. It's been pouring in your life. Why then are you not blooming? I think maybe you are when I see you look at Jim. I'm sorry for my transgressions…the birds and the bees, all that pollinating but no love. I hope you can one day forgive me," he said.

Molly was stunned. A tiny, solitary tear seeped from her left eye and carved a rivulet of pain and sorrow down her cheek.

"Well, thanks for your tithing to our little church in these wild woods, Jim. I worry for you and Molly. The revolutionaries will make the water in the Pearl River turn red. Make sure there is blood over your door when our angels of death pass over, but I'm happy to sell you all you need to tide you over, preacher. You need the powder and God knows we need the money," he said.

"God knows?" Michael asked with a smile.

"Good catch, Jim. It was a Freudian slip, an echo from childhood, but who knows, maybe I'm hedging my bets. I've fallen into the deep end of the pool without my life preserver, and all of us are crying 'help' and looking for a Lifeguard as we go down for the third time, aren't we, Jim?" he said.

Michael thought it was more than a Freudian slip. There was a lacquered hardness to the surface of Milkwood and his madness, a striving for moral indifference in his mocking words as he tried to shield his insecurities and doubts behind a veil of confused emotion. Michael thought he caught glimpses of a little boy peeking from behind a well-drawn curtain, but Milkwood had lived in darkness so long he had become darkness.

"Anyway, I know you want to save me from hell, but people like me couldn't be happy in heaven. Y'all just walk backwards out of this place like Noah's sons when you leave today and don't look back," Milkwood said.

A violent wind whipped down into the valley, rattled the doors and shutters, and made an eerie howl like a banshee. A yellow haze settled over the compound and seeped in through the cracks of the windows. The big guard burst into the room shouting:

"Men are coming, Mr. Milkwood! They got guns!"

CHAPTER THIRTY-ONE

"If your enemy offers you two targets,
strike at a third."—Robert Jordan,
Crossroads of Twilight

"Always keep your foes confused. If they
are never certain who you are or what
you want, they cannot know what you are
likely to do next."—George R.R. Martin,
A Storm of Swords

Otis was wedged in between two large oaks on the banks of a drainage ditch across from Moondog Square. He'd left his car in the drive of a vacant house on the hill, fought his way through the undergrowth, and walked to Moondog to kill or be killed. He'd come for the Stone brothers or Corndog or any villain who gave them safe harbor.

Otis looked up from his perch at a strange yellow fog settling over the valley. He felt the end of things at hand. Maybe these were the end times his mama told him about when he was a child. He wondered what it would be like when the armies of good came. Maybe there would be rest then for soldiers like him.

He wasn't good at words or at tears. He had tried and cried them both. Revenge was a bitter weed, choking out every flower in his garden, but justice was finally at hand. Otis closed his eyes to open his senses to Sheler's stardust from yesterday, to make her live again—to kiss her, hear her, see her, and feel her with his heart one last time in case things didn't go well, but it wasn't working today. He couldn't seem to see her face or remember what she looked like. He panicked and hyperventilated.

His heart had rusted from his secret tears. He'd held on too long to what was killing him, but it was the only thing that made him want to live. The prison chaplain at Parchman had talked to him about heaven and hell and asked him if he had thought about where he wanted to go when he died. Otis said, "I already been through hell on earth, so anywhere is fine, as long as it's someplace else."

  Otis settled his case of the shakes and adjusted the sights on his BAR. He put in a fresh clip, set the gun to automatic, and said out loud what passed for a prayer: "If it's three strikes and you're out, I struck out long ago, Lord, but I remind myself what Babe Ruth said: 'Every strike brings me closer to a home run.' Let today be a home run. Thank you. Amen."

****

  Corndog was dodging federal agents and gangsters who he was sure wanted to kill him. Something strange had happened behind him in the dark when he was driving north on 49. There were fast cars, strange lights, and a crash. He wasn't sticking around to figure it out, but he didn't feel safe anymore at his Greenwood home. He thought maybe he should've gone to his Greenville gin to hide out, but they could get to him there, too. Just like he separated the white lint from the trash and the seeds at his gin, those federal boll weevils were good at separating a man from his liberty.

  He decided to go back to Jackson, to lay low at Moondog Square. Before he left the Delta, he searched through his garage and found a small .25-caliber pistol he kept to shoot snakes and other undesirables. The small automatic was a poor choice for varmint control. It was loud and inaccurate at any distance, but Rose had given it to him on one of her visits, and he kept it in a rare moment of sentimentality. On the trip to Jackson, the slight weight of it beneath his jacket caressed his churning stomach and comforted him. Since Red had abandoned him, he thought the little pop-gun might be the last friend he had.

  As he drove down the winding street to Moondog Square, he itched all over and thought he was an old dog who kept sleeping under new porches, trying to lose his fleas, but like his sins, the fleas just kept on biting him. He turned on his windshield wipers, trying in vain to remove a sticky yellow film raining from the sky.

****

The message Split Nose was given when he called New Orleans to tell them he was in Jackson was straightforward: "Finish it and come home."

He and Jake the Rake said little to each other on the drive to Jackson. Both could've used a hot shower and a fresh change of clothes. Split Nose still had on the same shirt from the night before, and the stains of Booger Bob's blood showed on his sleeves. He knew Corndog was compromised and would likely squeal to the feds about them. The senator's little paramour had been dealt with, and now Split Nose was called to bat in the cleanup position. It was strictly business, but if the hippie cop from Biloxi happened to be at Moondog, he would be a bonus. He would be personal.

As they began their descent to Moondog Square, they could see a man who looked like Corndog exiting a car, and beyond him in the bushes, Jake saw movement. It was hard to make anything out because of the yellowing air in the depression.

****

The news of armed men approaching Moondog caused Milkwood lose it.

"It's the appointed time. The government armies have come for us, the last true remnant of the resistance. The earth is thirsty for blood. Power to the people! Repel the invaders, Sergeant Bodacious, until reinforcements arrive," he shouted.

"Yes, sir, I will," Bodacious said. He saluted and charged out the door with his sidearm and an Uzi with a full clip.

Michael grabbed Molly's hand and moved to leave, but Milkwood whipped out his pistol and pointed it at them. "No one move until we sort this out. There may be spies among us. If our forces are overwhelmed, we all may have to die together in our bunker. We can't fall into the hands of the enemy of the people's liberation forces," he screeched.

Molly looked at Michael as the sound of gunfire erupted outside.

"Milkwood, is there a back way out? Maybe we can all slip away," Michael said.

"No, Jim, we sealed it against intruders and those who tried to escape from our little community, to keep people out and to keep people in," he said.

Milkwood looked around the room with the eyes of a man who no longer had any oars in the water and wagged his gun at everyone in the room.

"Besides, Jim, out back is the holy ground, the tower of skulls and our place of sacrifice. We dare not disturb the spirits sleeping there," he said.

"Milkwood, we've got to get the girls to safety. We don't want to let the enemy capture our women. You know what they would do to them," Michael said, trying to find something to reach him.

Milkwood turned and looked at his followers. "Yes, you're right, Jim. We can't allow that to happen."

Without warning, he raised his pistol and shot one of his girls. *Bang!*

The sound of the shot was deafening, and the other girls screamed and cried. One crawled to the body of her friend, cradled her head, and rocked back and forth, wailing.

"There, they will never get her. She's safe now," Milkwood said, saluting the dead girl.

Molly rushed to the wounded girl's side, but she was dead.

"Why did you shoot that helpless girl?" Michael asked him.

Milkwood looked at him, bewildered at the question. "She was anonymous. I tore the scabs off her wounds, and she clapped like a trained seal. She was in the newspaper when she was born, and if I allow it, she will be in the paper in death, but I will be the one known far and wide when the rebellion comes. Don't cry for her. She's dead. It's not like you were going to see her at the tailgate party for the State–Ole Miss game," he said.

CHAPTER THIRTY-TWO

"Hand-to-hand is how it will be, a life-and-death fight with the fiend. And he whom death bears off will submit to the judgement of the Lord."—Beowulf

"We've got to start thinking beyond our guns. Those days are closin' fast."
—The Wild Bunch

When Otis looked up, he saw the rental car come down the hillside. He could see the Hertz sticker on the window. The windshield was heavily tinted, and in the pea soup of yellow, he couldn't make out how many were in the vehicle. The car stopped in the parking area, and the driver sat motionless for the longest time.

Finally the door opened and out stepped Corndog. Otis had him in his sights just as he saw Sammy and Marty Stone coming down the stairs. Then a ghost car appeared from out of nowhere and slowly coasted down the lane toward Corndog. Two men emerged, and an animated conversation began. The big guy said something to Corndog, who was protesting loudly and backing away. Corndog clutched the tiny pistol in his pocket and said, "We can work it out, Split Nose. Jake! Talk some sense into him!"

A theater of life and death was unfolding before Otis's eyes. It was too choreographed to be pure chance. The curtain was rising on the operatic production, and the players and extras were taking their places and reciting their lines.

The senator retreated to the other side of his car, drew his small pistol, and waved it at Split Nose and Jake. Otis laughed at the sight of Corndog, who couldn't find his backside with both hands in a real fight, with a gun. Corndog was packing heat. The big man called Split Nose laughed at the senator's peashooter.

Otis first aimed at the Stone brothers. Then he swiveled to aim at Corndog. He swung the muzzle of the BAR back to cover the two men who had produced their own guns. He licked his dry lips and wiped his sweaty palms on his pants legs. His heart was racing and the pumping blood was squishing in his ears. These people were gumming up the works. This wasn't how he'd planned it.

He forgot himself and stood up in his confusion just as the whine of a bullet buzzed by his head. The Stone brothers had seen him and were firing at him with 9mm semiautomatic pistols. Due to the distance, most of their rounds were falling short or wide and kicking up dust and debris around Otis. Call it luck or the home team advantage, but it wouldn't be long before they compensated. Otis's football coach always said life and football were just a matter of inches.

The die was cast. All the slugs were in one place, and Otis figured he was a big, gun-toting pillar of salt that had stared at and lived in Sodom and Gomorrah too long. He opened up on the Stones with a full burst from the BAR. Shell cases went flying, and the rounds splintered the rails and stairwell and slammed Marty Stone against the wall of the first floor like a ragdoll.

The screeching of ricochets around and in front of Otis sounded as if he'd been caught in a cloud of giant, angry mosquitoes. The BAR rounds were punching through the outer walls of the building, and the screams from inside the buildings were bloodcurdling.

Corndog thought someone was firing at him, so he fired two rounds at Split Nose and his partner. Corndog had arrived at the O.K. Corral, never having fired a shot, but even a blind pig stumbles into a mud hole now and then. One of his rounds grazed Split Nose along the side of his neck and cut right through the mark of Cain he bore.

Jake grabbed Split Nose, fired at Corndog, and retreated behind their vehicle. Jake kept tugging at the big man's arm, trying to get him in the car, urging him to leave the area.

As rounds buzzed past his ears and clipped the trees behind him, Otis moved from his position to one on an embankment behind Corndog's car. Sammy Stone retreated behind the stairs and was firing wildly at everything that moved.

Suddenly a dark-complexioned man appeared on the second floor landing and fired a short burst from an Uzi at the visitors from New Orleans and then at Otis. One round caught Otis high in his left shoulder and knocked him down.

Split Nose and Jake returned fire at the new gunman and at Sammy Stone, who was shooting at them. Shards of glass from his car hit Corndog in the face, and he rolled around on the ground like a wounded animal. It was a bloodbath.

Otis was dazed. Everything seemed to be moving in slow motion, but he propped up on his elbows and emptied a full clip in the direction of the second floor shooter and everything around him. The man came tumbling down the stairs face first, his chin bouncing off each step. His gun came clattering behind him until the man in the army clothes lay sprawled on the ground in front of the teepee. The Nod City Limits sign jarred loose, fell on top of the man, and covered his body. The gunman shuddered, went into a violent muscle spasm, and then was still.

Sammy Stone rolled out from under the stairwell, tore at the collar around his neck, exposing a gaping hole that had been his windpipe. He tried once to stand and fell dead beside the man with the Uzi.

Just as Otis was about to pass out, he thought he heard sirens, and he heard a voice from beyond ask, "What are you thinking right now? Are you silently pleading for one more chance, for just one more minute of life?"

CHAPTER THIRTY-THREE

*"Time flies, death urges, knells call, heaven
invites, hell threatens!"*—Edward Young

*"If you will not die for us, you cannot ask us
to die for you."*—Jacqueline Carey,
Kushiel's Dart

Milkwood had snapped. As the gun battle raged outside, the atheist revolutionary, like Nietzsche on his deathbed, quoted Scripture.

"All is lost, Jim! All is lost!" he cried.

"'For without are dogs, and sorcerers, and whoremongers, and murderers, and idolaters, and whosoever loveth and maketh a lie,'" he shouted like a preacher at a Saturday night tent revival.

Milkwood grabbed his walkie-talkie and said, "Come in, Bodacious. Are you there, Sergeant?"

His two followers were crying, and Molly had hugged the floor to avoid the stray rounds from outside. Michael could hear the screams of residents across the hall. He wondered where his backup was.

"Plan the wake, raise your glasses in a toast, play the dirge, and bear us to our holes in the ground. It is the appointed hour," Milkwood proclaimed.

"Milkwood, it may be too late for us, but let's get the women out of here," Michael said.

With a sudden burst of drug-fueled energy, the gaunt man swirled and backhanded Michael across his head with the pistol, knocking Michael to the floor.

"This is the Alamo. How dare you suggest we surrender to Santa Anna? Traitors will be shot on sight!" Milkwood shouted.

He raised the gun to shoot Michael, but Molly jumped in front of him and cried, "No!" just as a barrage of bullets from

Otis's BAR punched through the walls of the room and shredded all the trappings of the would-be deity of Moondog Square.

****

Michael was out cold, but he was being interviewed by a man in white who said the bill for his naïveté and carelessness had come due. The man said he could backdate the checks if he wished. They wouldn't be cashed if Michael found his way to Yeshua, where his debts had all been cancelled. "Where is He? How will I know Him?" Michael asked.

Then he heard someone calling his name.

"Michael, Michael. Can you hear me?"

Michael opened his eyes to see a fuzzy image of Clay Strickland standing above him.

"You're going to be all right, buddy," Clay said.

"What happened, Clay? I feel like I ate a bucket of ice cream too fast. My head is pounding," Michael said.

"It was a massacre. Your body unit went out, and we were flying blind and late to the rescue," he said.

"Casualties?" Michael asked.

Two men were standing behind Clay and looking at Michael.

One of the men had high, sharp cheekbones and a beaked nose. He had a hard jawline and a look of rapacity in his eyes, a man who wanted to control everything in his exclusive world of "I and not I."

"I'm FBI Special Agent Carlson Palmer from Washington. I'm assisting the organized crime task force out of New Orleans, and this is DEA Agent Tom Brooks from the task force. We'll want to debrief you later on cases we're working on. There are many overlapping concerns here, and you people have mucked up a long and meticulous investigation, but I can answer your questions. The Stone brothers are dead. The man called Bodacious is dead. Your CI, Otis, is wounded and on the way to the ER. He caught a break. The round that hit him went clean through.

"Your friends from New Orleans are under arrest, and Johnny 'Split Nose' Gagliano is already under guard in the ER. He took a round to the neck, narrowly missing the carotid artery. He'll recover to stand trial for the murder of Arnold and related drug and murder charges. Local FBI and DEA agents have been tailing the Marshmallow men for weeks. They had bird dog tracking devices underneath their car, and your race track theatrics on Highway 49 almost ruined their investigation," Palmer said.

Clay shot him a look, and the agent pursed his thin lips and nodded.

"After you turned the local area into a demolition derby, task force members waited and tracked them again as they made their way to Jackson. Agents lost them for a while but finally got a fix on their coordinates using the bird dog units. It took a while to narrow the field and wind up here late to the party. We hope to flip one or both of your racing buddies to turn on Marcello," Palmer said.

Agent Brooks said, "We arrested Senator Cornelius Ball for conspiracy to smuggle heroin. He was treated for minor wounds and is being interrogated at another location. The only thing he wanted to know was if you were an agent," DEA Agent Brooks said.

"But they're all bit players, as you are, Agent Parker, in our investigation of the Weather Underground fugitives who were here," Palmer said.

"Corndog was here, too?" Michael asked, ignoring the FBI agent and rubbing his aching head.

"What about Milkwood?" Michael asked, looking at Clay.

"Dead from a stray round from Otis's BAR or from shots fired by one of the other combatants firing at the building, we think. All his girls are dead, too. He shot one in the back, and it appears the other two committed suicide by slitting their wrists with razor blades and bleeding out," Clay said.

"Milkwood fell here," Clay said, pointing to men finishing a chalk outline on the floor next to Michael.

Michael looked at the outline of an empty man, a chalk outline looking for a floor to die on, his delusions of grandeur spilled onto the bloodstained floor of a house of horrors. Michael closed his eyes to stop the room from spinning out of control.

"Where's Molly?" Michael asked without opening his eyes.

The agents looked at each other, and FBI Agent Palmer snapped, "My toddlers are grown. I can't take you on to raise, Agent Parker. There are consequences. Your CI is dead. You're losing a lot of CI's, aren't you? The MBN is going to have to issue hazardous duty pay to work with you."

Michael opened his eyes in time to see Clay shoot Palmer a dirty look.

"What? No, she was just here. I remember now. As I was passing out, she jumped in front of me when Milkwood was about to kill me," Michael said.

"She wasn't hit by the BAR. It appears Milkwood killed her. She took a bullet meant for you. We found her body draped across yours," the FBI agent said.

"No! No! She's here somewhere. We have to find her, put out an APB on her," Michael said.

"Why don't you get the dream you're nursing out in the open where you can pet it. She's dead, Agent Parker. Let her go and get back to your local dope dealers and stay out of the big leagues," Palmer snapped, sighing and hooking his thumb under his belt next to the gun on his hip.

"Help me up, Clay. We've got to look for her. I know her haunts. We can't have another Rose," Michael said.

"I'm sorry but we can't allow that. Her apartment's now sealed. This is a federal matter now," the FBI agent said.

"Just help me up, Clay," Michael said.

Clay motioned the agents to a far corner of the room. As Michael struggled to get up, he could see an intense argument was taking place between Clay and the agents.

The red-faced FBI agent stormed off to talk on his radio. When he returned, he said, "Assistant Director Tollison authorized it, but if this blows up again, it's on you, Agent Strickland."

"Come with us, Agent Parker. They're holding up the hearse wagons for us. We'll take you to her body so you can get some closure," the sour-faced FBI agent said.

"C'mon, buddy, lean on me. Don't mind him. Drugs and organized crime are not his focus. The DEA doesn't like him any more than we do. He's a COINTELPRO operative after radicals and terrorists," Clay whispered.

When Michael got to his feet, Clay steadied him and said, "Remember, Molly's like a half moon. There's always half of her hidden away."

CHAPTER THIRTY-FOUR

"From the ashes, a fire shall be woken. A
light from the shadows shall spring."
—*J.R.R. Tolkien*, Fellowship of the Ring

"'Dig it! Manson killed those pigs, then they
ate dinner in the same room with them,
then they shoved a fork into a victim's
stomach."—*Bernardine Dohrn, Weather*
Underground co-founder, to an SDS
gathering in Beverly Hills

The walls of the buildings looked like Swiss cheese. They were riddled with bullet holes. Fragments of glass from the windows dusted the floor like fine-powdered snow garnished with red flecks of blood.

Somber-faced officers of every denomination in the alphabet soup of agencies stretched yellow crime scene tape around the area. Forensic experts picked through shell casings and meticulously photographed the carnage. Other officers canvassed the neighborhood and made notes.

Michael eased his way down the stairs with Clay and the federal agents. A sea of uniformed Jackson police officers and medical personnel were scurrying about. The flashing of red and blue lights was mesmerizing. Dave Best, Carl Burns, Dean Smith, and Chief Larry Burnside came up to pat him on the back and whisper awkward but kind expressions of support and condolence.

On the far side of the compound parking lot, there were three ambulance/hearses. Their back doors were closed, and the emergency lights lining the vehicles were blinking red and yellow. The entire grizzly scene was bathed in a strange dense yellow hue Michael had once seen in the aftermath of a tornado that had ripped through Parker Grove.

"How does it feel to be a part of, a catalyst for all this, Agent Parker?" the FBI Agent sneered.

Michael didn't answer. He was watching a man high on the hill watching them. The man was holding a sign that said, "Repent now. Judgment is at hand."

Agent Palmer knocked on the back of one of the long ambulances, and the door opened.

"Step out and give Agent Parker a moment," he said.

Michael stepped up and into the hearse, and Clay closed the door behind him. The stagnant air smelled like death. He was claustrophobic and bottled up with two corpses covered by shrouds. He sat there on his haunches for a moment and then leaned over to look at the toe tags visible at the end of the sheets.

There it was. The tag listed Molly's name and the time and date of her death. He couldn't bear to pull the sheet back. He bowed his head and cried softly without making a sound.

"Why are you crying, Michael?" a voice said from beneath the sheet covering the other body.

Michael almost jumped out of his skin. His heart was pounding like a jackhammer. He felt dizzy and thought he was hearing voices because of the blow to his head.

The sheet covering the other body rustled and the body beneath it rose up like a scene from a bad B horror movie. Then the sheet fell away, and the smiling face of Molly was staring at him.

"Surprised?" she said.

"What? How? I don't understand, but you're alive! Thank God, you're alive!" he said as he moved to take her outstretched hands.

Molly squeezed his hand so hard he thought he heard bones cracking.

"I don't understand, Molly," he said.

"How much have they told you?" she asked.

"They told me you were dead. Nothing else," he answered.

"It's a long story. Officially, I am dead," she said.

"I suppose I should make the bad joke then. What's a nice girl like you doing in a hearse like this?" he said.

"When Milkwood hit you with his gun, I could see he was going to kill you. I jumped in front of you and pleaded with him not to do it. I thought at first he was going to kill me. I walked toward him and told him it wasn't too late. I told him he'd taken me in when I was broken, and I could now walk him to the light and away from the darkness," she said.

Agent Palmer knocked on the ambulance door and said, "Five minutes, Agent Parker."

"As I was talking to Milkwood, his eyes softened. I was right in front of him, the barrel of the gun touching my chest. He began to cry, and then he said, 'Oh, little Molly. What have I done?'

"Before I could stop him, he turned the gun on himself and shot himself in the head. His blood was all over me. The girls shrieked and moaned, and they pulled razors out of their gowns and opened their veins. It was part of the suicide pact he made us sign in case the government ever came for our god. I tried to help him and the girls, but they were gone, an efficient and practiced exit he once drilled into us," she said.

"But why are you here? Why are they showing you as dead?" Michael asked.

"Agent Palmer showed up when all the police burst into the room. He was from Washington and knew all about me. He told me they'd been watching Moondog since the bombing of the Capitol, and he could get me out of everything, wipe the slate clean. It blew my mind when he said they wanted me to go away for a while for training and come back as an undercover agent to infiltrate the Weather Underground. He acted like it was the most normal thing in the world and said J. Edgar Hoover had authorized the plan because he believed the radicals to be a grave threat to national security.

"Agent Palmer said the men who visited Moondog would remember me and due to my history here, they would let me in. He also told me he knew some of the men had slept with me in the old days and inferred that they, the FBI, had tapes of everything. Palmer said intimacy was a powerful drug to numb their paranoia. He told me this was a chance to wipe the slate clean, to start life over. He knew I was now a Christian and told me this offer was like being born again in the service of God and country. I knew he was playing on my new faith, but I didn't care. My sorrows always knew how to swim, but I drowned them in the giant baptismal that stormy night in the stadium. He's just tying up the loose ends," she said.

"I don't know, Molly. This is too much, too fast," Michael said.

"I know. He said people were watching Moondog. The word would spread like wildfire, and we had to move fast. I'm scared, and it's a blind dart throw, but it feels right, Michael. It seems like a Divine window opening to give my life meaning, to make it count, to make what the world meant for evil…good. I'm just a caterpillar with a chance to become a butterfly," she said.

The FBI knocked on the door with urgency and said, "It's time, Agent Parker."

Molly pressed his hand to her cheek and said, "I was Cinderella looking for her glass slipper, but you and I could never be. I will always think of you and wonder about what-ifs, and I will worry about you. Please don't put those rose-colored glasses of idealism back on when I'm no longer around, Michael. When you take them off, you can see the true colors of the people who approach you because you will see them in black and white. You can't fix people like me. You can't give us what you can't spare, and you can't scratch an itch from childhood by trying to save others. There will always be trash fires burning around you, and you can't put them all out, running here and there with your water buckets."

She leaned forward and kissed him lightly at the corner of his mouth and then turned his hands over. "See, my M&M kiss melted on your mouth, not in your hands," she said.

They laughed too loud, like two people who would never see each other again.

"I used to think I was a squirrel because I attracted so many nuts, but you're the only nut I ever wanted to keep to get me through the harsh winters of life. Love can be ugly and beautiful, Michael…just like me," Molly said, her long lashes fluttering with the rapid blinking of her eyes.

The door opened. Michael stepped out as agents jumped in the back. The doors closed. The last glimpse he had of her was without his rose-colored glasses. Her head was tilted to one side. A sheath of red hair hung across her bowed head to mask the tears blurring her emerald eyes. All her clocks had been rewound, stains washed away, and her skin was as white as snow.

The yellow haze outside had vanished. He thought he heard the sun say, "I resign." The azure sky was cloudless, the world was clueless, and his heart suddenly hurt worse than his head. He thought life was never fair, but sometimes second chances are awarded to broken girls…girls who taste like M&M candy.

CHAPTER THIRTY-FIVE

*"Once to every man and nation comes the
moment to decide, In the strife of Truth with
Falsehood, for the good or evil side. Truth
forever on the scaffold, Wrong forever on
the throne—Yet that scaffold sways the
future, and, behind the dim unknown,
Standeth God within the shadow, keeping
watch above his own."—James Russell
Lowell,* This Present Crisis

"Truth crushed to earth will rise again."
—William Cullen Bryant

The smell of smoke and charcoal filled the air, and the burgers and dogs were on the grill at Clay's ranch, his castle in the wilds south of Jackson. As Clay tended his meal, he watched Michael play a card game with his daughter. He thought Michael was all patched up, but he could still see the cracks.

"Le, run in the house and help Mommy with the desserts. I need to talk with Mr. Michael a moment," Clay said.

When she went inside, Clay said, "I've been meaning to talk with you, and I wanted to do it away from the office. How're you feeling?"

"I feel good, Clay. I'm looking forward to seeing these Weathermen at the big antiwar march in Jackson and to the rumored assignment in Tylertown," he said.

"I talked with Agent Palmer," Clay said.

"What did he say?" Michael asked, perking up.

"Well, not much, as you can imagine, but he said things were going well. He also said Hoover himself authorized the operation with Molly. He told me Hoover remembered you from your time in Washington at the FBI," Clay said.

"Really? I know I'm unforgettable, but how in the world would Hoover remember a lowly former fingerprint tech?" Michael asked.

"Hoover said he remembered you from the day you met him at church on East Capitol Street. It was the site of Hoover's birthplace, a place and time he'd remember. Hoover said he was greeting guests and saw you standing beneath the giant stained-glass window dedicated to him at the service. He said you were standing there looking up at the towering image of Jesus, and the sun shining through the glass bathed you in a glowing ochre light. Hoover told Palmer he never forgot that. He said you were humble and nervous when he talked with you, but dedicated," Clay said.

Images of that day and the church service flooded Michael's mind. "That's something. Long ago and far away," he said.

"Palmer said the Weather Underground issued a formal declaration of war on the United States. He said people like Molly will prove invaluable to the FBI. Palmer said members of the Underground had gone to Cuba to work the sugar cane fields and to be schooled by visiting North Vietnamese Communists. He wouldn't say if Molly was one of them. They were trained, armed, and funded by the Cubans and schooled in propaganda and incendiary explosives.

"They're also trying to start a race war. The revolutionaries have pushed identity politics to pit neighbor against neighbor. They are trying to make their war not just ideological but racial. Hoover called Bernardine Dohrn the 'most dangerous woman in America.' She said, 'White youth must choose sides. They must either fight on the side of the oppressed or be on the side of the oppressor.' American against American, bombings, collaboration with Communists, and sowing racial unrest...they're cutting a wide swath," Clay said.

"If these radicals have such good intelligence, won't they wonder why Molly was declared dead but suddenly shows up to join forces with them?" Michael asked.

"As I understand the plan, she was to tell them she put her ID on one of the dead girls to throw the FBI off her trail and went on the run. She's the perfect recruit because she no longer exists. Most of the Weathermen are living under assumed names. They go into cemeteries to take the names of babies who died about the time they were born," Clay said.

"Fascinating. What will life be like for Molly?" Michael asked.

"From what Palmer told me, they badger their members and try to mold them into hardened revolutionaries. They have self-criticism sessions, 'Weatherfries,' they call them, to break down resistance and build cohesion in the collective. These are Maoist techniques we saw when I was in Vietnam. The Weathermen go at their members for hours on end to purge what they consider racism, individualism, and chauvinism in their ranks. They use these sessions, as long as twelve hours or more, to ridicule and bully their members and force them to toe the party line. They also use the sessions to root out informants. So that's something Molly will almost certainly have to endure, if she hasn't already.

"They live lean, and personal property is renounced. So she'll live a Spartan existence. She will live in safe houses full of propaganda, essays by Malcolm X and Ho Chi Minh, and rooms with Che Guevara's picture on the wall. They will eat rice and fish dishes they were introduced to in Cuba. All the money they beg, borrow, steal, or get from the Communists goes to the collective. Despite the Utopian ideals they profess, the men in leadership positions are all-powerful. They won't allow monogamy and view it as a threat. Couples are split apart, and women are rotated among the groups to break up affections and to provide sex partners for the leaders. This is a cult.

"Molly's young and pretty, so there will be jealousy from other women who make up about half the membership. The men will want to use her. I know that's hard to hear, but she's a survivor and has lived in a similar subculture for a long time.

She'll get martial arts training and opportunities to prove she's just as tough as the male revolutionaries. She will move a lot. They have been one step ahead of the FBI, but they've tracked them through fifteen states. It won't be an easy existence. She has undergone training by the FBI, and she has probably undergone training by the radicals. She'll never be the same person she was, but if she survives, she may have a long career in the intelligence services," Clay said.

Michael imagined these former children of privilege playing deadly games, sitting around at night chanting, "Hurrah for terrorism. Stick a fork in America, she's done." He thought of Molly in the middle of it all.

"Molly is now officially dead, but unofficially resurrected by Uncle Sam. If something happens to her, we'll never know. No one will. That's a lot to digest," Michael said, taking a big swig of fresh-squeezed lemonade.

"There is something else I haven't had a chance to tell you. When Rose was on the run before she was killed, she mailed a letter to the DEA. She detailed all she'd seen when she visited Corndog at his gin in Greenville, heroin in the cotton bales and so on," Claude said.

"That's incredible! Little 'Nosy Rosy' brought him down?" Michael said.

"Yep, Corndog talked too much and was trying to impress her. It's an age-old story. Because of her letter, he was indicted, turned state's evidence, and has been singing ever since about people in New Orleans, the Leg Room, and other cesspools," Clay said.

"I wonder if Molly knew what Rose did to redeem herself," Michael said.

"Yes, I told her after the FBI offered her the deal. I think that may have encouraged her to make her own contribution. If so, I plead guilty," Clay said.

Clay's daughter brought out the first desserts and then ran back to the house for more. Clay smiled and watched his only child scurry and skip away. Then he looked at Michael.

"Something else I didn't tell you. I called your family to tell them you had been injured so they wouldn't hear it from someone else. Your father answered the phone. I told him you were okay. He was real quiet, but I could hear him crying," Clay said.

Michael took a bite of apple cobbler and wiped something from his eye. He thought about when he was five years old, watching his father crank his tractor. His father reached down for him, sat him in his lap, and let him drive the family tractor down to the watermelon patch. Watermelons never tasted so good.

Clay's wife, Pat, stuck her head out the back door of her kitchen and said, "The news just said J. Edgar Hoover died."

Clay and Michael sat in silence for a moment, and then Clay said, "Your detective friend in Los Angeles, Harry Falkner, called and asked about you. He said you were a fellow traveler in the shadow lands, whatever that means. He sent you a note with this package."

Michael read the note.

Something to light your path. My friend Donald Keller with the Los Angeles Sheriff's Department created it for police officers. I used it while working the Manson murders when I almost got consumed by the darkness. Be careful. Sometimes the monsters get in your head and follow you home.

Your Friend,

Harry

When Michael opened the package, there was Harry's old Kel-lite flashlight. There was engraving down the side. *"One word of truth outweighs the world. Let the lie come into the world, let it even triumph. But not through me."—Alexander Solzhenitsyn*

EPILOGUE

"In the beginning God made man in
His own image, and since the fall, man has
been seeking to return the compliment."
—Alistar Begg

"You don't need a weatherman to know
which way the wind blows."—Bob Dylan,
"Subterranean Homesick Blues"

On May 19, 1972, the birthday of Ho Chi Minh, the Weather Underground planted a bomb in a bathroom in the Pentagon. A young woman matching Molly's description was seen coming out of the bathroom. No one was hurt, but classified files were destroyed. Michael never heard from Molly again.

After he retired, FBI Special Agent Palmer visited Tupelo. Michael showed him the original Citizens Bank that Machine Gun Kelly robbed. Kelly coined the term G-Man. Palmer wouldn't talk about Molly except to say the operation had been fruitful, and broken birds can learn to fly. He said caterpillars can become butterflies, and sometimes they fly overseas.

Otis recovered from his wounds and testified against what was left of the Hattiesburg syndicate. The government deemed the gun battle at Moondog to be self-defense, and after the parents of deceased young boys met with the local Forrest County District Attorney, no charges were filed in the death of Percy the Pervert. It was ruled a suicide. The body of Rose's hit man was never recovered and an attempt to serve a search warrant on a suspect gator failed, so no complaints were filed in Yazoo County. Otis was given a year in Parchman for parole violations and assigned to his old bunk. When he was released, he went to Memphis, collected his girls, and they settled near Hernando. Otis wrote Michael to tell him the girls looked more and more like little

Shelers with each passing day. Michael heard a surgeon in Memphis offered to try experimental surgery on his eye. It was successful, and no one ever called him "Bad Eye" again.

The Leg Room burned. Arson was suspected. The men of the Leg Room agreed to shut down their operations in lieu of prosecution for entertaining underage girls.

The Sun-n-Sand motel closed and remains abandoned. The legislature leases the old motel's lots for parking for state employees. Stories persist among legislators about the "good old days." They were old days, but they were not good.

After Corndog testified against the boys from New Orleans, he was fined a hefty sum and given a new name and a house in the desert of Arizona as part of the witness protection program. Even if they'd known where he was, it was too taxing a trip for his older friends from the Delta. He was lonely and became a regular at every baptism, wedding, and funeral. Just before he died, he told healthcare workers Melba would be along for him soon. A Mississippi newspaper published an article on the senator after his death. An acquaintance was asked if the senator was corrupt. He said, "Just rake through the ashes of his life. The embers of sin still smolder there." A menu from a Greenville restaurant lists one of its popular specials as "Corndog's Chili," and neighbors in Arizona remember him as the stoop-shouldered old man shuffling around his rock garden, tending a plastic cotton plant he watered every day.

Split Nose made bail but became a liability. His friend Jake the Rake was given the contract. After they left a house of ill repute in Metairie, Louisiana, "Thin" shot "Thick" in the back of the head and dumped "Cain's" body in the same sinkhole where Split Nose had buried his brother. Jake retired from active duty not long after the hit. He was given a small nightclub to manage in Biloxi, and he helped imprisoned Dixie Mafia members with a lonely hearts club scam they operated out of Angola Prison.

Rose's mother, Carla Addington, renounced the temptations of the Bohemian wave that swept the country, joined a fundamentalist church, and reunited with her husband. They started the "Wild Rose Foundation" for addicted girls in memory of their daughter. They were on a short list of suspects after the Leg Room fire.

The remnants of the Weathermen came out of hiding in 1980 when FBI surveillance methods were found to be illegal. They were never held accountable for the bombings or their declaration of war on the United States. Some died when a bomb they were making to kill army officers accidently exploded in their Greenwich Village townhouse. Bernardine Dohrn was jailed for eight months for refusing to testify before a grand jury investigating the Weather Underground's robbery of a Brinks truck. A guard and two New York State Troopers were killed in the robbery. She married Bill Ayers, who said, "I don't regret setting bombs; I feel we didn't do enough," and "Maybe I'm the last Communist who's willing to admit it." The Weather Underground code for dynamite was "ice cream."

Dohrn and Ayers became professors in Chicago and friends with State Senator Alice Palmer, a member of the Communist Party who visited Moscow during the Cold War. At a brunch at the home of Bill and Bernardine, Palmer introduced the man who would succeed her. He won her state senate seat and served on the board of the Woods Fund with Ayers. He later moved to 1600 Pennsylvania Avenue, where he named John Brennan as CIA Director. Brennan had voted for Gus Hall, Communist Party USA chief, who said he wanted to kill all Christians.

Some thought they felt a tremor from an earthquake near the Congressional Cemetery in Washington, but it was only J. Edgar Hoover rolling over in his grave.

Charity, the little girl from Moondog Square, became a champion for abused children and an evangelist who spoke all over the South to bring uncomfortable subjects out of the shadows. Michael heard her speak at a revival in Holly Springs, but he sat at the back and left before she finished. She was a strong and beautiful woman, invincible in her full armor of God, and he didn't want his presence to drag her back to the time when she was a scared and vulnerable child.

Red Winter tried to leave his past behind but couldn't make a clean break. He wiretapped for politicos until one of Michael's fellow agents promised to send him back to Jackson in a body bag. Red retired and was a private investigator until the road of life began to run out. In a nursing home near Jackson, he entertained his fellow residents with endless stories, one about the night he helped an agent in trouble, a Boy Scout who needed a friend.

Rachel the witch wrote a popular book on the occult, and Michael saw her on late-night television promising to read her tarot cards and predict the future for a small fee.

Moondog Square was shut down. Some of the residents were reunited with their families. Others went to the Mississippi State Hospital at Whitfield. Bodies were excavated. Many could not be identified and were buried in a local pauper's cemetery. Moondog Square was sold to the Good Shepherd Home, a shelter and orphanage for troubled boys. The valley was scrubbed clean, washed as white as snow. The Light came, and the darkness left.

After the fiasco at Moondog Square, Michael Parker took some time off. He thought a lot about growing up in Parker Grove. He thought about reading "Hardy Boys" books, listening to Elvis, the Platters, and the Ink Spots, and singing "Happy Trails" with Roy and Dale at the end of their TV show. He thought about firecrackers, Roman candles, and sparklers at Christmas, riding his new JC Higgins bicycle with playing cards pinned to the spokes, pitching horseshoes, and carving his name on old trees next to his family's initials. He remembered searching Parker Grove for hours with his axe to find the perfect family Christmas tree, and swinging through the forest on grapevines like his hero, Johnny Weissmuller.

Michael thought about carrying a baby calf in the driving rainstorm to get her to the barn before she drowned and how she soiled his brand new rain slicker. He thought about thumping watermelons on the vine, picking blackberries, figs, and muscadines for Pearl's jams and jellies, and scooping clean, white flakes from the hood of the family car to make snow cream. He thought about dogs, cats, hunting, fishing, pinky promises, and sneaking eggs out from under angry setting hens in the chicken house. He thought about all-night movies at the Lee Drive-In, seeing Elvis at the Tupelo Fair, his first kiss, and the giant army knife he got for selling subscriptions to *Grit* magazine.

Michael thought about church picnics on sawhorse tables, ice cream churns and rock salt, and he remembered RC drinks and Moon Pies, Tootsie Rolls, Saltine crackers with peanut butter, Ritz crackers with cheese, lightning bugs, tadpoles, frogs, playing outside barefooted until dark, looking for crawdads in muddy puddles, softball games, and Pollyanna games with Pearl.

He thought about heroes who leapt tall buildings in a single bound, knights without armor in a savage land, the breakfast of champions, and his childhood belief that good guys always wore white hats, vanquished evil, saved the fair maiden, and won the day.

He thought about bitter apples, serpents, the first grave, and the grave conquered. He thought about Nod as a place and a state of mind. He thought about Dixie Lee, lost lambs, and M&M's.

He thought about searching and seeking, wanting to escape—from what he wasn't sure, maybe ordinariness. He thought about wanting to be heroic, to matter to someone whose heart beat just for him, and he thought about wanting to return to all the things he couldn't wait to get away from.

In an interview forty-odd years later, Michael talked about a life that had passed so quickly. The old reporter had used up four notepads and two pencils as he listened to Michael talk about struggles and trials of the heart that time forgot. The reporter worked his sore fingers and cramping hands and asked, "Whew, did you leave anything out?"

Michael said, "Yes, but strolling down memory lane is a lot like hunting in a baited field in the land of forgettery. We remember how it was but also how we wish it had been. The two collide and get all tangled up. I don't want to talk about it anymore."

Michael picked up the ancient Kel-lite by his chair, shook the reporter's hand, and said, "Maybe I'll write some books about it all one day."

"The past beats inside me like a second heart."—John Banville, The Sea